Forgotten Angel

Forgotten Angel

A Northstar Novel

SUZIE O'CONNELL

ISBN-13: 978-1-950813-22-3

Dedicated to all the fans who have been waiting so patiently for Shane and Becky's story.

One

BECKY ABSENTLY HUMMED the national an-
them along with the singer on the TV and attempted
to quell the flutter of anticipation. She glanced again at
her cell phone, but its screen remained stubbornly
dark. Moments later, her boyfriend and his friends
cheered as the singer belted out the final notes, and
Becky ground her teeth as she dumped a jar of salsa
into a bowl and tore open the bag of tortilla chips.
Normally she enjoyed football more than Justin, but
he'd used the game—his cousin's first start as running
back for the University of Wyoming—and his little

sister's volleyball game on Monday as excuses against going to Northstar for her aunt's and cousin's birthdays. Justin always made the four-and-a-half-hour drive out to be a bigger deal than it was, and she had resolved to ignore her irritation like she always did when he refused to visit her family… until Uncle Ben called her in the middle of the night to inform her that her cousin's wife was in labor.

Justin strode into the kitchen to retrieve the chips and salsa, and her phone blared a snippet of her favorite pop song, a tune that had topped the charts her freshman year of high school when her friendship with Luke had first sprouted. She smiled fondly and snatched the phone off the counter, not needing to see the familiar number on the screen to know it was her cousin.

"You really need to update your ringtone, Becks," Justin remarked.

She scowled at him and answered the call. "Well?"

"I have a daughter," Luke replied. The pride and happiness in his voice created a distinct image of the broad smile undoubtedly plastered on his face. "And Ryan is doing great. Everything went as smoothly as we could hope."

Becky beamed. "Congratulations, Papa. I'm

guessing everything went quickly, too, because Uncle Ben didn't call me until midnight to say you'd just left for the hospital."

"I wasn't sure we were going to make it. Sorry I didn't call you earlier, but we didn't get to sleep until after five this morning, and—"

"I get it, Luke. No need to apologize."

"I know you said you and Justin won't be coming up this weekend, but if you can convince him otherwise, we'll be bringing her home on Monday, and we'd really love to see you and introduce you to this beautiful little girl."

"You know I want to be there, Luke. I really do. Maybe we'll be able to make it up next weekend. It won't be the same, I know, but…."

"I'll send you a picture as soon as I can, but right now, I have to go. Shane and Austin just arrived."

"What is *Shane* doing there?"

"He's in the process of moving back. I thought I told you that. He's home for a visit to look for a place to rent."

"Did he find one?"

"Yeah, Pat and Aeli are going to rent him the Bedspread's vacation cabin for at least a few months."

"Damn. *And* the jackass gets to meet your

daughter before I do." Her words were harsh, but her tone was teasing. She might not want to have anything to do with Shane, but it was good for Luke that the two old friends were working through the issues that had derailed their friendship. She couldn't even begrudge him his return home to Northstar, not when it made her squirm with envy and longing. With a sigh, she added, "I am missing too much."

"We keep having this conversation, and it always ends the same. Listen. If you do make it up this way, try not to be too hard on Shane, all right? He *is* trying."

"I'll keep that in mind. That's all in the past now, anyhow, right?"

"Exactly."

"Go enjoy your daughter."

She bid him goodbye, ended the call, and set her phone gently on the counter, frowning as regret and anger and envy mingled with joy. She should be there with Luke and Ryan and their new baby right now, not four and a half hours away making game-day snacks for a boyfriend who ignored her need to spend time with her family. The fact that she'd let this become the status quo of their relationship only heightened her frustration, and she clenched her teeth at the thought that followed. *I've given up precious time with my family for a man I have no plan to marry.*

The potent stew of emotions constricted her chest and made it hard to breathe. She tapped her fingers lightly on the counter and took several deep breaths before lifting her gaze to Justin, who hadn't yet returned to the game.

"They had a girl?" he inquired.

"Yep."

She studied him for several long moments, noting the disinterested, placating smile. Why was she still with him? They'd been together for six years, and though she loved him well enough, she had never given herself entirely to their relationship. She'd done that once before and had her heart broken, so when she'd followed Justin here to Jackson Hole to take a job on his family's ranch, she had refused to move in with him and had instead rented a tiny, one-bedroom cottage in nearby Wilson. The more important question wasn't why she'd stayed but why she'd followed him in the first place.

I was afraid my family had changed so much that I wouldn't fit into it anymore.

"I have to go home to Northstar," she said slowly. "Luke and Ryan will be bringing their daughter home on Monday, and I want to be there."

"Becks, we've talked about this. My sister's volleyball game—"

"My best friend and his wife just had a baby," she snapped, "and that little girl will never be this new again."

"Becks—"

"No, Justin. We *did* talk about this. We decided against going to Northstar for Aunt June's and Luke's birthdays to save the trip until after Luke's baby arrived so we could meet her, since it's apparently impossible to go for both."

"I don't remember that discussion."

"Of course you don't. You only remember the discussions you *want* to remember." She lowered her voice, narrowing her eyes as she carefully selected her words. "Consider this a conversation you'll want to remember, Justin. I don't care if you come or not, but I'm going home. And if you don't come with me, I won't be coming back."

He brushed that aside and responded with such a mollifying tone that her lip curled. "If you need to go, then go. I'm sure the ranch will survive without you for a few days, and my family will understand."

Becky leaned back against the counter, folded her arms across her chest, and glared at him. Right now, she didn't see the rich dark hair, the devastatingly be-guiling blue eyes, or the dreamy, chiseled face. All she saw was a disappointment, and she understood with a strange serenity that there was no love between them that would last.

This is it? This is how a six-year chapter of my life comes to a close? Somehow, this detached, half-assed argument was a fitting end.

Shaking her head, she shooed him out of the kitchen. "Go watch your Pokes."

He smiled, kissed her cheek, and returned to the living room. She stared after him for a while, ponder-ing her options. She enjoyed her job on the Teton South Ranch, leading trail rides, showing guests the ins and outs of ranch life, and tending to the horses, but she could do that back home on the Royal R or for the Ramshorn Hot Springs and Lodge. How many times had her aunt and uncle and cousin asked her to help out with that end of the business? A slow, satisfied smile lifted her face as a refreshing calm brushed away her anger.

Becky pushed off the counter, grabbed her jacket, phone, and keys, and strode through the house.

"Where are you going, babe?" Justin asked.

"Home."

"You're not going to stay and watch the game with us?"

"Nope."

As she walked out the door, she squared her shoulders. Without giving herself the opportunity to change her mind, she climbed into her truck and drove straight to the main house of the Teton South Ranch. It was an attractive structure, wrapped completely in a covered porch littered with Adirondack chairs and scarred, weathered end tables adorned with horseshoe art. Two-storied with eight-bedrooms and four bathrooms, the monstrosity looked every bit like a quintessential ranch house… and nothing at all like the more modest main house of the Royal R Ranch, which was similar in style but had the genuine wear and tear of a working ranch instead of the too-perfect affectation of the Sutherlands' ranch house.

Becky climbed up the broad stairs, crossed the porch to the front door, and entered without bothering to knock. Unsurprisingly, she found Justin's parents, sister, aunt and uncle, and half a dozen of the ranch's guests lounging on the plush, L-shaped couches wrapped around the TV in the sprawling living room to watch the Wyoming Cowboys' football game.

"Becky, dear, what are you doing here?" Justin's

mother asked. "I thought you were going to spend your day off watching the game with Justin and his friends."

"That was the plan, Sherrie, but the plan has changed. Can I talk to you for a few minutes?"

"Sure, honey."

Becky led the way into the house's enormous kitchen and turned to face her boss, leaning casually against the counter with her ankles crossed and her thumbs hooked in her pockets. "I need to go home to Northstar. My cousin and his wife had their baby… and I need to be there with them."

"Is everything all right?"

"Everything is fine. I just need to be with my family right now."

"How long do you need, dear?"

Becky opened her mouth, then closed it again. Was this what she really wanted? Because there would be no going back once she quit. She truly did love her job and Justin's family even more, and maybe she didn't think of them as her second family, but she *did* value their friendship, and if she moved back to Northstar, it would likely fade into memory.

"I'm not going to like your response," Sherrie said. "Am I?"

It wasn't a question.

After taking another moment to test her decision and finding it solid, Becky shook her head. "I'm very sorry for the short notice, but this is it for me. It's time to move back home to Northstar."

Sherrie studied her for a long time with lips pursed. Disappointment warred with anger and resignation for control of her expression, and Becky waited patiently while the battle played out.

Finally, Sherrie asked, "And what about Justin?"

Becky hesitated, well aware of Sherrie's defensiveness of her precious son. "I think we all know it wasn't going to last. Our priorities conflict too strongly with each other, and I've let his devotion to his family keep me from mine long enough."

She didn't add that she was tired of Justin's selfishness in other areas, but there was something in Sherrie's face that led her to believe the older woman suspected it. After a moment, her shoulders dropped.

"I was afraid this day would come," she said quietly. "Is there any way either of us can change your mind?"

Becky shook her head.

"You're not even upset."

"Not particularly. I'm disappointed, but I think

this has been coming for a long time." Glancing down at her feet, she added, "I'm sorry to do this to you because I love you all and my job here."

"But you love your family more. I can't fault you for that." Sherrie embraced her. "You can come back whenever you want, you know. I hope you do. I hope my son realizes what a mistake he's made with you."

Sensing that she was walking on a thin line, Becky hugged her back and replied, "Thank you. For everything."

"Keep in touch."

Becky nodded but doubted either of them would.

As quickly as she could without being rude, she escaped the house. She drove to the local supermarket to pick up something for dinner, since she had no intention of going back to Justin's, and grabbed some boxes while she was at it. The implications of what she'd done didn't hit her until she was sitting in the middle of her living room surrounded by half-packed boxes. At once, a broad grin curved her lips, and she leaned back with her head tilted up and her eyes closed as she reveled in the promise of freedom and fulfillment.

I am going home, she thought with something close to glee. *And right now, I don't even care if that means I'll have to deal with Shane.*

Truth be told, she was curious to see for herself if Luke and Ryan were right that he'd finally started taking responsibility for his mistakes. Of course, if anyone called her on that, she would heartily deny it. No matter what feelings she might still have for him, she doubted she'd ever be able to trust him not to hurt her again. His track record was too full of broken hearts.

* * *

Shane parked his truck in front of the log cabin Pat and Aelissm O'Neil had purchased and renovated as an extension of their inn. It was small but more than adequate for his needs, and he imagined he'd be spending a lot of his free time lounging in one of the chairs on its covered front deck, which—like the large windows that took up most of the front wall—faced northeast with a commanding view of the Northstar Mountains. He shut the engine down and climbed out of his truck, pausing a moment before he ascended to the deck to take in that spectacular view. It was so familiar, but it was with an entirely new appreciation that his eyes roamed over the mountains and valley. He inhaled deeply, smiling as his lungs filled with the soothing fragrances of wild places, and all at once, he understood just how much he had missed home. The

Bitterroot Valley was stunning, and he'd grown accustomed to it, but it never would have replaced Northstar's place in his heart.

And yet… he'd been gone so long now that he felt like an outsider. He could count the number of times he'd been home on both hands, and on his brief visits, he hadn't given himself the chance to get reacquainted, afraid that if he did he wouldn't be able to gather the strength to leave again. How foolish he had been to think he *should* leave.

Shane set aside those thoughts and bounded up the stairs to the deck just as Pat stepped out of the cabin. In contrast to Aelissm's blunt, somewhat chilly reception when he'd walked into the Bedspread Inn just a few minutes ago, Pat regarded Shane with a relaxed smile. Even so, Shane hesitated a heartbeat before shaking the man's offered hand, looking for any sign that Aelissm's qualms were shared by her husband. While Pat hadn't gone out of his way to be friendly to Shane, he'd always been polite. But Pat was like that. A kind and gentle soul, Shane's father called him.

"Well, this is it," Pat remarked, gesturing for Shane to head inside. "It's small, but you said you weren't looking for anything big."

"Small works well for me. And it's actually bigger than my cabin in the Bitterroot."

The layout of the cabin was simple. Below the loft over the back half of the cabin were a tiny bedroom with bunk beds, the bathroom, and the small but functional kitchen. The front half was an open living area with a vaulted ceiling. The couch, coffee table, and television sat to the left, and the dining table and chairs and the woodstove were to the right in front of the kitchen. In addition to the windows that made up most of the front wall, two big, square windows let in yet more of the view and light on each side wall of the living area. All in all, the cabin was quite similar to several others in Northstar, including the one Luke and Ryan Conner had built, though theirs was considerably larger with two full-sized bedrooms downstairs.

Shane stepped over to one of the front windows with his hands in his pockets to admire the view. Yep, he'd definitely be enjoying that deck… at least until the weather turned colder. It was decidedly refreshing to think that he'd be here when the seasons changed instead of landing for a day or two before flitting off again as he usually did, and a broad and unexpected smile curved his lips. He let his eyes drift closed as the smile turned poignant and a welcome peace settle over him.

"Glad to be moving home?" Pat inquired, noting his preoccupation.

"Definitely." Shane turned his attention to the tall man. "But that doesn't mean it's going to be as easy as it feels like it will be right now."

Pat offered him a sympathetic smile. "I'm sorry if Aeli was less than welcoming to you when you stopped down at the inn. I hope she wasn't too surly."

"Not really, but I'm grateful you volunteered to show me the cabin." Shane shrugged. "I can't blame her. She's protecting people she loves."

"Yes, she is, but people make mistakes, and trying to make up for them is an admirable endeavor. Takes a lot of guts."

"I'd like to think you're right, but it's probably more desperation than guts. I'll be turning thirty in March, and after Dad's cancer scare…. Let's just say I've come to realize a few things I wish I'd understood years ago."

"Don't be so hard on yourself. Your thirties are for fixing the mistakes you made in your teens and twenties. And your forties…." Pat grinned. "Well, by the time you hit forty, you might finally have a clue about what's really important in life. If you're lucky."

"I'm not sure I deserve to be so lucky," Shane murmured. Abruptly, he changed the topic. "You and Aeli did a great job on this place."

"Thank you. You're sure you don't want us to move the furniture out so you can move yours in?"

"Positive. I'm trying to get back on your wife's good side, and I don't think making more work for her would be a smart move."

Pat offered a sympathetic smile. "Aelissm will come around. If Luke and Ryan can find it in their hearts to let go of the past—and I believe they will and are—she'll have no reason to stay mad."

"Thanks, Pat. I mean that."

"Well, I don't want to keep you too long. I know you need to head in to town to visit Luke and Ryan, which I have to say makes me a little envious. You get to meet their daughter before I do."

Shane looked up sharply. "How'd you know about that?"

"Luke told us when he called the inn a few minutes before I came up here."

"Ah."

He wondered what emotion had tinged Luke's voice when he'd mentioned it, and Pat answered his unspoken question before it had fully formed in his mind.

"He sounded excited about it."

"That was probably just his excitement about his daughter."

"Could be, but I doubt it."

"Come on, Pat. It hasn't been so long since Seth was born that I'll believe you've forgotten how consuming that joy is."

"I remember it like it was this morning, and that's why it's even more striking that he would ask me not to keep you too long."

"He's probably more excited about my dad meeting his—"

"Shane," Pat interrupted. "Just go, would you? And while you're at it, try to remember that there's a reason why you two were best friends once upon a time."

Laughing a little, Shane nodded. He thanked Pat for his time and promised to sign the lease and bring it back this afternoon. Pat handed over the keys to the cabin and laid a hand on his shoulder for a moment with a keen glint in his hazel eyes that said more than any words could.

Welcome home.

Then he headed back to the Bedspread Inn.

Shane poked around the cabin for a few minutes with anticipation and nerves tingling through him until he realized he was delaying his visit with Luke and Ryan. Scolding himself, he stepped outside and locked the door behind him, then drove to the bunkhouse on the Lazy H that his father had called home since Shane had gone off to college. While he missed the tiny, one-bedroom cabin located at the foot of the Northstar Ski Hill that he'd grown up in, he was glad his father had decided to take the Hammonds up on their offer to bunk with their then-inexperienced new ranch hand Jerry Mackey. It had saved Austin a lot of money, and Jerry had been good company for him. It was possible that he'd also saved Austin's life.

Maybe someday I'll remember he prefers to go by Jeremiah, Shane mused.

His father must have heard him pull up because he stepped out onto the bunkhouse's covered porch just as Shane shifted his truck into neutral and set the parking break. Since Austin was already hopping down the stairs, Shane waited in the truck, trying not to think about what that fresh pink scar above Austin's right eyebrow represented. His father was—thanks to Jeremiah's concerned observation—in good health with every expectation to remain so for the foreseeable future.

"You ready for this?" Austin asked after he'd closed his door.

"Not really," Shane admitted.

His father studied him for a moment before voicing the question that had plagued Shane since Luke had called early this morning to invite him to meet his new daughter. "Is it that you don't feel like your relationship with them is stable enough yet... or that it should be you in that hospital room with Ryan instead of Luke?"

Shane clenched his jaw. It wasn't that he coveted Luke's wife. He had long ago given up any right to call Ryan his, and at any rate, the same reason that had spurred him to walk away from her remained. He knew exactly why the idea of meeting Luke and Ryan's daughter made him uncomfortable, but it wasn't something he was prepared to share, so without responding, he backed his truck away from the bunk house and drove up the gravel ranch road.

"Can I ask you a question, Shane?"

He only nodded.

"Why now?"

"What do you mean?"

"You know what I mean. Why did you decide to

come home now? You've been talking about it for two years, and this is the third time a forestry tech position has opened up in Devyn, so what's changed to make you stop talking and act?"

"You know what."

Austin fingered the new scar, frowning. "I'll be fine. Thanks to Jeremiah, we caught it early. A quick snip and all I have to show for it is this pretty little scar."

"I know that, Dad. It's just…." Shane tightened his grip on the steering wheel and glanced over at his father. Austin's hair was now more gray then dark blond, but his brown eyes were as keen as ever. Countless hours spent riding the range under the blazing Montana sun or in the biting winter wind had etched lines into his face, most noticeably at the corners of his eyes, but none of it made him look as old as Shane had felt he was when Austin had broken the news three weeks ago that he'd had an operation to remove a spot that had turned out to be cancerous. In fact, Austin looked as indeterminately ageless as ever. He didn't know what he'd expected when he'd arrived in Northstar yesterday, but that barely noticeable scar wasn't it. The news that had finally shaken him out of his melodramatic stupor seemed far less shattering now. Except that he couldn't dispel the nagging sense that too much time had slipped away while he avoided dealing with the issues that had kept him from coming home for so long.

He didn't respond until he'd turned onto the main road through the valley. "I know there's nothing to worry about now, but it scared the hell out of me."

"Well, you ain't getting rid of me any time soon, boy-o."

Chuckling, Shane replied, "I'll hold you to that."

"Let me ask you something else. If that job with the Forest Service hadn't opened, would you still have decided to come home?"

"Yes," Shane responded without hesitation.

"I'll be damned. Maybe I should've gotten cancer sooner."

"Dad…" he groaned.

"What? It's about time you pulled your head out of your ass. Northstar is where you belong, Shane, and if it took me getting cancer to make you see it… well, I'm glad it happened."

Shane glanced at his father, and the smug expression on Austin's face made him laugh a little harder. Shaking his head, he said, "I haven't said it enough in my life—especially not in the last ten years—but I love you, Dad. Sorry I've been such an ass for so long."

There was more he wanted to say, but old habits were hard to break, and they fell into companionable silence. Thoughts of the relationships he wanted to repair occupied him all the way into Devyn, and before he knew it, he was parking his truck in the hospital's lot. Austin undoubtedly knew how awkward this was going to be for Shane, but he didn't let that slow him down. He was out of the truck and striding toward the door of the hospital before Shane had even gathered the brainpower to pull his key out of the ignition. He had to hurry to catch up with his father. They stopped only briefly to check in with the nurse and to ask for specific directions to Ryan's room.

This was the first real test of his decision to move home to Northstar, and he hesitated in the hallway outside the hospital room where the woman who had nearly become the mother of his child was ensconced with his former best friend and their hours-old baby. He found himself once again on the outside of two people he loved, and the fact that it was all his own doing did not make it any less unsettling to face them.

Memories assaulted him, bringing with them a torrent of agonizing emotions, and try as he might, he couldn't help but think that it was in this very hospital that Ryan had lost her first child. His child, he thought, though he had no more claim on that tiny girl than he had on her mother. Angel Rose, Ryan had called her. The image of Ryan going through that alone and terrified threatened to overwhelm him. Two years ago, when she and Luke got together, she had said she needed to forgive him, and he believed she had or was at least in the process, but he knew it would be much longer before he forgave himself, if he ever did.

"You coming?" Austin asked him.

Shane swallowed the memories and took a hesitant step toward the open door of the room and another until he could see inside. Ryan was sitting up with a tiny baby girl snuggled lovingly in her arms while Luke perched on the side of the bed beside his wife, talking on the phone and absently stroking Ryan's hair with his gaze frequently shifting between his wife and daughter. Shane's first thought was that things really had turned out for the best for them both. They were entirely in tune and relaxed with each other in a way he and Ryan had never been. He shut the second thought down the moment he felt the first tickle of it; he'd never be able to get through this if he allowed it to gain even a tentative foothold.

"If you do make it up this way," Luke was saying,

"try not to be too hard on Shane, all right? He *is* try-ing."

Becky, Shane knew without needing confirmation. There was only one person currently residing outside of Northstar whom Luke would need to ask to be nice to him. Just thinking her name brought an entirely different kind of heartache because it was inescapably en-twined with longing and desire. One night of awkward and fumbling but exquisite passion after three years to-gether was all they'd had, but nine years could not make him forget the feel of her silken skin against his or the way the fragrances of their home melded with the warm, natural scent of her. Not even Ryan had been able to make him forget Becky, and they'd been together as long.

"Are you going to come in or are you going to just stand there in the doorway staring with that stupid look on your face?" Austin asked with an unsettling combi-nation of concern and laughter in his voice. A heart-beat later, the latter won out, and he grinned. "Get your ass in here."

Austin's adoration for Ryan had not dimmed in the least, Shane noted, and for that reason alone, he knew it was good that he had taken that first step to-ward earning her forgiveness. With her married to

Luke, living at least part-time in Northstar, and maintaining her friendship with his father, she would always be a part of his life.

Finally, Shane strode into the room. Ryan and Luke met his gaze with broad grins, and he breathed a *little* easier.

"I'm glad you came, Shane," Ryan said softly.

Shane stepped over to the bed to peer down at the baby in Ryan's arms. "What's her name?"

"Guess you're going to *have* to come to the party on Monday," Luke replied. "We've picked a name—picked it right after we found out Ryan was pregnant—but we're not telling anyone until Monday."

"Let's just see how this goes first, all right?" Shane said. "Where are Alex and your parents?"

"Out getting something a little more palatable than hospital food for lunch."

"Can't say as I blame them." Shane shifted his weight.

"Want to hold her?" Luke asked.

"Uh…."

Before he could say it wasn't a good idea, Luke took his daughter from Ryan and with a tenderness that seemed impossible for a man of his size, settled her in Shane's arms. Shane tensed when his old friend returned to his wife's side with a surprisingly assured smile.

Not so bad, he thought. *I can do this.*

He hazarded a glance at the bundle now tucked against him, and his breath caught in his throat. Though she was only hours old, he saw her parents' beauty in the delicate features of her face. She was a perfect blend of them, and Shane felt a spark of amusement at the trouble Luke—and probably Alex, too, as her older if adopted brother—was going to have chasing the boys away when she was a teenager. When her eyes opened, he had only a moment to wonder if they would stay blue like Luke's or change to a silvery green like Ryan's. As those big, gorgeous eyes met his, it felt like someone punched him in the chest, and all at once, he understood with a precision that had previously eluded him just what he had lost the day Ryan had miscarried.

"I'm sorry," he said, hastily but carefully handing the baby to Austin. "I can't...."

Overcome by the urge to flee, he strode from the room, and by the time he found a chair just down the hall and sank into it, he was gulping for breath. He hunched over his legs and curled his arms around his head, fighting against the panic and the raging sense of loss. He knew in his heart that if he hadn't walked away from Ryan, she wouldn't have taken the job in Devyn and wouldn't have fallen down the stairs of her rented house, which had caused the total placental abruption that had ended her first pregnancy in a heartbreaking miscarriage. He had thought of that lost child so many times over the years and mourned her, but until this moment, he had never let himself consider that he'd actually wanted her.

He had just begun to get hold of himself when he sensed he was no longer alone. Someone sat beside him but said nothing, and he figured it was his father. He couldn't yet bring himself to look up to see, so he said, "Just give me a few minutes, Dad. Please."

"Well, I'm someone's father now, but considering the fact that you're older than me, it's biologically impossible that I'm yours."

Shane lifted his head and glanced to his left to see Luke sitting in the chair next to him. Despite the bitterness and self-loathing pulsing through him, he found the energy to offer his companion a weak smile.

"Smart ass," he muttered fondly, grateful for Luke's lighthearted teasing. "My dad's still in the room with Ryan?"

Luke nodded. "And making a fool of himself over

my daughter."

Shane wanted to ask Luke what it felt like to be a father now, but he couldn't bring himself to say the words, so they sat silently for several minutes.

"I get the feeling that losing Angel grieves you more than you knew," Luke said quietly.

He was every bit as insightful as Shane recalled, and as uncannily intuitive as June. Since there was no point in trying to lie and because he was unable to give voice to the renewed ache of loss, he simply nodded.

"Then why did you walk away?"

Shane couldn't answer that. He wasn't sure how Luke would react to the knowledge that he'd left because Ryan's pregnancy had forced him to admit that he would never stop loving Becky. It didn't matter that he might never get another chance with her; he couldn't do that to Ryan. *But I could walk away from her and leave her to raise our child alone… or mourn her, as it turned out.* "When I figure that out, I'll let you know."

"I hope you don't think I'm judging you, Shane. To be honest, once I got past the anger that you'd hurt someone else I'd come to love, I was selfishly grateful you and Ryan didn't make it. When she came into my life, I finally began to heal—truly heal—and now I have everything I was beginning to think I never would."

They fell into silence again, and Shane knew Luke was right. Even if he and Ryan had lasted a little longer, he believed in his heart that they would have eventually grown apart. Ryan deserved so much more than that. So did Luke, and for those reasons, Shane had done the right thing even if he'd done it in the worst possible way.

After several minutes, Shane noticed that they hadn't said another word to each other and admitted that he'd missed Luke's quiet, unassuming friendship all these years. The animosity that had torn them apart was gone, and without it hanging over them, the old camaraderie was returning. Just like old times when he'd been pissed at who knew what, simply sitting with his friend and knowing Luke understood him helped ease the grief. Though his friend hadn't said it, Shane sensed that Luke cared about him. Even after every stupid thing he'd done.

"You're a better friend than I've ever been," he said. "I wish I'd realized it sooner. I wish I'd realized a lot of things sooner."

Luke gripped his shoulder for a minute, then grinned. "Better late than never. If you're up for it, come back in."

Shane watched Luke walk away. He took a few minutes to gather the shreds of his courage before he followed his friend. For a moment, he leaned in the doorway and watched his father—as Luke had said—make a fool of himself over the new baby and recalled that it wasn't only how Shane had left Ryan that had nearly destroyed his relationship with his father but also how deeply Angel's premature birth and death had broken Austin's heart.

Abruptly, he pushed off the doorjamb and entered the room. "I'm sorry for a minute ago," he said. "Old feelings caught me off guard."

"Not one of us in this room is a stranger to old feelings," Ryan remarked. She glanced at her daughter cradled so tenderly in Austin's arms and smiled. "Well, *one* of us is a stranger to them."

"Let's hope she stays a stranger to them," Shane murmured.

"That's probably too much to hope for," Luke said. "And at any rate, it's the pain in life that gives you the deepest appreciation for the good things."

"I'm going to have to take your word for that." Shane's lips curved. "But this little girl right here…. I'd say she's pretty good proof of it. She's so beautiful."

The conversation turned, as it should, to Luke and

Ryan's daughter, and though Shane was able to subvert the lingering ache of grief and the surprising twinge of envy enough to laugh with his companions, he was glad no one asked him to hold the baby again. Those feelings were too close to the surface, and he didn't think he could handle another breach. Regardless, it was good to talk and laugh with Luke and Ryan, and in this moment, he felt like they had put the past where it belonged.

Dad's right, Shane thought. *This* is *where I belong. Maybe I'm not such an outsider after all.*

Two

BECKY CLOSED THE CANOPY on her truck and returned to the tiny cottage that had been her home since she'd moved to Wyoming. She couldn't decide if it was admirable or pathetic that all her belongings fit easily in the back of her truck. She also couldn't decide if she should be disappointed that she had neither seen nor heard from Justin since she'd left his house on Saturday, but she wasn't surprised.

I wonder how long it will be before he realizes I'm gone.

With a shrug, she returned her attention to her landlady as the two of them completed the final walkthrough.

"Everything looks great, Becky," the middle-aged woman said. "Thank you."

"If it's all right, would you mind just mailing the refund for the security deposit to this address?" She tugged a small sheet of paper out of the back pocket of her jeans and handed it to the woman. "My parents' phone number is on it, as well, because there's no cell service in Northstar."

"Absolutely. I'm sorry to see you go, but I'm happy for you. Call me if you ever need a reference."

"Thanks, Jody."

"Good luck, honey."

Becky dropped the keys to the cottage into Jody's upturned hand and watched as the older woman locked the cottage, waved goodbye, and climbed into her Subaru. After Jody drove away, Becky wondered if she would even miss Wyoming. The Jackson Hole area was stunning, but she'd always been a visitor here. Of course, that's all she had been in Northstar for the better part of the last decade, and apprehension quivered through her. Would she be able to find her old balance, or would the shift in her family that had happened with the birth of her little brother, who was now nine, require her to find a new one?

Time to find out. Becky slid in behind the wheel of her truck.

She'd said her goodbyes to the rest of Justin's family yesterday, her truck's gas tank was full, and there was nothing left to do, so she drove toward the pass between Wilson and the Swan Valley. She turned her music up and enjoyed the drive with thoughts of home floating delightfully through her mind as she passed through Idaho Falls and continued north on I-15 across the sagebrush plains rimmed by distant, summer-bare mountain ranges. Relief mingled with joy and blossomed into excitement the closer she came to home, escalating as the interstate climbed the deceptively formidable Monida Pass and crossed the border into Montana.

The skies remained a stunning blue littered with a few popcorn clouds all the way to Northstar, and Becky mused that, after a string of sullen, overcast days, it appeared that even the weather was in a better mood now that she was going home. Beneath those pristine skies, the Northstar Valley was every bit as breathtaking as her heart remembered, and a weight she hadn't been conscious of lifted.

Because it was well after six, Becky headed directly to the cluster of cabins at the secluded end of Wellman

Creek Road where everyone would be celebrating her cousin's birthday. She navigated her way around the rocks and bumps with the effortless assurance of years of practice. There was one thing new, however, that gave her a bit of a jolt and drove home that things had changed in her absence. Instead of heading straight up to the gate and beyond to Uncle Ben and Aunt June's cabin to see Luke, she followed the old logging spur that curved away to the left just before the final climb up to the gate.

As she came around the hairpin corner that was Luke's favorite thinking spot, her cousin's cabin came into view. It sat up the hill a little ways with a commanding view of the Northstar Valley to the south. Since the driveway was packed with vehicles, Becky pulled her truck off to the side of the road in the pullout at the edge of the switchback and stepped outside. A soft breeze brought the mouthwatering and smoky scents of the barbecue to her, and her stomach growled, reminding her that she hadn't eaten anything since breakfast.

She hiked up to the cabin with a grin plastered to her face as she took in the sight of so many of her loved ones gathered on the deck. Her parents and little brother were there along with the entire Hammond clan, the O'Neils and their brood, Luke's parents and siblings, and Ryan's parents, grandparents, and twin brother. Coach Wells was also present, and Becky was as happy to see him as she was to see everyone else.

As soon as she reached the deck, she went directly to her cousin. Ryan was perched on his lap, curled in his arms, and even as tired as she undoubtedly was, she was beautiful, perhaps more so now than ever before because the same undimmed happiness and pride that shone brightly in Luke's blue eyes also glowed in her green ones. Becky couldn't be more thrilled for them both. When they started to get up, she motioned them to remain seated and leaned down to hug them.

"Sorry I'm late," she said. "But I couldn't miss this."

"I'm glad you're here," Luke replied. "Where's Justin?"

Becky sighed. Now was not the time to go into detail about *that*, so she said simply, "Let's just say I won't be missing anything else from now on."

"You're moving home?"

"I am."

Luke beamed. "*Now* it's a perfect birthday. Great timing, by the way. Ryan and I are about to announce our daughter's name."

"Finally," Luke's little brother muttered.

Becky nearly laughed, overcome by a robust giddiness at being surrounded by her family. She glanced around to locate the baby and found her tucked possessively in the arms of Ryan's mother. Becky couldn't see much of her but a dusting of fine blonde hair and was impatient to hold Luke's daughter, but she didn't ask just yet, figuring she'd have far more opportunity to do so than Jillian. She listened as Ryan explained why she and Luke had chosen their daughter's name—to honor the two women who'd supported them through every trial they'd faced in their lives—and nearly choked up.

"We'd like to officially introduce our daughter to you as Ashleigh June Conner," Ryan said.

"Perfect," Uncle Ben said, voicing Becky's immediate thought.

While congratulations were offered, Becky stepped away from her cousin and his wife to embrace her parents. It wasn't like she'd hadn't seen them at all since she'd followed Justin to Wyoming, but today was so remarkably different than any of her hasty visits. Her father didn't say a word but hugged her for a long time with a strength that said plainly how much he'd missed her and how glad he was that she was home.

She clung to him, realizing just how thoroughly she'd missed the comfort and protection of his arms. That, at least, hadn't changed, and she knew it never would, no matter how much her family changed.

It's a special kind of love between a daughter and her father, Becky mused, glancing briefly over her father's shoulder at her cousin, who had regained his daughter from his in-laws.

"I love you, Daddy," she whispered, tilting her face up to meet her father's adoring gaze.

"I love you, too, darling," Andy replied. "Always."

"Why didn't you tell us you were coming?" her mother asked, shoving her husband aside to hug Becky as tightly. "Not that I care. I'm just glad to see you."

"Well, you're going to be seeing a lot more of me," Becky murmured. "Honestly, I just made the decision two days ago, right after Luke called to tell me about his daughter's birth."

"You're really moving home?" her brother asked.

"Yep. Which means you and I are going to be spending a lot of time together bonding, little man. I've got a lot of lost time to make up for."

James, evidently, had not yet reached the stage of being too cool to be completely ecstatic about his sister's return and launched himself into Becky's waiting arms. She lifted him off the ground with his arms wrapped tightly around her neck. In that moment, all her worries about no longer fitting into her family seemed silly and childish.

"I can't wait," he said. "We're gonna have so much fun!"

"You bet we will."

"All right, James," said a masculine voice behind her. "It's my turn."

Becky set her brother down and swiveled on her heel to see her uncle and his wife standing patiently beside her. She first embraced her uncle, suddenly reminded of the day more than twelve years ago now that he'd shown up in Northstar as unexpectedly as she had today. That day was perhaps even more momentous because Becky had gotten her uncle back that summer and gained an aunt and a cousin she adored.

"What's wrong, Becky?" Ben asked softly.

"Not a damned thing," she answered. "Everything is right. My family is whole and happy again, and I'm here to see it."

Ben chuckled knowingly and stepped aside so she could hug June.

"It's so good to have you home," her aunt said with a bright smile. "Why don't you go steal Ashleigh away from her father before someone else does? I'll bring your dinner over in a minute. Burger or steak?"

"Uh, burger, I think. Thanks, Aunt June."

Becky joined her cousin and his wife at the table and held her hands out, wiggling her fingers. "All right, Papa, my turn."

Ryan stood up for a moment to stretch, and Luke leaned over to carefully hand his daughter to Becky, then pulled his wife back onto his lap and kissed her soundly. Shaking her head and beaming, Becky turned her attention to their daughter. She was so tiny and so new but utterly perfect. As her eyes swept over Ashleigh's delicate face, she wondered if this little girl would ever understand how truly special she was. Tears threatened, and she hastily blinked them away as adoration and joy and a love as deep as any she imagined she'd feel for her own child swamped her.

"She's a beautiful little girl," Becky murmured. "And so much more precious for everything the two of you have been through."

"I couldn't agree more," Luke said. He lightly took his wife by the chin and kissed her again, then touched his forehead to hers. "I am truly blessed."

"I think you two get worse every time I see you," Becky said with a laugh. "You *do* know that you have the rest of your lives to be together, right?"

"Yep," Ryan replied. "And we plan to enjoy every second."

She rested her head on Luke's chest again for a few moments, and a poignant, blissful smile softened her features. Becky glanced away, feeling like she was intruding on a private moment.

"Um, Becky?" Luke asked. "I'm not sure he'll show up, but we invited Shane to the party. I'm sorry. I didn't know you were coming."

"I appreciate the heads up," she replied quickly in an attempt to avert the usual ache of regret. She sighed, then trailed a finger over Ashleigh's silken cheek as she accepted the inevitable. "Since he's moving home, too, I suppose I'll have to get used to dealing with him on a regular basis."

"It certainly seems that way, and maybe that's not a bad thing even if it feels like one right now." There was something decidedly prodding about his tone, but in his way of telling her to think about it, he didn't give her a chance to respond before shifting topics. "So… Justin. What happened?"

Becky shrugged. "I finally got tired of the bull-shit."

The arrival of June and Ben with dinner

interrupted their conversation. Becky's stomach growled again when the delicious aroma hit her, but she was in no hurry to hand Ashleigh back to her parents or to anyone else, so she let her burger sit while Luke and Ryan ate. The rest of the families gathered closer around the table to eat, and the chatter centered on the newborn with occasional wise cracks about Luke's age. He took them all in stride, as was his nature, and Becky's face ached from smiling.

Luke and Ryan's adopted son, Alex, who was now a junior in high school, offered to take his new sister so Becky could eat. Grudgingly, Becky gave her up as her hunger at last won out. There would be plenty of time later to hold Ashleigh, she reminded herself, all too aware that it had become a habit to squeeze as much time with her family as she could into a few ridiculously busy days that never left her satisfied. As soon as Alex took Ashleigh, the same dopey grin shared by everyone present spread across his face, and for a moment, the changes in him were sharply apparent. The last vestiges of boyhood were fading fast, she mused and wished she'd had more time to get to know him. She was pleased to see that he'd entirely shed his initial shy wariness just as Luke had after June had adopted *him*.

"So, Becky, where will you be staying until you find your own place?" Aaron Hammond asked, yanking her back to the present.

"Um…." She ducked her head sheepishly. Usually, she and Justin stayed in one of the guest cabins on the Royal R because her parents' small house was too cramped for five people, but her father had told her just last week that the cabins were all booked solid through the end of October. There would be only four people to squeeze into her parents' house now, but James's room—her old room—was barely big enough for him, and the couch wasn't comfortable to sleep on for more than a night or two. "I have no idea. Honestly, I *just* decided to move home two days ago, so I haven't gotten that far yet."

"She's gonna stay with us. Right, Becky?" James asked. "You can have your room back, and I'll sleep on the couch."

"I appreciate the offer, little man, but I'm not going to take your room."

"I have a better idea," Ryan said. "We have a spare room here in the cabin."

"No, you don't," Becky said. "You have a daughter now."

"Who will be in her crib in the loft with us for a

while so we don't have to tackle the stairs in the middle of the night," Luke said. "Besides, it'll be great for Ryan to have you around since Alex and I will be gone a lot with school and football. Unless your parents and James would rather you stay with them."

Becky glanced first at her parents, who were almost comically conflicted between their desire to have her close and the relief that they wouldn't have to rearrange their house to make room for her.

"It *would* be a lot more comfortable for you," her father remarked. "And we'll still see a lot of you—more than we've been able to in years—because you're home now."

Becky nodded, then turned her attention to her little brother. James fought to contain his disappointment, but it was a battle he was doomed to fail, and after a moment, his shoulders drooped.

"What about you and me spending time together?" he asked so quietly she barely heard him.

Grabbing his hand, Becky yanked him into her lap and hugged him tightly. "We're going to spend so much time together that you'll be sick of me and glad we don't live under the same roof. I promise."

"Impossible," he muttered. "I can't ever get sick of you."

"You say that now, James, but you're about to that age when you're going to start wanting more and more space." Becky turned to her cousin and his wife and son. "As long as you three are sure, that'd probably work out better than me trying to squeeze into my parents' house." *Or blowing my savings on rent*, she added to herself. *I really did not think this through.*

"We wouldn't have offered if it would be a problem," Ryan assured her. "Of course, you may change your mind after a few days of dealing with a crying baby and a hormonal new mom."

"Bring it on," Becky said, laughing. "Seriously. I wouldn't miss it—any of it—for the world. I don't want to miss anything ever again."

After dinner, as the sun sank below the western ridges and bathed the eastern peaks in light that shifted enchantingly from rich gold to vivid rose, Ryan excused herself to feed Ashleigh while June, Ben, Luke, and Alex cleared the remnants of the meal, and Coach Wells bid everyone good night, hugging Becky before he left with a heartfelt *glad you're back.*

She leaned back in her chair with her hands knitted behind her head and her legs stretched out in front of her and crossed at the ankles. Contentment settled wonderfully over her as she watched the shadows crawl up the eastern foothills. Closing her eyes for a few minutes, she inhaled deeply. It was as if the very bones of the earth beneath her were a magnet and she a piece of iron hopelessly unable to resist its pull and only truly at peace when she embraced it. Whatever it was, she had no trouble admitting that she had made the right decision to come home… even if she *hadn't* thought it out very well. Hell, she was newly single and not remotely upset about it.

She chatted with her parents, and the O'Neils and Hammonds updated her on the goings-on of Northstar, and for a handful of moments, it felt like she'd never left. She hadn't had time to indulge in this on her too-brief trips home over the last six years, and she was amazed at how much had changed… and how much hadn't. There were some new residents, a few new additions to longtime families, and several new hiking trails, and business at the Bedspread Inn, the Ramshorn Hot Springs, and the Royal R Ranch was booming. But otherwise, life in Northstar went on as it always had—at a blissfully unhurried pace.

Her aunt and uncle came back out with Alex right behind. Ryan came out a minute after and gingerly sat in the chair beside Becky.

"You know, for a woman who just gave birth two

days ago, you are remarkably energetic, Ryan," Becky observed. "Is it just a show or are you really that amazing?"

Ryan laughed heartily. "At least a little of the first, and I hope some of the second. I'm tired and sore, and my body feels totally strange and unfamiliar and a bit fragile, but I have this curious energy that makes me feel like I can conquer the world."

"She's just that amazing," Luke said as he stepped out the door with his daughter.

Becky stood up to meet him. "My turn again. Gimme."

Just as she took the baby from her father, a tingling at the base of her neck alerted her that someone was watching her, and she looked toward the road. Her heart lurched, thumping against her ribs with a flood of tangled emotions at the sight of that familiar face with its pleading brown eyes and cap of tousled dark blond hair. The last time she'd seen him, he'd been wearing a suit at Luke and Ryan's wedding, and as handsome as he'd been in it, he was far more appealing to her in those worn jeans, blue-gray and white plaid button-up shirt with its sleeves rolled up past his elbows, and scarred work boots.

Damn, she thought appreciatively. Then she jerked

herself back to reality. *That's exactly the kind of thinking that got your heart broken.*

"I'm sorry, Becky," Luke murmured. "I know this is awkward for you."

She met his concerned gaze with a smile. "Don't worry, Luke. I won't ruin your party."

"It's not my party that I'm worried about."

"I know. But I'll be okay." She grinned. "I'm too damned happy to be home to let even Shane ruin my night."

* * *

"It's late enough in the day now that you might as well go to Luke's party and head back to Hamilton in the morning."

After spending the day in Devyn meeting with his new coworkers and bosses, Shane was inclined to agree with his father about waiting until morning to drive back to the Bitterroot because the last thing he felt like doing was spending another four hours in his truck. No, there was one thing he was less inclined to do.

"Considering who's on the guest list for Luke's party, I don't think it's a good idea that I go, Dad."

"Horse shit," Austin muttered. "I thought the whole point of you moving back was to stop running from your troubles and face them."

Shane growled, but his father was right. "Fine. Let's go. Party's probably half over by now, anyhow."

Austin drove up to Luke's cabin, and Shane stared out the passenger-side window, watching the flicker of blue sky between the bottlebrush branches of the lodgepole pines and trying hard not to think about what awaited him at his old friend's cabin. His father parked behind a silver pickup Shane didn't recognize, and as he stepped out of his dad's truck, he habitually glanced at the other vehicle's plates to see where the truck was from, thinking maybe June's parents had driven out from Washington. It became immediately evident that it wasn't Luke's grandparents; the truck had Wyoming plates, and his heart dropped into his stomach as soon as it clicked what that meant.

Becky.

"It'll be fine," Austin remarked when Shane didn't immediately follow him. "So let's get a move on."

"I wouldn't be so quick to say it'll be fine, Dad. Becky's here." Shane's voice was strangled by a myriad of emotions that he hungered for with the poisonous fervor of addiction.

"So?"

"That's a lot more trouble than I feel up to handling right now."

He didn't say it, but he was tired of seeing hatred in Becky's enchanting gray eyes every time she looked at him. They'd seen each other only a handful of times since they'd broken up, and each time, she'd greeted him with a cold glare or a snarled "go to hell." He'd last seen her at Luke and Ryan's wedding, and if the cold shoulder she'd given him was any indication, time had not yet dimmed her anger.

"Well, get over it."

"I think it might be best if I just wait for you…" A glance up at the cabin stalled the words in his throat; Becky stood out on the deck with her cousin and holding Luke's daughter, echoing the day he'd so stupidly broken both their hearts. "…in the truck," he finished slowly. "I don't want to wreck Luke's party."

"You're not waiting in the truck."

Panic warred with thrill, and the desire to go to her and wrap her in his arms like he once had conflicted nauseatingly with the urge to flee. When she glanced up and their gazes met, his moment to escape ended abruptly, leaving him no choice but to follow his father up the hill.

He clenched his jaw and set off after Austin, whose ground-eating strides were a welcome reminder that his father was in very good shape. Dread and nervousness grew with each step he took, and by the time they reached the party, his heart was pounding too erratically to be explained by the little bit of exertion it had taken to climb the short hill. Luke greeted him with a grin.

"I'm glad your dad dragged you up here," he remarked.

"Yeah," Shane said. A smidgeon of the tension tightening the muscles of his neck and shoulders eased. "Sorry we're so late, but I *just* got back from my meetings in Devyn."

"Not a big deal. Dinner's over already, but there may be a steak left if you're hungry."

"Thanks, but I ate in town, and I think Dad already ate, too."

"I did. Got hungry waiting for you to get home," Austin confirmed.

"Well, make yourselves comfortable," Luke said, stepping out of the way so they could join the rest of the party on the deck.

Ryan, June, Ben, Pat, and the kids all greeted Shane warmly enough as did the Hammonds and Coach Wells and even Aelissm. Ryan's family was polite, except for Matt, who only nodded in greeting with a dark scowl on his face. No surprise there, Shane thought. Having said hello to everyone else, Shane turned at last to Becky. At the moment, she was too busy gazing at Luke and Ryan's daughter, and he expected that tender smile would turn into the cold, flat expression she seemed to reserve just for him as soon as she lifted her eyes.

"Hello, Becky," he said softly.

To his shock, the smile didn't disappear, and when she replied, her voice was disconcertingly gentle. "Hello, Shane."

"I assume we also missed the announcement," Austin said before Shane could make any further conversation with Becky, perhaps trying to stave off any awkwardness. "What'd you name her?"

"Ashleigh June," Ryan replied.

"Beautiful," Shane murmured. "She's got some big names to fill, though."

"Yes, she does," Luke agreed, "but she'll have all the love and support she'll need to make it happen."

Shane nodded and leaned against the post of the roof over the deck with his arms folded across his chest. The mood on the deck of Luke and Ryan's cabin was celebratory and at the same time completely mellow. Maybe it was the glorious evening, but he doubted it. The love and affection that bound these people together was palpable, and for the time being, they all seemed content to set aside whatever resentments they harbored against him.

This isn't so bad, he told himself as he listened to the relaxed chatter.

"Do you want to hold Ashleigh?"

Shane blinked at Becky, unable to recall her joining him at the edge of the deck. He stared blankly at her, wondering what she'd just asked and why she was willingly talking to him. Finally, he asked, "What?"

"I asked if you wanted to hold Ashleigh," Becky repeated. "Everyone else has held her at least twice, including your dad. So… it's your turn."

"Uh… I don't think I'm quite ready to try that again," he replied, eyeing the baby in her arms.

She shrugged. "Suit yourself."

Becky took the baby back to Luke and, to Shane's further surprise, rejoined him with her back to the cabin and her thumbs hooked in the back pockets of her jeans. They stood in surprisingly pleasant silence for several minutes, mutually enjoying the sweeping view of the valley and its guarding mountains. Sensing that he was holding on to his angst in preparation to defend himself against her hatred, he took a deep breath and let go of those instincts as he exhaled, deciding to appreciate this moment of serenity with her for as long as it lasted.

Unbidden, his gaze shifted to his companion, tracing every cherished line of her that was within sight. Her eyes were the same stunning gray as he remembered, but her hair was longer than she'd ever worn it, and loose, it probably fell to her lower ribs in soft, nearly black waves. She was nearly as tall as he was— just two inches shorter at five-nine—and had an athletic body honed by a lifetime spent working on a ranch. There was a startling femininity about her, however, and the tomboyish ponytail, T-shirt, jeans, and stained, lace-up cowboy boots did nothing to cover it up. Instead, it allowed her natural beauty to shine through.

Damn, she was sexy. She was even with anger darkening her features, but with that contented smile—something he hadn't seen in close to a decade—she was the most remarkable woman he'd ever laid eyes on. In the years they'd spent apart, Rebecca Epperson had grown into the beauty her coltish adolescence had only hinted at. With a bemused grin, Shane imagined her old "friends" who had so mercilessly teased her now seethed with envy. Amusement gave way to longing, and he understood with a new clarity just how much he'd missed her.

Shifting his weight, he said, "No one mentioned you would be back in Northstar. I'm guessing that means it was an unexpected trip."

"It was definitely unexpected, but it's not a trip," she replied, glancing at him. Her smile deepened. "I'm moving home."

Given their more recent past history, her admission should have made him shudder with panic, but instead, it brought him tranquility because she belonged here as much as he did, and Northstar had been missing something without her. He lifted one corner of his mouth. "Somehow, that makes me feel like things might someday be right in the world again."

"You and me both," she said with a laugh. "I hear I'm not the only one moving back. Why now, Shane?"

"Didn't you hear about Dad's cancer scare?"

Becky glanced sharply over her shoulder at Austin, then she turned her gaze fully on him, and her eyes widened with shock. "No, I didn't. Why didn't anyone tell me?"

"I think he tried to keep it quiet, and it sounds like he might have actually succeeded."

"What was it? Is he going to be all right?"

"Yeah. Jeremiah noticed the spot above Dad's

eyebrow, and the docs were able to get it early, and they say he'll be just fine."

Becky offered him a sympathetic smile. "I'll bet that scared the hell out of you."

"It really did. Made me realize that he won't always be around and that I haven't spent nearly enough time with him in the last ten years, so… here I am."

She lowered her gaze to the deck and pushed a piece of gravel off with the toe of her boot. Was that a flash of guilt that crossed her face just now?

"I hope I'm not the reason you stayed away," she murmured with her eyes still lowered. "If so, I'm sorry for that. No matter how angry I was with you, I never would have wanted you to give up time with your dad because of me."

She *was* the reason he'd stayed way, but that didn't make it her fault. He was entirely to blame. Of course, admitting any of that would likely take their conversation down a path that he had no desire to ever tread again, so he simply shook his head and said nothing, unwilling to jeopardize this tentative truce even to put her mind at ease. After a minute passed in silence, he said quietly, "It's a gorgeous evening."

"Yes, it is," she agreed with something that sounded like relief. "All the more so because, two years ago, I was beginning to fear Luke would never find a way to fully get past what JP did to him. And now… he loves his job and he's happily married with a brand-new baby girl."

"And an adopted son," Shane added. "I haven't gotten to spend much time with Alex yet, but he seems like a great kid. He reminds me so much of Luke before all that crap happened."

"I agree… on all counts."

Becky let her gaze wander out over the valley, which was quickly darkening into twilight. Behind them, lights blazed from inside the newly finished cabin, coaxing golden highlights from her dark hair. She glanced briefly over her shoulder, then turned back to Shane, and when she smiled, his heart tripped over itself in delight.

"It's good to see you and Luke getting along again," she murmured.

Shane nodded in agreement and studied her for a moment, wondering when this refreshing camaraderie was going to end. There was no sign of the emotions he'd come to expect from her, only that beautiful and unwavering joy. Unable to stand the suspense, he decided to risk triggering her anger. "This is the longest conversation we've had in years. Actually, it's the first *real* conversation we've had. Do you mind if I ask what's changed?"

For a long time, she didn't answer. She simply stared out across the valley with her lips pursed and her brows lightly pinched in a contemplative frown. As the seconds ticked away, Shane began to relax again as it became clear that she wasn't going to take offense to his inquiry.

"I guess I finally got tired of holding on to my anger. Maybe I'm old enough and wise enough now to understand that it was taking too much energy to maintain it. I haven't been home nearly enough in the last several years, and every time I came home…. I let my anger take some of the joy out of the few visits I made." She twisted her lips in amusement. "And Luke might have chastised me at his wedding about it."

"He did?"

"Yeah. After you left early from the reception. He told me that I'd never be free from what happened in the past if I kept trying to hold on to it."

"Sounds like something he'd say."

She laughed, and Shane briefly closed his eyes to enjoy it. It had been so long since he'd heard her laugh, and the sound was more cherished than even the sighing of the summer evening breeze through the pines and the distant calls of the cattle that populated the Northstar Valley.

"Besides," Becky continued, "since we're both back in Northstar, it'd probably be best for everyone if we set our differences aside and find a way to get along."

Shane chuckled, lightheaded with relief. "That's for damned sure."

"Truce?"

He turned to face her and saw that her hand was extended. Grinning perhaps too broadly, he shook her hand and said with complete honesty, "Truce."

Three

"ABOUT TIME YOU TWO GOT HOME," Becky chided teasingly when Luke and Alex strode through the front door of the cabin at a quarter after seven.

Luke braced his hands on the back of the couch and leaned down to give his wife a kiss before he turned a tired smile on Becky. "Sorry. Practice ran a bit late."

Alex dropped his backpack on the floor beside the front door, then sprawled on the loveseat with his arms flopped out to the sides, his legs stretched out in front of him, and his head resting on the back. After only a moment's respite, he bounced to his feet again and strode over to Ryan to take Ashleigh. Becky smiled fondly. Yesterday, when she had jokingly remarked that Alex was making a habit of spoiling Ashleigh, he had replied that not long ago he'd thought he would never get the chance to spoil a sister. It was the same thing Luke had said after *his* little brother's birth, and the same thing Becky had thought when she'd been surprised by James's arrival. The fact that neither Kyle nor Ashleigh were Luke's or Alex's biological siblings did not seem to matter one bit, and maybe that minor detail actually made them more appreciative.

Speaking of younger siblings, I need to go pick mine up.

"Well, dinner's in the oven, and it'll be done in about five minutes," Becky remarked, pushing to her feet. "Chicken enchiladas, which I know are a favorite."

"Everything's a favorite with these two," Ryan quipped. "Thanks for cooking again, Becky."

"Don't I know it," Becky said with a laugh. "And you're welcome. I have to do *something* around here to earn my keep so I'm not inconveniencing you too much."

"Not possible," Luke said as he walked into the kitchen to grab plates and silverware, "We're too glad you're here to be inconvenienced."

"Yes, we are," Luke's wife agreed. She got up and helped her husband set the table while Alex indulged in some sibling bonding.

"I'm glad to hear it, but I'm going to depart and give you all some quiet family time because I need to go get James. I'm already running late."

"Have fun," Luke told her.

Becky grabbed her windbreaker and dashed out the door. She'd been home only a week, but already, she was falling into a comfortable routine. On weekday mornings, she helped out down at the Ramshorn, and in the early afternoons, she spent time with Luke's wife, cherishing the opportunity to get to know the woman who'd captured her cousin's heart and finally torn down the last of the walls he'd built to protect himself. Becky found herself quickly forming a strong friendship with Ryan built as much on a natural compatibility as their mutual fondness for Luke.

She'd also had plenty of time to reconnect with her parents and brother, the latter of whom she now picked up from the Northstar School every day. She spent at least an hour—usually two—with him every afternoon, often helping him with his homework or exploring the ranch with him before she headed back to Luke and Ryan's to assist with dinner. Saturday and Sunday, she'd led trail rides for Ramshorn guests, and James had tagged along, proving quickly that he was a good hand to have around. Though he was only nine, he was a skilled rider and commanded the respect of the greenhorns with the same quiet confidence their father exuded. Becky couldn't be more proud of her little brother. To top it off, their mutual love of being ranch kids made it a genuine pleasure to spend time with him despite the age difference of nearly eighteen years.

James sat on the steps of the porch reading a book while their mother and Jessie Robinson sipped glasses of lemonade in the chairs. Becky took in the familiar sight of her old home with its cheerful yellow siding and covered porch and, with her mother and brother sitting as they were, was reminded of another day many years past when her uncle had picked her up for her first of many weekends at his and June's cabin. That day had been the beginning of her incredible friendship with Luke.

"That's a smile I haven't seen on your face in a long time," Jane mused as Becky climbed out of her truck. "What are you thinking about?"

"Good times with my family," she replied.

"Have a seat, if you can spare a few minutes."

Becky sat on the steps beside her brother with her back against the handrail, facing both James and the two women. With a happy sigh, she let her gaze wander briefly over the broad, summer-browned field between her parents' house and the main house. Buildings rimmed the field—five small staff cabins and five larger guest cabins that sat between her parents' house and the main house on the southern and western sides, and the barn, corrals, and machinery garages stretched across the northern side. A gravel road looped around the field just inside the circle of buildings, connecting them all, and Crystal Creek flowed from northeast to southwest through the center of it with a man-made pond stocked with trout for kids to fish right smack in the middle. Two thick bands of lodgepole pines and alpine spruces bordered the entire compound, one to the north beyond the barn, garages, and livestock pens and corrals, and the other to the south behind the staff housing. Beyond, surrounding the compound, were several hundred acres of grazing pasture and forest. For Becky, it was heaven on earth.

Jim and Jessie Robinson had purchased the land in their early twenties for a rock-bottom price from an old rancher who hadn't been able to turn a profit. It was simply too high in the mountains for what he wanted to get from it. The Robinsons had stubbornly eked out a living with the assistance of only two employees—Becky's maternal grandparents, James and Eleanor Conner—for many years until they'd had the brilliant idea to turn the place into a dude ranch. It had taken a few years to build up the business, but gradually through persistence and hard work, they'd turned it into a resounding success.

James's recurring shoulder injury and the failing health of Eleanor's parents had forced them to leave the ranch with their two children—Jane, then fourteen, and Ben, only eight—and move to Washington. Her family's tie to the ranch might have ended there, but Jane had returned at nineteen to take the Robinsons up on their open offer of a job. By that time, Becky's father, who had lost both his parents in a car accident, had taken over James's position as ranch foreman.

And the Robinsons themselves… they had become part of her family long before her birth, and she'd grown up thinking of them as her surrogate grandparents, replacing the ones she'd lost in that car wreck. They were probably closer to her than her Conner grandparents, whom she hadn't seen nearly enough until they'd moved back to Northstar the summer before her senior year. They'd been there for all her birthdays and watched her graduate from high school *and* college, and more importantly, they had inspired in both her and her parents a deep and enduring love of life on a ranch.

This place and these people are in my blood, my heart, and my soul, she mused. *Always pulling me back. One more reason Justin and I never would have worked out.*

"I know I've said it since you've been back," Jessie said, leaning forward in her chair to rest her hand on Becky's shoulder, "but it's so good to have you back, Becky."

"It's good to *be* back. I missed this so much—everything and every*one*. I know I've been home a few times, but those trips didn't give me the chance to just sit here and reconnect." She tipped her head back and groaned. "Ugh. I never should have left."

"You were young and adventurous and you needed to stretch your legs and see what else was out there," Jessie observed thoughtfully. "I'm sure Justin's ranch was more exciting, but the Royal R does have a certain quiet charm that our guests seem to appreciate."

Becky shook her head. "This place is much more than the Teton South will ever be. It's special and real.

The Sutherlands' place is too commercialized."

"Yeah, Jessie," James piped. "It's way fancier, and believe me, that's not a good thing. This place is so much better."

"Thanks, kiddo."

"It's getting late, so if I'm going to keep my promise to James about our brother-sister dinner at the Bedspread, we should probably get going." Becky stood and hugged Jessie and her mother, then turned to James. "You ready to go, little man?"

"Yeah! I'll be right back."

He got up to take his book inside, but Jane held out her hand. "Just go. I'll put your book away."

"Thanks, Mom. Love you!"

"Love you both. Have fun."

"We will," Becky vowed.

By the time they arrived at the Bedspread Inn, it was just after eight—much later than she'd hoped to eat dinner. James, being the growing boy that he was, quickly announced that he was starving, so she chose a table beside the front windows to best enjoy the fantastic view of the Northstar Mountains aglow with the last, fading light of sunset. To her surprise, Pat and Aelissm were both working tonight.

After Aeli greeted them, she held up the menus in

her hand. "Do you two even need these?"

"I don't think so," Becky replied.

"James, I know you want a bacon cheeseburger with fries, right? And a Roy Rogers to drink."

"Right."

"And for you, Becky?"

"That sounds really good, but I think I'll have the rib eye. Medium rare with the rice pilaf and salad with ranch dressing. And I'll take an iced tea with just a pinch of sugar and lemon."

Aelissm nodded and disappeared into the kitchen.

"So, did you get the rest of your homework done after I left this afternoon?" Becky asked James.

"Yep. Which means we get to play games after dinner, right?"

"If there's time," she replied. "It's already getting pretty late, and you have school tomorrow."

James growled. "There's not enough time in the day."

Becky laughed loudly at that. "You, mister, are far too young to have that problem."

"Obviously not," he retorted with a sass that reminded Becky strongly of their mother. Maybe he wasn't so quiet spoken after all.

"If you think it's bad now, just wait until you're

my age."

"Are we going on any more trail rides this week-end?"

"I don't know yet. Maybe."

"If so, do I get to go again?"

"James, as big a help as you were *last* weekend, I would happily *beg* you to go."

He grinned widely in reply.

The bell on the front door jingled, and Becky habitually glanced over her shoulder to see if she knew who'd entered. Her heart skittered when she saw Shane and Austin striding inside, but before she had time to decide if their arrival might put a damper on her evening with her brother, James called out to them.

"Hi, Austin! Hi, Shane!"

"Hi there, James," Austin replied. "Evening, Becky."

"Austin," Becky said, standing to embrace him. Her issues with Shane had never diminished her fondness for his father. "It's good to see you again, although I'm a little miffed I didn't hear about your cancer scare until Shane told me last week."

"It was nothing to worry you or anyone else over."

"Bullshit. *You* are worth worrying over." Before

Austin could shrug her off again, she turned to his son. "How are you, Shane?"

"I'm good. You?"

"Good. Just spending some quality time with my date for the evening."

"Handsome date you've got there," Shane said with her favorite playful gleam in his eyes. "We're just here for a couple of beers, so we'll leave you to it."

"Wait," James said. He shifted his gaze from Shane and Austin to Becky. "Can they sit with us?"

"James, I don't—"

"This is your time with your sister," Austin interrupted. "We don't want to intrude."

"Please, Austin? You still haven't told me the rest of that story about how Beth got lost in the snowstorm and how Nick found her."

"No, I haven't because that's a story you should hear from them. They tell it better."

"No one tells better stories than you do," James said with conviction. "Please sit with us."

"It's up to your sister," Austin said.

James turned hopeful eyes on Becky. "Please, Becky?"

Sighing, she acquiesced. "He's not going to let it go, so you might as well join us."

"Are you sure that's all right?" Shane asked.

She nodded and told James to scoot around to her side of the table. Austin sat across from James so he could finish the story, leaving Shane—to Becky's simultaneous irritation and delight—the chair across from her. For a moment, they listened as Austin picked up the tale they both knew well of how, when Nick and Beth Hammond were a couple years younger than James, Beth had gone out in a snowstorm to check on an orphaned kitten and how Nick had known just where to find her. It was a good story, Becky thought, but she knew how it ended—with them returning safe and sound after riding out the storm snuggled together in one of the sheds on the Lazy H Ranch—so she instead directed her attention to Shane.

"He idolizes the two of you," Becky observed. With an amused roll of her eyes, she added, "He thinks it's awesome that you sort of grew up on all the Northstar ranches instead of *just the one* he's stuck to."

"It was a good way to grow up," Shane said. "I certainly have no complaints."

"And now you work for the Forest Service." She shook her head. "I never would have seen that one coming. Not from a gifted artist like you."

"It's too hard to make money with art."

"Sad, but true. Why forestry, though? That's such a science-heavy degree, and I seem to remember you hating science for a long time."

"I like being outside even more than I like art," he replied with a grin. "And thanks mostly to June, that forestry degree wasn't nearly as difficult as I thought it would be. Plus, it opened the door for a job I really enjoy."

"Somehow, that doesn't surprise me. I know you're a forestry tech for the Forest Service, but that's a pretty broad description."

Shane grinned again. "I'm one of the guys who gets to maintain trails, campgrounds, fishing access sites, and the like."

"Which means you get to spend the overwhelming amount of your time out of doors."

"Yep."

"Lucky you."

Aelissm returned with Becky's and James's beverages as well as a Trout Slayer each for Shane and Austin drink orders. Undoubtedly, she'd seen them walk in and knew exactly what they would order; Austin, at least, was a regular, and Becky knew his son shared his taste in beer.

What does it say about me that I know what kind of beer

he likes even though I haven't ever bothered to ask? Becky wondered.

When Aelissm left again, Shane resumed the conversation, but shifted the focus to Becky. She marveled at how easy it was to talk to him now that she'd decided to let go of her anger; it was actually a relief to not hate—or rather, pretend to hate—him anymore.

She hadn't allowed herself to take notice on the few occasions they'd crossed paths, too aware that paying him more than a fleeting glance would destroy her ability to shut him out. Even back in high school, he'd been fit—the result of playing football with a dedication that rivaled Luke's—and though he hadn't played in some time, he'd maintained his physique, but there was something *unfamiliar* about him. It was a subtle change, but maturity had erased the last traces of boyhood, and with her pulse escalating, Becky admitted that she liked the more rugged masculinity, which was enhanced by a few days' stubble that dusted his jaw.

He's the same old Shane, she thought, *but different, too.*

"And you have a bachelor's in animal science now, right?" Shane inquired, yanking her attention back into a safer zone of thought. "Like Nick Hammond."

"Yep, and I'm certified in AI like him, too."

"Have you looked into doing that? I imagine it'd pay very well, although impregnating cows doesn't seem like a fun career."

"It pays very well, and I *should* look into it, but no, it's not what I want to do," Becky replied. With a wiggle of her eyebrows, she added, "Besides, it takes all the fun out of breeding for the bulls, and let's face it, Northstar has some prime bulls."

"Uh-huh. Something tells me you aren't talking about cattle anymore."

Busted. Because she didn't dare admit that he was right, she only grinned smugly at him and was rewarded by a smile that was both devilish and adorably embarrassed.

"So, anyhow…" he said. "Do you have any plans for work yet, or are you taking some time to enjoy being home?"

"A little of both." Becky was grateful *one* of them was able to stay on track because she certainly wasn't. "I'm helping out at the Ramshorn—leading trail rides and taking care of the horses, mostly. It's not full time, but I like that. It's not like I have any bills other than student loans to pay at the moment since I'm staying with Luke and Ryan, so it's nice to have the time to get reacquainted with Northstar."

"Is it easy being back or is it an adjustment?"

"In some ways, it's a lot easier than I thought it would be… but it's an adjustment. I haven't been home much since I left for college, and it's different living with Luke and Ryan instead of with my parents and brother."

"What do you mean you haven't been home much? Didn't you come home during the summers while you were at MSU?"

"Other than that first summer, I only came home on the weekends and over the holidays. I got my AI certification and took a few extra classes in hospitality and tourism thinking they might be useful to the Royal R. Instead, they got me a job on a guest ranch in Wyoming."

"I didn't know that."

"Well, home was a bit awkward. My family had changed, and I wasn't around enough to fully adjust to that, I guess."

Shane lowered his gaze and twisted his beer around in his hands for a moment. "I remember the day James was born. You said you were afraid everything would change again."

"Yeah, a lot changed that day," she replied icily. "And the next day, too. Didn't it, Shane?"

He swore under his breath, but instead of avoiding the topic like she expected, he met her gaze head on. "I'm sorry, Becky. I was so—"

"Did you two used to date before I was born?" James asked cheerfully, abruptly cutting into their conversation.

Becky felt like she'd been kicked in the chest by a horse. She stared at her brother's bright, expectant face for several pounding beats of her heart and wondered if the world had turned over.

"Wh-what?" she sputtered at last.

"Austin said you used to be good friends," James explained. "Why did you stop being good friends? Good friends usually stay friends, but boyfriends and girlfriends break up, right?"

She glanced at Shane and saw her shock reflected.

"That's some interesting logic, James," Austin said slowly. "But sometimes even good friends go their separate ways, too."

James frowned thoughtfully, and thinking he'd let the subject go at that, Becky took another sip of her iced tea.

"It woulda been cool to have Shane as a brother," James remarked.

Becky inhaled sharply, and a trickle of her tea tried

to go down the wrong pipe. She coughed until her eyes watered, and all the while, James looked at her in confusion. Shane took a long drink of his beer, then stared at the bottle as if it was the most interesting thing in the world. The crimson that climbed up his neck and threatened to spread across his face, however, belied his unconcerned expression, and after she recovered, Becky was gleefully delighted to see that she wasn't the only one who didn't know how to handle her brother's remark.

"What?" James asked. "What'd I say wrong?"

"Not wrong," Austin corrected. "Awkward."

"Why? I like Shane, and he *would* be a cool brother. Or I guess he'd be my brother-in-law, though, right? That's what you call a sister's—"

"Yes, that would be the correct term, James."

Mercifully, Aelissm arrived with their food, and Austin was able to redirect James's attention with another story, this time the one about John Wellman, the penniless miner who had partnered with a wealthy doctor to claim the silver at the end of the road where the Conners' and O'Neils' cabins were. Becky let out a sigh of relief and settled in to her meal, determined to keep the conversation from returning to topics that were sure to ruin the evening.

James finished well before she did, proving just how hungry he'd been, and while she ate, she listened as he quizzed Shane about his job with the Forest Service. Shane indulged him with good humor and seemed like he genuinely enjoyed the conversation, and Becky shook her head, smiling when their talk took a turn into the territory of male bonding. Fishing quickly became the topic of choice, and they told tall tales about all the gargantuan fish they'd caught in their lives.

"I've got you both beat, and unlike you two, I have photo proof," Becky remarked. "Remember that twenty-three-inch lake trout I caught a couple years ago when we all went fishing out at Armstead Canyon Reservoir?"

"Oh, man, Shane, you shoulda seen that bugger," James piped, holding his hands out to show the size of the fish. "It was *huge*."

Shane chuckled. "As I recall, your sister has always been a top-notch fisherman."

After that, their conversation shifted to Becky's fishing prowess, so she humbly returned her focus to her meal while they talked. Shane was so good with James, and the way he focused on her little brother had the boy chattering away. James wasn't what she would call shy, but he was usually quiet spoken like Andy, so to hear him talking a million miles an hour soon had Becky's cheeks aching with ceaseless mirth. She glanced at Shane and mused that, had Ryan not miscarried, he probably would have made a good dad.

The thought bounded exuberantly and unwelcomed into her head, and Becky jerked back and scowled. It didn't matter what kind of father he would have been because he'd coldly turned his back on that responsibility. Shaking her head, she chided herself for letting her guard down for even a moment. Allowing such thoughts to take root would certainly destroy the good mood of the evening, so she reminded herself that, despite how traumatic loosing her child must have been for Ryan, things *had* otherwise turned out for the best. She and Luke were as happy as any couple Becky knew, and considering the love her parents shared or that between Uncle Ben and Aunt June, that was saying something.

Despite her admonishment, she couldn't entirely keep Shane out of her thoughts, drawn to him as she'd always been, so she focused on other things about him.

There was something else perhaps more fascinating than the physical changes she'd noted earlier. When he and Austin had first joined her and James, there had been a noticeable tension about Shane that had since dissipated, and for the time being, he was as laid back as she remembered him to be. Though she and Ryan hadn't officially agreed upon it, they tended to avoid the topic of their mutual ex, but Becky recalled Luke's wife once comparing Shane to Luke, calling Shane intense and edgy while noting Luke's innate serenity. At first, she hadn't been able to reconcile the Shane Ryan knew with the one she'd known, but after some thought, she knew Ryan was right.

When had he changed?

She opened the door to their past just a tiny bit to peek in, and in doing so, she understood that he hadn't been the same after Mike's and Carol's deaths. There *had* been an unusual intensity about him when they were together, but the only element of it she'd noticed—or bothered to pay attention to—was the strain between him and Luke. Now she thought he'd become quieter and more introspective after Mike and Carol died, bottling things up instead of letting them breathe.

I guess that's understandable, she thought.

Of the five people he should have been able to count on to help him through that tragedy, two had been murdered and a third had had even more trauma to work through, leaving Shane with only his father and Becky. Austin had tried to understand but hadn't known how because he couldn't imagine how it affected Shane… or any of them. Shane hadn't been able to talk about it with Becky much, either, because every time the subject came up, it only turned into another failed attempt to find closure and understanding, and they'd ended up burying it again like scar tissue around a sliver, shielding themselves from the pain but never removing the cause.

The moment sympathy flared, she doused it because they'd all been hurt deeply that summer and in the weeks, months, and years that followed. No matter the reasons, he *had* broken her heart and he *had* walked away from Ryan in a most heartless way, and Becky refused to get caught in that trap a second time… even if her heart leapt every time she saw him.

Austin once again claimed James's rapt attention with another story, so Shane turned back to Becky.

"I guess you did a good job of keeping your loathing for me a secret from your brother," he said quietly. "Thank you for that."

"I didn't do it for you," she replied. "I did it for self-preservation."

"I'm aware of that, but thank you anyhow."

Becky sat up and studied him for a moment with

her last bite of steak skewered and forgotten on her fork. That was—for the second time tonight—*not* the reaction she'd expected.

"Why are you looking at me like that?" he asked warily.

"You're not…." She paused, pursing her lips. "After Mike and Carol died, you were so defensive all the time, and you bottled everything up. Now you're not. At least not right now."

He smiled sadly but offered no explanation, and she didn't push the matter even though it made her incredibly curious. What had he started to say earlier when he'd apologized the first time? He'd been so…. So what? Messed up? Selfish? Stupid?

Abruptly, she closed her mind to the questions popping up like her mother's crocuses through the snow in spring and hurriedly finished the rest of her dinner, then flagged Aelissm down. Since James had to be in bed by ten at the latest, Becky paid the check, and announced that it was time to call it a night.

"Thanks for joining us," she told Shane and Austin. "It was fun."

"Yes, it was," Shane agreed. Leaning in a little so only Becky could hear, he murmured, "Even if your brother *did* almost give us both a heart attack."

"What's life without a little excitement?" she replied playfully, surprising herself. "Have a good night, boys. Come on, James. Time to go home if you want to play even *one* quick card game before bed."

With her hands on James's slender shoulders, she ushered him out the door. Before they headed down the stairs to her truck, she paused and glanced over her shoulder at Shane and was unsurprised to find him watching her. When their gazes met, he looked away, and regret swept unrestrained over his face. Her brows dipped in a frown momentarily before a subtle smile erased it. For the first time since the night he'd broken her heart, Becky found something to like about him, and while that made him incredibly dangerous, it also made her believe he might have at last become the man she'd always suspected he could be—the kind of man who could rebuild her trust and reclaim her heart... and be worthy of it.

* * *

Shane watched Becky walk outside for a moment before forcing his attention from her just as their gazes met. He hadn't yet recovered fully from the shock of her brother's announcement, and her observation that he wasn't as defensive as he used to be didn't help. Neither had her not-so-subtle appraisal right before that comment about the quality of Northstar's bulls. Where in all holy hell had *that* come from?

His face warmed uncomfortably at the blatant innuendo behind the remark, and he took a few deep breaths to slow his racing heart and quell the lingering jitters. It didn't do much good, so he drained the rest of his beer in a swallow, set the bottle at the edge of the table, leaned back in his chair with his hands knitted behind his head, and sought *any* distraction.

He glanced up at the dark-stained ceiling beams, and his eyes skipped from one familiar, teal-emblazoned ranch brand to the next—the Lazy H, C Diamond, Royal R, Bar E, and Marsh among others. He'd worked them all alongside his father as a boy and as a teenager, and he would have been content to work them again had the forestry tech position at the Devyn Forest Service office not opened. More than content, but the life of a ranch hand was hard and uncertain, and he wanted to have something more to offer his future wife because, as puerile as it might be to include it in his thought process, the financial instability had likely been a contributing factor to his own mother's decision to abandon her husband and son.

"Now, that was something I thought I'd never see again," Austin remarked.

"Oh? And what is that?" he inquired. *So much for distraction.*

"The two of you getting along." His father took a drink of his beer, and when he set the empty bottle down. Austin's eyes narrowed with smugness satisfaction. "Not just getting along but entirely absorbed with each other."

"What are you talking about?" Shane asked even though he already knew the answer. While he and Becky had been talking, he hadn't paid attention to anything but her, which was how James had managed to catch him so entirely off guard with that question.

"You know exactly what I'm talking about. There's still a very powerful bond between you, and don't you dare try to deny it because I'm not blind. The question isn't whether or not any feelings remain but rather what you should do about it."

"Nothing, Dad. There's nothing to be done about it because, until recently, Becky hated my guts. And rightfully so."

"Until recently…" Austin repeated. "If you ask me, I don't think she ever hated you. I'd be willing to bet the ranch that staying angry with you was a defense mechanism."

"Then it's a good thing you don't have a ranch to

bet."

Austin held up his hands in a show of peace. When Pat walked by on his way to another table, Austin lifted his empty bottle, and Pat nodded in acknowledgement. To Shane, Austin said, "I won't push it, but you'll have to excuse me while I sit back and watch the show."

"Another Trout Slayer, Austin?" Pat asked, striding over.

"Yep."

"Shane, how about you?"

"No, thanks. I'm driving."

"Can I get you something else, then?"

Shane's eyes sidetracked to Becky's empty glass. "Yeah. How about an iced tea?"

Pat left with the empties expertly clutched in one hand and Becky's and James's plates balanced on the other. He returned moments later with their drinks before leaving again, and Shane watched the man glide from one table to the next as he took over for his wife, who must have ducked into the back to work on other Bedspread business. With a twist of his lips, Shane mused that his wish to enjoy a couple beers with his dad in a quiet bar would remain unanswered. The Bedspread's restaurant was packed, just as it had been every night since he'd made his final return to Northstar on Thursday with all his belongings tied down to the trailer he'd borrowed from the Hammonds.

"For a slow night," Shane said, "it isn't very slow."

"Business has been good for Northstar in recent years."

"Obviously."

Shane nursed his iced tea, glancing out at the deck even though Becky and James were long gone, smiling as he thought back on his conversation with the kid. He reminded Shane strongly of Becky at that age and made him long for the days before tragedy had shattered their lives. Where would they be now if Mike and Carol hadn't died? Would he and Becky have stayed together, gotten married, and now be regaling their own children with tales of past adventures? Or would things have turned out exactly as they had?

"You're still thinking about her."

Shane glanced sideways at his father. "Believe it or not, I think about her a lot. Always have."

"Then why in the hell did you break up with her? I used to think you were blind to how much that girl loved you, but now I think there was something else entirely going on."

Because it would only open up old wounds more than they had been already tonight, Shane didn't respond. His father took his silence as confirmation.

"And yet you're going to sit here and tell me there's nothing you can do—are *willing* to do—about it."

"I thought you said you weren't going to push it."

"I did," Austin replied. "But I'm watching my son lose himself in thoughts about a woman he gave up and should have pushed from his mind a long time ago."

Growling in frustration, Shane asked, "Why can't you just let this go tonight?"

"Because I firmly believe there is something between you and Becky worth fighting for. Something your mother and I never had." Austin took a long swallow of his beer, and his expression turned thoughtful and slightly remorseful. "It's taken me a long time to see it, but Kelly never loved me like that, and I've come to realize I didn't really love her, either. For your sake, I wish we'd realized it sooner… before you were old enough to be hurt by her leaving."

The tension that had vanished while he'd talked with Becky and James returned, aching in his neck and shoulders. If there was one subject guaranteed to get his mind off Becky, it was the woman who had taught him at a very young age how to leave when things didn't go his way.

"I never told you," Austin continued, "but we've been in contact a few times over the years. The first time she called was about four years after she left. She was engaged, and I guess her fiancé wanted her to clear the air or make sure she was firm in her decision to cut ties with her first family."

Shane stared at his father for several moments, wondering if he'd actually heard his father say he'd talked with his ex-wife since she'd run off. "Why are you telling me this now?"

Austin met his gaze, and the regret that briefly shadowed his eyes sparked a surge of disgust for what his mother had done to his father when she'd so abruptly decided she couldn't handle marriage and a kid anymore. Another, more troubling thought followed on its heels. Hadn't he done the exact same thing to Ryan? No, not exactly, but close enough and just as reprehensible if not more so.

"Maybe that cancer scare made *me* realize a few things, too," his father said. "She's asked about you a few times, and I think she feels guilty about leaving you even if she never wanted a kid in the first place."

"So?"

"Well, it's not my place to decide whether or not she's worthy of your time, and I've kept that choice from you."

"What choice?"

"Whether or not you want to reconnect with her."

"How can I reconnect with her? I don't even *know* her."

"Maybe not, but she *is* your mother, Shane."

"No, she's a stranger. And didn't she give up parental rights, anyhow?"

"Yes, she did."

"Then what is the point of reconnecting with her… assuming she even wants to?"

"Maybe there isn't any point," Austin conceded. "I'm not saying you *should* reconnect with her. I'm just saying it should be your choice. Not mine."

Shane probed his feelings regarding his absentee mother, and other than the anger over how she'd hurt his father, he felt nothing for her. Undoubtedly, since he seemed prone to do as she had, he'd inherited something from her, but that was something he was determined to conquer. Aside from that, he'd had a great life with his father, and he wouldn't trade even a second of it to change the past because it would have been different had his mother stayed. Her unhappiness would have taken some of the joy out of life for both him and his father.

"Dad?"

"Hmm?"

"Why didn't you remarry? I used to think it was because you still loved her."

Austin shook his head. "I realized I didn't love her like I thought I did when, as the years went by, I stopped thinking about her."

Unwilling to be dragged into another conversation about Becky, Shane ignored the pointed look his father gave him. "Okay, but why didn't you move on with someone else?"

"I never found anyone I wanted to spend the rest of my life with. I married your mother because I thought it was the right thing to do. It wasn't, of course, but at the time…."

"As I recall, you weren't exactly out there looking for someone new, either. I think I can remember you going on *maybe* five dates my entire childhood."

"Had no desire and no reason to. It might be foolish, but Kelly made me a little gun-shy of women." Austin paused to finish his beer. "Besides, I had my son and a life I loved, and that was enough for me."

"Thanks, Dad," Shane murmured. "We *have* had a pretty good life, just the two of us."

"Yup, we have. Barring a couple of hurdles, we've done all right."

He didn't have to ask to know what hurdles his father spoke of, and he deeply regretted that his stupid decisions had damaged his relationship with Austin. "I'm working to fix that."

"And you're doing a good job of it so far, too."

"Looks like you two are having quite a serious conversation."

Shane glanced up to see Luke striding over and realized he hadn't noticed the other man's arrival. When Luke slid into the seat Becky had occupied not too long ago, Shane asked, "What are you doing here so late?"

"Mom got a call from a panicked client whose daughter's wedding the Ramshorn is hosting at the end of the month, so she asked me to come down here to double-check a few of the details with Pat and Aelissm, since they're in charge of the reception."

"At a quarter to ten at night?"

Luke shrugged. "They're an hour behind us."

"And you couldn't have just called down?"

"No. It's something I need to see—a matter of

logistics. Speaking of the wedding, it's a trail ride, and we're short-handed even now that Becky's hired on. You wouldn't be interested in a job for a day, would you, Shane? That is… as long as you and Becky can continue to be civil to one another. I don't imagine the bride and groom would appreciate their guides getting into an argument and spoiling their special day."

"I think we'll be all right," Shane replied. "She seems to have gotten over her desire to rip my heart out, so we've actually been able to have a couple of real conversations now."

Luke quirked a brow. "Interesting choice of words."

"Don't read too much into it."

"Read as much into as you want, Luke," Austin remarked. "We joined her and James for dinner, and we all had quite a nice time."

"Fascinating," Luke said. He glanced between Shane and his father, but didn't press the matter. "Anyhow, are you interested? Your dad already said he'd help, but we could use another guide, especially an experienced one."

Shane regarded Luke with narrowed eyes for a moment, then shook his head and laughed. "Do you ever slow down?"

"You know me," Luke replied. "I like to be busy."

"Nerd."

"Takes one to know one."

"True enough. In answer to your question, sure I'll help. Sounds like fun."

Luke stood, clapped Shane on the shoulder in thanks, and excused himself to track down Aelissm to ask her whatever he needed to know for the wedding. Shane's lips lifted in another smile. While it was too new to fully believe, he appreciated that his strengthening friendship with Luke made it a lot easier to come home to Northstar than he'd imagined it would be.

"Things are at last getting back to normal," his father observed as if he'd heard Shane's thoughts. "So, let's end our night on a high note, shall we?"

Shane agreed and headed to the bar to pay for their drinks. When Aelissm stepped out of the kitchen and actually smiled at him, he found himself agreeing with his father. *The day's definitely ending on a high note. A few more days like this and I might actually feel like I belong here in Northstar again.*

As he followed Austin out into a night that clung to summer's warmth, he allowed himself to hope that he might do more than simply make amends to the people he'd hurt. Maybe it was crazy to think it was remotely possible, but he hoped he could prove to Becky that she could trust him again and that they could, at the very least, find a way to be friends again. Of course, that wasn't all he wanted, but he didn't dare get *that* far ahead of himself.

Four

SHANE'S INITIAL WORRY that having a wedding on a trail ride with sixty-some guests would be a monumental disaster was quickly proven wrong by the Conners' effortless organization. June, Ben, Luke, and their staff had set up a straightforward routine to get the wedding guests ready for the ride, and they executed it flawlessly with the kind of polite command that left no room for argument. While the guests dressed for the ceremony, Shane, Becky, Ben, Luke, and the other guides saddled the horses. Then all Shane had to do was wait for the time to mount up when he would go down the line and give those riders needing one a hand into their saddles.

In the meantime, he followed his fellow guides back to the lodge for the pre-ride check-off and perched on a stool at the thick log-slab bar. His father and Jake Sterling stayed out with the horses to make sure none of the other Ramshorn guests got curious and disturbed them.

"So," Luke said, claiming the stool beside him. "What do you think of the circus?"

"I'm impressed," Shane replied. "More so because I was afraid it *would* be a circus."

"Aunt June is so good at this," Becky remarked as she joined them, "that even the weather cooperates. It's *gorgeous* out!"

"What would have happened if it wasn't?"

"We would have moved the wedding up to the pavilion," Luke answered.

"What pavilion?"

"The one we built last summer up the hill behind the corrals."

Shane shook his head. "There've been a lot of changes in the last few years for a place that never changes."

Becky laughed. "I've been thinking that same

thing. But at least they're good changes. Small ones. Northstar is still Northstar."

"Always," Luke said. "We're all too stubborn to let it change too much."

With a dizzying sense of déjà vu and a pleasant nostalgia, Shane glanced at Luke on his right and Becky on his left and thought of the last time the three of them had sat in this lodge together. It had been twelve years—more than a third of their lives—and they had all changed. For one, they were adults now, but there were other, less obvious changes. Gone was the carefree jubilation of their teens. Well, Luke had never been entirely carefree, but at sixteen, he'd certainly been a lot less taciturn than he'd become following the murders of Mike and Carol. Really, they hadn't had much time together as a trio, but their friendship had formed quickly and deeply and given Shane the impression that together they could conquer the world, and he had felt the loss of it even more keenly than Mike's and Carol's deaths. Afraid he'd jeopardize this moment, he didn't mention it but was glad for the peace it brought him.

Wedding guests began arriving for the pre-ride meeting, and Luke pushed to his feet to lead it. Before he joined his father in front of the dark fireplace, he leaned in and whispered to Shane, "Watch out for the redhead."

Before Shane could ask what he meant, Luke walked away. Turning to Becky, he posed the question to her, but she only grinned in response. He received his answer moments later when a young woman with glossy red curls spilling down her back from beneath an ivory, narrow-brimmed hat strolled through the open door of the lodge. She wore an ivory-colored dress with a wide, ruffled V-neck and layers of a frothy material he had no hope of naming that, while quite modern, was strongly reminiscent of Montana's gold rush era fashion. A short veil flowed from the rear of her hat, and it dawned on him at once that she was the bride. She shortened her strides to give him the most blatant appraisal he'd ever been the subject of.

Unsettled, he looked away and wondered, *What is a bride doing staring at another man like that?*

What surprised Shane even more was that the slender man he guessed was the groom—judging by his crisp beige suit, ivory dress shirt, bolo tie, brand-new cowboy boots, and brown cowboy hat—didn't seem in the least bothered by his bride's unabashed perusal. And he *was* aware of it, Shane noted as he caught the man occasionally following his bride's gaze with a patient, faintly smug glint in his eyes.

Shane was glad to escape outside at the end of the pre-ride meeting, and after he settled his cowboy hat on his head, he immediately got to work helping wedding guests onto their horses. When he arrived at the bride before any of the other guides, he nearly groaned.

"Hey there, gorgeous," she purred after he gave her a hand up onto the back of her bay gelding. "I don't remember seeing you around here before, and I'm sure I wouldn't forget a cutie like you."

"I've been gone a long time," he replied, deciding polite conversation might be the best way to handle her. "Just moved back a few weeks ago."

"Why am I not surprised you're from Northstar?" she inquired, wiggling her eyebrows. "This valley sure does breed some fine-looking men."

Shane swore under his breath as his face heated uncomfortably. It had been a *long* time since a woman had made him blush. "Thank you. I think."

"Okay, Chloe," Becky called, striding over. "Leave the poor boy alone."

"Becky, right?" the redhead asked. "Luke's cousin."

"Yep."

"Is this one yours?" Chloe nodded her head

toward Shane.

"Does it matter?"

Shane glanced sharply at Becky, surprised by her answer. Where was the quick, definitive *no*? A confirmation would have much more firmly established boundaries, so he doubted her ambiguous response was meant to dissuade Chloe from flirting with him. If her vagueness was intentional, why? If it was a slip…. Shane shook his head, refusing to let himself go down that path.

"I think you'll agree that we need Shane here clear-headed and not all discombobulated because a pretty girl is flirting with him," Becky was saying. "We need him to help keep an eye out for mountain lions, don't we? I'm sure you remember the one we saw on the trail ride two years ago, and I would hate to have a repeat of that on your wedding day."

"I'm just having a little fun with him."

"I know that, but I'm not so sure *he* does. I hear it's been a while since someone as beautiful as you paid him any attention, so I'm afraid he won't know how to handle it."

"You're a riot, Becky," Shane muttered.

She beamed at him with mock innocence, then continued to address the bride. "Anyhow, we're about ready to go if you're ready to get married."

The redhead's expression shifted immediately from sultry to excited. "You bet I am."

Right on cue, Luke called for everyone's attention. A hush fell over the sixty-some guests, who now turned their horses to face him. When all eyes were on him, he tipped his head forward to let his hair fall into his hat with a practiced flair that made Shane certain it was for show—an intentional shift into character. Straightening in his saddle again with his hat securely on his head, Luke asked, "Are y'all ready to take Ryder and Chloe up the trail and bring them back as Mr. and Mrs. Williams?"

A cheer met his inquiry, so he shouted, "Then let's get a move on!"

"Y'all?" Shane asked, turning to Becky, who would be riding beside him immediately behind the wedding party. "Since when does Luke say *y'all?*"

"He doesn't," she replied, laughing. "It's part of the show. Just wait."

Luke gestured to Ben, and father and son headed to the front of the double-wide column at a lope. With the synchronized grace and precision of a well-rehearsed routine, the guests fell into line behind them, and many of the swimmers climbed out of the pools to watch the spectacle. Even Shane found himself caught up in the excitement of it, and the familiar rocking gate of the horse beneath him reminded him that, though it had been too long since he'd been in a saddle, riding was as natural and easy as it had ever been.

"I almost miss the days when the Ramshorn was just a rustic lodge and hot springs tucked away in the mountains," he called to Becky over the thunder of hooves, "except that it still is."

"It really hasn't changed," she replied. "It's just that more people know about it now. Uncle Ben and Aunt June and Luke all love the essence of this place too much to let it become anything else."

"Makes me very glad they—and not someone who would see only the potential to make money—bought it."

"Amen to that."

A hundred yards up the Meadow Lake Trail, Luke and Ben slowed their horses to a walk, and Shane briefly closed his eyes to allow his other senses to soak in his surroundings. The cherished sounds of creaking leather and the occasional snort of a horse were all around him, complimented by the gurgling of the creek the trail followed and the sighing of the breeze through the pines. The late morning sun beat down on him with a blissful, soothing warmth, and the breeze carried a crispness that kept the day from getting too hot. Opening his eyes again, he glanced at Becky. The gentle smile that graced her features when she met his gaze said quite plainly that she understood exactly how he felt, and something that he had buried years ago clawed its way free. In this moment, they were connected again, bound by their shared love of their home.

"It's good to be back," she murmured.

He only nodded because no words were needed. Turning his gaze forward again, he caught the bride watching him over her shoulder. When she winked, Shane averted his eyes.

"What's her deal?" he asked Becky.

"Whose deal?"

"The bride's."

"Do tell what you mean."

"I mean she's getting married today, and yet she can't seem to…." He paused, wondering if it would sound completely vain to say the redhead had been ogling him most of the morning.

"She can't seem to what, Shane?" Becky asked with her eyes twinkling. "Stop staring at your gorgeous self?"

He pressed his lips into a flat line and regarded

Becky with narrowed eyes, not nearly as amused as she seemed to be. She laughed and kept laughing until he feared she'd fall out of her saddle as mirth slackened the muscles she needed to stay upright. He couldn't help but smile even though he had no idea why she was laughing; her merriment was contagious, so open and honest, and he had no more hope of resisting it now than he ever had.

"What is so damned funny?" he demanded, trying hard not to laugh with her. He nearly succeeded, but his voice trembled with the effort.

"You getting all flustered over Chloe flirting with you."

"How is that funny? Thank you, but I have no desire to get into a brawl with the groom because his fiancée can't keep her eyes to herself."

"Ryder's a teddy bear, and anyhow, you've got him by a good thirty pounds of muscle, Shane. I'm sure you could take him."

"Just because I can doesn't mean I want to."

"I wouldn't worry. She is a notorious flirt, and Ryder is very well aware of that," Becky explained. "You should have been here two years ago when she went on her first Ramshorn trail ride. Poor Luke did everything he could to escape her, and Ryan was too busy talking to your dad to rescue him."

Shane glanced to the head of the column at Luke and chuckled a little as he pictured his old friend trying politely to stave off the girl's advances. "Okay, I see why it might be a *little* funny. Seriously, though, Ryder doesn't have a problem with it?"

"Not that I've heard. Luke says she's completely smitten with him, and Ryder knows it. I guess her outrageous flirting is how they got together in the first place."

"That doesn't tell me why he's okay with it."

"She chose him," Becky replied as if that were all the explanation necessary.

He didn't understand, so he asked for clarification.

"He knows her flirting is nothing more than meaningless entertainment because he claimed her heart. It belongs to him, and no one will ever take it from him."

Now that *I understand.* Shane let his gaze linger on Becky. *Too well because mine still belongs to you.*

Their conversation dwindled, but the silence was as pleasant as their discussion. Perhaps more so because it allowed him to focus on Becky and not on the bride and groom. He'd always liked that about her, that she was content to enjoy the peace and didn't feel the need to fill every moment of the day with meaningless chatter. The rejuvenating sense that they were in tune returned, and Shane let out a contented sigh even as a tiny voice in the back of his mind worried that reconnecting with his home—with Becky—had so far been too easy.

It's too beautiful a day to think like that, he told himself.

The site for the wedding ceremony was at the end of the trail beside the tiny and aptly named Meadow Lake. Nestled in a shallow bowl, the lake was barely larger than a pond but rimmed with lush meadow still vibrantly green even this late in the year. The aspen gathered around the inlet and outlet streams were a riotous mixture of brilliant yellow and fiery orange, contrasting sharply against the vivid azure sky. Benches made of log halves had been gathered in the widest portion of the meadow around an arbor of woven willow branches that had been artistically decorated with golden aspen leaves and delicate, deep-purple flowers. Shane noted the craftsmanship of the arbor and the logs and decided Aelissm O'Neil had had a hand in their construction.

A spacious corral had been built a little away from

the arbor and benches, half in the meadow and half in a stand of aspen, and Luke and Ben led the column of riders to it before dismounting. Shane and Becky briefly parted ways to help wedding guests off their horses while June and the photographer, Skye Hammond, got the guests situated on the benches. After a rider dismounted, his reins were secured to the saddle horn, and his horse was turned loose in the corral.

When the guests were seated on the benches and waiting for the wedding to begin, Shane perched beside Becky on the top rail of the jackleg fence that enclosed the corral to watch the goings-on.

"I'm guessing this isn't the first wedding to be held here," he remarked, gesturing to the corral.

"Nope."

"If I recall correctly, this is a new trail. Only about two years old, right?"

Becky nodded, glancing at her uncle and aunt, who were talking with another of the guides. "The owners of the Ramshorn may have been instrumental in both its conception and its construction."

"I'm surprised they were able to get it done because it seems like the government is determined to *close* trails rather than open new ones." Shane chuckled. "But it's not the first time that's happened, I hear.

There's a rumor going around that they and the good people of Northstar were able to get a much better trail put in up to the Hall and Hopkins Lakes."

"Yep. Of course, there's a mountain lion who seems to think the den right along the trail is a great place to raise her cubs."

"Is that the mountain lion you were talking about earlier?"

"The very same. She had two more cubs this year and chose the same den."

"I'm slated to repair a bridge on that trail next week, so thank you for the heads up."

"Wouldn't want you to become dinner," Becky said.

As the wedding ceremony got under way, they stopped talking again. Instead of watching, Shane let his gaze wander around the bowl of Meadow Lake and the forested ridges that surrounded it and tried not to think about how beautiful a bride Becky would have made had he not broken her heart.

"They're lucky," she said quietly.

"Who?"

"Chloe and Ryder. They have such an effortless love. Just like my parents. And Uncle Ben and June. And Luke and Ryan. I can't imagine anymore what it must be like to trust your partner so completely or to have that level of commitment."

Her tone was that of introspection, so Shane knew her words weren't a jab at him, but he grimaced anyhow. He hadn't realized it then, but he'd since come to understand that the love they'd shared had that potential if he had just given in to it and let it blossom.

"Why didn't Justin do that for you?" Shane asked. "You were together for, what, six years?"

As soon as the questions spilled out of his mouth, he wished he could snatch them out of the air and take them back. Becky's eyes turned cold, and her mouth flattened into a defiant line.

"Let's not talk about Justin, all right?" she said.

Shane wanted to slap himself as she jumped down off the fence and strode toward her aunt and uncle. Dropping his head into his hands for a moment, he snorted.

It has *been too easy.*

After almost three weeks of surprising peace between them, this setback should have filled him with hopelessness and despair and a renewed sense of loss. Instead, it ignited a desire to convince her to give him a chance to earn her forgiveness. The usual urge to give up and run was gratifyingly absent, and the need to fight for what he wanted was delicious, so he hopped down off the fence and started after her to apologize for crossing a line.

"Becky, wait. Please. I'm sorry."

She turned slowly to face him, waiting expectantly for him to elaborate.

"I didn't even think when I asked that. It's none of my business why you and Justin didn't work out."

"No, it isn't."

"I know where the line is now, so I won't mention it again. Just… please don't shut me out again."

Her scowl turned quizzical, and she studied him for a long time, undoubtedly pondering the plea he had tried and failed to keep from his voice. When she didn't move away, he began to relax a bit, but the way she continued to search his face gave him no clue what she was thinking.

"What?" he asked at last, unable to ignore his curiosity any longer.

"You keep surprising me, Shane."

"Is that a good thing?"

"So far… yes, it is." She jerked her head toward the corral, and he again joined her atop the fence. "All right, I won't shut you out again. What do you want to talk about?"

To hide the dazzling triumph that shimmered through him, he flashed her only a brief smile. "We don't even have to talk. I'm perfectly happy just sitting here with you, but I *am* curious about something."

"Oh?"

"How bummed is James that he didn't get to come today?"

Becky turned her gaze out across the small lake, and the expression that passed over her face was an exquisite combination of sisterly fondness, amusement, and something else he thought might be approval of his inquiry. "He is doubly bummed because he didn't get to come *and* because he's missing out on spending time with you."

"No accounting for taste," Shane remarked, hoping the self-deprecating humor would get him a little deeper into her good graces. "But it's nice to know that *someone* in Northstar other than my dad likes spending time with me."

"Don't get any ideas," she said slowly, "but since we've been back, I've actually enjoyed spending time with you, too. Like old times."

It took everything he had to keep a broad grin from spreading across his face, but he managed with only a glimmer of one as hope was kindled.

One step at a time, Shane.

* * *

To say that Shane had surprised her when he hadn't just let her walk away after he'd asked about Justin was a monumental understatement. He hadn't only surprised her, though; he'd intrigued her, too, and several hours later, she was still pondering it. She was also wondering why, since he'd only been hired for the trail ride, he had volunteered to assist with the wedding reception. He usually avoided this kind of thing, yet here he was standing across from her and holding the other door of the Bedspread's restaurant for guests as they headed outside. The smile that flashed across his face from time to time and the way he touched the brim of his cowboy hat when someone thanked him mesmerized her. Occasionally, he lifted his eyes to meet hers, and his smile widened and became more playful.

What are you plotting? she wondered and was just as curious to find out as she was to discover if this mellower and more humble Shane was here to stay.

After the last guest headed out to the lawn in the center of the U-shaped driveway where the band was warming up, Luke joined them at the doors, and together, they strolled out onto the deck to the railing. For several minutes, they stood comfortably without talking and surveyed the goings-on. The tension that had plagued them for twelve years was noticeably absent. She'd noted it this morning when they'd sat together in the Ramshorn Lodge, and it was wonderful. This was how their interactions *should* be… and had been for those too-brief months the summer her uncle had returned to Northstar. Relaxed, easy, and natural.

"This is nice," she remarked.

"What is?" Shane asked.

"Us. Together with no scowls or angry words. Just peace and happiness and… just us."

Neither of her companions said anything, but she sensed they understood her and agreed. Faint, poignant smiles gentled both their faces as they glanced at her and each other in unspoken agreement. This was what they'd lost that summer and what should have bound them together as they helped each other heal from those tragedies.

Instead, they had let JP win.

She had thought of this bond a lot throughout the years and recognized that she'd missed it, but until she'd been faced with the reality that she and Shane—and Luke and Shane, for that matter—would have to find a way to coexist in Northstar, she hadn't understood how much. For all his faults and hurtful decisions, she had never stopped thinking of Shane as her friend. Not even when he'd accused her of choosing Luke over him or on the rare occasions she'd seen him in the years since and hated him for hurting her.

Ryan pulled up in the black Dodge pickup Luke had purchased the weekend he'd first met her family, and Becky watched as her cousin's countenance shifted into reverence. With the arrival of his family, Becky's moment with him and Shane ended.

That's not a bad thing, she told herself as her heart dropped a little. *He's so happy now. At last.*

Still, as Ryan, Alex, and Ashleigh joined them on the deck, Luke's attention shifted fully to them, and it dawned on Becky that it would never be her and Shane and Luke again. Those days were over, but they had a chance now to find a new balance. Just like the one she was building with her family.

"So, how did everything go?" Ryan asked.

"Flawlessly," Shane replied. "I can see why word's gotten around that the Ramshorn is the place to hire to host a wedding."

Becky glanced between the two former lovers and marveled that there didn't seem to be any strain between them. She wondered if they had really set their past aside or if they had simply perfected the ability to pretend none of the heartbreak had happened.

"You're free to go any time, Shane," Luke said. "We really appreciate your help today, but I'm sure you're ready to escape."

"Actually, I'm quite enjoying myself, so if it's all right with everyone, I thought I'd stay a while longer."

"Suit yourself," Luke remarked with a shrug.

"Hey, Luke," Alex said. "I know I said I'd watch Ashleigh so you and Ryan could dance, but Iris is here."

"Go," Ryan said with a knowing wink.

Alex flashed them a grin and bounded down the stairs, then sprinted toward the crowd of people gathering near the band for the bride and groom's first dance as husband and wife. Becky turned to Luke with brows lifted. "Iris? As in Iris O'Neil, Pat and Aeli's daughter?"

"Yep."

"I thought he was dating that Bree girl."

"They broke up this spring," Ryan explained.

"I don't think he was *that* interested in her to begin with," Luke added. "Even if they *were* together for a year and a half."

"It was comfortable," Becky said. "I can relate to that."

"Comfortable has its uses," Shane remarked. Hastily, as if he didn't want to give anyone the chance to question his statement or what he meant by it, he said, "Why don't Becky and I take Ashleigh for a little while so you can dance?"

Ryan and Luke eyed Shane for a moment before their eagerness for a chance to indulge in some one-on-one time won out. After Ryan handed her sleeping daughter to Becky, she twined her fingers with her husband's and led him to the lawn. Becky glanced at Shane and nodded her head to one of the picnic tables near the area that had been cordoned off for dancing by hay bales and strings of clear, round garden lights. They didn't talk for a long time, content to watch the dancers.

After a while, Shane turned his gaze on Ashleigh, and a tender smile settled over his features, making him at once devastatingly handsome and irresistibly desirable. There was a trace of sadness mingled with the joy, but it was so faint that she wondered if she was imagining it. Real or not, she couldn't shake the feeling that she was getting another rare glimpse into his heart.

"If you want to hold her, just say so," Becky offered quietly, sensing that teasing him right now would make him close up again. "I don't mind sharing."

"Thanks," he replied, "but I'm not ready for that yet."

"I'm sure you won't drop her," she remarked playfully, unable to help herself.

His lips twitched with amusement. "Believe me, Becky, I'm not worried I'll drop her."

"Then what *are* you worried about?"

At first, she thought he wouldn't answer as a frown darkened his expression, but after a moment's hesitation, he did.

"That I'll hate myself more than I already do."

Intrigue became ravenous curiosity, but Shane returned his attention to the dancers with his jaw set and distance in his eyes. She could ask him until she passed out from lack of oxygen, and he wouldn't explain his response. So she followed his gaze and watched Luke and Ryan dance for a while. Her cousin and his wife moved together as one with a fascinating grace and love radiating from them as brightly and warmly as the westering sun.

"You know, everyone says John and Tracie or Nick and Beth are the best dancers in Northstar," she mused. "But I think Luke and Ryan are tough competition."

"Without a doubt."

"Is it weird seeing Ryan with Luke?"

Shane shook his head, and his expression turned contemplative. "I gave her up a long time ago, and I never felt like she was mine to begin with. Besides, she and Luke are truly beautiful together, and since I care for them both, how can I be anything but happy for them?"

"They *are* beautiful together," Becky said. Turning again to Shane, she asked, "Do you really mean that?"

"Yes, I do." He met her gaze, and a mischievous gleam danced in his eyes. "What? Did I surprise you again?"

"Yeah, you did."

"Good. Now I'm going to surprise you once more." He waved to catch Alex's attention and beckoned him over. "I hate to interrupt you and Iris, but can I ask you a favor?"

"Sure."

"Would you mind taking your sister for a few minutes so I can dance with Becky?"

"Yeah, of course."

Alex lifted Ashleigh out of Becky's arms while she stared at Shane, dumbfounded. When Shane stood and faced her with his hand extended, she snapped her mouth closed.

"Since when do you dance?" she blurted.

"Since now. Will you please dance with me?"

"But… you don't dance."

"I didn't," Shane corrected. "Ryan taught me, and while I wasn't particularly interested at the time, I *did* pay attention."

Hesitantly, Becky took his hand and let him pull her to her feet.

"Thanks, Alex," Shane called over his shoulder as he pulled Becky to the edge of the throng of dancers.

With a confidence she did not expect, he took her into his arms and led her through the basic box steps of the tango. Like Shane, she hadn't danced much in her life, but thanks to Tracie Hammond, she knew how and was able to follow her partner's lead with a semblance of the grace required. She was certain, however, that they couldn't hold a candle to how effortlessly Luke and Ryan danced.

The song was fast, and despite her reservations, Becky found herself caught up in the dance. She barely had the focus left to think that this was a hundred eighty out from any dance she and Shane had shared at her ill-fated prom, and as the comfortable familiarity of being in his arms merged with the newness evoked by their time apart, Becky admitted that she'd missed him. Not just the friendship they had shared or the memories they'd made. She missed the smell of him, the warmth, and the firmness of muscle beneath her hands and against her body. She'd just missed *him*.

"So, back to this thing about you spending time with me and enjoying it," Shane said in a smooth voice.

"What about it?"

"I have this thought that we should go out to dinner in Devyn some Friday and catch a Wolves football game."

Becky jerked back. Surely he couldn't be asking her on a…. "What, like a date?"

"No, like friends. And I want James to come so you two can have some sibling bonding time while we're at it."

She let him guide her back into the dance—now a slower waltz—and searched his face for any sign that he was hoping for more than what he'd proposed. She found only patience as he waited for her reply.

"Are you sure that's a good idea?"

"Why isn't it? We used to be friends once upon a time, and I'd really like to be friends again because that would make us both living back here more enjoyable, wouldn't it?"

Had she not, only two minutes ago, been thinking

of how much she'd missed him? Of course, that probably just made being friends again a very stupid thing because it wasn't so great a step from there to dating again. No, she promised herself, she wasn't dumb enough to give her desire for something more than friendship even the tiniest bit of rein.

"So long as you have no other intentions…" She paused to let her words sink in. "…that would be fun, and I'm sure James would love it."

"That's the idea. So, since you live with one of the coaches and one of the players, I'm going to assume you know when the next home game will be."

"Friday after next."

"How about we plan for that?"

"All right."

Shane twirled her as the band picked up a lively tune, and Becky found herself laughing delightedly.

There's no harm in being friends, she told herself. *Right?*

Five

SHANE HADN'T SET FOOT in this stadium since his last high school football game—the state championship the Devyn Wolves had won his and Luke's senior year—and the moment he took a seat on the front-row bench at the fifty-yard line, the memory of that night enveloped him. His friendship with Luke had been in tatters, but they had managed to set aside their problems for the sake of the team and the game, and for those few short hours that night and every Friday night prior for the duration of the season, they had been able to resurrect some of their old harmony.

Even with the fresh agony of Mike's death hanging over them and Luke stepping in as the starting quarterback. Perhaps it was those differences that had helped them find a new cohesiveness on the field.

Too bad it didn't carry over to the rest of our lives.

Becky had been the team's manager, and that night had been their last moments of untroubled unity as a trio. That night, Shane had hoped they might find a way to overcome what JP had done to them, but Luke had closed the door on him even more firmly after football season ended, sinking Becky deeper into the divide between them. When it had come time to decide which school to play for, Luke had chosen the Montana State Bobcats, and Shane had picked the University of Montana Griz, believing they'd never be on the same team again.

Thank God we were wrong. Shane located his old friend on the sidelines with the other coaches, and instinctively, he reached for Becky's hand, stopping himself just short of taking hold of it. Lord knew how she'd react to *that*.

"Whatcha thinking about over there, looking so serious?" she asked during a lull in the game.

"That last state championship before Luke and I went off to separate schools. That was the last time we were all on the same field, you and Luke and me."

She scanned his face, and without a word, he knew she understood that he wasn't talking about the football field. Nodding, she returned her gaze to the game, but after a moment, she said, "That was a great night—the last great night. All the rest after that were only good at best and sometimes just plain bad."

The Wolves' defense forced their opponents to punt, and Ant O'Neil ran for a forty-yard return on the kick. The roar of the crowd drowned any further conversation, and Shane set the memories aside, resolving to enjoy the game. It wasn't hard. He'd loved every second he'd played in college, but there was a wholly different feel to high school games, a less clouded excitement that permeated the air that he'd dearly missed. This was his turf in a way Washington-Grizzly Stadium had never been.

"See? Wasn't this a good idea?" Shane asked Becky as Alex sprinted into the end zone for his second touchdown of the game.

"I never said it wasn't!" she yelled over the roaring crowd.

"Uh, close enough. You doubted."

She stuck her tongue out at him with a teasing glint in her eyes.

"What do you think, James? Was this a good idea or what, bud?"

James yanked his attention from the game to grin at Shane. "Heck yeah! It's even cooler that I know so many of the players."

"Yeah. Hey, Becky, how many of the starters are Northstar boys?"

"Well, there's Alex, of course, Will Hammond, Ant O'Neil, and Hunter Fitzwater. So, four. Last year, there were five because Noah Ulrich—Henry's step-son—played, but he graduated this spring."

"That's pretty impressive, since there are more kids at Devyn High School than there are people in Northstar."

"This coming from one of two Northstar players who were good enough to earn full-ride scholarships to play college football," Becky said, nudging her brother with her elbow.

"That's right! You played for the Griz, didn't you, Shane," the boy piped. "And you played all four years, right?"

"Yep, but I was what they call a red-shirt fresh-man, meaning I didn't actually play any games until my second year because they had a senior player in my po-sition."

"So you went to college for five years, then?"

"Right. Well, sort of. I took off for a semester my last year and went back the following fall to finish."

"How come you didn't just finish like normal?"

When he realized where the conversation was heading, Shane cursed himself for mentioning it. He hadn't thought anything of answering James's questions honestly, but now he faced finding a way to explain that he'd gotten Ryan pregnant and had been too big a coward to accept the responsibility. Not only was it a difficult situation for a nine-year-old to comprehend but the topic was also sure to trigger Becky's defensiveness of Luke's wife and remind her that he had a bad habit of running away.

"It's a long story," he said carefully, "but the short of it is that I was stupid. Very, very stupid."

"Were your grades bad?" James asked.

"No, nothing like that. People make mistakes, bud, and I made a couple *big* mistakes."

James seemed satisfied with that answer, and even if he wasn't, his attention was diverted when Will Hammond intercepted a pass and ran the ball for fifty-six yards before he was tackled.

"You actually left school when Ryan got pregnant?" Becky asked close to his ear.

"Yes, I did," he replied with gritted teeth. Why had he told James about that?

"That was a dumb thing to do."

"Yeah? Not any dumber than walking away from her like I did."

"At least you went back and finished your degree."

Shane eyed her for a moment, wondering if she was going to let it go at that. She was apparently of a mind to keep it from ruining their evening out, but he was certain the subject would come up again when they didn't have an audience, and he dreaded that moment. There was no way that conversation would end well.

Best to not worry about it until you have to, he told himself. With a deep breath, he focused on the game and let the excitement of it push the memories and dark thoughts from his mind.

The Wolves scored again on the possession begun by Will Hammond's interception, and the half ended seconds later. Claiming a desire to stretch and move around, Becky offered to fetch drinks and snacks for them. Shane watched her stride away through the crowd of people who undoubtedly had the same idea and tried his best not to notice how sexy her backside was in those jeans. That kind of thinking would only leave him frustrated and hopeless.

"Having a good time, James?" he asked, turning his attention fully on the boy.

"The greatest. I don't get to go to too many football games—just the state championships."

"I take it that you're a pretty big fan like your sister." When James nodded emphatically, Shane asked, "Do you play?"

"Just with Alex and Kyle and Ant and Seth and Will and Eric Hammond and a few other boys... not real games. I wanna play when I get to high school, but I'm not very good.

"Says who?"

He shrugged. "No one says it, but I know I'm not very good."

"I'll bet you can change that if you wanted to."

"Yeah? How?"

"You work at it and you practice a lot. I'll tell you a secret. Okay, it's not really a secret. I used to suck at science, but I worked hard to get better, and now I have a bachelor's degree in forestry, which is pretty much all science."

"You really think I could get better just by practicing?"

"I know you can. And I'll bet you Luke would

work with you when he has time if you just ask him."

"What about you?"

"Luke would probably be able to help you more since he's a coach," Shane said. James's shoulders drooped in disappointment, so he quickly added, "But if you don't mind my crummy coaching skills, I'd love to."

Becky's little brother grinned broadly. "I knew you'd make a good big brother… or brother-in-law. Whatever."

"How about a friend?"

"I like that." With a sly smile, James added, "But I'd prefer to have you as a brother."

"Thanks, but can you do me a favor and not mention that in your sister's hearing?"

"Why not?"

"I don't think she'd appreciate it."

James eyed him with suspicion. "You two *did* used to go out! Come on, Shane, admit it. I've heard people talk, and I'm not dumb."

With a chuckle, Shane said, "You are most definitely *not* dumb. In fact, you're too stinkin' smart."

He sighed, admiring the kid's persistence even as it exasperated him. James was far too insightful and— if the excitement shining in his gray eyes was anything to go by—far too hopeful. For the second time in less than twenty minutes, Shane found himself searching for a way to explain his mistakes to Becky's too-smart-for-his-own-good brother, and this time, he doubted he'd get away with the same *it's a long story* line.

"What happened?" James prodded when Shane didn't reply quickly enough. "Are you glad it happened? Because it doesn't seem like you are to me."

"No, I'm not glad."

"Did she break up with you?"

Shane shook his head. "No, I did it. I screwed up, bud. Big time. Some bad things happened, and—"

"You mean the murders, right? Of Mike Thompson and Carol Landers?"

Of course the kid knew about them. They might have happened before his birth, but the people of Northstar had long memories and still talked about that summer. It had shaken the community to its core that one of the Valley's own had so coldly killed two teenagers and tried to kill a third.

Nodding, Shane said, "I let that and everything that happened right after get in the way. I let those things become more important, and I let them control…." He choked on the words a little, so he cleared his throat. "I let them control me and made stupid decisions because I was scared that we—your sister and Luke and I—wouldn't be able to overcome them. Maybe I was right, but I didn't give us a chance to prove one way or another, and because I didn't, I hurt Becky."

"Did you love her?"

"Much more than I realized until it was too late."

"And… now?"

Shane smiled sadly. "I think you know as well as I do that you don't ever stop loving someone like your sister."

James grinned again. "She *is* special."

"Yes, she is."

"So why don't you make it up to her?"

"I don't think I can, bud."

"Why not? You got a degree in science even though you weren't very good at it at first, right? And you worked hard at football and got so good that you got a scholarship to play for the Griz. Look how far a little hard work got you with those things."

He had a point even if it was too simple, and Shane wished it were that easy. "Unfortunately, James, relationships don't work that way. I had control over football and science, but to make it up to your sister…. Well, a lot depends on her. She'd have to forgive me, and I just don't see that happening."

"How do you know if you don't try?" James asked with a sass that nearly made Shane laugh out loud. "She likes you, you know."

"She's *beginning* to like me again," Shane corrected. "Until recently, she hated me, and I can't blame her. I would hate me, too."

James shook his head with a certainty incongruous with his young age. "She never hated you. I would know."

"I'm thinking she was just very good at hiding it from you." He spotted Becky making her way back to them with three bottles of water and nachos. The chill of the mid-October night had coaxed a beautiful rosiness from her cheeks that made her gray eyes glitter. Yanking his gaze from her, he said quietly, "We should probably keep this whole conversation between ourselves, all right?"

"Even the part about you helping me with football?"

"That part's probably okay to mention. It might get me a little further into her good graces."

She had barely reached them before James blurted, "Hey, Becky, guess what! Shane's gonna teach me how to play football better!"

"That's great, James," Becky replied as Shane took the nachos and a bottle of water from her. "And very generous of him."

As the game got back underway and they shared the nachos, Shane considered the wisdom of confiding in Becky's nine-year-old brother. In all fairness, the boy was a great listener, and kids his age had a straightforward way of looking at problems that adult brains tended to complicate.

Despite the excitement of the close game, Shane couldn't seem to pay attention to it; his mind was preoccupied with too many questions and too many perturbing memories. What he'd told James about letting the traumas of Mike's and Carol's deaths become more important than his relationship with Becky was true. Had he and Becky been doomed to fail before he'd even asked her out?

He thought about the tension that had sprung up between him and Luke and how Becky had been plunged into the middle of it, pulled from opposing sides by her love for them both and unable to heal the rift no matter how hard she tried.

Did we ever have a chance?

Shane shook his head. He wasn't going to take the easy way out and blame JP for his mistakes anymore.

Perhaps he could blame JP for a lot of what had happened—manipulating him and Luke and Becky and Mike and Carol into doing the things they had, making them doubt each other—but JP hadn't made Shane sleep with Carol nor break up with Becky. And he certainly hadn't made Shane walk away from Ryan. The blame for those stupid decisions rested squarely on Shane's shoulders.

By the time the game ended with a Devyn Wolves field goal to clinch a twenty-five to twenty-one victory, Shane couldn't remember most of the second half. It was a statement to how much power Becky had over his thoughts that his ponderings about how he'd failed her had kept him from enjoying the game. Usually it was football that distracted him, but before he knew it, Luke and Coach Wells were standing right below him and inviting him, Becky, and James down to the field.

As soon as they'd made their way over to the stairs and down to where Luke and Greg waited, Shane found himself wrapped in a bear hug by his old coach.

"It's about time I get to see you again, Shane. It has been far too long."

"It has," Shane agreed. "And I'm sorry."

"I must also say that it's good to see you and this young lady here together again," Greg said, giving

Becky a hug, too, before shaking James's hand.

"We're just friends, Coach," Shane corrected lightly.

Greg regarded him with a brow lifted and his lips quirked. "That's what I meant," he said in a distinctly sly tone.

Deciding it would be smart to change the subject and quickly, Shane turned to Luke. It was weird to see him wearing a semi-shimmery navy and gold coach's shirt and matching ball cap instead of a uniform, pads, and helmet, and it drove home how much had changed since that last game they'd played together. *Change isn't always bad*, he reminded himself. "You look good wearing a coach's hat."

"I enjoy wearing it, too. It took twelve years, but things are finally getting back on track." Luke glanced between Shane and Becky with the subtlety of an air horn. "Just a few things left to be righted, and we might all be able to put that summer behind us at last."

Coach Wells clapped them both on the back, beaming. "It does my old heart good to see the two of you fixing your friendship. It's been a worry of mine that it wouldn't ever happen."

"Old?" Shane, Becky, and Luke chorused.

"If you're old, I'm a monkey's uncle," Shane

quipped.

"I'm pretty sure concessions was selling bananas," Coach Wells retorted without missing a beat. "Would you like one?"

They all laughed, and Shane couldn't agree more with what Luke and Greg had said. All of it. Being able to call Luke and Becky his friends again made him believe that anything was possible. If they could find a way to forgive the past and revel in the blessing that had been their friendship, maybe—just maybe—he *could* find a way to rebuild Becky's trust and show her that he'd never break her heart again.

On the ride home to Northstar, with Becky's brother asleep in the center of the bench, Shane finally asked the question that had plagued him since his talk with James.

"Do you think we actually had a chance?"

"What do you mean?" Becky asked absently, staring out the window at the stars.

"Mike's and Carol's deaths really screwed with us all. How could we have hoped to overcome that when we were so young?"

"You think we—you and I—failed because of what JP did?"

"Is it that big a stretch to think it? Luke couldn't

stand to be around me, and I couldn't understand then why… and you got caught between us."

"Luke couldn't stand to be around you because you slept with Carol when JP was using her to screw with his head."

"I didn't say he was wrong to react that way, Becky." He glanced at her, searching for a way to explain what he felt. The glare she gave him didn't help. "I'm just asking if not knowing how to deal with everything that happened prevented us—"

"Please don't fight," James mumbled, sitting up and rubbing his eyes.

"We're not fighting, bud," Shane said gently. "We're just talking about old and unhappy memories."

"Well, stop. We had fun."

With a chuckle, Shane said, "Yes, we did. Go back to sleep, James. I promise we won't talk about it any more tonight."

He met Becky's gaze over her brother's head and held it. She nodded in agreement as she interpreted his unspoken remark.

But we will have to talk about it eventually if we ever hope to put it behind us.

* * *

By the following Saturday, Becky hadn't managed

to stop thinking about what Shane had asked after the football game. Was he right to question if they'd ever had a chance? Maybe so, but if it was true, it was just as true that his actions had made it so. No one had forced him to do what he'd done.

Becky swore under her breath and chastised herself for letting the past distract her when the cow and calf she was driving toward the main herd doubled back toward the spring. She spun her horse around and tapped her heels to his sides, and being the superb cow horse he was, he knew what to do with only the slightest command from her and lunged forward to cut off the stubborn heifer and her calf. Getting her turned back toward the herd became a dance as Becky and her mount anticipated the cow's moves as if they shared the same mind. At last, the cow broke into a run as she reached the meadow and the rest of the herd. She let out a grumpy bellow as she and her calf joined the others.

Becky grinned triumphantly, thrilled to be dusting off abilities she hadn't gotten to use nearly enough in the last ten years. Sure, she'd helped move cows for the Teton South Ranch as part of her job there, but that was different—mostly a show put on for guests with cows that were so accustomed to being moved from one pasture to another that they rarely provided her with the opportunity to flex her ranching muscles. More was the pity because the Sutherlands trained some excellent cutting horses.

These cows, on the other hand, had spent all summer fattening up for winter in the lush alpine meadows with such rare interference from humans that they were half wild, and the natural instincts honed by the need to protect themselves and their calves from predators made them a gratifying challenge to wrangle.

"I'm betting your talents were wasted on that dude ranch in Wyoming," Shane called as he chased two young cows out of the trees and joined her for a moment's rest. "Must feel good to be working cows with some sense again."

"God, yes!" she replied, beaming.

"Yeah, Justin's cows are totally dumb," James announced as he rode over on the heels of a calf that had gotten separated from its mother. "And all those city slickers think it's so cool and so hard to move them when all you have to do is get behind them and yell once or twice to get them going."

"I take it you've visited his family's ranch?" Shane asked.

James rolled his eyes. "Yeah, and I wasn't

impressed."

Becky and Shane laughed long and loud at her brother's cheek. They were still laughing as they turned their horses around and headed toward a band of particularly ornery cows that had bunched in a smaller meadow on the other side of the strip of forest Becky had just chased the cow and the calf out of. Andy joined them while his wife, the Royal R's three other regular cowhands Liam, Chris, and Max, and the pair of border collies stayed with the main herd to keep the cattle they'd already gathered from getting any ideas about wandering off.

Becky and her brother trotted their horses to the rear of the cows and startled them into a run with a few calls of *whoop-whoop!* and a bit of hat waving. At first, the cows and their calves seemed to think it was safer staying together, but it wasn't long before a couple tried to make a run for it. She and James remained in their places at the rear to keep any cows from doubling back while their father and Shane headed off the runaways' escape attempts.

Though Shane had had even fewer opportunities to keep his skills sharp than she had, he was as gifted a cowhand as he'd always been and utterly fascinating to watch as he and his agile buckskin mare outmaneuvered, outsmarted, and outlasted the cantankerous cows. He was grace and power, intensity and patience. And sitting as effortlessly in his saddle as if he were glued to it, he was sexy as hell.

"You're doing it again," James remarked, angling his little paint gelding closer to Becky.

"Doing what?" she asked.

"Staring at Shane."

"I am not."

"You are, too."

"Fine. Maybe I am."

Justin might be a champion roper, but Shane was the all-around better cowboy, Becky mused, still watching him.

"I don't care, you know. Because I like him a *lot* more than Justin," James continued. "Shane never would have kept you from us."

Becky snapped her head around to stare at her brother. James hadn't exactly made it a secret that he wasn't too fond of her ex-boyfriend—the most recent one, she thought with a jab of chagrin—but he'd never so bluntly blamed Justin for keeping Becky from her family.

"I'm so sorry I let that happen, James," she said. "I hope you don't think I stayed away because I didn't want to see you and Mom and Dad. Because I really did. I missed you all so much."

"I don't think that at all. I *know* you didn't come home very often because Justin doesn't like us."

"Sure he does."

James shook his head. "If he did, he wouldn't have always been in a hurry to leave as soon as you guys got here."

Becky growled. "I broke up with him, didn't I? And I'm home now with no plans to ever move away again. I love my family too much to be apart from you anymore. And yes, I'm beyond sorry it took me so long to figure that out. Is that what you want to hear?"

James gave her one of those smiles that made her feel like she'd taken a simple observation and blown it out of proportion.

"I think you have one of those…. What do they call it? A guilty conscience. All I said was that I like Shane better than Justin," he remarked, confirming his suspicion. "I know *you* like Shane better than Justin, too."

"Oh? And what do you expect me to do about that, wise one?"

James shrugged. "Go out with him again. Not as friends like last Friday, but as boyfriend and girlfriend."

"Again?" Becky asked pointedly with her brows lifted. "Who says we were together before?"

"No one."

"Then why did you say *again*?"

"I know you dated him."

"Yeah? How do you know that?"

"I just know things."

"Uh-huh. Well, little brother, I hate to disappoint you—I really do—but *again* isn't going to happen."

"Why not? Don't you love him anymore?"

"You're not going to let this go, are you?"

"Nope. Why won't you go out with him again?"

"Because I can't trust him!" she snapped. Her horse hopped sideways at her outburst, and she took a deep breath to rein in her anger, then patted the gelding's neck.

"But you still love him," James persisted.

"It doesn't matter if I do or not because love can't grow without trust. Without trust, love shrivels and dies."

"What if trust is rebuilt? Wouldn't love be able to bloom again? Or rise, I guess, like a phoenix from the ashes."

Her mouth fell open. It wasn't James's disturbingly mature comments that shocked her. It was his choice of an analogy. She turned her gaze toward Shane and heard again the question he'd asked her the night they'd slept together—the night he'd given her that beautiful phoenix necklace he'd designed for her.

Don't you always say we're like a phoenix risen from the ashes of what JP did?

"Becky? Did I say something wrong?" James asked. His voice was full of concern, and she was sure she'd see worry pinching his brows together if she could tear her eyes away from Shane long enough to look.

"Not wrong," she replied as she gathered her wits. She at last shifted her gaze back to her brother and offered him a reassuring smile. "Just very unexpected. Can we leave this topic alone for the time being, little man? We *do* have a job to do here."

"I guess."

No sooner had they put the conversation away than three cows broke away from the band. Andy and Shane quickly turned back two, but the third—the ever obstinate and frustratingly smart number five-sixteen—immediately took advantage of their preoccupation and bolted. Shane heeled his horse and gave chase.

"Get her, Shane!" Andy yelled, laughing.

It had been so long since Becky had seen her

father react so warmly to Shane, and it wasn't just that he was grateful for Shane's skilled assistance today. Andy had been warming up to Shane since her ex had come back to Northstar, and even as memories and less-than-kind thoughts about him lingered, she couldn't help but wonder if she was being unfair by holding on to the past. He *had* changed again and for the better this time. She'd noticed it on numerous occasions, and it looked like her father had, too.

I think Dad was as heartbroken as I was when Shane left, Becky recalled as she watched Shane drive the cranky heifer back toward the rest.

When Andy high-fived Shane after they'd joined the band of cows with the main herd, Becky couldn't stop the broad smile that spread across her face. Of one thing she was certain, and watching Shane and Andy work so seamlessly together only made it more obvious. Her father had *never* held Justin in the same high regard as he'd once held Shane, and she knew Andy wouldn't have condoned her marrying Justin.

Recalling the one time Justin had been invited to join them on a cattle drive, she snickered. His arrogance, seated firmly in his collection of roping trophies, had quickly crumbled as her father had put Justin's abilities and stamina to shame. Exhausted by lunchtime, Justin had ridden back to the ranch early and by himself. He hadn't been asked to help again.

In contrast, Shane had assisted the crew of the Royal R Ranch numerous times in his life, and had proven himself a valuable hand every time. Modest, too, Becky added, remembering that one of her favorite things about working with him compared to working with Justin was that Shane didn't brag; he just worked until the job was done. She believed he would have had her father's heartfelt approval if he had asked for her hand instead of breaking her heart.

Since that line of thought wasn't going to lead her anywhere but back into the painful past, she shoved it from her mind and stubbornly prevented it from coming back by focusing on the task at hand. Having saved the most difficult bunch of cows for last, they now had the entire herd gathered, and it was time to drive them home to the ranch.

They made it back without incident and pushed the herd into the designated pasture, then unsaddled their horses, brushed them down, and turned them loose in the smaller pasture closest to the main house. Shane joined Becky and her family for dinner with the Robinsons, Max, Chris, Liam, and the two housekeepers Mae and Belle, and they all sat down to eat just as sunset burned across the sky. Jessie and the house-keepers had spent the day preparing a delicious barbe-cue in between entertaining the ranch's fourteen guests, who were now back in their cabins having had their dinner before the staff. The Royal R's employees usually ate with the guests, but on cattle drive days, it was impossible to know exactly when they'd return.

Becky pondered the logistics of bringing guests on the drives like they did on the Teton South. The cattle were wilder and unpredictable, certainly, so there was no way guests would be able to assist, but they could ride along and watch—a trail ride with a twist. That would certainly give them a greater appreciation of the work that went into moving cattle than hearing about it.

Jessie set a plate in front of her with a rack of baby back ribs, garden-fresh corn, and homemade cottage fries and patted Becky's cheek lovingly with a cool, soft hand before she took her seat beside her husband near the head of the table. Jim said a short but heartfelt grace, and told everyone to dig in. Becky nearly purred as she took her first bite. It made her forget that she was tired and sweaty and allowed her to shove her de-sire for a long, hot shower to the back of her mind.

"I can't believe we were able to leave the cows in

the high country for so long this year," Max remarked. "I don't remember the last time we had so little snow this late into October."

"I'm sure Mother Nature will make us pay for it. Seems like the later winter starts the worse it is," Jim said. With a wistful shadow in his eyes, he added, "What I wouldn't give to have been able to go with you today."

"Quit your belly-aching, old man," his wife retorted and passed him the salad. "Maybe if you stuck to your diet, your cholesterol and your blood pressure wouldn't be so bad and your old heart might be able to handle that much excitement."

"Get off me, woman," Jim grumbled as he piled salad on his plate.

"That's not what you said this morning when everyone else was out working," Jessie said with a wiggle of her eyebrows.

Jim swore under his breath as chuckles rose around the table, but he was grinning. Becky met Shane's gaze across the table and saw amusement sparkling in his eyes. Tired as he surely was, there was an enticing energy about him. It felt right having him here, sharing this time with her family and the Robinsons and the rest of the staff. The only person who didn't seem too happy about his presence was her mother. Jane watched him with a thoughtful frown that occasionally shifted into a look of concern when she glanced at her daughter. Becky could well imagine what thoughts preoccupied her mother, but Jane was gracious enough to keep them to herself throughout the meal.

Becky stood and started to clear the table, but Jessie wouldn't allow it.

"Don't worry about that, dear. I'll get that in a minute. You've already done plenty around here today, and it's getting late, so you should probably get headed back to Luke and Ryan's."

"Yes, ma'am."

"I should probably get headed, too," Shane said, pushing to his feet with a groan.

"You're not... out of shape... are you, Shane?" Becky teased.

"For this? Yeah, I am. Do you know how long it's been since I've spent all day in a saddle chasing cows? Let's just say it's been so long that I can't remember exactly the last time."

The others rose from their chairs and stretched. Andy was the last to stand, and Becky noticed that he absently massaged his knee—the one a cow had crushed back when he and Jane were dating—for a few moments before he pushed to his feet. She frowned in concern. The injury had nearly ended his career as ranch foreman and had almost cost him Becky's mother because Jane had had to choose between him and the home she had left her family to return to. It was a testament to the love between them that Jane had chosen Andy fully believing they'd have to find a new life off the ranch just as *her* parents had. As it turned out, the doctors had been able to repair the knee, and with intensive physical therapy, Andy had been able to ease into work six months later. The Robinsons, who had by that time folded Andy into their family, had held his job while he recovered and given him lighter chores until close to a year after the incident when the doctors cleared him to return to full duty.

"You all right, Dad?" Becky asked quietly.

"The old knee's aching a bit tonight." He offered her a reassuring smile and wrapped his arm around her shoulders, hugging her close. "I know I've said it more times than I can count, but I'm so glad to have you home. It was wonderful riding with you again today. I've missed that."

"I have, too."

With his arm still around her shoulders, they walked out onto the covered porch together, and Becky was keenly aware that his limp was more pronounced than usual. Most of the time she barely noticed it, but tonight, it was obvious his knee was hurting him. He leaned out over the porch railing to look up at the mostly clear sky aglow with a soft lavender twilight. The scattered clouds that had been alight with fiery hues not long ago were now dark and moody grays, and the first stars twinkled between them.

"I think we brought the cows down just in time, Jim. Weather's changing," he remarked, leaning down to rub his knee again. "I think you're going to get your snow soon, Max."

The cowhand followed Andy's gaze. "You think so?"

"Yep. Feel the damp in the air?"

"I do," Becky said, suddenly realizing that a chill had set in since they'd gone in for dinner. The balmy warmth that had made today's cattle drive so enjoyable had disappeared entirely.

Jim extended his hand to Shane, who shook it. "Thanks again for your help today, kid. Are you sure we can't pay you?"

"I'm sure. That delicious dinner and the chance to

get out and do what I love is payment enough. I'd say the stiff muscles are evidence enough that I don't get to do it often enough anymore."

"Thanks, Shane," Andy said. "Come back any time."

"I will. James, are we on for a little football practice tomorrow afternoon?"

"You bet." With a wink, James added, "If you're up for it."

"See you about two, then. I'd be over earlier, but I told Dad I'd help him and Jeremiah fix a fence on the Lazy H."

"Just like old times, huh?" Becky asked.

"You bet."

"Good night, Shane," Jessie said. "And again, thank you."

With a wave, Shane trotted down the steps and across the yard to where his truck was parked beside the barn. Becky watched him go with a light smile before she turned to her parents to hug them and James before she headed out. When she embraced her mother, Jane implored her to be careful and sensed she wasn't talking about driving back to Luke and Ryan's cabin in the dark.

"What do you mean?"

"You're getting attached to Shane again," Jane said too quietly for anyone else to hear.

"We're just friends, Mom, which I think is something we both need." Becky glanced at James with an amused twist of her lips. "Your son, on the other had, seems to have all kinds of schemes for getting Shane and me back together."

"He does, does he?" Jane glanced at her youngest with brows lifted. James's eyes widened, and he scooted closer toward Andy, unaware of the source of his mother's consternation but nervous all the same. Jane returned her attention to Becky. "Just be careful, all right?"

"Don't worry, Mom. I have no plans to get involved with him again. I learned my lesson last time."

She bid her parents and the Robinsons and the Royal R ranch hands goodnight and climbed into her truck. As she drove home to Luke and Ryan's, she thought about her mother's concern. Given Shane's reputation, Jane was right to be apprehensive, but Becky wasn't so sure of her own conviction. She *knew* she should keep her distance from Shane, but she still loved him—she'd never stopped loving him—and it became clearer the more time she spent with him. The connection to him she'd felt as a teenager was as strong as ever, the same deep and consuming love her parents shared… the same her aunt and uncle had found and the same that had helped her cousin finally let go of the past to fully embrace the joys in life again. She wished it were possible to open her heart to Shane and let that love envelope her again.

Just one problem, she reminded herself. *I can't trust him.*

Six

THE SNOW HER FATHER had predicted had arrived—a foot in the lower Northstar Valley and a foot and a half in the higher Crystal Valley over the past eleven days. The skies had been overcast, dusting the world with snow every day since the cattle drive, so today's clear skies and bright sunshine were a very welcomed change even though the snow that covered everything in billowy whiteness was blinding.

Becky navigated her way over the snow-covered roads between Luke and Ryan's cabin and the Royal R Ranch with a faint smile, thoroughly enjoying the wintry weather. Jessie had called her at Luke's last night to ask her to come over for a chat, and she suspected it had something to do with the impending departure of the Robinsons' ranch hand Liam. She parked in the looped driveway of the main house and climbed the shoveled steps to the porch. Jessie opened the door before she had a chance to knock.

"Thanks for coming over, dear," Jessie greeted, giving her a hug. "How are the roads?"

"Snotty," Becky replied. "They plowed the main road last night, but it snowed again this morning, so it's snow-covered and slick. Not that I'm complaining."

Jessie chuckled. "You always did love the snow. I'm glad to see that hasn't changed. Jim! Becky's here, so get your butt down here!"

Becky followed Jessie into the living room and sank into one of the plush Lay-Z-Boys. Jim ambled down the stairs and joined them moments later, and Becky stood to briefly embrace him.

"It does my heart good to see you, girl," the rancher said, claiming his favorite recliner. "As always."

"We'll try to make this quick because we know you're taking James trick-or-treating in Devyn this evening."

"I'm sure you've heard that Liam will be leaving his job," Jim said. "His father's health has taken a turn for the worse."

"Ah, damn. How much worse?" She knew the ranch hand's father had been battling an invasive and incurable form of cancer for over four years, and that he'd had to have a valve in his heart replaced with one from a pig just six months ago because the treatments used to prevent the cancer from spreading further than it already had had irreparably weakened his heart. Poor Liam. He was just twenty-five, and his father was only forty-nine—far too young to be facing this. She was just two years older than the ranch hand, and she couldn't imagine losing one of her parents so early in life.

"They've had to stop the cancer treatments to save what's left of his heart and give him a little longer to settle his affairs. It has always been a matter of time, but time just got a lot shorter, and now it's months they're talking about instead of years. Liam has said he'd like to come back after but doesn't know when that might be. It might take a month, or it might take six, and he'll likely need some time after his father passes."

"Indeed it is, but there's nothing anyone can do that hasn't already been done. Anyhow, this leaves us a hand short, and we'd love to hire you."

"What about when Liam comes back? You *are* going to hire him back, aren't you? He's a good hand."

"He's a great hand," Jessie replied. "And his job will be waiting for him. You won't actually be replacing him, though we'll need you to fill in for him until he's able to return."

"If I'm not taking over his position, what will I be doing?"

"We'll be adding a new position just for you—guest liaison—because we're looking to expand that side of operations. We've wanted to bring you on in that capacity for a while, but it was only recently that we made the decision to grow the tourism side. The business the Ramshorn has been bringing to Northstar has been good for us as well, and we've been booked solid, and we're already starting to fill up for the spring. If we're going to do it, now's the time, especially with you back home. We're hoping you can help us make it happen."

"How much are you looking to expand? Because you don't want to lose the Royal R's coziness and authenticity. That's what makes this place special. Guests come here not only to experience ranch life but also to be treated like part of the family. If they want the luxury ranch experience, they go some place like the Teton South."

"We completely agree. And the fact that you understand that just proves that hiring you to do this is the best way to bring this idea to fruition. You're not only a gifted ranch hand; you also have the business and tourism skills we need, and you understand what we're about."

"You're part of the family," Jim added, "so we know you care what happens to this place."

"In answer to your question, we're not sure yet. A lot depends on the demand, but the way business has been going, if we have the space to house guests, we'll start with adding at least one more housekeeper and another cowhand. We've already started looking into having another couple cabins built, both guest cabins and staff cabins.

"The job is full time, and for now, you'll move into Liam's cabin. Once we get another staff cabin built, you and he can decide who wants which."

Becky had anticipated the offer to fill in or take over for Liam, but she hadn't foreseen any of the rest of it. Giddiness thrummed through her veins even as sympathy for Liam's situation made her heart ache. How wonderful would it be to return to the ranch she'd grown up on and to work beside her mother and father and brother? She loved working with Uncle Ben and Aunt June and Luke at the Ramshorn, but that job was temporary. She knew they'd keep her on as long as she wanted to work, but she missed ranch work.

"Business is winding down a bit at the Ramshorn," she said. "I hope you know I want nothing more than to take you up on the offer right here on the spot, but I made a commitment to Uncle Ben, Aunt June, and Luke, and I'll need to talk to them first. In the meantime, I'll definitely help out on the days I can."

"We completely understand," Jessie said. "And we certainly don't expect you to leave your aunt and uncle hanging."

"I should have an answer for you within the next couple of days, if that's all right."

"That's perfectly fine. Liam will be here for another week or so, anyhow. That's all for now, dear. We can discuss the particulars if or when you decide to take the job."

Becky stood and walked with Jessie to the front door. She paused, staring out at the fresh snow and smiling. Turning to Jessie, she said, "Thank you for the job offer, Jessie. You and Jim are as close to my heart as my own grandparents, and I hope you know I'd do anything for you."

"We do know that, as much as we'd love to have you work for us, we wouldn't want it to be at the expense of your commitment to other members of your family."

"Thank you. I'll let you know as soon as I can."

"In the meantime, you'd best get moving. I think I saw your mother returning home with your brother just before you pulled up, and I'm sure James is anxious to get going."

Becky climbed into her truck and drove over to her parent's house. Her heart soared with the exhilarating promise that every dream she'd had about working this ranch again might soon become a reality. It was too good to be true, but she pushed that and everything else about the prospective job from her mind. This afternoon and evening, she had to be a big sister, and the rest could wait.

Sure enough, James was home and in his room working on his homework when she strolled inside. Their mother sat at the computer in the living room, staring intently at the screen, probably working on something for the ranch—bookkeeping most likely. Her father stood in the tiny kitchen talking on the phone, and by the sour expression on his face, he wasn't happy about the call.

"If she wants to call you, she'll call you, but I'm pretty sure she has no desire to talk to you, Justin," he was saying.

Becky's heart tripped, and she froze midstride between the living room and kitchen.

"Well, she just walked in, so let me ask her." Her father met her gaze and said, "It's Justin. Do you want to talk to him?"

"No, I really don't."

"There you go. She doesn't want to talk to you. Goodbye."

Before Justin could argue, Andy punched the call-end button and set the cordless handset back in its cradle. He then turned to Becky with an expression that quickly shifted from irritated to remorseful.

"I owe you an apology. That's the third time he's called here looking for you, and I should have told you before now, but I wanted to give you time and space from him so you didn't do anything foolish."

Becky didn't respond for a moment while she considered whether or not she should be upset that her parents hadn't told her Justin had been calling. No, she shouldn't, but it was a bit insulting that Justin had only called her three times in the month and a half since she'd left him. *I guess that says pretty clearly where I rank on his list of priorities.*

"When did he call the first time?" she asked.

"About a week after you came home."

"And the second time?"

"About three weeks ago."

"Wow. That's pretty… pathetic."

"I'm sure he's been busy."

"Busy. Right." Becky sighed. She studied her father with narrowed eyes. It spoke more of Andy's innate graciousness than of Justin's worth that he'd made an excuse for him. In light of her father's well-known dislike of her ex, it rang false, so Becky assured him that he didn't need to defend Justin to her. With a sigh, she added, "It's probably just as well you didn't tell me. I wouldn't have wanted to talk to him, anyhow, and it would have put me in a bad mood."

"So, what did Jim and Jessie want to talk to you about?" Andy inquired lightly.

Becky was grateful for the change in topic. "Don't pretend like you don't already know exactly what they wanted, Mr. Ranch Foreman," she replied teasingly.

"They offered me Liam's job and cabin until he comes back, and then they want me to be their new guest liaison."

"And?"

"Well, I have to talk to Uncle Ben and Aunt June first, don't I?"

"Yes, but do you want the job?"

"Of course I do. You know I've always wanted to work this ranch just like you do. I love it here, Jim and Jessie are family, and… what else can I say? I was born and raised to love ranch life." Becky grinned. "I found it."

"Found what?"

"The one good thing about sticking with Justin for so long."

"And what is that?"

"Lots of experience on a high-grossing dude ranch. I saw a lot of different things in action, so I know firsthand what works and what doesn't, and I know the Royal R well enough to apply that here."

Andy nodded, and she could picture the gears turning in his mind as he considered the ramifications of her experience. Excitement washed through her again, erasing her annoyance at Justin for the time being.

"Is that what you're wearing?" Jane asked, at last looking up from whatever financial report she was working on for the Robinsons and effectively ending their conversation.

"I thought I'd pull on my ski gear and borrow Dad's cross-country skis and go as a ski bum," Becky replied.

"Well, you'd best get to it. James doesn't have much homework, and with the roads as crappy as they are, you'll want to take it slow."

"Yes, Mom," Becky said.

She jogged out to her truck to get her gear, which she'd piled haphazardly on the passenger seat in her rush to get over here, and headed back in to pull it on. At least her snow pants were lightweight, she mused, or she'd end up roasting. She was just settling her knit hat and ski goggles on her head when James came out of his room to announce that he'd finished his homework. He was dressed as a medieval king, and his costume, which their mother and Ryan had helped him put together, showed far more forethought and effort than hers, and he looked her over with a brow raised.

"That's all you could come up with?" he asked.

"Hey, consider yourself lucky I put even this much effort into my costume," she retorted.

"Halloween's never really been my thing."

"Well, are we ready to go? We still have to stop and get Shane."

"I guess I'm as ready as I'll ever be. Love you, Dad. Love you, Mom."

"Drive safe," her parents replied.

"Get your coat, kid," Becky told her brother.

The temperature had dropped in the short time she'd been in her parents' house, and Becky elbowed her brother. "Bet my costume doesn't seem so dumb now, huh?"

James rolled his eyes.

When they were buckled in, Becky turned to her brother and asked, "You're sure you're not too old and too cool to go trick-or-treating yet?"

"Heck no. I'm just glad I have an awesome big sister who isn't too cool to take me."

She reached over to affectionately ruffle his mop of dark hair. "Thanks, little brother."

Becky admired the snowy scenery as she drove, wondering how long it had been since she'd had an opportunity to get out and enjoy Northstar under a thick new blanket of snow. She and Justin had visited in the winter months a few times, but he'd never wanted to go out and explore, claiming that it was nuts to freeze their butts off when they didn't have to. If he wasn't working or skiing, Justin avoided the cold and snow like he might a visit to a torture chamber. They had so little in common beyond being ranch kids that she asked herself for the umpteenth time since she'd walked out of his house that afternoon how she had put up with him for so long.

I closed the door on that chapter of my life, she vowed. *So there's no point in rehashing it over and over.*

Except that Justin hadn't gotten the message. She would have thought what she'd said when she'd left and not hearing from her in a month and a half would have convinced him they were over. Sure, she hadn't known he'd called, but he didn't know that, and anyhow, she hadn't once called him, and she'd had her cell phone disconnected—no point in paying for it, since there was no service up here. What did he want? It wasn't as if he really loved her. More likely, he missed the status and comfort of having a longtime girlfriend... much like he might miss a possession.

Becky sneered.

"Uh, are we gonna go in to see Shane's cabin or just wait for him to come out?" James asked.

She blinked, confused. When had she pulled up and parked in front of the Bedspread Inn's small guest cabin? "Wow. Yeah, we'll go in."

She followed her little brother onto the deck and glanced at the chair and small table while they waited for Shane to answer James's knock. With a smile, she noted the half-empty, steaming mug of coffee, pencils, eraser, and open sketchpad. Undoubtedly, Shane spent a lot of time out here when he wasn't working. Curious, she took a couple steps toward the table and saw that he was working on a magnificent bull elk with the familiar peaks of the Northstar Mountains in the background. She heard the door open but couldn't pull her eyes away from the drawing until she'd taken in all the details.

"You're still sketching, I see," she remarked, turning to him.

"More since I've been home," Shane replied. "I didn't for a long time after I left, and it's been slow getting back into it."

Before she could ask why, James glanced over Shane's attire. "You, too?"

"What?" Shane said, holding his arms out and glancing down at his hastily put together lumberjack costume. "Halloween's not really my thing."

"You and my sister seem to have a scary amount of things in common."

Becky groaned. "Don't start on that again. Please. I am not in the mood for it right now."

Shane eyed her warily. "Everything all right?"

"Everything's just peachy." She forced a smile, then glanced at the sketch and kept it in her mind's eye to subvert her annoyance at Justin. She and James and Shane would have a good time tonight, she vowed. "I'll be fine as soon as we get this show on the road."

"You sure about that?"

Nodding, she said, "A little distraction will go a long way."

Shane gathered his sketching supplies and coffee and invited them in for a tour. Becky pretended to be more interested than she was, but even in her daze of irritation, she found enough brainpower to appreciate the work Pat and Aeli had put into fixing up the place. It was beautiful. She guessed he'd opted to keep their furniture because the log pieces fit the cabin a little too perfectly, as if they'd been made for it. The décor suited him, though, and he'd added a few of his own personal touches here and there to make the space his—that first lasso his father had bought him and taught him to use when he was a little boy, a couple of framed drawings she'd watched him create in high school, a bowl full of crystals from crystal park sitting in the center of the dining room table, and a few other knick-knacks he'd collected in his life.

Sensing that Shane was watching her, she glanced at him and saw a faint frown pinching his brows. Her heart beat a little faster at the thought that he was sincerely concerned about her state of mind and not merely playing the sympathetic friend. The quickly returning and strengthening bond between them should terrify her, but instead, it soothed her, so this time when she smiled at him, it was genuine and open. What did concern her was the way her pulse accelerated as she took another look at his costume and noted how it fit him just a little too well. The thick wool flannel, a red and black plaid that brought out the rich brown of his eyes, accentuated strong shoulders, and the tan Carhartt work pants hugged narrow hips and long, slightly bowed legs. Even the suspenders, scarred boots, and bright yellow hardhat added to his brawny appeal. It wasn't fair.

Easy, girl. He's off limits.

"My costume all right?" he asked, noticing her appraisal.

"Even if it wasn't, I'm not in a position to say so, am I?" She gestured to her own hastily put-together outfit.

After Shane locked the cabin, they piled into Becky's truck. James glanced between them.

"Should Shane drive, Becky?" he asked.

"What do you mean?"

"You're a little distracted, and the roads suck."

"I'm sure she'll be fine," Shane said. "Your sister knows these roads, and she's a heck of a good driver. I trust her."

Becky met Shane's gaze over her brother's head, and she smiled widely at his compliment. "Thank you, Shane. At least *someone* has some faith in my abilities."

"I guess," James muttered.

"Better be careful, little man," Becky said. "I know all your fears… and being Halloween, who knows what might happen."

As Shane launched into a series of local ghost stories—including the one about Matilda, the ghost who haunted Mathews Hall on the university campus where they would be trick-or-treating later in the evening—Becky found a reason to let go of her vexation. She was finally getting to spend the quality time with her brother she had missed out on most of his life, and she and Shane were friends again. Maybe it was idiotic to let him back into her heart even as a friend, but no matter what he'd done, at one time he had been one of the best parts of her life, and she needed that connection right now.

* * *

A week and a half after their Halloween excursion, Shane carried the last box of Becky's belongings from her truck into her new abode on the Royal R Ranch, pondering the conversation he'd overheard between her and Luke about Justin when they'd taken James trick-or-treating at the high school after they'd made the rounds at the college. He'd mostly pushed it from his mind, but it was back—Justin had called her again this morning. Or rather, he'd called her parents and received the same response from them. *Becky doesn't want to talk to you.* When Shane settled the box on the floor beside the couch, he noted her expression. It was identical to the one she'd worn most of the evening on Halloween, a mixture of perplexity and irritation. He wanted to ask why Justin's calls so agitated her but doubted he'd get any more of an answer than he had when he'd asked the same question the last time.

Shane recalled leaning against the counter behind Luke's desk in his classroom, listening as Becky went off about her ex-boyfriend and trying to ignore the fact that she'd again relegated him to the outside, choosing Luke as her confidant just as she had so often in the past.

As old feelings and jealousies threatened, he doused them. That was the past, and they were working on rebuilding their friendship. It would be monumentally imbecilic to ruin this second chance by letting their—*his*, he corrected—past mistakes taint it.

"You're doing it again," he remarked.

"Huh?" She jerked her head up from the box of pictures she'd been staring blindly at for the last ten minutes.

"Exactly. Still thinking about Justin calling again this morning?"

"Yeah."

"Are you having second thoughts about leaving him?"

"No. Not one."

He waited for elaboration, but when she gave none, he asked, "Then why are you so flustered about him calling?"

"I'm annoyed," she snapped.

Glancing at him, she flashed a smile that was undoubtedly meant to apologize for her surliness, but it didn't reach her eyes, and it was gone in a moment as resentment again settled over her features. Shane shuddered, all too familiar with that expression.

At least it's not directed at me this time, he thought. "Would talking about it help?"

"Probably not."

"You want me to kick his ass? I know that's technically Luke's job, since he's your best friend, but I'd be happy to do it."

That brought a more genuine smile to her face, but it too faded quickly. "Thanks, but considering our history, that might be misconstrued."

Shane figured it would be best to let that comment slide without a response, so he sat on the floor to open and unpack the box he'd brought in. He was about to change the subject to anything that might get her mind off her ex when she continued with the topic.

"Why won't he accept that it's over? It's not like either of us was really *that* committed."

"And yet you managed to stay together for six years."

Snorting, Becky lifted her lips in a humorless, self-mocking smirk. "What can I say? It was comfortable, and I was stupid." She took a deep breath, and when she continued, her voice was slightly less bitter.

Ignoring post-breakup anger, the picture Becky had painted of Justin in the bits and pieces of conversation Shane had overheard between her and Luke made him all the more confused about why she'd stayed with the guy for six years. Then he thought of her two "friends" from high school, Jenny Thompson and Andrea Hirsch, and realized that perhaps she had more patience for the self-absorption of others than he gave her credit for. *It was comfortable,* she'd said. That sounded about right. Just like her so-called friendships with Jenny and Andrea, she'd accepted the hassles of her relationship with Justin as a tolerable cost of the benefits. For someone who was so strong and independent, she had a surprising willingness to overlook the faults of others no matter how they might hurt her.

When the thought crossed his mind that she might have overlooked his faults had he given her that chance, he rejected it immediately, appalled by it. Accepting a person for who they were—the good and the bad—was one thing, but subjecting herself to the bad when it far outweighed the good was something else. He would never want that from her, would never want to cause her pain just so he could have her love. If he had to hurt someone, he'd rather do it once rather than continually hurting her because he was too afraid to hurt himself by letting her go. No matter what he was and no matter what he'd done in his life, he wasn't *that* selfish.

"Maybe he won't accept that it's over because he realizes what a remarkable woman he's lost," Shane remarked casually.

Becky glanced at him and rolled her eyes. "Yeah… I doubt that's it."

"Then he's an idiot."

She laughed. "Getting warmer. Let's not talk about him anymore, all right? It's done and over, and I have a great new job and a cozy new cabin to focus on."

"Yes, ma'am," Shane concurred. He lifted the box of pots and pans he'd brought in. "Where do you want these? And don't tell me 'in the kitchen.' *Where* in the kitchen?"

"In those cupboards just to the right of the stove."

While they unpacked her belongings and stowed them, they chatted about her new job. Shane smiled at the vibrant, childlike joy in her voice that contrasted the maturity and confidence in her sturdy, long-limbed body. He glanced over her while she was distracted by finding homes for her belongings, appreciating every line of her. She was the quintessential born and bred ranch girl with that athletic build—he'd seen her buck more than a few hay bales, wrestle calves at branding time, and throw a few thousand blocks of firewood—

and her body was a physical representation of the strength within. Time had softened the boyish straightness of pre-adolescence with feminine curves, making her irresistible. The fact that she had no idea of how strikingly beautiful she was made her even more so.

How did I manage to convince myself I'd ever get over her?

Shaking his head, he listened to her talk, enjoying the smooth timbre of her voice as she told him how Ben and June and Luke had been completely supportive of her taking the job on the ranch—no surprises there, Shane thought—and how it was perfect timing because their need of her skills as a horse wrangler was dwindling as the summer tourist season at last began to wind down. The Ramshorn was still busy, but with the snow piling up on the ground, there wouldn't be any more trail rides, so the Conners would soon be turning their horses out with the Hammonds' herd on the Lazy H for the winter.

"And I have no desire to clean and stock cabins or cook and wait tables," Becky announced as she helped him set out her pictures. "I love Uncle Ben and Aunt June and Luke, and I'm grateful for the work because I needed it, but that's not my idea of an ideal job. Not when I could be ranching."

"I completely understand. The Ramshorn job

requires too much time indoors."

Shane grabbed the last framed photograph out of the final box. He and his father had plans to go out to dinner in Devyn, and he was looking forward to it, but he was disappointed that his excuse to spend time with Becky was coming to an end. Glancing at the photograph, he inhaled sharply. Grinning out at him was a set of young faces he hadn't seen since high school. Mike Thompson—dressed in his navy blue graduation robe and matching mortarboard—had graced the photographer with one of his rare, wide-open smiles as he stood between Luke and Shane with his arms around their shoulders. Carol Landers had her head on Luke's shoulder with her hands tucked possessively around his arm while Becky stood beside Shane with his arm around her waist. Mike's little sister, Jenny, and her best friend Andrea stood on chairs behind Mike, and both gave him rabbit ears.

Just six days after the photo was taken, the first of the traumas that had shattered their lives that summer had happened when Carol had broken up with Luke, convinced by her uncle that Luke was turning away from her in favor of Becky. Shane hadn't ever believed that, but that hadn't stopped him from accusing Becky of the very same thing three years later.

"We all look so young," he murmured.

Becky glanced at the photograph over his shoulder. "Of course we do. We were in high school."

"I know, but it feels weird. You and Luke and I have all grown up, and even Jenny and Andrea have, but Mike and Carol never will."

"Don't you have any pictures of them?" she asked.

"Just our old yearbooks, and I haven't looked through them in ages."

"I guess we all have our own ways for remembering the ones we lost. Pictures, a patch on a college football jersey…." Becky paused, and though he didn't look at her to confirm it, he sensed her gaze on him. "Or a tattoo."

He didn't respond and didn't move, but he could almost feel the tattoo high around his right bicep.

"I saw the interview you did your last season with the Griz when that news anchor asked about it," Becky murmured. "I was surprised because you never seemed open to the idea of tattoos."

"I wasn't," he replied. "I never felt like I was home after I left Northstar, never settled down enough to put out pictures, so a tattoo seemed like the only way to keep them with me."

"Do you have any others?"

Again he said nothing, only offered her a sad smile as he took in every detail of the image. When Becky leaned against his arm with her head on his shoulder in silent commiseration, the image blurred as his other senses claimed control of his mind. Old sensations wrapped around him like a long-lost, beloved blanket, and he let them saturate him and dull the edge of his more painful memories. How long had it been since they'd sat like this? The warmth of her body pressed to his even so platonically and the natural scent of her, imbibed with the faint fragrances of pine and horses, took him back years.

"I know you don't think so, but our relationship was built on a broken foundation," he said, staring with unfocused eyes at the picture. "I'm not trying to put the blame on anyone but me… but how did we stand a chance with that much pain wedged between us?"

She sat up abruptly, and he pinched his eyes close, already missing their moment of closeness.

"That's not what created a wedge between us, Shane."

"Isn't it?" Taking a deep breath to calm the tremble in his hands as he set the photograph on the coffee table, he met her gaze head on. "I am more sorry than you know for all the shitty things I've done. I hate hurting you, Becky, and it broke my heart to do it."

"Then why did you do it?"

"I couldn't stand putting you through any more pain."

"But you didn't. Not until—"

"Yes, I did. I hurt you every single day because I didn't do everything I could to mend my friendship with Luke. I didn't really do *anything* to mend it, and instead of admitting that, I blamed him and I blamed you for pushing me away, for choosing each other over me." Shane hunched over his knees, unable to sit fully upright beneath the weight of his failures and every moment of happiness they had cost him. Scrubbing his hands over his face and through his hair, he glanced briefly at Becky and tried to put his frustration into words. "I was seventeen, for God's sake, and you weren't quite fifteen yet when Mike and Carol died— when they were *murdered* by someone we all called a friend and thought we knew and could trust. How in the hell were we supposed to comprehend that let alone figure out how we *should* react? We all did the only thing we were old enough to understand and shied away from the pain instead of facing it."

Shane expected to see anger or bitterness or

accusation on Becky's face when he looked at her again, and he did, but alongside those things he saw grief and a hint of shame as she stared at the far wall without seeing it. There was too much pride mixed in, too, for her to admit that she might have been wrong to treat him as she had even though he hadn't given her much choice but to push him away. At any rate, he didn't want that from her.

In a moment of stunning clarity, he not only knew *exactly* what he wanted but was also brave enough to say it out loud.

"I want a second chance, Becky. A chance to start right by fixing what broke that summer… what's still broken."

She jerked back. With her mouth hanging half open and her mist-colored eyes wide, she stared at him for a long while. Whether she waited for an explanation or was too shocked to begin processing his statement, he wasn't sure, but he didn't plan to give her a chance to figure it out.

"I don't deserve it, but that's what I want. Maybe I'm asking too much, and if so, I'll be happy to be your friend because I want you in my life in whatever way you'll allow. But I know there's something powerful between us, and I want to find it again and make it stronger and give it the chance it didn't have before."

He leaned forward a moment with his hands braced on his knees, still watching her face, then pushed to his feet. Impulsively, he leaned down and kissed her cheek, surprised and gratified when she didn't pull away in disgust. He pulled away just enough to see her face, and the surprise and innocent desire in her eyes hit him like a punch to the chest, confirming that their love hadn't died.

Daringly, he pushed his luck and brushed his thumb across her cheek where his lips had been only a moment ago. Close to her ear, he whispered, "Please think about it."

Then he bid her goodnight and headed for the door. She was still staring at him when he stepped outside into the frigid but exquisitely beautiful afternoon and quietly pulled the door closed behind him.

Seven

"SHE'S MAKING ME NERVOUS," Shane said, glancing over his shoulder into the living room of Luke's cabin. Becky sat with James, Ryan, Alex, and Ashleigh on the floor playing some board game or other. She wore a blue and gold Montana State Bobcats T-shirt to show her support for her alma mater just as Luke wore his Bobcats jersey. Shane had donned his maroon and silver Griz jersey for the first time since his last game, and Ryan was wearing her favorite Griz T-shirt—the same one she'd worn to many of the home games to cheer him on—putting them on the opposite side of the afternoon's rivalry game. Neither Alex nor James had picked a side, choosing instead to wear the Devyn Wolves T-shirts they'd bought at last night's state championship game.

Luke glanced up from the pot of melting cheddar cheese he was stirring. "Who? Becky?"

"Yes, Becky." Shane handed him the peppers he'd chopped. "Who else?"

"Why is she making you nervous?"

"She hasn't once brought up what I said last week, and she's been nice, so I'm not sure if she's choosing to entirely ignore it or plotting to castrate me. You wouldn't be willing to help a friend out and let me know which, would you?"

"Nope."

"Dammit." Shane groaned, then chuckled. "God, I feel like I'm in high school again, asking if you think Becky would go out with me."

"That's because you're *acting* like we're in high school. You want to find out what she's thinking, maybe you should just ask her."

Shane shifted his attention to the living room. Again. His eyes lingered on Becky, taking in the carefree smile that ignited her silver eyes, while he pondered his inability to figure out how she'd taken his admission. For the moment, she was entirely unguarded again, like she used to be, and he cherished the beauty that radiated from her, the kind that glowed from within. Not so long ago, he'd believed he would never see that light again, but he'd seen it often in the last two months.

"She used to be so easy to read, but now I have no idea what she's thinking."

"She learned how to better hide her thoughts," Luke said with a shrug.

I wonder when she learned that, Shane nearly asked, but he already knew the answer. He started to ask if Luke was supportive of him and Becky getting back together, but the woman in question strolled into the kitchen before he could, so he held his tongue, opened a bag of tortilla chips, and started arranging them in a casserole dish.

"You know, it was better when you were both in navy and gold," Becky remarked, snatching a chip and dipping it in the sauce as Luke briefly left it unattended while he stepped over to the opposite side of his kitchen.

Shane glanced down at his jersey. "Maybe so, but I'm proud to wear this."

"I didn't say you shouldn't be. You earned it. I'm

just saying it was better when you two played on the same team instead of against each other." She grabbed another chip. "And, yes, for a while in there, it *was* against each other."

"Makes it even more incredible that we're *all* on the same team again now, doesn't it?" Luke replied, glancing at Shane over Becky's head as he poured the cheese sauce over the chips. "Despite the fact that we're wearing opposing jerseys today."

"That's my point, Luke," Becky said. Wrapping an arm around Luke's and Shane's waists, she pulled them close to her and sighed contentedly. "I'm glad to have my two favorite guys together with me again. It makes me believe that we might actually have a chance to find our way back."

"Not back," Luke corrected. "Forward. With a chance to make what we had even better."

Shane glanced sharply at Luke to find his friend watching him with an unsettling intensity. If he read it right, Luke *did* condone his decision to again pursue a romantic relationship with Becky. Interesting. However, as much as he wanted to ask for clarification, he was too chicken to do it with Becky standing between them… even though Luke's support might sway her to give it a shot.

Clearing his throat, Shane instead changed the subject. "I heard someone say last night that you promised the team they could cut your hair if they took home the championship. Is that true?"

"Yep," Luke said.

"It's easy to say that now because they lost, but c'mon, Luke. That haircut's like… your security blanket."

"Exactly," was all Luke replied.

Shane jerked back and stared at the other man. If Luke noticed his shock, he gave no sign and went about adding toppings to the nachos entirely unbothered. Shane couldn't imagine what Luke would look like without that haircut; he'd had that exact style as long as they'd known each other—seventeen years now. It hid a scar, a memento from the man Luke had believed was his biological father until two years ago, and the fact that he was willing to let the world see it was an incredible thing. For the first time possibly in his entire life, he was truly secure.

"Wow," Shane said quietly. "That's… huge."

Luke shrugged. "I figured out that I'm strong enough to overcome anything life can throw at me… because I already have. When I married Ryan, I made a promise to her and to myself and to everyone who loves me that I would never again let the traumas or the anger or the fear stop me from appreciating and enjoying all the blessings in my life." He paused in his task to glance pointedly between Shane and Becky. "That's a promise I think you should both make, too."

Becky pressed her lips into a flat line, then said, "I'm working—"

"Don't just 'work' on it," Luke interrupted. "Do it. I wasted a lot of years 'working on it.' Now, if you'll excuse me, I need to go change a diaper while you two finish the snacks. Becky, you should know where everything is."

"Yes, sir," she replied. After he'd left the kitchen, she turned to Shane and asked, "Is it just me, or is he getting a little bossy in his old age?"

"I heard that!" Luke called from the steps up to the loft.

"Of course you did," Becky muttered fondly.

"Since he's right," Shane answered, "I think that actually makes him wise rather than bossy."

She pointed a salsa-filled spoon at him. "Just this once, I'm going to admit that *you* are right, but I'm still going to call him bossy because I feel like teasing him."

Shane held his hands up and chuckled. "Tease away."

He helped her finish the nachos, then carried them into the living room and told Ryan to keep her backside planted before he returned to the kitchen to assist Becky with the rest of the snacks.

"So, how come your dad didn't come?" Becky asked. "I know Luke and Ryan invited him."

"He'd already made plans to watch the game with Jeremiah and the Hammonds and the Sterlings down at John and Tracie's."

"Ah. You know, one of these years, we need to find a way to get everyone together again to watch the Brawl of the Wild now that Northstar's very own Cat and Griz boys are back home."

"Wouldn't *that* be a blast?" Shane agreed. "Dad says it was a bigger party in Northstar than the Super Bowl when Luke and I played."

"It still is, even if it isn't as fun to watch now. But with you both here…." She smiled. "Northstar is whole again."

He watched her a moment as she pulled plates, silverware, and napkins out, wondering if broaching last Saturday's conversation would cast a shadow over their fun evening with James, Luke, Ryan, Alex, and Ashleigh. And Bridger, he mused as the golden retriever bounded in the front door Alex held open for him.

"You wanna give me a hand with the drinks?" Becky asked. "Then we'll be all ready for game time."

Shane headed to the fridge to take the requisite beverages from Becky. "Since I haven't seen you much all week, how's the new job going?"

"It's amazing. I've been spending most of my time with Mom, Jim, and Jessie talking about how to incorporate some of the things the Teton South Ranch—Justin's family's spread—does, like allowing guests to get more of a hands-on appreciation of how hard it is to work a ranch. I mean, there's obviously a lot they won't be able to help with because, unlike the Teton South, the Royal R is a working ranch first and a guest ranch second, but there's no reason why guests can't join us on a cattle drive to watch or ride the fences. Right now, all they get to do is watch from a distance or listen to Jim and Dad and the hands talk about it."

"And raid the chicken coop for eggs."

"Exactly. Some guests have said in the past that they'd like to get their hands dirty while they're staying on the ranch, that that's why they chose the Royal R over a more…. What's the word I'm looking for?"

"High end? Fancy? Fake? Oh, how about manufactured?" Shane supplied.

Becky laughed. "We'll go with manufactured. The Royal R—like the Ramshorn—has a more rustic, rough-and-tumble appeal, and like Jessie said, they're not taking full advantage of that yet."

"Sounds like you're in heaven."

She grinned. "You bet your ass I am."

"I'm happy for you, Becky. And I have to say it's pretty incredible seeing you so animated about it. You're getting back to your old self again… back to the Becky I first fell in love with."

Shane realized what he'd said too late and held his breath as he waited for her reaction. Shyly, she ducked her head as her grin softened and warmed. He took that as a good sign. It was certainly better than the reaction he would have expected from her just a few short months ago. He reached into the fridge to grab another can of soda and nearly dropped them all when he felt her fingertips on his right arm as she gently tugged up the sleeve of his jersey. She must've seen just enough of his tattoo to make her curious. Because he wasn't quite ready for her to see it—or the other two, which she would undoubtedly ask about if he let her glimpse the one on his arm—he set the can down and swatted her hand away.

"Knock it off," he said playfully.

"Why can't I see it?"

"I don't want Mike and Carol's memory to intrude today."

"You two gonna get your butts in here or what?" James asked from the living room. "The game's about to start."

"Yeah, we're coming," Shane replied. With the cans of pop balanced carefully on one arm, he hooked Becky's finger with the pinky of his free hand and drew her into the living room. She didn't object, nor did she pull away, and he took *that* as a good sign, too.

I'm still waiting for her to turn on me, though, he noted. Because sitting with his arm pinned to his side wasn't comfortable, he cautiously laid it on the back of the seat behind her, surprised again when she didn't seem to mind that, either. Maybe he was foolish to worry she wasn't open to the idea of giving their love another shot. Maybe all those years of animosity from her made him jumpier than he needed to be. Or maybe he *was* right to be nervous and she was lulling him into a false sense of security so it would hurt more when she ripped his hope apart.

It was pointless to allow what might or might not be prevent him from enjoying the game and the company, so he didn't. He cheered his Griz on as they scored the first touchdown of the game late in the first quarter and joined Ryan in urging them to stop the Cats' relentless drive toward the end zone, groaning at both the resulting touchdown and the extra point that tied the game with seconds left in the first half.

Not two seconds after the first halftime commercial began, James asked, "So, Shane, Luke, which was more fun to play? High school or college football?"

"High school," they replied in unison.

"How come?"

"Luke, you want to take this one?" Shane asked.

"Sure. For one, college football is a lot more like a job, which takes some of the fun out of the game. And, for me at least, the coaches made a big difference. Our college coaches might have been better versed in the game itself and the technical and tactical sides of it, but the game and winning were their priorities. Their jobs require it. However, there's something that makes Coach Wells a better coach—he genuinely cares about his players."

"Why does that matter?"

"You get a coach who really cares about you and puts your safety and well being above winning," Shane said, "you'll play your heart out for him."

"That makes sense," James said thoughtfully. "I

wouldn't want to play for a coach who didn't care if I got hurt."

"Exactly," Shane remarked.

"So, Shane, did you play any other position besides cornerback?"

"Yeah. In high school, I also played at left tackle."

"That's the one that protects the quarterback, right? Like in that movie?"

"A left tackle protects a right-handed quarterback like Luke or Mike Thompson, yes. If you have a left-handed QB, it's the *right* tackle's job to protect him."

"How does he do that?"

Luke explained, demonstrating how, particularly when throwing the ball, he was vulnerable from behind and that it had been Shane's job to guard his blind side. "And he was good at it, too. When he was my left tackle, I never worried."

Shane glanced at Luke. Was his friend intentionally trying to talk him up... and if so why and for whose benefit? There had been plenty of times that he'd used the blind side analogy when thinking of Luke and Mike, and it was never a happy line of thought, so he pushed it aside before he started thinking of other things that had no place in his mind today.

"If he was so good, how come he didn't play that

position in college?" James asked.

"I wasn't going to ever be big enough to play it at the college level. Which is why Coach Wells put me at cornerback, too."

"That and you were smart and fast," Luke added. "Shane here was the only Griz to intercept any of my passes… and he did it to me three times in the four years we played."

"Yes, I did," Shane said smugly. "And yet you still kicked the snot out of us."

Even after the game started up again, they continued to talk about Shane's and Luke's football careers, mostly ignoring the game. To James's surprise, Ryan and Becky participated with equal zeal and nearly equal knowledge, detailing for him what Shane and Luke were too humble to talk about. Gradually, Shane exited the conversation, content to listen and watch. He loved how energetic Becky was about the sport, and it made him hope all the more fervently that she was amenable to giving him another chance.

When the game ended in a sixteen to seven Bobcat victory, Shane helped clean up before he announced his departure.

"This was a lot of fun," he said, "but I should go spend some time with my dad."

"Tell him hi for us," Ryan said. "And tell him next year he'd better watch the game with us."

"Will do. Thanks for inviting me over."

Becky followed him outside into the murky afternoon, and awkwardly, they stood at the edge of the deck much like they had on her first night back in Northstar. For a while, they didn't speak, but Shane sensed there was something she needed to say. He shifted his weight and stuffed his hands in the pockets of his jeans and prepared himself for the worst.

"Thank you for being so patient with James and putting up with his endless questions about football," she said.

"Like I've told you before, I enjoy it. He's a good kid, Becky."

"I know he is. I just don't want him to be lonely like I was before I got to be good friends with you and Luke."

"He won't. He's got Kyle and Seth and a bunch of other boys to hang out with. And an incredible big sister who isn't afraid to play in the mud."

Becky only nodded as their conversation again dwindled, but when Shane glanced at her, he found her watching him intently. Her eyes were darker than usual, reflecting the overcast skies, but it wasn't just the dismal weather that stole the silver glow any more than it was only the threat of snow on the biting wind that made him shiver.

"I overstepped my boundaries last weekend and made you uncomfortable," he said softly. "Now we're at an awkward stage again, and I'm sorry for that, but I don't take back what I said because I'm tired of hiding what I feel in my heart, and I'm tired of trying to pretend I don't feel it."

"You're sure this is what you want?" she whispered, taking a step toward him.

His heart leapt, thudding against his ribs. She stood so close…. "Yes," he breathed.

"Absolutely certain?"

"Completely."

He saw it coming, but that did nothing to lessen his shock when she curled her fingers around the back of his head and dragged his mouth down to hers. She was so forceful and demanding that he stumbled back and slammed into the pole supporting the deck's roof, uncaring when a knot on the log bit into the flesh between his shoulder blades. The way she kissed him with such intoxicating confidence and command left him incapable of doing anything to save himself even as a warning sounded deep in his mind. A moment later, however, it too fell silent when Becky pulled away just enough for him to see the blatant desire in her eyes. Her pupils dilated until her irises became slender rings of pewter around bottomless pools of black. Consumed by that desire, Shane dove after her mouth again, drawing her body against his and reveling in the contrasting familiarity and newness.

Abruptly, just when he thought he'd completely lose his mind, she slid her hands up his chest and shoved, pressing the knot deeper into his back. The jab of pain was nothing compared to the agony and despair that lanced through him when his eyes focused enough to see the tears brimming in hers.

She spun away and strode to the front door of Luke and Ryan's cabin. She yanked it open, then whirled to face him again and hissed, "You really think a half-assed apology is going to fix us?"

"No, I—" The door slammed behind her. His shoulders dropped, and for a moment, he stared at the closed door. Then he tipped his head back against the post and closed his eyes. "—don't."

How long he stood there, he didn't know, but it was long enough for a squall of wind-driven snow to swirl down from the mountains. Tiny flakes stung the exposed skin of his face, and at last, he pushed off the post and headed out to his truck. The hope that had flared so brilliantly just moments ago sputtered.

But it didn't die.

Clenching his jaw and straightening, he slid in behind the wheel of his truck and gunned the engine to life with anger and purpose tightening his muscles. It took every effort to drive away and not barge back into Luke and Ryan's cabin and demand she talk to him, but she hadn't changed so much that she would allow that. Knowing Becky, her stubbornness would kick in and he'd kill any chance he might still have.

His father hadn't yet returned to the bunkhouse when Shane parked in front of it, but he arrived within a few moments. Shane didn't immediately get out of his truck, instead staring at the plumes of snow obscuring the peaks of the Northstar Mountains for almost a minute before he stepped out into the frigid air to join his father on the deck. Without saying a word of greeting, he dropped into the old spindle-legged chair beside Austin.

"I guess I don't need to ask how your afternoon with Luke and Ryan and Becky went," his father remarked. "Except that you've been gone long enough to watch the entire game with them."

"Oh, I did. And we had a great time. Right up until

it was time for me to leave."

"Yeah? What happened?"

"Becky kissed me." He took a deep breath, hoping that might calm his agitation. It didn't. The disappointment that settled over him when he recalled Becky's words did, obliterating the energy that bolstered him. Without it, he sagged against the back of the chair. "Then she called my apology half-assed."

"I know that look, Shane. Don't you dare think it."

"What if I'm wrong, Dad? What if I really did kill whatever love she had for me?"

"Then you bring it back to life. Isn't that what *this* means?" Austin prodded him in the chest directly over his heart hard enough that it hurt even though his coat and the jersey beneath. "I wasn't fond of the idea of you getting tattoos, but yours mean something, and right now, I think that one's the most telling of them. You can't give up now or she'll never see that you've changed."

Shane massaged away the lingering ache from his father's poke and thought of the design Austin referred to, a timeless symbol of hope and rebirth he had drawn himself. He let his eyes drift closed, picturing its elegant lines in his mind's eye… and smiled. "I have no intention of giving up."

He turned his head toward his father and opened his eyes. Austin stared at him in undisguised shock. Slowly, as the meaning of his words became clear, a smile to match his own lifted his father's lips.

"I'll give her a little time and space to think about it," Shane said. "But I'm not going to let her go again. Not this time."

* * *

Not once in their six years together had Justin *ever* inspired the same ravenous desire Shane could with only a kiss. It quivered through her, restless and empowering. One night. That's all they'd had together, but her body hummed with the memories of it and with the promise of what could be again if she would just give him the chance he'd asked for.

Becky fell back against the door with her head tipped back, gulping air as she tried to keep the tears from falling and the scream of frustration locked in her throat. Slowly, she slid to the floor and drew her knees up to her chest. She pinched her eyes closed, but a tear seeped out anyhow with more threatening to follow. How could she have been so stupid as to kiss him? She *knew* it was dangerous to give her attraction to him even an inch… but she'd gone and given it a damned mile!

"Alex, why don't you and James take Bridger outside and throw the ball for him for a little while," she heard Luke tell his son.

"But Becky—"

"You're a good brother to want to help her, James, but give her a little space right now, all right? Alex?"

"Yep. C'mon, kiddo. Let's let the adults talk about adult things."

God, he's a good kid, Becky thought. *Not much of a kid anymore, though. And James....*

She was lucky to have a brother who wanted to help her even if he was far too young to have any idea how. She was lucky, too, to have a friend as supportive and understanding as Luke, whom she opened her eyes to see squatting in front of her with a worried frown shadowing his face.

"If there was nothing left between you and Shane, it would have been easy to tell him no when he asked for a second chance," he said gently. "Tell me again that you can fight this."

"I have to," she replied. Her voice trembled, and she cursed her weakness.

"Why?"

"You know why."

"I know why you *think* you have to fight it, but Shane's not the same boy who broke your heart."

"How do you know that? People don't change *that* much."

"Do you think the Shane who walked away from you and who walked away from me would have *ever* apologized to either of us?" Ryan asked, joining them on the floor. "No, but Shane's apologized to us both, and he *is* trying to right the wrongs as best he can."

She knew it wasn't a betrayal, but Ryan's defense of Shane felt exactly like one. With a sheen of tears making her vision waver, she lifted her eyes to meet her cousin's gaze.

"He hurt Ryan far worse than he ever hurt you, Becky."

She winced.

"But she's forgiven him, and I'm pretty sure she'll tell you she's happier for it."

"Of course she's happier. She has you."

"And in order to fully appreciate what we have— or could have, in your case—you have to first let go of the past because holding on to that hurt takes away some of the joy," Ryan said. "Shane *has* changed, and I heard you say as much to Luke the other day. How'd she say it, love?"

"I believe she said he's surprised her quite a few times recently and even went so far as to tell me she hoped it's real."

"He *has* surprised me," Becky admitted. "And I *do* hope it's real."

"Why do you hope that?"

"Because… if it is, he might be the man I can feel safe to love. But what if it's not real? What if it's too weak to last and he gives up again?"

"Something tells me he's not going to give up this time." Luke held out his hand to help her up and hauled her to her feet when she took it. "So maybe it's time to blow the conversation wide open."

"How?"

"Start with what the hell happened with you and him that set you off just now."

Becky eyed her cousin warily, not sure if she was quite ready to divulge that piece of information just yet because it would only prove him right. And she wasn't strong enough right now to admit that or deal with the consequences of admitting it. Stubbornly, she clenched her jaw and shook her head to try to convince Luke to leave it alone.

Less than a second later, he took that choice away

from her. As if she were the proverbial open book, her ever-insightful best friend read her guarded expression as easily as if it were words written on a page.

"You kissed him," Luke observed.

"Why do you say *I* kissed *him*? Why couldn't it be the other way around?"

"Because I know you and I know Shane… and I know he's determined, so he wouldn't do anything that stupid because he doesn't want to screw this up."

Becky snorted and muttered, "You've definitely got the stupid part right."

Luke's lips twitched in amusement, but his somber frown quickly returned.

"To be fair… he *did* kiss me back."

"Of course he did," Ryan said. "He loves you."

"The question here is why you kissed him," Luke said before Becky could deny Ryan's declaration.

Becky opened her mouth, then closed it. The answer was embarrassing in its cruelty. "I wanted to hurt him."

With that admission, the tears broke loose. When had she become so callous that she would premeditate wounding someone she *did* care deeply for? She had never in her life believed in revenge because it took far more strength to refrain from retaliating than it did to return the pain—to show if not kindness then mercy to the one who'd hurt her.

"I've thought about what he said so many times this week and how I couldn't do it, couldn't give him that chance. And I thought maybe I could show him…."

"Show him what, Becky?"

"It failed miserably, okay? Is that what you want to hear, Luke?" She sank onto the loveseat where she had enjoyed the warmth of Shane's casual embrace not so long ago. "All I did was prove you right."

"Yeah, you kinda did."

Becky laughed miserably at that. "Smart ass."

"Look, I know it hurts—more now that both of you being back in Northstar has forced you to reopen old wounds—but I firmly believe you and Shane have something incredible. I suspected it when we were kids, and I've sensed it every time the two of you have been together in the last two months. When you're not *trying* to be angry at him, it shines through."

She turned her face back to him, trembling with hope that he was right and fear that he wasn't.

"I see it in your eyes right now," he whispered. "But you will never be able to get over what happened if you keep trying to bury it again by pretending you are content being friends."

"Yeah? What do you suggest I do instead?"

"Talk to him. About everything. Tell him exactly how he hurt you so he knows what he has to do to heal it."

She shook her head as fresh tears threatened to join the ones that had already fallen. "I can't...."

"Yes, you can. And somewhere, behind all those walls you've built, you want to." Luke sat beside her and hugged her tightly. "Take it from someone who became a master at building walls. You cannot understand how freeing it is to tear them all down until you do. So do it."

"Do you have any idea how much like your mother you sound?" Scowling, Becky added, "I really hate you right now."

"Why? Because you know I'm right?"

"Yeah. Do you *always* have to be right?"

"It's a surprising benefit of all the nightmares I've survived. I get to be wise beyond my years."

His teasing tone was exactly what she needed right now, and she rested her head on his shoulder like she had so many times since the day they'd found Carol's body atop the mine tailings just a hundred or so yards through the forest outside his cabin. When Ryan sat on

Becky's other side and took her hand, Becky hugged her, too, wishing she could accurately explain to Luke's wife just how glad she was Luke had found her.

"Give Shane that second chance," Ryan whispered. "Or, at the very least, give him the opportunity to prove he deserves it."

She didn't make any promises—her thoughts were too chaotic—but she mulled over everything they'd said as she drove home through the murky snow squalls. James sat quietly in the passenger seat all the way down the mountain, and she exhaled in a sigh of relief that he kept the questions that obviously plagued him to himself.

He maintained his silence all the way home. She had planned to stay a while to visit with her family, but right now, she had no desire to be sociable, preferring instead to sulk and attempt to work through her tangled thoughts in solitude.

As soon as she pulled up in front of their parents' cottage, however, James's concern and curiosity got the best of him.

"Why were you upset? Was it something Shane did?"

"No, it was something *I* did. Can we please not talk about this right now?" The scowl he gave her elicited a grimace from her. "Hey, don't look at me like that."

"Why not? He's trying to make up for whatever he did, but you keep pushing him away. That's kinda mean, Becky, especially because he makes you happy… or he could if you let him."

Becky shifted in her seat, uncomfortable with the accuracy of her brother's innocent statement. At one time, Shane *had* made her happy. He'd been able to brush her worries away with a kiss or bolster her confidence with a handful of words. He'd given her the fortitude to draw a line with Jenny and Andrea and, with the reverence he'd treated her with, made her believe she was worth more than she'd ever thought. He'd shown her how strong she could be.

Then he'd taken it all away.

Did no one understand that? Why were Luke and Ryan both so adamant about her giving Shane another shot? When had they decided to take Shane's side over hers?

"Everyone just needs to leave me alone about this," she growled, tightening her grip on the steering wheel until her knuckles whitened.

"Fine," James snapped. He jumped out of her truck, and just before he slammed the door, he added,

"Keep wallowing in your misery."

Becky stared after him. *Keep wallowing in my misery? What nine-year-old says things like that?* It was even more shocking that he understood exactly what it meant, and ignoring the youthfully narrow shoulders and slight, almost skinny build, Becky knew she was seeing her first real glimpse of the man he'd grow to be—as generous and compassionate as he was strong and determined. *Lord help the world when that boy comes into his own.*

She shifted her truck into gear and drove to her small cabin, which like her parents' house, sat at the edge of the tree line across the wide field from the main house on the gravel access road that connected all the ranch's buildings. After parking her truck in front of her new home, she headed inside. It was comprised of just four rooms—a combination living room and dining room at the front and a single bedroom in the rear at the end of the short hall between the kitchen and bathroom. It was nearly identical to her little cottage in Wilson, Wyoming, but instead of cool white walls and Bavarian charm, the cabin was constructed of squared logs and glowed with the cheeriness of golden wood tones. It was much more her style, she thought, expecting the coziness of it to chase away some of her angst. It didn't. If anything, it felt lonely with the memory of kissing Shane still too fresh in her mind.

She thought of making a snack but wasn't hungry, so she flopped on her sinfully squishy couch and let her head fall back. Her eyes drifted closed, and she thought back to the conversation they'd had on this very couch only a week ago. Rarely in the past had he been so open, risking that she might decide to tear him apart. The vulnerability of it stunned her. Shane *never* let his guard down so completely—his mother had taught him from a very young age the danger of doing that—so how could it be anything but real?

Rising to her feet, she stepped across her living room and retrieved the picture that had captured his attention last week. With shaking hands, she plucked it off the hutch behind the dining room table. As her eyes tracked from one familiar face to the next, anger sparked.

How did we stand a chance with that much pain wedged between us? he'd asked.

"The problem is that you created a lot of that pain," she said when her gaze came to rest on Carol.

She returned to the couch and set the picture on the coffee table. Tilting her head, she noticed a slip of folded paper sitting there, and she picked it up.

Justin called again. Love you. Dad.

Anger exploded into fury, and she snatched her cordless from its cradle on the end table beside the couch, quickly punching in Justin's cell phone number.

"Hello?"

"Since you obviously haven't gotten the message," she said, "let me reiterate as clearly as I can. We are done and over."

"Becks?"

She sneered at the nickname, no fonder of it now than she'd ever been. "Yeah, who the hell else?"

"Baby, I'm so glad to hear your voice. I was beginning to think you'd never call me back. We need to talk."

"What is there to talk about, Justin? I'm done letting you control my life and keeping me away from my family and my home."

"But, baby, I love you. I know I screwed up, and I want the chance to make it up to you."

What did it say about her that she now had not one but two exes trying to convince her to let them fix things with her?

"Please, Becks. I want to work on us. I promise we'll visit your family as often as you want. I know how important they are you, and I was stupid before for not considering it."

Visit as often as she wanted? Somewhere in the back of her mind, she understood that she needed to explain to him in the firmest words that that was no longer an option, but at once, exhaustion descended on her. It was too much, and the words that would clarify that she had no intention of ever going back to him faltered into skittering pieces she couldn't catch. "No, Justin."

"Don't say no. Please don't say it without even thinking about it."

I can't handle this right now, she thought. "Fine. I'll think about it. Just… stop calling me, all right?"

"All right. That's all I can ask for," Justin said.

Relief was plain in his voice, and Becky thought again that it wasn't smart to give him even that much hope. She didn't say goodbye and simply ended the call. She wondered, had Shane not opened this can of worms, if she would have honestly considered going back to Justin. The answer was a solid no. A sly voice informed her that Shane's admission only made it easier to close the door on Justin, and Becky groaned.

What a mess, she thought and stretched out on the couch with her arm across her eyes.

Eight

HE'D GIVEN BECKY five days of privacy with only one phone call on Sunday morning to ask her to genuinely consider what she wanted. It fortified his hope that she'd promised she would and thanked him for giving her the space and time to work through it. They'd both been busy with work, so it had been easy in the physical sense to maintain his promise to avoid unduly influencing her one way or the other. Emotionally, however, it had taken far more willpower than he'd anticipated to stop himself from calling her.

Today, at last, his waiting would end.

Shane ascended the steps to the deck of the Bed-spread's restaurant with his father right behind him. The dining room was more crowded than usual, but today it was filled with locals attending the annual Thanksgiving potluck. Jake Sterling, who had always been kinder and more understanding when the rest of Northstar had turned a cold shoulder, was the first to greet them. Before Shane had exiled himself, he never would have imagined that he'd end up with so much in common with Jake, but their paths had taken them in the same direction and earned them the apathy of their friends and neighbors, and in the couple of years their stints at the University of Montana had overlapped, they'd gotten to be pretty good friends. Jake had since humbled himself and apologized to the people he'd hurt, and in so doing, he had worked his way back into the good graces of the loyal and long-remembering residents of Northstar. That gave Shane hope that he'd be able to do the same.

I already am, he reminded himself. *And it feels incredible.*

"Too bad you aren't still playing with the Griz," Jake remarked conversationally. "We might've won on Saturday."

"I don't know about that since Luke and his Cats

beat us three of the four years I played." Shane nodded his head in greeting to Jake's wife and six-year-old son. "Melissa, Tommy, how are you?"

"We're good, Shane. And you?"

"Can't complain, but I don't think I've ever been so glad to see the closing day of hunting season just around the corner. I'll be glad to get back to my regular duties at work."

"Is the check station terribly boring?"

"Horribly so. But I suppose it's not all bad because I've had plenty of time to do some drawing."

Melissa, whom he'd first met at college when he'd taken the art class she'd taught while she worked on her Masters of Education—the only one he'd had the heart to take—smiled proudly. "I'd love to see what you've been working on. I heard a rumor that you've been drawing a lot more lately."

"I have indeed."

"I'm glad to hear that. I know you lost the heart to do it for a long time, so it makes me happy to hear you've found it again."

The bell on the front door jingled, and Shane looked up to see Becky, her parents, and brother strolling inside, shedding their heavy winter coats as they entered the blissful heat of the restaurant.

"Thank you," he mumbled to Melissa, his eyes locked on Becky.

She wore crisp new boot-cut jeans, a glittering Western belt and buckle, and a fitted mist-gray V-neck sweater that called attention to her eyes and hugged her athletic body in a most enticing way. With her dark hair plaited into a long braid currently flopped over her shoulder and her favorite old pair of cowboy boots on her feet, she was the embodiment of everything he loved about Northstar and entirely breathtaking.

Someone gripped his shoulder, and his heart nearly fell out of his chest. He turned to find Luke grinning beside him, and Shane doubted the source of that smile was amusement at having spooked him. His friend's words confirmed it.

"He's definitely *found* his heart again," Luke said in response to Melissa's observation. "Now he just has to win it back."

Jake glanced between Becky and Shane. "I'm not the least bit surprised."

Unwilling to be the center of their gossip—or at least not wanting to hear it—Shane excused himself to make the rounds. It immediately became clear that the tides had turned when Aelissm O'Neil put her task of arranging potluck dishes on hold to greet him with a smile.

"I'm hearing some things about you that impress me," she explained when he inquired about her change of heart. "Seems you might have rediscovered your honor."

Word of his indiscretions had burned through Northstar faster than a lightning-sparked wildfire, and it appeared the steps he'd already taken toward reparation were spreading just as quickly. Right now, in contrast to before, the speed of Northstar's grapevine was a major benefit of living in such a small, tight-knit community.

"Does that mean I can call you Aeli again instead of Mrs. O'Neil?" he quipped.

"God, please. You know I hate formalities," she replied. "And I don't recall ever saying you couldn't call me Aeli."

"No, but you didn't have to use words to make it quite clear that Shane was no longer worthy of that privilege," Pat remarked.

"Well, I apologize. In cases like yours, Shane, it is a pleasure to be proven wrong."

"Happy to do it," Shane said, nodding once while he attempted to hide the smug grin that threatened.

He walked away from them after a few more

pleasantries with a bit more bounce in his step. He located his father again and said a quick hello to the Hammond and Carlyle clans before following Austin to the table beside the one Becky, her parents, her brother, her Conner grandparents, and the Robinsons had claimed. Luke and his family—his wife, son, daughter, parents, and siblings—also sat nearby, and Shane wrapped the companionship they offered freely around himself, soaking up every last drop. With the exception of Becky, they all treated him with unreserved joviality and fondness, and he readily acknowledged that he'd missed their wonderful brand of love. The conversation flowed uninterrupted even when everyone got in line to fill their plates from the myriad of dishes people had brought, and they talked and laughed and lingered over their meal as the sun sank behind the western mountains and day gave way to starlit night.

Becky was polite, friendly even, but there was a disheartening distance in her voice whenever she and Shane spoke to each other, and it troubled him. Either she hadn't decided what she wanted or she had come to the conclusion that friendship was all she could give him. He ached to know which, firm in his decision to remain friends if that's all she wanted, but he resolved to be optimistic until it was time to ask her.

"This right here," Austin remarked, lifting his steaming coffee mug in a toast, "is what life is all about. Cherished family and friends, engaging conversation, and a cup of strong coffee. For these things, I will always be thankful."

Everyone in their group and those close enough to hear raised their drinks to his toast. Smiling so broadly that his face hurt, Shane sipped his coffee and glanced from one treasured face to the next. Some might say he'd missed out on a lot by having no other close family but his father, and two years ago he would have agreed, but in this moment, he understood and appreciated exactly how wrong such a statement was. All of Northstar was his family, and he counted himself lucky to have benefited from the love of the Conners especially. His own mother might have walked away, but he'd been blessed to have had June fill that role even in the limited capacity she had.

How differently would everything have turned out if only he had let her and the rest of them help him instead of pushing them away?

Maybe he and Luke would have found a way to overcome their issues, and Shane would have then been able to accept that Luke would always hold a piece of Becky's heart, comfortable in the knowledge that she could love them both simultaneously in their own way. It sounded like a dream, but if Shane hadn't broken up with Becky, he would have had no reason to get involved with Ryan. And while that meant he wouldn't have hurt her—something he didn't know if he ever could or should forget—it also meant she wouldn't have taken the job in Devyn with the hope of repairing their relationship and she wouldn't have met Luke.

Shane glanced at the couple, who were currently entwined and either oblivious or uncaring of the amused glances of their friends and family. Even if he and Becky were destined to remain nothing more than friends, the love that Luke and Ryan had found was worth every broken heart along the road that had led them to it.

"Things happen for a reason," June murmured, leaning close with her granddaughter in her arms while her son and daughter-in-law enjoyed each other.

"Are you *certain* you can't read minds, Mom?" he asked with a chuckle. "Because that's exactly where my line of thought was leading me."

"I promise I can't. I'm just uncommonly observant."

"It's good to see Luke so happy. And Ryan, too."

"Yes, it is." June glanced down at Ashleigh, then back to Shane. "Are you ready to try again?"

Shane tilted his head and studied the sleeping baby's angelic face, prodding the peace that had settled over him the moment he'd accepted that it was better that the "what ifs" would never happen. "You know… I am."

June settled Ashleigh in his arms, carefully so as not to wake her. Shane let the weight and scent and beauty of her saturate him and consciously opened himself to all the grief and fear and self-loathing that he'd caged for so long now. He allowed himself to wish his child had survived and to admit that he could have found a way to do right by Ryan without destroying any chance of reuniting with Becky. He acknowledged his cowardice and cruelty. He'd done that much—to some extent—before, but as he brushed his fingers through Ashleigh's dusting of impossibly fine golden hair, he took it a step further.

He let it go.

Closing his eyes, he pictured all those destructive emotions as a pile of ash in his hands and then pictured casting them to the wind, watching as they drifted away and faded into nothingness.

The back of his neck tingled with the peculiar sensation that he was being watched, and when he opened his eyes to seek the source, his gaze met Becky's. He'd never seen that exact expression and could not begin to decipher it, but it bored straight to his heart, igniting at once triumph and trepidation. Briefly, he tightened his arms around Ashleigh, not yet willing to give her up now that he'd found the nerve to hold her.

But it's time, he knew.

Grudgingly, he handed Luke's still-sleeping daughter back to June, met Becky's gaze again and inclined his head toward the door. Her brows dipped, but she stood and walked around the tables to him, folding her arms across her chest and regarding him with a gleam in her eyes that he could only describe as defiance wrapped in apprehension and curiosity.

"We need to talk," he said quietly so only she could hear as he rose to his feet. "Now."

"This really isn't the time or the—"

"Then when, Becky? We need to, and between your job and mine lately, it has been too easy to avoid it." He was careful to keep his voice gentle and even. "I'm tired of avoiding it and wasting time."

He held his hand out, offering her the choice and the control. He'd made the mistake of deciding for her once before and vowed he never would again. His heart beat several times while he waited, each thud harder and faster than the last as she hesitated. Doubt slithered through him.

"All right," she said, curling her fingers around his.

"We'll be back," Shane told June.

Luke's mother only nodded knowingly and offered an encouraging smile. Shane guided Becky to the doors and helped her into her coat before shrugging into his own, then took her hand again and led her outside into the bitterly cold night. He didn't let go of her until they reached the corner of the broad deck closest to the eastern Northstar Mountains, and even then, he only did it so she could put her gloves on and tuck her hands into her coat pockets to keep them warm.

Before he could decide where to start, she blurted, "I owe you an apology… for kissing you on Saturday."

It might not be wise to say it, but he couldn't help himself. Nor could he stop the smile that accompanied it. "No apology necessary. I enjoyed it immensely."

"I'm sure you did, but I *do* owe you an apology because I did it to hurt you."

"I'm guessing by the look in your eyes right before you slammed the door that you hurt yourself as much or more than you intended to hurt me."

Becky flicked a trough in the snow that had piled up four inches on the railing. "Yeah, I did."

It would probably be best not to respond to that—not because he felt even remotely triumphant but because she deserved her privacy on the matter. He lifted his gaze to the heavens and let his eyes wander amongst the dazzling stars. Absently, he jerked his gloves out of his coat pockets and stuffed his hands into them. The wind was calm, but the air was frigid with the temperature a few degrees below zero.

"You ever notice how the stars seem to burn with a brighter fire on cold nights like this after a wet snow has cleared the air?" he asked.

"It's freezing out here, and you're stalling?"

"I'm not stalling. I'm taking a moment to appreciate something simple and beautiful." He shifted his gaze back to her. "Because I didn't do that nearly enough when I was younger."

"Bullshit. I've seen your drawings. If anyone could see the beauty in even the tiniest things, it was you."

He shook his head. "I saw it, but I didn't appreciate how important those little things are. Just like I didn't know how important you are to me."

Despite accusing him of stalling only moments

ago, Becky didn't reply, and he sensed that she was in fact delaying the conversation they needed to have. As they stood in silence, staring up at the stars, the cold began to seep into his body, but he ignored it, unwilling to rush her.

"I was surprised to see you holding Ashleigh," Becky remarked. "What changed?"

"I finally found the courage to do it."

"Why would you need courage to hold that beautiful little girl?"

"I'm not surprised you don't realize that Ryan wasn't the only one who lost a child when she miscarried. But we're not going to talk about that tonight because we need to talk about us first."

Becky eyed him with suspicion. "Fair enough. So what gave you the courage to hold Ashleigh?"

"I accepted the fact that I can't change the past no matter how much I wish I could. All I can do is take the lessons from it and try to be a better man for them." He turned fully toward her. "Maybe what I said at your cabin *was* a half-assed apology—I don't know because that's for you to decide—but even when I made it, I didn't expect it to fix us. I only hoped it might open the door so I can show you that I'm prepared to do whatever it takes to make things right."

"That's all well and good in sentiment, but what happens when things don't go your way, Shane? And they will because that's life. Shit happens." Anger warred with pain for control of her voice, and even in the dim glow of the porch light, he saw the shimmer of tears in her eyes. "What will you do when something goes wrong? Will you run away like you always have?"

"No. I'm done running. It only creates more pain."

"No doubt about that, but people don't just change who they are."

"That's not who I am, Becky. It never was."

"The hell it isn't. Only a runner walks away from his pregnant girlfriend. Because he's afraid of commitment."

Shane swore as anger and desperation simmered together in a vicious concoction, and he balled his hands into fists to contain it. So much for hoping they would be able to have a civil conversation. "That's not why I left Ryan."

"Then why, Shane? Huh? Tell me how you could do that to such an amazing woman."

"Because of you, Becky," he snapped. "Because I realized that I would never be able to bury my love for you deep enough."

He paused to rein in his temper and watched as shock and confusion and doubt contorted Becky's face in a shifting kaleidoscope of raw emotion.

"I didn't know if I'd ever have another chance with you," Shane continued more gently, "but I was certain that if I stayed with Ryan, whatever hope there was would die. I couldn't do that to her. Melodramatic as I'm sure it sounds, I couldn't condemn her to being stuck with a man who was in love with someone else. She deserves so much more, so I walked away because a quick, straight cut heals cleaner and faster than a scrape made over and over."

* * *

Becky felt like she'd been stabbed in the heart with an icicle. She stared at him and wondered if she'd heard him right. At first, she didn't believe it, but slowly, guilt coiled around her, constricting her chest and making it hard to breathe. *No,* she thought, shaking her head to dispel it. She didn't believe for a second that she was in any way responsible for the pain Ryan had suffered, and when she probed a little deeper, that wasn't the source of her mortification.

She felt guilty for doubting that Shane's words were one hundred percent the truth.

She searched his face for any sign that this was all

a masterful act and found nothing more than a plea and the same vulnerability that had preoccupied her thoughts after she'd kissed him. Shane was many things, but he'd never been a manipulator or a liar. So why did she now doubt him?

With the brutal force of a blizzard, all the emotions from the night he'd broken her heart howled through her. Tears burned in her eyes and strangled her voice as she demanded, "Then why did you break up with me, Shane? Why did you say those things to me?"

"I knew they'd hurt you, and I knew that hurting you was the only way to make you give up on me."

"Well, you definitely hurt me. I have never felt so worthless or used as I did that day." She cursed her trembling voice. "Can you even imagine how I felt? We made love for the first time after three years together, and the very next day, you broke up with me."

"Becky, I—"

"Do you know how long it was before I stopped believing you'd compared me to Carol or Heather or any of the others and found me so disappointing that you couldn't stand to be with me anymore? Four goddamned years, Shane. It took me three years to rebuild enough confidence to say yes when Justin asked me out and another year after that before I was brave enough to let him do anything more than kiss me."

Shane winced and looked away. For a long time, he stared silently at the mountains glowing dimly in the light of the stars and the waxing gibbous moon.

"I'm sorry I ever let you think that, all the more because it could not be more wrong," he said quietly. "I have *never* compared you to anyone. You took my breath away, Becky, in the most amazing way possible. No one has ever or will ever compare to you."

He reached to tuck a strand of hair that had pulled loose from her braid behind her ear and exhaled in a cloud of silver when she jerked away.

"Carol was a mistake. I didn't enjoy it, and if it had been up to me, it never would have happened."

It struck her as absurd. If he hadn't wanted it to happen, he could have stopped it. And yet… it was such a lame explanation that it struck a chord, and curiosity overpowered her accusations. "What do you mean, *if it had been up to you?*"

Shane shook his head. "She thought Luke would never take her back, so she shifted her sights to finding someone new to take care of her. You remember what Pete—JP—said about her being a survivor always in search of the most advantageous arrangement?"

Becky nodded. "Aunt June mentioned something like that, too."

"I didn't understand until that night exactly what they meant. Mike broke up with her just that morning, and Luke wasn't ready to forgive her… and I was ignorant enough to try to be a good friend. When she left the potluck in tears, I just wanted to be there for her—as a shoulder to cry on, nothing more—because she didn't really have anyone else she could talk to. She never let anyone in other than Luke, and to some extent because of my friendship with him, me. Not even Mike."

Was that true? She'd never really given Carol that much thought, but the pretty redhead had spent most of her time hanging around with Mike and the popular crowd. Shallow, Becky realized now. Those friendships were about as deep as the ones Becky had with Jenny and Andrea. No, not even as deep as that. At least Becky had stuck with Mike's little sister and her best friend. Most kids had a couple of close friends they spent the majority of their time with, but aside from whomever she was dating, Carol hadn't. She'd bounced from one set of friends to the next. Until Luke and Shane—just like Becky in that respect.

"We talked for a while," Shane continued, "and I

told her she just needed to give Luke some time, that he'd come around, but she was so certain they were over for good."

He leaned back against the railing and folded his arms. Becky shivered, suddenly realizing in the lull of their conversation that she was cold. When he held out his arm, beckoning her to him, she hesitated. The little bit of warmth he offered was preferable to stubbornly freezing, but oddly, the cold helped level her emotions, distracting her just enough that she was able to listen with a more open mind, so she shook her head and hugged herself more tightly.

"The next thing I knew, she was kissing me and trying to take my shirt off," he said. Was that a note of disgust in his voice? "She shot down every argument I made about betraying Luke and you and how stupid it would be to keep going the way we were and said it was what she wanted. At the risk of sharing too much information, she was relentless. Frenzied, and it was paralyzing. So I got up and was headed out the door when Pete came home and told us Mike had been found dead in his truck out at the turn-off… that he'd killed himself."

This time, it wasn't the bite of the winter night that made her shudder. Even twelve years removed, it required no effort to recall that horrible afternoon—an afternoon that had started off so fantastically with her Uncle Ben proposing to June. She hadn't considered Mike a friend, but she'd known him well enough through her friendship with his little sister that the shock of his death had tormented her dreams until other, grimmer nightmares had overtaken them. It had seemed so incongruent that a kid with as much going for him as Mike had would commit suicide… and as it later turned out, he hadn't. But that day and the days that followed, the communities of Devyn and Northstar had reeled.

"When it hit us…. Chaos. It felt like the world had fallen out from under us."

Yes, it did, Becky agreed silently. *And I'm sure it was worse for you because he was a good friend and teammate.*

"All my good intentions were lost in the confusion, and we both sought any anchor we could, and emotional turmoil became physical. It's as simple as that. I didn't initiate it, but neither was I able to stop it. I used to think I was too inexperienced to know how to stop or control it, but true or not, that's a weak excuse."

Following along intently and wrapped in the embrace of lacerating memories, Becky almost missed his last statement. When she had snap-analyzed the rest and reached it, her line of thought came to an abrupt halt. "Wait. What? How inexperienced? You can't tell me...."

Shane didn't reply, and as she watched his face, he raised his guard for the first time since they'd stepped outside. To this point, he had been entirely candid, but now he clenched his jaw, hardening his expression. The regret in his eyes, however, was clarification enough of what he meant by *inexperienced*.

"What about the others? Those girlfriends you had back in high school?"

"There *were* no others," he replied softly. "Carol was the first. And I wish she hadn't been."

"But...."

Becky tried to recall the girls he'd dated. Mostly, he'd only gone on a handful of dates with any one of them and kept things casual, but there was one she knew of that he'd been serious enough about—Heather Brown—that he'd gone out with her close to a year. Memories of them making out in a shadowed corner, though laced with a tint of her teenaged envy, were clear enough, but looking back from a more mature perspective, she picked up on things she'd been too young to grasp before—the way he hadn't initiated any hand holding and had usually been the one to put the breaks on those make-out sessions. And she couldn't recall him ever admitting to sleeping with any of them. In fact, on the rare occasions when the topic had come up, he'd squirmed his way out of talking about it.

"What about Heather? You were with her almost as long as Luke was with Carol."

Shane shook his head. "Not even her."

"Why didn't you ever tell me?"

"Tell you what? That I was a virgin until that night?"

"Well, yes. And the rest of it."

"Seventeen-year-old boys who are still virgins—unlike girls, for whom virginity is still acceptable and even admirable—are mocked and teased and bullied. It was easier to let people believe I wasn't. Besides, it was no one else's business, and I didn't figure it would matter to you one way or the other."

"It didn't. Doesn't. I'm just surprised because I'd assumed... like everyone else."

"You know what they say about assumption, right? That it makes an 'ass' out of 'u' and 'me'?"

With a twist of her lips, she replied, "I am familiar with that concept, yes."

"As to the rest of it, I underestimated you."

He glanced in the windows of the dining room to where their friends and family were enjoying each other's company. Becky followed his gaze and smiled, warmed by the love that radiated from them all.

"And you were right. I betrayed my best friend. I knew how screwed up the situation was, and I wasn't strong enough to protect his blind side."

"Is that why you felt like I should give up on you?"

He nodded. "People in pain make stupid decisions. All I could see was the strain I was putting on you because I couldn't fix my issues with Luke, and I didn't know how you could possibly love us both."

"I never chose him over you," Becky said defensively.

"Didn't you?"

She started to reiterate that she hadn't, but he held his hand up.

"I didn't know why then, but I get it now. What happened that summer bound you and Luke together in a way I doubt I'll ever fully empathize with because I wasn't there. I didn't see what you did, and that put me on the outside." Shane paused, and as his eyes darted over her face, she saw him struggling with the past. The compulsion to hold him close until the memories went away was powerful, but suspecting it might also derail him, she refrained. "It was my job to chase away your nightmares, and I couldn't do that. I didn't know how. But Luke did."

This time when he moved to tuck her hair behind her ear, she let him do it, holding his gaze while he did so. She'd never thought about it like that, and while it made her uncomfortable to think she had ignored how the traumas of that summer affected him, she couldn't deny it. Her heart told her everything he said was the truth, but she had spent so long believing otherwise that her brain doubted. So, because she couldn't yet begin to unravel everything he'd told her let alone make sense of it all, she folded her arms around his neck and held him close for a long while. The cold seeped deeper into her, but where their bodies touched, heat chased it away.

"I don't have an answer for you, Shane," she said. "I can't wrap my head around all this right now, so I don't know how much of what you said I believe. I need some time to figure it out. Can you accept that?"

"I'll have to, won't I," he replied with the faintest of smiles. "Honestly, it's more than I deserve."

You still can't see your own worth, she thought. "I may not know if I can give you a second chance, but whatever I—*we*—decide, I am certain that I want us to remain friends. I need that, and until recently, I didn't know how much. Just like Luke has his piece of my heart, you have a piece of it, too, and I want my heart to be whole again."

With a disarming tenderness, he clasped her face in his gloved hands, brushing his thumbs across her cheeks. The emotional bonds might be tattered, but the physical ones were as strong as ever, and her pulse hummed in anticipation. He didn't kiss her on the mouth, however, instead pressing his lips to her chilled cheek. As he took her gloved hand and led her back inside, it shocked her to realize she was disappointed.

The body and heart are in agreement, she mused, *but will the brain fall into line, too? And what happens if it does?*

Nine

WHEN SHANE STRODE into the Bedspread Inn to pay rent, Pat was up on the stepladder hanging the mistletoe in its traditional place in the center of the first beam. For once, the restaurant was nearly empty, but being just after three on a Monday, it was well past lunch, and the dinner rush hadn't begun. Most locals were still at work, and the skiers hadn't yet come down off the Northstar Ski Hill, nor had the snowmobilers and cross-country skiers come in from the trails.

"Isn't that the same sprig your brother-in-law first kissed your sister under?" Shane asked.

"The very same," Pat replied as he climbed down.

"Maybe I should try it on Becky since it seems to have worked so well for Ty and Shannon." Shane pulled his wallet out of his back pocket and took out the requisite cash. "Anyhow, I have rent for you."

"You do remember it's not due until the fifteenth, right?"

"I do, but I'm rather enjoying being back on your wife's good side."

With a chuckle, Pat said, "Come on over to the bar, then, and I'll get you a receipt."

Shane followed the older man around the fireplace to the back of the restaurant where his wife was currently assisting a customer. She flashed him a smile in greeting, and he returned it. He perched on a stool at the bar while he waited for Pat to write out his receipt, idly studying the O'Neils' customer. The woman was dressed in soft slacks and a loose-fitting blouse beneath a Columbia down coat—comfortable for travelling but not the durable clothing people usually wore while visiting Northstar. She might simply be passing through, but Northstar was off the beaten path. No wedding ring, he noted with a quick glance. She appeared to be in her early fifties and had a lithe build. Her hair was a vibrant if silvering red in a short, stylish bob and contrasted rich emerald eyes. With her pale but flawless complexion, she had the quintessential Irish coloring, so he was not in the least surprised that her last name was of Irish origin.

"What's in Seattle, Dr. Brennan?" Aeli asked. "And wouldn't it have been easier to fly?"

"I'm on my way to give the keynotes speech at a medical conference, and yes, it would have been easier to fly, as I usually do, but I had a little free time, so I decided to drive with the thought that I might stop here on my way through to see an old friend."

"Who do you know in Northstar, if you don't mind me asking?"

"Austin McGuire."

Shane swiveled on his stool to face the woman, now thoroughly intrigued. He started to ask how she knew his father, but Pat interrupted.

"Here you go, Shane."

"Thanks," he replied, taking the receipt and folding it before tucking it into his wallet, which he then returned to his back pocket.

While he'd been momentarily distracted, Dr. Brennan had suddenly noticed him and now studied him with a disquieting interest.

"Shane is it?" she inquired.

He nodded.

"You look so much like Austin. Shockingly so."

"I hear that a lot."

"I assume, then, that you are of relation to him."

"I'm his son."

"I thought as much." She extended her hand, and he shook it. "Kelly Brennan."

"My mother's name is Kelly," he remarked. He caught a faint whiff of gardenias and barely refrained from curling his lip at the fragrance.

"Yes, I know." She smiled. "It's a good Irish name."

Irish, yes, but not so good in my experience. Because it would be rude to say it, he acknowledged her quip with only a brief nod before changing the subject. "How long are you in the valley?"

"Just for tonight."

"Does my father know you're coming?"

"Yes, although I wasn't sure when I spoke to him on the phone a few weeks ago if I would be able to stop on the way through or if I'd have to wait until the return trip. I do hope I haven't missed him."

"No, you haven't. He's out working on the ranch, but he should be finishing up soon. I'm headed over there now. Would you like me to tell him you're here?"

"Please," she said. "And thank you. I'll give him a call, as well, as soon as I get settled. I'd like to invite him out to dinner so we can catch up. You're welcome to join us, of course."

He was insatiably curious to find out how this woman knew his father, thinking they must have met before his birth because he didn't recognize her. Dinner would be the perfect opportunity, but her comment about her *good Irish name* and the faint fragrance of gardenias that seemed to be coming from her agitated him, so even though it was mostly a lie, he said, "Thank you for the invitation, but unfortunately, I have other plans."

"Perhaps some other time. I'm hoping to visit again in the coming weeks."

"Perhaps," he echoed, standing. He shook her hand again. "It was nice meeting you, Dr. Brennan."

"Likewise, Shane."

He bid Pat and Aelissm farewell and escaped the Bedspread Inn. It *was* an escape, too, he admitted, unsure why Dr. Brennan so unnerved him.

It's the reminders of my mother, he reasoned.

He was so young when she left that he couldn't remember anything more about her than hazy sensory details like long, soft hair the color of tarnished copper and the scent of her favorite gardenia perfume. To this day, he'd never liked that smell, though he did not have the same aversion to women with red hair—Carol was proof enough of that with her mane of auburn curls. At any rate, it wasn't polite or fair to judge a stranger simply because she happened to have a few things in common with the woman who had abandoned him and his father.

Regardless, those similarities gnawed at him all the way to the Lazy H. Austin was already home having finished his task of fixing the carburetor on the hoist truck for the Hammonds' beaverslide early. Shane entered the bunkhouse without knocking and found his father at the sink in the kitchen scrubbing the grease stains from his hands and forearms.

"We're still on for dinner at the Ramshorn," Austin said. "Looks like I don't need to head in to Devyn to pick up those pulleys for the beaverslide after all. They aren't in yet."

"Actually… I think there's been a change in plans."

"Oh?" Austin dried his hands on a dishtowel and turned to him. One look at his son brought a frown to his face. "You look troubled."

"I am. I ran into a Dr. Kelly Brennan at the

Bedspread just a few minutes ago when I stopped in to pay rent. She says she's an old friend of yours."

"In a manner of speaking," Austin said, "yes, she is an old friend."

"She'd like to have dinner with you. She also said she'll be calling as soon as she gets settled in her room at the Bedspread. You want to tell me what's going on, Dad?"

"You didn't recognize her?"

"No. Should I?"

"Maybe not. It's been a long time, and you were very young."

"Who is she?"

The way Austin hesitated with that guilty shadow in his eyes made Shane squirm. Why did he get the feeling that he wasn't going to like his father's answer?

"She's your mother."

He stared at Austin with his mouth working to form words that his brain was unable to string together. It couldn't be true.

"She still wears gardenia perfume," he heard himself say. Voicing that single observation scattered his thoughts into a thousand different directions. He fought to gather them again and organize them into something recognizable, but it was a useless endeavor as the ramifications of his father's words permeated his brain. With his legs threatening to give out in the shock of it, he pulled out one of the chairs at the table and dropped into it hard enough to jar his back. Nearly two minutes ticked by in silence while he stared unseeing at the flames flickering behind the glass in the door of the woodstove in the small living room.

"It isn't perfume. She grows gardenias. I'm surprised you remember it, but I suppose that explains why you've never been fond of them."

Shane brought his gaze back to his father and gaped, unable to regain his wits.

"What the hell?" he sputtered. "You've got to be kidding me. Please tell me you're joking."

"Brennan was her maiden name. I guess she decided to keep it after she remarried."

"What is she doing in Northstar?"

"I told you. It isn't my place to decide whether or not she's worth your time. Remember? We had this conversation right after you moved back."

"I remember the conversation, but that doesn't explain why she's in Northstar."

"She called me a few weeks ago and asked if it would be all right if she stopped by on her way to Seattle for a conference or on the way back."

"So she said. Why is she here, Dad?"

"I think she wants to explain to you why she left."

"Why? Would good does she think it will do?"

"You'll have to ask her that at dinner."

Shane shook his head vehemently. "No. I'm not going. I have nothing to say to her."

"Shane, just give it—"

"No." He jumped to his feet and headed for the door as something close to panic seized him. He had to get out of there.

"Shane!" Austin barked just before the door slammed shut.

The tires of Shane's truck spun in the gravel as he sped away from the bunkhouse, but no matter how fast he drove, he couldn't leave behind one nauseating thought.

I'm running away from my problems again...just like she taught me.

He had no particular destination in mind, but he wasn't surprised when he pulled up to Becky's cabin and shut the engine down, suddenly afraid she might not even be home even though her truck was parked beside her house. It was nearly dinnertime, but ranch work rarely followed the regular nine-to-five shift clock. He sat in his truck for a while, watching her front door indecisively. Since their talk on Thanksgiving, they had been able to slip back into a comfortable companionship, unhindered by her uncertainty about a romantic relationship because, true to his word, Shane was content for the time being to enjoy her friendship. He'd kept his hands and his hopefulness to himself to give her the freedom she needed to work through everything he'd told her, and perhaps it was that habit that made him hesitate to intrude on her sanctuary.

I need her, he admitted and climbed out of his truck.

He trudged up the steps to the tiny deck, and for a moment, the anticipation of seeing her quieted the confusion that had exploded upon learning the woman he'd spoken to in the Bedspread was his mother. He'd spent more time with Becky since Thanksgiving than he had since she'd taken the job on the Royal R, and it seemed that the more he was around her the more he missed her when he wasn't.

She answered his knock wearing only a deep red towel. "Shane," she stated with dark brows lifted in surprise.

He knew he shouldn't, but he couldn't help glancing over every inch of exposed skin.

God help me, he thought, *because she's even more*

beautiful than I remember.

Her face was smudged with grime, and her hands and forearms sported numerous red marks and what appeared to be splotches of blood. Since he couldn't see any obvious cuts, he assumed the blood wasn't hers and most likely from an animal. None of it dimmed her appeal.

Noticing his perusal, she splayed the fingers of the hand not clutching her towel closed and inspected it. "We had a mare deliver early," she explained. "And by some miracle, her foal is actually quite strong—only slightly premature. The vet is checking him over now but thinks he won't even need to be on a ventilator."

"That's good news, considering December's just barely started."

"Yes, it is. This mare has a history of foaling earlier than most, but this was early even for her." Becky tilted her head. "What are you doing here? I thought you were supposed to be having dinner with your dad at the Ramshorn tonight."

"I was, but I…." He snapped his mouth closed, seeing the goose bumps now rising over her skin. "Can I come in?"

"Now's not really a good time, Shane. I'm covered in afterbirth, and I'm about to hop in the shower."

"My mother's in the valley."

Shock then disbelief passed over her face. "How do you know?"

"I talked to her."

After only a momentary hesitation, Becky stepped back. "Yeah, come on in."

She closed the door behind him and sat with him on the couch. He was acutely aware of the hand she rested on his back in silent support, but even that couldn't keep the confusion at bay. As he knew it would, that debilitating mess of emotions slid back into his mind.

"Are you all right?" Becky asked quietly.

"No, I'm not." He hunched over his legs with his forearms braced on his thighs. "I didn't recognize her, and she didn't say anything, but I'm sure she figured out who I was even before I told her that her 'old friend' is my father."

"How did you find out it was her?"

"Dad. I stopped by his place after I talked to her to pick him up for dinner." He glanced briefly at her. "Go take your shower. I'll be all right for now."

"Do you want to stay for dinner?" she asked, standing. "Since it sounds like your plans with Austin have fallen through...."

"Uh, sure. That'd be great. What's for dinner?"

"After today… microwave TV dinners."

"How about I cook something a little more satisfying? You just restocked yesterday, didn't you?"

She nodded. "I think I put one package of pork chops in the fridge, too, instead of the freezer."

"I can work with that."

While Becky ducked into the bathroom to bathe, Shane installed himself in the kitchen and used the task of preparing fried pork chops, mashed potatoes, and salad to distract himself. By the time Becky emerged from the bathroom again and disappeared into her bedroom to dress, Shane had dinner well under way and was in a much calmer frame of mind. Of course, it was nearly impossible to stop himself from thinking of Becky toweling off and slipping into her fleece pajama pants and tank top just a few feet away behind the closed door of her bedroom.

Down boy, he told himself. *Until further notice, she's a friend only.*

Stubbornly, he kept his back to her room and set the table while he waited for the potatoes to boil. Just as he set about breading the pork chops, she joined him in the kitchen. Without a word, she stepped behind him and tucked her arms around his waist with her chin resting on his shoulder to watch him cook. His pulse jumped, but he ignored it and continued working.

"Feeling a little better now?" she asked with soft concern.

Because he didn't trust his voice, he simply nodded.

"How can I help?"

"Talk to me," he replied. "Tell me more about your day."

"I meant with dinner."

"I know, but I've got it handled."

The phone rang, and she stepped away to answer it. Shane immediately missed the warmth of her body against his.

"Hi, Austin," she said into the phone. "Yeah, he's here."

A chill seeped through him. He didn't know how his father knew Becky's number, nor could he decide if he should be amused or mortified that his father had guessed where he'd gone.

"Not at all. Mmm-hmm. Right now he's cooking me dinner, and after, I think we'll watch a movie. Yep, of course. Talk to you later," Becky said and ended the call. She set the cordless handset on the coffee table and returned to the kitchen, leaning against the counter near Shane. "This is quite a pleasant change. Justin never cooked."

"Really?" he inquired lightly. "I'm no great chef, but I enjoy it, and at times like this, it's surprisingly therapeutic."

"Well, he's not creative like you, so I suppose creating a meal doesn't have the same benefits for him." With more amusement than disdain, she added, "That and he's an ass."

Shane smiled at that, smugly noting that there was at least one favorable thing in Becky's estimation he had that her ex did not. "Sounds like it." Sobering again, he asked, "Did my dad tell you to send me home to deal with my mother?"

"No, he asked if I minded keeping you here for a while and if I would help you calm down. He also told me to remind you that he loves you."

With brows lifted, he eyed her. Then he snorted. "I guess it bothers me more than I ever knew."

"Do you want to talk about it, or would distraction be more effective?"

"Since I don't have any idea why she's here or what she wants, distraction would probably be the way to go."

"You know, when you *are* ready to talk, Luke would be able to help a lot more than I can since he went through something similar not so long ago with Allen Maxwell. Anyhow, back to distracting you. I figure we could watch one of the *Lord of the Rings* extended editions after dinner and you can tell me again why it's such an amazing story."

"You say that like it will be about as fun as watching paint dry."

"Not at all. I love them as much as you do." She pushed off the counter and turned to him, sliding her hands up his chest and hooking them around his neck. "I love them *because* you do."

He lowered his head and pressed his forehead to hers, and when she tightened her arms around him, he tucked her against him and shuddered. She had an ability to soothe him like no one else could, and he was immeasurably grateful that they had found their way back to being friends.

After dinner, they did the dishes together, then retreated to the couch. Sensing perhaps that he needed to have her close, she sat on one end and let him stretch out with his head pillowed on her thigh, absently combing her fingers through his hair. They watched the movie, and other than the occasional comment to note their favorite scenes, they didn't talk. Shane felt a bit like he was using the situation as an excuse to force their relationship into a more physical territory, but that was a fallacy. Becky said nothing about it, and he hoped that meant it hadn't crossed her mind. He had vowed that he wouldn't push her into a decision, and he intended to hold to that.

But it's healing to be so comfortable together again.

"Mmm. Yes, it is," she murmured.

"Yes what is?" he asked. When he realized what she was talking about, he groaned. "Shit. I'm sorry. I didn't mean to say that out loud."

"It's all right, Shane."

"But I said I wouldn't—"

"You're not. Besides, you're right. This *is* healing." She leaned down to hug him, and her still-damp hair fell across his neck, eliciting a shiver from him. "So much so that I'll be sad when the movie ends and you head home."

Hope flared, scorching away the questions and confusion about his mother's presence in Northstar, and he wrapped his arm around her waist in gratitude. If she was leaning toward a second chance… well, he could and would deal with Kelly Brennan because nothing she had to say could bring him down if he had

Becky's love to support him.

* * *

Nearly two weeks after Shane had shown up so unexpectedly at her cabin, the topic that had brought him to her door seeking solace was still on Becky's mind. Because she'd been pulling all-nighters to keep an eye on the premature foal, who was struggling a bit, she had neither seen nor spoken to him on the phone for more than a few minutes at time—not long enough to ask even how he was handling it or if he'd found out exactly why Kelly had decided now was the time to reconnect. He had seemed like his normal self, but she didn't know if that meant he was okay or if he was simply too happy to see her to let it get in the way.

She'd find out shortly, however. They'd both set aside their duties for a few hours today to go swimming at the Ramshorn. Intentionally, she'd arrived early so she had a chance to talk to Luke, whom she hadn't seen much of lately, either. She located her cousin behind the bar in the packed lodge going over the information packet for one of the cabins with a party of four. Her aunt and uncle were also working, and she saw a brief glimpse of their cook, Jason Paulsen, when he brought out an order to a customer sitting at the bar while Luke was busy.

"Becky, sweetheart, how are you?" June asked.

"Good, Aunt June." She glanced around. "It is *packed* in here today."

"It's been like this since the ski hill opened."

Luke sent the guests off to their cabin and ambled over to Becky and his mother.

"Why don't you take a quick break to go check on Ryan, Luke?" June said. "We can handle everything here for a few minutes."

"Thanks, Mom," he replied.

Becky followed him outside, amused at the length of his strides. If she didn't know any better, she might think he was glad to get out of the restaurant for a bit. As they headed up the snow-covered driveway toward the pools, she asked, "Ryan's working, too?"

"Yep. Nate called in sick this morning, so she's covering the pool house."

"I thought this was supposed to be the off season."

"It used to be. Days like today, I almost miss the time when we were lucky to have one or two of the cabins booked and two or three tables taken."

"Just how busy is it?"

"We have no vacancies through New Years."

"Wow. That's insane."

She glanced around the wide parking area beside the pools and pool house, and guilt prickled her for taking the job on the Royal R. Cars lined the entire span from the two RV hook-ups to the very end of the pool enclosure and more were parallel parked across the parking area down from the corrals half-hidden in the trees nearly to the lodge.

"If you guys need a hand from time to time, you can call me, you know," she said. "I could have taken Nate's shift this morning to help out so Ryan didn't have to."

"I would have, but Shane told me you and he had plans today, and since it sounds like neither of you have seen as much of each other lately as you'd like, I wasn't about to take what time you *do* have."

"Has he talked to you about his mother showing up?"

Luke nodded.

"I probably should have asked you before I told him to talk to you, but I thought you might be able to help him more than I could."

"I sincerely doubt that." Luke smiled. "It sounds like she wants to explain why she left. Supposedly, it's for Shane's benefit, but I don't see what he has to gain. He doesn't need her, and he doesn't want her in his life."

"How's he doing with it?"

"Better when I talked to him yesterday than when he called the day after. If you want my honest opinion, this isn't about Shane. It's about her. She needs to ease her guilty conscience."

"That's what I'm afraid of."

They'd reached the pool house, so Becky abandoned the conversation for the time being and stepped through the door Luke held open for her. She strode down the narrow hallway with its large, square windows overlooking the pools and turned the corner toward the dressing rooms. There were at least a dozen people in the wider lobby, and Becky had to fight her way through them to sneak into the office immediately to her right. By the guests' damp hair, she guessed they were on their way out. Good. The fewer people there were in the pools the more relaxing it would be for her and Shane. While Luke paused to chat with a guest who'd recognized him as one of the owners, Becky sequestered herself in the safety of the office with Ryan. Ashleigh snoozed soundly in her mother's arms with the assurance of the complete devotion of her parents, and Becky spared a moment to marvel at how quickly Ryan had adjusted to motherhood and that she could work around her sleeping daughter with such ease.

"I can't believe she's already three months old," Becky said, perching on the stool beside Ryan. "And seeing how much she's already changed makes me all the more thankful that I decided to come home because I would have missed so much."

"We're glad you came home, too," Ryan replied. "I've really loved getting to see exactly why you're Luke's best friend."

"Speaking of your husband," Becky remarked, glancing at the man now at the center of their conversation, "for being such a total introvert, he does this whole gracious lodge owner thing very well."

"Yes, he does. I got my first taste of that on our very first date when a guest cornered him in the pool to ask about the Ramshorn's wedding packages. So I guess you could say I got used to it right from the beginning."

Becky chuckled. "I remember hearing about that."

The guests headed out to their vehicles, and Luke joined his wife and Becky in the office. For a few moments, all was quiet, and the relief on her cousin's face made Becky laugh. Luke leaned down to kiss his wife, then leaned against the snack counter. Becky folded her arms and tapped her fingers, wondering if the question she wanted to ask Luke would be uncomfortable for Ryan. She desperately wanted to know the answer, and now that she had time to get one, she decided to go ahead.

"Ryan, is it all right if I ask your husband a question about Carol?"

"Why wouldn't it be?"

"Um, it's a personal question. *Very* personal."

"Just ask it, Becky. I'm quite secure in my marital status."

"What if *I* don't want to hear it?" Luke asked playfully. "Or answer it?"

"Tough. You're the only person alive who can answer it for me, but I wanted to give your wife the chance to leave the room if she doesn't want to know."

"She knows everything." He held his hands out, palms up, and closed his eyes, making a show of taking several deep breaths before he met her gaze. "All right. Ask away."

"What kind of lover was Carol?"

"In a word… assertive. Especially at first."

"Can you be more specific?"

"She wouldn't take no for an answer."

"She initiated your first time?"

Luke nodded.

"Of course she did," Becky muttered. "I hate to press for details, but this is kind of important."

"Is it?" Luke regarded her with a lifted brow, and she could almost feel him digging around in her thoughts. "I wanted to wait because my life was complicated enough, but she persisted. Honestly, she was overwhelming—so adamant that I'd call her possessed. Why do you ask?"

"Something Shane said about the night he slept with her made me curious. Do you think she would have done the same thing with him? I mean… kept after him until he gave in?"

She expected him to wince at the mention of the act that had fractured his friendship with Shane, but the only reaction Luke gave was a contemplative frown.

"Absolutely I think she'd do it," he said. "Carol was a survivor, and sex can be a way to acquire security." He pushed off the counter and reached for Ryan's hand. Threading their fingers together, he pulled her hand to his lips and kissed her knuckles before again turning his attention to Becky. "Life never really gave her much chance to be anything else. Pete and Jake and Tammy did everything they could for her, but they couldn't even hold themselves together."

A couple walked up to the counter, interrupting their conversation with excited questions about the lodge and pools, and Luke let go of his wife's hand to take their payment for swimming and answer their questions. When they left, he picked up where they'd left off.

"Factor in the emotional hurricane of finding out about Mike, and I'm not at all surprised it happened. I wish I'd figured that out a long time ago because I was mad at Shane for giving in… just like I did. But enough about Shane and me. I'm much more interested to hear about Shane and *you*."

"Don't get your hopes up just yet, Luke," Becky replied flatly. "I'm still deciding whether or not I dare take a chance on him again."

"What's to decide?"

"He's run so many times."

"That may be," Ryan said, "but he's come back to you, hasn't he? Not only that, he's opened up about everything, and you know as well as I do—or you should—that he doesn't do that. Believe me, Becky, the man's in love with you. When we were together, he rarely talked about his past or anyone from it, but he mentioned you more than anyone else. And it used to make me a little jealous the *way* he talked about you—

with such reverence and regret in his voice."

Becky shifted her weight. She'd become so used to thinking of Ryan as Luke's wife that she didn't like to think of Ryan with Shane, and recalling that she'd been with him for three years—as long as Becky had been with him—was so awkward that she squirmed. She shoved the thought away because, in the brilliant aura of Ryan's love for and with Luke, Ryan's relationship with Shane meant nothing anymore.

"You believe that?" Becky asked. "You honestly believe I can trust him?"

"I do. He's not going anywhere this time unless you send him away."

"And before you start questioning if you want to give him a second chance again," Luke asserted, "you might want to remember all those talks we've had about him over the last, oh, twelve years. Even in the last couple of months, you've been happier just being friends with him again."

"Slathering it on thick today, aren't you?"

Husband and wife regarded her with matching mischievous grins. A second later, those grins—if it was possible—widened as Shane strode up to the window. Becky's heart leapt, as it usually did, but this time, she didn't try to subdue her pleasure at seeing him. He greeted them all, letting his gaze linger on her before jerking his attention away.

"You guys aren't hosting another wedding this weekend, are you?" he asked.

"Nope. This is all regular business."

"Unbelievable." He pulled his wallet out of his back pocket to pay for swimming.

"Employees swim for free," Luke said.

"But I haven't ever worked here."

"You helped with Chloe and Ryder's trail ride wedding, didn't you?"

"Yeah, I guess, but that was one day."

"Would you just shut up and go swim?"

Rolling his eyes and laughing, Shane told Becky he'd see her out in the pools in a few minutes.

"This is going to be so much fun to watch," Ryan said gleefully to her husband. "He was trying so hard to play like he's not interested in her."

"Mmm-hmm," Luke replied.

"I'll see you later," Becky muttered, grabbing her swim bag off the floor by the desk where she'd set it.

Despite her feigned chagrin, a delicious giddiness bubbled through her as she pieced together the information Luke and Ryan had shared with what Shane had told her on Thanksgiving. She had thought about it plenty in the three and a half weeks since, and though she hadn't *actually* believed he had been anything but truthful, it was reassuring to have confirmation from Luke and his wife.

She changed quickly into her deep red two-piece swimsuit, wrapped her matching towel around her waist, and left the dressing room. By the time she passed the office, Luke had returned to his duties at the lodge, leaving Ryan to man the pool house office alone. For the moment, however, all was quiet, and Becky only waved as she headed out to the pools to give the other woman a chance to enjoy the brief lull. Because most of the forty or so swimmers were gathered in the smaller and hotter of the two pools, she made her way around the boardwalk to the stairs of the larger pool.

Much better, she thought, counting only four other people.

The hinges on the door screeched, and Becky glanced over her shoulder to see Shane stepping outside in a pair of plain black swim trunks with his towel over his left shoulder. For once, she was okay with admitting she was attracted to him. With that physique, how could she not be? As her eyes took in every line of him, she agreed with what Ryan had once said about

Luke because Shane was the same—it was a rare and charming quality when a man could take pride in his body without letting that pride turn into arrogance. Her heart fluttered again, more so when she caught sight of a tattoo on his upper left arm. He was too far away yet for her to make it out, but it wasn't the armband she remembered the reporter mentioning in the interview when he'd played for the Griz. Curious, she shivered as the cold air coaxed goose bumps from her skin and waited for him to reach her instead of jumping into the steaming water.

"I finally get to see your tattoo. Or should I say *tattoos*?"

"I have more than one, yes."

"So… lemme see them."

First, he turned his right arm to her, and she studied the ink that stained his bicep where there had been nothing but smooth skin the last time she'd seen this much of him naked. Stubbornly, she refused to think about that last time and instead focused on the tattoo, which she was certain he'd designed himself. The style was what she thought of as Celtic tribal—simple lines with curves and sharp angles. Two wolves, a slightly smaller one lying and howling while the larger stood guard over her, with a backdrop of familiar peaks and what she guessed by the arrangement of those mountains was a lakeshore encircled his arm. The wolves—their high school mascots—undoubtedly represented Mike and Carol, though there were no accompanying numbers or text to confirm it.

"I get the wolves, but why Sawtooth Lake?" she asked, tracing the saw-blade teeth that had inspired the mountain's name. "I know Carol hiked up once or twice with Luke and Aunt June, but I'm pretty sure Mike never did."

"Sawtooth is where it all ended, and when I was designing this, I couldn't stop thinking of how close Luke came to joining them."

She glanced sharply at him. He'd gotten the tattoo long before he and Luke had begun to even think about repairing their friendship. Shuddering as memories of that terrible time threatened, she twirled her finger in the air, commanding him to turn so she could see the other. It was more delicate than the wolves but in the same style and perhaps more heartbreaking—angel wings folded around a rosebud.

"Angel Rose," she murmured. "Your daughter with Ryan."

This time when she lifted her eyes to meet his, she simultaneously wanted to step back in shock and throw her arms around his neck. The first impulse faded quickly, and she refrained from acting on the latter, unsure how he would react.

"I never knew…" she whispered.

"Never knew what, Becky? That it broke my heart when she was born too early?" He lifted his hand and caressed her cheek with his thumb. "I haven't seen you nearly enough recently, so I'd rather not ruin our few hours together with sad memories."

"But—"

"Get in the pool before I decide it would be fun to throw you in again like I used to when we were kids," he said with a playful challenge in his voice. "There will be plenty of time later to talk."

"As you… wish…."

When he'd brushed his thumb across her cheek, his towel had shifted enough to reveal a peek of more ink. Frowning, she gently pulled the towel from his shoulder, inhaling sharply. Stretching across his left pectoral nearly to his collarbone was an even more delicate, more ornately detailed design. With the same curves and angles present in the other tattoos, it followed the shape of a backwards S, and while others might not immediately guess specifically what kind of bird it was, Becky knew exactly because it matched the necklace he'd given her the night they'd made love. The same one she'd given to Austin to give back to him the morning after he'd broken her heart.

"It's a phoenix." She traced the lines with her fingertips, mesmerized by the design and the implications of it. "When did you get it?"

"About four months after we… broke up. It took me that long… to get the design… how I wanted it." He shivered. "Uh, Becky?"

"Hmm?"

"That is *very* distracting."

Grudgingly, she withdrew her hand, but averting her gaze was not so simple. She thought about how they used to say their relationship had risen like a phoenix from the ashes of JP's horrific plot. Had Shane, even so soon after he'd broken her heart, held on to that idea and hoped they might rise again? With the evidence right in front of her, it was difficult to doubt that… or anything he had revealed to her since he'd first asked her to give him a chance to fix what was broken between them. Was he right, too, that they hadn't had a chance before to make it work and that, with many of the wounds either healed or dulled by time, they might now be able to build something stronger?

At last lifting her gaze to meet his, she saw the memories in his eyes, but she also saw hope. Ryan's words returned to the front of her mind. *He's not going anywhere this time unless you send him away.*

Was a second chance possible? Hope sparked, but Becky shook her head. She couldn't make that decision just yet, not until she'd had a chance to integrate what she'd learned today with everything else. She needed to let it all simmer together for at least a few hours. Preferably a few days so she wouldn't make the mistake of deciding on a knee-jerk reaction.

"Let's go swim, shall we?" she remarked. "And after, I think I *will* take you up on your offer of dinner at your place. It's still open, right?"

"Yes, it is. I've even got the steaks waiting in the fridge for us."

She yanked her towel from her waist and tossed it over the railing, then turned back to him to say that steak sounded delicious, but the amusement and desire in his eyes stole the words from her tongue. "What?"

"As your friend, am I allowed to say that you are sexy as hell?"

"I suppose so."

"Good, because you are."

She laughed to hide the blush that threatened.

Justin had been very good at complimenting her, so one would think she should be used to being called sexy or beautiful, but the way Shane said it made Justin's words seem hollow and contrived. When Shane said it, she didn't feel like he was trying to win her favor but rather like he couldn't help himself even though it might instead earn him the opposite. She leapt into the pool with Shane right behind her, and as they enjoyed the hot water together, she noted the sadness that lingered in his eyes and considered something she never had before. He'd hurt others, most especially Ryan, but with all those heartbreaks combined, his decisions had hurt him far worse. It was instinctive to want to soothe away his troubles, to wrap him in her arms and hold him until the pain went away, and she had to remind herself that they were only friends.

Is that my answer?

Ten

BECKY STEPPED THROUGH the front door of Shane's cabin, which he held open for her, and shrugged out of her coat. He took it and his own and hung them on the hooks beside the door, then turned away to stoke the fire while Becky lounged on the couch. Her body was marvelously relaxed from their soak in the hot springs, and her mind was also surprisingly at ease, though that had very little to do with the hot water.

She'd made a decision about Shane.

"Make yourself right at home," he teased when he

rose to his feet again.

"Mmm. I am."

It was early in the afternoon—not quite four—but neither of them had eaten lunch, so Shane stripped out of his thick wool shirt and ensconced himself in his kitchen to start dinner. Becky wished he'd take off the sleeveless Under Armor shirt beneath as well, then chided herself. It was a bit premature to be thinking like that, so with her arms folded on the back of the couch, she settled for admiring the view she had. It was disgusting, really, how graceful he was as he moved around his kitchen, pulling out whatever dishes and utensils and ingredients he deemed necessary. Weren't women supposed to be the elegant sex?

"Have you heard anything else from Kelly?" she asked to distract herself.

"She called Dad again last night to say she and her husband have rented a cabin up at Georgetown Lake for ten days over Christmas and New Years." He smirked. "I guess they tried to get a cabin at the Ramshorn, but they were all booked."

"Lucky you."

"Yep. Supposedly, they made these plans quite a while ago, but of course, she wants to sit down and talk while they're in Montana."

"Of course."

Frowning, Becky let the matter drop for a few moments while he prepped dinner, but she was too curious to let it rest for long.

"What does she expect to happen?"

He shrugged.

"Luke thinks she just wants to ease her conscience."

"So he said."

His back was to her, but the way he stood with his head tipped slightly back and his shoulders held stiffly compelled Becky to join him in the kitchen as if she could drive away his troubling thoughts with her presence. When she leaned back against the counter beside him, he glanced at her with a forced smile.

"You could just tell her you have no desire to talk to her," she said.

"Believe me, that's exactly what I want to do. I don't need anything she has to offer." The muscle in his jaw jumped, belying his nonchalant declaration. "I stopped needing her the day she walked out on us."

"But…?"

"I'm curious," he replied. "She says she wants to explain why, and I guess there's a part of me that wants to know because I've done the same thing she did."

"Then maybe there's something she *can* do for you after all." Becky laid her hand against his cheek and turned his face to her. "She can prove that you aren't like her and that you don't need to run away from your problems again."

"That's generous coming from you. But what if her explanation shows that I'm exactly like her?"

"It won't. Your biggest problem has always been that you think you're not worthy of those who love you."

She hesitated, searching his eyes and her own mind for every detail of what he'd said recently, and knew she was right. The confidence he'd built on the football field did not extend to his personal life, and Becky remembered that even back in high school he'd struggled to see his own value in the arena of relationships.

"You thought you couldn't chase away my nightmares and be everything I needed you to be, and you couldn't offer Ryan the love she deserved, so you left us, thinking we would be better off without you."

The vulnerability had returned to his visage alongside a plea for something her brain was just beginning to comprehend, something her heart had believed all along.

"Your mother, on the other hand.... Well, as I recall your dad saying once or twice over the years, she left because her life wasn't going the way she'd hoped. That is entirely selfish." She let her fingertips dance over the rose tattoo with its delicate angel wings. "I used to think you left Ryan when she told you she was pregnant because you were...."

"Scared shitless of becoming a father?"

"I was going to be a *little* nicer and say 'terrified of that level of commitment,' but yes. I know differently now."

"Oh? How?"

"A man who's afraid of fatherhood doesn't get a tattoo memorializing his lost daughter." Becky studied his face as she spoke. *There's that guarded look again. Which means I'm right.* "Especially a man who used to claim he'd never get *any* tattoos. I never considered how much *you* lost when she died, and I don't think anyone else did, either. Perhaps we would have been kinder had we known."

"I didn't realize it, either, until Ashleigh was born and Luke sort of... dropped her right into my arms," he murmured. "Or at least, I didn't admit it. If I admitted that I wanted her, I would have to admit that I could have found a way to make *something* work with

Ryan, but instead, I ran."

"People in pain make stupid decisions," Becky said, holding his gaze.

"True enough, but I will regret how I handled the situation until my dying breath," he said. "I will not, however, regret that I did it because she found Luke, and *that* is what was meant to be."

He'd said as much before, but this time, she didn't doubt him. He believed every word of it, and that genuine gladness for their friends went a long way to quieting her remaining fears.

"Aren't those two things one and the same?"

"Maybe they are."

"Then maybe you should cut yourself some slack."

Shane regarded her with brows lifted. "You're being awfully sympathetic tonight. What's going on?"

Because the words to explain felt awkward and inadequate, she pushed off the counter and pressed her lips gently to his. When she stepped back, understanding brightened his expressive brown eyes while amusement lifted one corner of his mouth.

"You're not going to accuse me of making a half-assed apology again, are you?" he quipped.

"No. No more accusations." She kissed him again,

just as lightly. "Because I figured out it *wasn't* a half-assed apology."

His brows dipped in a frown, and for long while, he didn't respond. "You're sure?"

"My brain isn't fully on board," she admitted. "But my heart is. And since so many people I love and respect always say we should trust our hearts, I'm going to do just that. Like I used to."

Shane glanced over her face, then trailed his fingers lightly along her jaw before claiming her mouth with a sweet intensity that left her breathless. In the absence of anger and resentment, she was free to savor every sensation and to appreciate how effortlessly he fanned her desire. He made her feel cherished in a way Justin never had, strengthening her courage and inspiring her boldness.

"You always were an incredible kisser," she whispered against his lips.

He rested his forehead against hers with his eyes closed and his brows again drawn together. Instantly, the old doubts and disappointments reared, and her heart thumped erratically with an entirely different emotion than what had captured it just moments ago.

"What? What's wrong?" she asked. Her voice trembled with nervousness.

"I've been hoping for this for so long, but I was afraid you'd never be able to forgive what I've done," he replied. "So I'm afraid that this is just a dream and that I'll wake up to you still hating me."

Relief eradicated her worries, and to her surprise, she grinned as mischief shimmered through her. She slipped her fingers under the hem of his shirt, pinched tender skin between her fingers, and twisted.

With a yelp, Shane jumped back and rubbed the sore spot. "What the hell?"

"Did that hurt?"

"Yeah, it did!"

"Good. That means you're awake."

He stared at her with his mouth hanging open in disbelief, which made her ridiculously proud of herself. As his expression shifted into amusement, he shook his head and smiled. "Thank you."

"You're welcome. For the record, though," she added, grabbing a fistful of his shirt and pulling him back to her, "I never really hated *you*. I hated what you did."

"There's a difference?"

"Mmm-hmm. A big one." Noticing that the previously mouthwatering aroma of dinner had turned acrid, she glanced at the frying pan, then tilted her head toward it. "You might wanna flip the steaks."

"Shit," he muttered, releasing her to tend to their dinner. "You are distracting me. If you don't want dinner charcoaled, you should probably go relax in the living room."

"I think you're right."

She kissed his cheek, then exited the kitchen and left him to his task. With everything that had happened recently, what she had learned, and the ramifications of it all, shouldn't she feel like her world had shifted again? Shouldn't she be staggering against the disorienting swirl of jumbled thoughts? Instead, her mind was serene, and she smiled as she imagined what Luke and Aunt June would say.

This is the right decision.

She made her way back to the couch and noticed something she'd missed before. A sketchbook sat on the narrow coffee table. Too tempted to see what Shane had been working on to leave it alone, she picked it up.

"Hey, Shane," she called, lifting the book. "Do you mind if I snoop?"

He glanced over his shoulder. "Help yourself."

She briefly regarded him with a raised brow before sinking into the couch's marvelously squishy cushions to peruse his artwork. There had been a time when he'd been reluctant to let anyone see his drawings. Like many artists, his work offered a glimpse into the deepest reaches of his spirit, and she believed that showing it to anyone left him feeling exposed and vulnerable. It amazed her that he had become comfortable enough with himself that he could now open himself so freely. Maybe he *had* changed enough to render her fear of him breaking her heart again hollow.

While he finished dinner and set the table, she leafed gently through the sketchbook, which was nearly full; there were only three blank pages at the end. The rest contained a wide and beautiful array of styles from stunningly life-like wildlife and landscape drawings to geometric patterns to the tribal style of his tattoos. Some were basic line art while others—like the elk she'd seen back in October before he'd completed it—were breathtakingly detailed. He'd always been talented, but he had definitely improved.

"What do you think?" Shane asked, studying the elk over her shoulder.

"They're incredible," she murmured. "Every single one of them."

"Thank you. Unfortunately, I'm a better artist than a cook, but I hope dinner will be edible."

"I'm sure it will be great," she responded distractedly, enamored with his drawing. The more she looked, the more there was to see, including a tiny chipmunk on the trunk of the lodgepole pine at the left of the image.

"Get your ass to the table, then, because it's getting cold."

Laughing at his playful tone, she carefully closed the sketchbook and set it on the coffee table.

Contrary to Shane's worry, their meal was fantastic. Afterward, they cleaned up together and adjourned to the couch as the sky outside let loose a curtain of tiny, windblown snowflakes. They briefly discussed watching a movie, but conversation quickly pushed the idea from their minds. They told stories from their college days and discussed the routes they'd taken toward their respective careers, laughed at high school antics and adventures, and shared anecdotes about people they'd met in their time apart. Becky was surprised to learn that Shane had taken only one art class in college, and he hadn't known that she had maintained her own residence off the Teton South Ranch.

"It's like you had no intent to stay with Justin even from the beginning," Shane remarked.

"Maybe I didn't. I certainly didn't immerse myself

into that relationship like I did with you."

"I'm sorry, Becky."

"Don't be. For once, it wasn't a jab at you." With a sardonic twist of her lips, she added, "Looking at it like that, it seems that us getting back together was inevitable."

"I'd like to think so," Shane whispered as if it wasn't intended for her ears. "Were there any other serious relationships besides Justin and me?"

"No. I went on a few dates, but nothing made it past a kiss or two. I just wasn't interested, and to be honest, it was kinda fun being single. Well, except for the couple of times when I had to lie to a guy I had no interest in. Poor Luke had to masquerade as my boyfriend for a couple weeks… and right after he'd made it clear he wasn't interested in dating *anyone* for a while."

"Sounds like an awkward situation from him, but I'm sure he was a good sport. He always is."

"He was. We've had a few good laughs about it. What about you? Any other serious relationships I should know about?"

"Just you and Ryan."

"What about the rebound after Ryan?"

"Of course you know about that," he muttered.

"That wasn't a serious relationship, and I broke up with her after a month. She was totally *not* my type, and I admit that I was probably a bit of a dick to her when I ended it, which seems to be my style. But she wouldn't take the hint when I tried to be polite about it." He cleared his throat. "Anyhow, since I know you're curious, no, we never made it to the bedroom."

Becky lifted her hands in a show of peace. "None of my business. Although… isn't that the point of a rebound?"

He shrugged. "Maybe. But I wasn't even attracted. And, technically, it *is* your business now."

"I hope you don't expect me to divulge all the saucy details of what happened in the bedroom with Justin."

"God, no. Not only would that be an invasion of your privacy, I just don't want to know." He held out his arms and beckoned her into them with a twitch of his fingers. "I don't *need* to know, either, because none of that matters. We—you and I together—are all that matter to me now. Really, we're all that's ever mattered."

She glanced up at him, warmed as much by that sentiment as she was by the heat of his body and the popping fire in the woodstove. Resting her head on his chest, she sighed contentedly, allowing herself a few moments of bliss before she put boundaries on it.

"As much as I feel like we can just pick up where we left off," she said slowly. "I think we should proceed cautiously."

"Agreed. I want to do it right this time," Shane replied. "And that means taking the time to make sure we've addressed and repaired anything that's still broken."

Again, she tilted her face up to him. "You mean that?"

"I do. I've spent a long time waiting and hoping for a second chance with you, so I'm not about to screw it up by rushing it."

She didn't say it, but it went a long way to rebuilding her faith in him to know how much he wanted this. Absently, he stroked the tips of his fingers over her shoulder and upper arm and stared at the flames dancing behind the glass in the door of the woodstove with a faint contemplative smile gentling his features. Only firelight and the hood light over the stove in the kitchen illuminated the living area of the cabin, and the play of shadow and golden glow was enchanting. So enchanting that Becky didn't mark the passage of time until she happened to glance over Shane's shoulder into the kitchen at the clock on the microwave.

"Holy crap!" she exclaimed, bolting upright. "It's two in the morning!"

"Is it really that late?"

"Yeah, and I need to get home."

"I thought you didn't have to work tomorrow."

"I'm not supposed to, but I have some housework to do, and we have a few guests who will be leaving this week who expressed interest in a sunset or starlight trail ride if the weather clears, which it's supposed to." She looked at Shane with one corner of her mouth lifted. "You wouldn't be interested in coming along, would you?"

"You know I would."

Becky leaned into him and pressed a chaste kiss to his lips, then stood, grinning at him. "I figured as much. I'll call you tomorrow when I know more…. Uh, today."

Unwillingly, Becky headed toward the door to grab her coat while Shane stepped over to the light switch to turn on the porch light.

"Well," he said, staring out the big window. "Either the weathermen were wrong again or I don't know the correct definition of 'flurries'."

Becky joined him at the window and gawked. The

tiny snowflakes that had begun falling shortly after dinner had grown and multiplied, whipped across her view by a brutal northwesterly wind. It was difficult to tell exactly how much had accumulated—she guessed eight to ten inches—because the wind had pushed it into drifts. On the lee side of their trucks, there was one such drift that must be at least three feet deep, while on the windward side right beside the tires the ground was nearly bare.

"But the storm was supposed to track north and east of us," she remarked. "We were only supposed to get a skiff!"

"When do they ever get our forecast right?" Shane inquired. "Looks like our old ranchers and cowhands were right again, however. Dad said we'd get a lot more snow than the forecasts called for."

"Yeah. My dad said the same just this morning."

"I think… maybe you should crash here tonight," he said slowly, staring outside. "Wait until they plow the roads in the morning."

"I'm a Montana girl. I know how to drive in crap like this." Becky eyed him. "Besides, I don't think me staying here is such a good idea."

"I'm well aware that you can handle a vehicle in the snow, but it's damned near blizzard conditions out there, and you know as well as I do that the pass will have gotten twice as much snow as the valley." At last, he turned to face her. "Why take the risk?"

"Shane…."

"Please, Becky, I need to know you're safe."

"So I'll call you when I get home."

"I have a spare room with bunk beds already made up or a very comfy couch. Or you can have my bed and I'll sleep downstairs. Hell, I'll even make you breakfast in the morning."

Driving home in the mess outside this late at night was *not* at all appealing, but the thought of breakfast with Shane in the morning was, so she said, "Fine. You win."

She returned her coat to its peg and again joined him at the window. They watched the snow fall for a few minutes before they both yawned. Laughing, they decided to call it a night. After showing her where the light switch was in the downstairs bedroom, Shane lingered a moment, leaning in with his hands braced on the doorframe. Clearly he wanted to say something, but whatever it was, he kept it to himself and pushed upright.

"Shane, wait." It probably wasn't a good idea, but Becky sidled up to him and asked, "Don't I get a goodnight kiss?"

"I thought we agreed not to rush this."

"We did, but is there really any harm in one more kiss?"

Chuckling, he indulged her, pressing his lips tenderly to hers. "Good night, beautiful. I'll see you a little later in the morning."

She watched him climb the stairs, then closed the door and leaned against it, quivering. *Take it slow*, she thought. *Yeah, right. I have about as much chance of doing that as I do of sprouting wings and flying.*

* * *

Shane didn't sleep. Instead, he lay in his bed and listened to his relief and joy argue with his doubt over whether or not Becky had decided to give him permission to prove himself worthy of her love. Sometime between three and four in the morning, the storm blew itself out; the wind died and the snow ceased to fall, and he listened as a muffled quiet descended over the valley and mountains. By six, he gave up on sleep and tip-toed downstairs, stoked the fire until its glow was bright enough to sketch by, and picked up his sketchbook and pencils, then settled down onto the floor in front of the woodstove to draw.

He had no particular image in mind when he put

sharpened graphite to paper, but unsurprisingly, a phoenix began to take shape. When dawn first began to brighten the world outside, he set the nearly complete and detailed outline aside to make coffee with the intent of breaking out his colored pencils later. He hadn't used them in years, but because Becky had given him the set for his birthday the spring before he'd broken up with her, he had always made sure they were among his meager belongings each time he moved.

With a steaming mug of coffee in hand, he went to the window to watch the new day break, more at peace than he'd been in a very long time. As his first day back in Northstar had turned into his second and his first week became his first month, that tranquility had grown like a sprout from a seed, watered and fertilized by rebuilding his relationships with his friends and neighbors, but now it burst into full bloom. Rather than the typical reds and oranges associated with phoenixes, he decided he'd color the one he'd drawn this morning with the hues that now saturated the tattered, eastward-racing clouds. Carmine, apricot, amaranth, and lavender. Maybe with a touch of aquamarine, jade, and sapphire.

"Good morning," Becky said brightly beside him.

He swore under his breath, caught completely off

guard by her arrival and unable to recall hearing her stirring. Glancing at her, he saw she was dressed in the flannel she'd worn yesterday and the Hot Chillys long underwear she'd had on under her jeans. He also noticed that she'd been up long enough to brush and braid her hair and pour herself a cup of coffee.

"Good morning," he replied after he recovered from his shock.

"What were you thinking about so intently that I was able to not-so-quietly sneak up on you?"

"What colors I wanted to use for the phoenix I drew this morning."

"How long have you been up?"

"I don't know. What time is it?"

"Ten to eight."

"Almost two hours, then."

"Can I see it?"

"Sure." He retrieved the sketchbook for her and kissed her cheek. "I owe you breakfast, so I'll get it going. Any special requests?"

"Nope. Surprise me."

He decided on Denver omelets, remembering they were her favorites. After inspecting his sketch, she dressed and called her parents while he cooked, and to Shane's dismay, Andy informed her that the plows had been out to clear the pass already. Becky's father also informed her that, yes, the trail ride was happening, which meant she needed to get home soon if she wanted to get any of her housework done before she had to help bring in the horses and get the tack ready for the riders. Shane wasn't ready for their time together to end even though he'd see her again in a few hours when he headed up to the Royal R to assist with the ride, but to his delight, she lingered over breakfast. He hoped that meant she didn't want to leave.

At last—a few minutes after ten—she announced that it was time for her to head out.

"You want to come tonight, don't you?" she asked as they stood beside the still-closed front door.

"You bet," he replied. "What time do you want me to be there?"

"Around three. We're going to take the Harrison Park trail to the Moose Pond warming cabin and have a fire and some hot chocolate as we watch the sun set, then ride back as the stars come out."

"Sounds beautiful."

"As long as the clear skies hold." Becky glanced out the window at the now cloudless sky. "Looks like they might. Although I suppose a couple of clouds to catch the sun's light would make for a prettier sunset."

She's delaying, Shane realized. "I'll see you at three, then."

He wondered if it would be inappropriate to kiss her goodbye, but she alleviated his quandary before he could think to ask her for permission. And she didn't kiss him on the cheek, either; she kissed him firmly on the lips, and though she didn't deepen the kiss, it was clear she wanted to.

"Let's wait a while to tell Luke about this, all right?" Becky asked.

"Uh… why?"

"Because I don't want to hear him say he told me so just yet."

Chuckling, Shane said, "Knowing him, he won't say it."

"Probably not, but he'll be thinking it."

With one more kiss, Becky vanished out the door. Shane stood by the window with his hands in his pockets and watched her drive away, wondering if this was all real or if it was only a vividly realistic dream.

Because he had no more desire to listen to his father say *I told you so* than Becky had to hear Luke say it, he decided against heading down to the Lazy H to while away the time with Austin. He did, however, call his father to reschedule their dinner for tomorrow after work. He then used the phoenix sketch to distract himself from thinking about Becky, and by a quarter to two, he finished it and was pleased with the final product. Wanting to have a talk with Becky's parents before things between them progressed any further, he quickly donned his cold-weather gear in preparation for this evening's chilly ride and was out the door by two.

Andy and James were home when Shane pulled up to the ranch foreman's cozy yellow cottage, but Jane and Becky were out bringing in the horses. Becky's father invited him in with a polite smile that made him just a little uneasy.

Maybe more than a little. The exact same apprehension that had quivered through him all those years ago when he'd first asked Andy permission to date Becky—the first and only time he'd bothered to ask a girl's parents for permission—now trembled through him again. Andy was both fair and good-natured, and Shane was a grown man now, so it was ridiculous how fast his heart began to pound when Andy asked James to go get ready for the ride. Of course, when he'd asked for Andy's consent to date Becky back then, he hadn't yet broken her heart.

To Shane's simultaneous relief and alarm, Andy

wasted no time getting right to the matter at hand. "Becky told me this morning that she decided to give you that second chance you asked for."

"I didn't know she'd told you I'd asked for one."

He only nodded in confirmation.

"I know I screwed up with her, Andy," Shane said. "And I've regretted it every day since."

"If you're here to ask for my permission again, it's not up to me anymore, if it ever was. My daughter is more than capable of making her own choices, and she has."

"I know that, but I value your opinion and your friendship, and I want to know that I have your consent."

"You do. I've always liked you, Shane, and I'm impressed by what I've seen from you since you've been back home. I *want* to believe you and Becky will last this time. However, past history compels me to let you know that if you hurt my daughter again, you will lose my support and my respect with no chance of ever regaining it."

"I understand completely, and I would expect nothing less."

"Good." When Andy smiled this time, it was much friendlier. "James will be thrilled to hear the news."

Shane glanced toward the boy's bedroom—Becky's old room where they'd made love while her parents were in the hospital with their newborn son all those years ago. "He's an amazing kid."

"He's also a good judge of character, even as young as he is. So it tells me a lot that he adores you." Andy gripped his shoulder for a moment and squeezed. "On a different subject, I'm glad Becky asked you to go on the ride because Jim and Jessie asked Jane and me to sit down with them to talk ranch business this evening."

"Everything all right?"

"As far as I know, but…. Let's just say I'm concerned."

"Is Jim all right?"

Andy glanced out the window across the field to the main ranch house. The frown that shadowed his features did not leave Shane with a good vibe, and it was more than concern for his own family's position and future that worried Becky's father. Shane recalled that Andy had moved to the ranch at just eighteen, two years after a car wreck had taken his parents' lives, and the Robinson's had filled the void created by their deaths.

"Andy?"

"I don't know yet, but he has a bunch of tests scheduled this week—blood work, an echocardiogram, and whatnot." Becky's father returned his attention to Shane. "Becky's already worried enough about Jim, what with his high blood pressure, so I'd appreciate it if you didn't mention this to her. There's no point in worrying her more until we know something."

"I really hope everything will turn out all right. Jim's a good man."

"Yes, he is." Andy glanced out the window and inclined his head toward the barn. "Jane and Becky are on their way back."

Right about the time the women strolled through the front door in a whirl of brisk air, James bounced into the living room dressed and ready for the evening's adventures. Becky stopped abruptly when she spotted Shane standing with her father, but a smile quickly replaced the shock that widened her eyes.

"You're early," she remarked.

"I wanted to speak with your dad for a few minutes… alone."

"Oh?" Becky asked, glancing between him and her father with a brow lifted. "About what?"

"Us," Shane replied.

"Us?" James piped. "Like a you-and-Becky-together kind of 'us'?"

"Okay!" Becky interrupted. She glanced between her father and Shane and hesitated a moment like she wanted to ask for more detail, but when her gaze flicked to her brother, she folded her arms across her chest. "Let's get this show on the trail, shall we?"

"It's just going to be you, Shane, and James," Andy remarked, then repeated what he'd said to Shane about needing to stay at the ranch to talk with Jim and Jessie.

Becky's brows dipped in concern, and though she didn't ask what could be so important that it couldn't wait to be discussed on Monday, it was clear that she was worried. They all headed out onto the porch, and James jogged out into the snow while Becky stood with her parents. To give her some space, Shane headed down the steps, grabbing a handful of snow on his way. He packed it into a snowball and chucked it at James, grinning when it exploded against the boy's shoulder. Becky's little brother stared at him for half a second before a delightfully mischievous grin flashed across his face. With a speed that shocked Shane, he scooped up a fistful of snow, packed it, and hurled it at him. Shane only had time to glance down as it hit him square in the chest.

"Oh yeah?" he asked, forming another snowball.

Voices behind him caught his attention, and before he could launch his second snowball, James hit him again. Shane glanced back at Becky and her parents. Though their voices were hushed, Shane didn't have any trouble hearing what they said.

"So, what did Shane want to talk about?" Becky asked her father.

"He asked my permission to date you again."

"And?" Jane asked.

Shane winced. There was a note of disapproval in her voice, and while he had earned it, he didn't like the reminder of his mistakes. Not today. Today was for celebrating the realization of his dream to get Becky back.

"It's not mine to give, but if it were," Andy said pointedly to his wife, "he'd have it."

Jane might be as stubborn and independent as anyone Shane knew, but she trusted her husband's judgment, and Shane noticed a lessening of her frown. "You really think that's a good idea, Becky?"

"I don't know if it's a good idea or not, Mom," Becky replied. "But I know that fighting it makes me irritable while giving into it makes me feel relieved and free and, yes, happy."

Jane regarded her daughter with one brow quirked.

"Stop pretending like you didn't see it coming, Jane," Andy said. "And stop trying to convince our daughter that you and I weren't saying *just last night* that it might actually be a *good* idea if they get back together even if the only thing that happens is they fix what broke that summer so it isn't hanging over them both for the rest of their lives."

Jane scowled briefly at having her bluff called, then turned her attention to Shane. "I know you're listening, so you may as well get your ass over here."

Obediently, Shane tossed his half-formed snowball at James, who easily ducked it, and joined Becky and her parents. With his chilled hands in his pockets, he waited for Jane to say whatever it was she thought necessary. Seconds ticked by, but she said nothing, only studied him with a frown that was distinctly more contemplative than disapproving, and gradually, Shane relaxed. When she finally spoke, the words were not what he expected.

"I hope it sticks this time," she said with a gentleness that surprised him as much as the sentiment in her words.

"Me, too," he murmured. "Thank you."

"All right," Andy said, gripping his shoulder. "You'd best go round up the guests and get those horses saddled."

"Yessir."

Hooking Becky's finger with his, he pulled her toward the corrals, snagging James around the shoulders on his way. Becky angled them toward the main ranch house where, she informed him, the five guests who'd decided to brave the cold trail were currently eating an early supper. He was unsurprised when she accosted Jessie in the kitchen rather than heading directly to the guests. James glanced questioningly after her, then turned expectantly to Shane, who shrugged.

"Everything all right?" he heard Becky ask Jessie.

"Everything's fine, dear," the older woman replied. "Jim has several appointments this week, so we'll be gone from the ranch a lot, and we just want to go over a few things with your folks. There's nothing to worry about."

"Uh-huh." Becky's tone was flat, unconvinced.

"The guests are nearly finished with their dinner, so I'll turn them over to you and Shane," Jessie said firmly.

She's worried, Shane decided. *Very worried.*

She turned to him with a grateful smile. "I'm glad to see you, Shane, even if it makes me feel like I'm asking you to work on yet another of your days off."

"You're not asking me to do anything. I volunteered. You know I love any excuse to get out and ride," he replied lightly. Taking Becky's hand and giving it a reassuring squeeze, he added, "Especially when it provides an opportunity to spend more time with this beautiful lady and her charming little brother."

"Well now." Jessie glanced between them with brows lifted. "This is a happy revelation. "And in that case, I shan't keep you any longer. It should be a lovely night, if a chilly one."

"Chilly or not, I'm very much looking forward to it. We'd better get to it, Becky, so Jessie can get her work done and have some time to relax."

The scowl overlying the worry was evidence enough that Becky was unhappy with the dismissal, but she obeyed and strolled into the dining room where they found the guests lingering at the table though they were all finished with their meal. Becky quickly introduced the five guests—George and Rhonda Crank, a newly empty-nested couple she'd once met in Wyoming at a wrestling tournament, young honeymooners Parker and Haley Morrison, and widow Gail Hickam

Fines, whose beautiful Shetland sheepdog Quinn would be enjoying yet more spoiling in the warmth of the ranch house with the Robinsons while her master was out in the cold and snow.

"Gail's kids surprised her with this trip as an early Christmas present," Becky explained. She hesitated just long enough to grip Shane's shoulder and drag her brother to her side. Addressing the guests, she said, "You all know my little brother, James, but allow me to introduce your other guide for the evening. My partner here is Shane McGuire, and he works for the Forest Service maintaining the trails—including the one we're taking this evening—and he's a native Northstar ranch kid just like James and me, so rest assured that you're in good hands with him. Since we have such a small, cozy group tonight, it'll just be the three of us guiding the trail ride. I have a couple of instructions for everyone. First, the snow makes the landscape look soft and smooth, but don't be fooled. Harrison Park, where we'll be riding, is littered with small boulders as well as a meandering creek, all of which are now buried under the snow and invisible. It's important that everyone stay on the trail except where we show you it's safe to leave it. We don't want anyone—people *or* horses—getting hurt."

"Just in case something happens, how will we know where the trail is?" Gail asked. "Is it marked?"

"Yes, it is," Shane replied. "It's also a groomed snowmobile trail, so while last night's snow will have filled it in some, it should be quite easy to see."

"Second instruction," Becky continued. "Have fun. This ride is all about making this a special experience for you, so if you want to stop to take pictures, we'll stop and take pictures. That's it, so if everyone is ready, get your cold weather gear on and meet Shane, James, and me out at the corral to saddle the horses."

On cue, Jessie returned from the kitchen with sacks full of their s'mores and hot chocolate fixings. Shane took the goodies from her and followed Becky and James outside. Immediately, he recognized the buckskin mare he'd ridden when he'd helped drive the Royal R herds down from the summer allotments back in October, and when the pretty little horse nudged his shoulder before nosing the sacks after the sweet treats inside, he asked Becky if he could ride her again.

"I figured you might want to," she answered. "Which is why I picked her for the ride even though she is *not* a trail horse."

"Don't worry, sweetheart," Shane said to the mare, patting her cheek. "That was a compliment.

Means you're too smart to plod contentedly along. You like more challenge than that."

They made quick work of saddling their horses and stowing the snacks, and by the time the guests arrived to help saddle their own horses, Shane was just securing an ax behind his saddle and his rifle in its boot. While he assisted Gail, who was refreshingly inquisitive about the process, his gaze wandered frequently to Becky. Out here on the ranch, she was in her element. The beauty her old friends and so many others had been too blind to see and that he now realized he'd noted but never fully appreciated shone more brightly than the fiery westering sun.

"So," James said, sidling over as Shane double-checked Gail's saddle and helped her into it. "You and my sister."

"Yeah, what of it?"

"You're together again?"

"Looks that way."

"So… I might *actually* get to call you my brother soon?"

Perhaps the comment should have exasperated him—James *did* tend to be a broken record on the subject of Shane and Becky getting back together—and on some level it did because he didn't want to rush things and screw up his chance to win her back. But he couldn't stop the smile from spreading across his face. James's expression flipped like a switch thrown from hopeful to giddy. "Don't go getting ahead of yourself, bud. Like I've said before, a lot depends on your sister."

"I know that, but you're gonna work hard for it, right? Just like you did with football and science. Because you want it."

"Yeah, I want it."

Apparently satisfied with that answer, James climbed into his saddle and backed his horse away from the corral fence with the smuggest grin Shane had yet seen. It was nice to know Becky's little brother was so firmly on his side, and at once, it struck him how much had changed since he'd last been able to call Becky his girlfriend. They weren't kids anymore with only a vague idea of what the future might hold, half excited and half terrified of what life after the relative safety and familiarity of school would bring. They had spent time apart, tested the waters of adulthood, and embraced the confidence that came with the certainty of knowing they could support themselves, make their own decisions, and own up to the consequences. That changed the game. And the prize.

Yes, a lot has changed, but there's one thing that never will.

It was that one thing that transformed the desired outcome. This wasn't a see-where-this-goes experiment.

Suddenly, he realized someone was talking to him and glanced up at Gail. "I'm sorry. What did you say?"

She smiled in a way that said she'd noticed his preoccupation. "I just asked how cold it's likely to get by the time we get back."

"Probably single digits above freezing."

Becky walked her horse over, and Shane realized he was the only one not yet mounted. "We ready?"

Despite the cold that threatened to steal the warmth from his body, he swung effortlessly into the buckskin's saddle. "Yep."

Eleven

THE TRAIL WAS EASY TO FOLLOW even without the markers; someone had been out on it on a snowmobile since the snow had fallen. Shane was in no more hurry than anyone else, and they took their time traversing the three-mile trail, pausing often for the guests to take pictures or simply to admire the sunset that exploded across the sky and tinged the wintry landscape with a reflected rosy glow. A slender, waxing crescent moon peeked out between the fiery clouds. Most of the trail wound through open meadows, but occasionally, it crossed through copses of lodgepole pine, Douglas firs, and spruces decorated with thick pillows of powdery snow that drifted in glittering curtains from the branches when disturbed by a horse's shoulder or a young boy's gloved hand.

When they reached the Harrison Park warming hut—a single-room, off-grid log structure currently occupied by the snowmobilers who had cut the trail—the sunset had faded into a dim ruddy light along the bellies of the tattered clouds in a sky that darkened quickly into indigo twilight. Shane dismounted in the small corral beside the hut and, at Becky's insistence, left her and James to help the guests down from their horses while he headed inside to start a fire... or to keep one going, as the case turned out to be.

"No need to put that out," he said to the occupants of the hut, who were just about to douse the fire in the hearth. Even in the dim light the dying fire provided, Shane immediately recognized Aaron Hammond and his family. "Saves me the trouble of having to start a new one."

Aaron's beautiful dark-haired wife, Skye, greeted Shane with a smile. "Fancy meeting you here. Whose group did you bring with you?"

"Royal R's. I'm giving Becky a hand. Skye, I know the photography business is booming, what with all the work the Ramshorn has been sending your way, but Aaron, how's sheriffing these days?"

"Blessedly quiet."

"Is it just me or has it been a *lot* quieter since you ran against ol' Rogers and won?"

"It seems that way, but if there's a correlation...." Aaron shrugged.

"I can think of two right off the bat. You're better at the job than he ever was *and* you're not a pompous ass." Shane glanced away, catching sight of Becky with her brother and the Royal R's guests staring up at the sky as the first stars appeared, and clenched his jaw. He hadn't been harassed as thoroughly as Becky and Luke had by the former sheriff Steven Rogers during the investigation of the murders of Mike Thompson and Carol Landers, but the way Rogers had questioned him and his father with that note of suspicion in his voice and the way he'd handled the case in general still made Shane a touch queasy. That wasn't the only case Rogers had mishandled. Aaron's older brother Nick and his wife Beth had had their own issues with the man. His lip curled. "Good riddance to him."

"Obviously, you aren't the only one who thinks that way," Aaron said. "But on an entirely different topic, I want to know something. I've heard a rumor that you and Becky might be getting back together. Is it true?"

Shane eyed Aaron, frowning as he glanced between the sheriff and his wife. There was nothing in either of their expressions that suggested they were against the idea, but the habit of nearly a decade slithered through him, and he tensed, anticipating rejection. Aaron had treated him with nothing but kindness and respect before, during, and after the investigation, but when Shane had broken up with Becky, both Aaron and Skye, who hadn't had much time to get to know him, had made it clear that their loyalty was with Luke and Becky. Shane understood it and accepted it as a consequence of his actions, but it hurt nonetheless. Cautiously, he remarked, "You say that like you think it's a good thing. Do you think I've changed that much since I came home?"

"I don't think you've changed at all. I think you've finally found your way back to yourself." Aaron gripped his shoulder so hard that Shane nearly yelped. "You were always a great kid, Shane, with the potential to be a great man. But everything that happened when Mike and Carol died and so much that's happened since made you lose sight of that. And you haven't answered my question. Is the rumor—"

"Shane!" Becky interrupted excitedly. "You might wanna…. Oh, hi, Aaron. Skye. And Jessie and Eric. You guys might want to see this, too."

Shane tossed the couple of slender logs remaining of what the Hammonds had brought in on the fire to keep it going until he could split some of the larger logs stacked outside, then followed them and Becky out.

Instantly, he was awestruck.

Ribbons of blue-green light writhed in the northern sky above the jagged line of mountain peaks. His amazement was echoed in the quiet murmurs of those around him. He reached for Becky, folding his arms tightly around her more because he wanted to have her close than because he needed the warmth of her body, and committed this magical, perfect moment to memory.

"I'd forgotten we might see the northern lights tonight," he murmured close to her ear. He was tempted to nibble on her neck and along her exposed jaw but refrained.

"Do you see them often here?" the newlywed Haley Morrison inquired breathlessly.

"Not really," Aaron replied. "Maybe once or twice every few years."

"This is incredible," Gail said. "I wish my kids

were here to see this."

The Hammonds watched the lights with them for a few minutes before calling it a night. They settled their gear on their snow machines and bid everyone goodnight. Just before Aaron climbed on his snowmobile in front of his teenaged daughter, Jessie—the Robinsons' only grandchild—he inclined his head at Shane and Becky. "I guess that's answer enough. G'night, all."

After the buzz of the snowmobiles' engines faded away, the Royal R group was left alone in the quiet of the brilliant night to enjoy the dancing, ethereal aurora. The guests were nearly as arresting, they way they stood in absolute amazement of the spectacle before them.

"I love watching how people who aren't from here react," Shane remarked. "Reminds me of how lucky we are to live here. I mean, you and I both *know* Northstar is beautiful, but seeing it through someone else's eyes really drives it home."

Becky nodded and wrapped her hands around his arms, resting her head back on his shoulder. "Yes, it does. And I think that's one of my favorite things about the Royal R being a guest ranch. Keeps me from taking this amazing life we have for granted."

Shane held Becky a long time, pleased that she was content to let him do it, but eventually and reluctantly, they ushered everyone inside where they could enjoy the show through the windows as they warmed chilled extremities. While Becky set out the treats, filled the two kettles with water, and set them on the grate over the fire, Shane stepped back outside and grabbed the ax off his saddle to split some firewood. It was relatively early—barely half past six—but thanks to the short December days, it was full night with the twilight only a smudge of indigo in the southeastern sky. The crescent moon smiled brightly amidst the stars, and Shane found it easy to ignore the plunging temperatures as he got to work. Because they planned to stay at the warming hut at least a couple hours—longer, now, if the aurora continued its mesmerizing show— he split a dozen logs knowing that any they didn't burn would be appreciated by whoever used the hut next. At any rate, it was a good distraction from his thoughts about what Aaron had said. While he appreciated the compliment in the sheriff's words, Shane didn't quite believe them. Old habits were hard to break, and on this most spectacular night, he refused to be pulled down into a pit of doubt.

He stacked the first load of log quarters onto his

arm and hauled them inside. By the time he completed his task, Becky had the hot chocolate ready and was pouring it into cups while James and the guests made s'mores and watched the northern lights.

After he'd brought in and stacked all the logs he'd split in the rack to the right of the fireplace, Shane dragged Becky outside with the pretense of checking on the horses and tucked his ungloved hands in the back pockets of her insulated Carhartt pants to draw her body into his. Resting the side of his head against hers as they watched the aurora in silence, he found it difficult to believe this was real. The stunning night with its glittering stars, slender crescent moon, and otherworldly banners of light and the feel of the woman he had yearned for and loved for so long standing at ease in his embrace was all too perfect to trust.

"This has to be a dream. A beautiful, impossible dream," he said softly, turning his face fully to her. "Because I broke your heart and you hate me."

"Shane…" she murmured.

He shuddered with longing when she brushed her warm fingertips over his jaw and down his neck before letting her hand rest on his shoulder with her thumb against his pulse.

"Don't talk like this. Not tonight."

"Did you really decide to give me another chance?"

"Yes, I did."

"And we're together again?"

"Yes, we are."

She leaned away, studying his face with a frown, and he couldn't recall her ever looking as beautiful as she did right now with the glow of the stars and aurora softening her often-proud features.

"Does Aaron's parting comment have anything to do with this sudden doubt?"

"A little, yes. There's a rumor going around that we might be getting back together… and we sort of proved it true."

"And this bothers you why?"

"Three months ago, I was the outcast of Northstar with only a slim hope I might be able to beg my way into everyone's good graces. Now, I have you back, and it just doesn't feel—"

Becky pressed her lips firmly to his, sliding her hand up his neck and curling her fingers around a fistful of his hair. When she angled her body into him, his worries evaporated, drowned out by a sudden and thunderous desire.

"Does this feel real?"

Her voice was distractingly husky, inviting him to kiss her again. So he did. She kissed him back, threading her arms around his neck and drowning him in sweet adoration. The taste of her, the heat of her body, and the intoxicating demand of her mouth were certainly real enough. Even the most vivid dream could not compare. He barely heard the squeak of the door's hinges and paid it no attention, too lost in the bliss of holding and kissing Becky to care if the universe was watching.

"Eh-hem."

Becky jumped, then pressed her forehead to Shane's and laughed breathlessly before turning to her brother, who watched them with his arms folded and brows lifted in inquiry. She let out a sound that was half sigh, half growl and laden with fond exasperation. "You know, this—" She gestured between Shane and herself. "—was a lot easier before you came along. And yet, without your nagging, this might not be happening. So I'm not sure whether I should say thank you or tell you to bugger off."

James stuck his tongue out.

"What do you need, bud?" Shane asked.

"Nothing from you two. Gail left her camera bag with her extra memory cards hanging on her saddle horn, so I volunteered to get it for her."

They watched him stride out to the horses and back, promising to follow him inside in just a moment. Becky took Shane's hand, knitting their chilled fingers together and gazing at them for a moment.

"It seems I'm not the only one with trust issues. You don't trust what's right in front of you."

He started to object, but she silenced him with a feather-light kiss.

"Is it always going to be like this, you kissing me to shut me up?"

"That's not a problem, is it?"

"Nope."

"Good. Because I really like kissing you. More now, I think, than before because I can make comparisons and know that no one else ever kissed me like you do."

"Oh?" He wasn't entirely sure he wanted to know the answer because he didn't want to think of her kissing other men, but he asked anyhow. "And how do I kiss you that is better than how anyone else has kissed you?"

"It's like you can't get enough of me, but at the same time, you're conscious of what I want and what I need from you. It's… heady. You're an amazing kisser, Shane."

"That or the others were just really crappy kissers."

"No. It's all you, babe."

Grinning, he clasped her face and kissed her soundly with an urgency brought on by the knowledge that they *were* technically on the clock even if this night felt like the furthest thing from work. "Kisses and flattery. I think I could get used to this."

"You *think* so?"

"I *know* so."

"Shane?"

"Hmm?"

"What did my dad mean when he said you stopped by to ask his permission to date me again? Did he mean again as in this is our second round or again like this isn't the first time you've asked?"

"Both."

"When was the first time you asked?"

"About twelve years ago."

Becky jerked back in shock, but it dissolved quickly into an incredible, gentle smile. "You keep surprising me."

"That's still a good thing, right?"

She nodded and hugged him. "It absolutely is."

"That's good news because I want this to work. I want it more than I've wanted anything in my life, and like I told your brother earlier, I will work to make it happen. You tell me what I need to do to prove to you I won't ever break your heart again, and I'll do it."

"As soon as I figure it out, I will." She draped herself around him and sighed with a reluctance to leave him that made him a bit smug. "But in the meantime, we should get back to work."

* * *

At ten to six on Friday, Becky unlocked the front door of Luke and Ryan's cabin and flipped on the lights as she stepped inside. The open living area with its vaulted ceiling and rich, pale golden wood tones was elegant but also rustic and welcoming, and it suited Luke perfectly. For a moment, completely alone in the cabin, she couldn't believe it was real. This was the material embodiment of her cousin's dreams come true, and even though she'd had two years to get used to the fact that he had achieved his every wish, she'd spent far longer watching him suffer as the traumas of his past held those dreams just out of his reach.

Skimming her fingers over the hand-peeled logs, she used the tactile confirmation to prove to herself that this place and his happiness were very real… and marveled at what else that could mean. Inevitably, her thoughts shifted to Shane. If Luke could come so far, could they, too?

It had been almost a week since she'd given in to her heart and agreed to see if she and Shane could repair their relationship, and in that time, her doubt had lessened considerably and was transitioning into a growing certainty that the risk of whatever pain might or might not lie ahead was worth the reward of his company and the pleasure it gave her. She wanted to be with him and had spent every moment she could spare with him—a few minutes here and there, an hour at most.

It hasn't been enough, she admitted. *But that's about to be rectified.*

He should be arriving any moment with Ashleigh and Bridger, whom he'd picked up on his way home from work. He and Becky had volunteered to babysit Ashleigh while Alex spent the night with Will Hammond, Ant O'Neil, and Hunter Fitzwater in one of the Lazy H's bunkhouses—a tradition for the first night of Christmas break—so Luke and Ryan could go on their first date alone since before their daughter's birth. Becky had thought of driving in to Devyn to get Ashleigh and Bridger, but for once, Shane had had to work in town, so there was really no point. Besides, with Jim and Jessie away from the ranch all week, she'd been picking up the slack and had only finished up for the day twenty minutes ago. She'd rushed over, hoping Shane wouldn't beat her here because he didn't have a key. Or maybe he did. Luke and Ryan surely would have given him one since he had their daughter.

"Whatever," Becky grumbled, wondering why she was suddenly so anxious.

No, she knew why—that momentary sidetrack of her thoughts to Jim. The rancher's doctor had ordered more tests. He was supposed to have been done with the last yesterday, but he and Jessie had received a call about some results that apparently necessitated more. No one had told her what kind of tests he'd had, and both the Robinsons and her parents assured her that Jim's doctor was just being thorough and that there was nothing to worry about. Becky wanted to believe them, but their eyes didn't lie. They were concerned.

"I have to stop thinking about it."

She busied herself starting a fire in the woodstove.

What seemed like only moments later but must have been several minutes because she now had a strong fire going, Shane strolled inside with Ashleigh's car seat hanging from one arm, his laptop bag slung over his other shoulder, and a bouncing golden retriever at his heels. Thinking of his reluctance to hold Ashleigh early on, she didn't offer to help him with her, though she did get up to close the door behind him.

"Hi, beautiful," he greeted, kissing her cheek. "Missed you."

"Missed you, too."

"Really?"

"Don't look so shocked."

Shane shrugged. "I keep waiting for you to change your mind."

"I won't… as long as you don't give me a reason to." She sighed. "It's actually a relief to have said yes, Shane. My heart wanted to the moment you asked, and the indecision was a lot more stressful than I was willing to admit."

"That's reassuring."

His gentle tone was equally reassuring and surprised her again because his otherwise jovial expression made her expect a teasing response. He said nothing else and carried the car seat over to the couch. He dropped his shoulder and let his laptop bag slide gently onto the cushion while he held the car seat steady with his other hand because Ashleigh was wiggling and kicking so much that she was in danger of rocking her seat right off the couch. Next, he shrugged out of his coat, first one arm then the other, contorting his body to do it so he didn't have to let go of the car seat. It was comical, but at the same time, more than a little arousing. Beneath his coat, Shane wore only a black T-shirt, and it wasn't what she would call form fitting, but it hugged his body just enough to accentuate his physique. He hadn't shaved in a couple days, and the resulting scruff added another layer of ruggedness to his well-used work boots and faded Wranglers.

Lordy, she thought. *That ass in those jeans.*

If she thought it was fascinating to watch muscle flex as he twisted out of his coat, it was even more so to observe him unbuckle Luke and Ryan's wide-eyed daughter like he'd done it a thousand times and lift her out without a trace of hesitation.

"Hey there, gorgeous," he cooed. "Bet it feels good to be out of that thing, huh. And I'm sure you're ready for a change, too."

Becky held her hands out to take Ashleigh, and Shane eyed her.

"I got it," he said.

She gaped. "When have you *ever* changed a diaper?"

"About an hour and a half ago when I picked her

up."

Becky followed him to Ashleigh's room—the room she'd stayed in when she'd first returned to Northstar—and leaned in the doorway while Shane cradled the baby in one arm as he pulled out a diaper and wipes. Bridger sat beside the changing table, watching the proceedings as intently as Becky.

"I promise I can handle this," Shane said to the dog. "No need to look so concerned."

Satisfied that his girl was in capable hands, Bridger wandered over to Becky for some pets. At first, she didn't notice him, too absorbed by Shane and Ashleigh, so he nudged her hand with his cold, wet nose. Absently, she obliged him and thought again that Shane would have made a good father had Ryan not miscarried.

Might still make a good dad someday, she mused with a twist of her lips as her pulse tripped. "This may be the most adorable, sexiest thing I've ever seen you do."

He glanced over his shoulder as he dressed Ashleigh again. "Seriously?"

"Well, you know what they say about men and babies appealing to women's biological clocks."

"Is that your way of saying yours is ticking?"

"Until recently, I thought it might never start."

Having finished his task, he brought Ashleigh over and settled her in Becky's arms, saying only, "I know you want her."

Something in the way he said it—a curious light in his eyes and a more curious hitch in his voice—led her to believe his remark was not a general observation but a response to her statement. She ached to know what he was thinking, to ask if he wanted kids after losing Angel Rose—how strange it was to consider it like that—but she suspected the answers would further erode her doubt, and as wonderful as things seemed to be going, she didn't yet trust him enough to abandon caution entirely. And talking about their hopes for the future would do just that.

Besides, we have more from the past to mend first, she reminded herself as she carried Ashleigh into the living room. She snagged the fleece throw off the back of the loveseat and tossed it to Shane, then gestured for him to spread it out.

"Tummy time," she said to the baby, settling her on the blanket.

Ashleigh immediately positioned her arms and hands under her body and pushed up, teetering a little.

"You're not going to..." Becky murmured.

Then she did it. She rolled onto her back. It

looked more like she fell over than rolled, but she was delighted.

"No way!" Becky cheered. "Good job, little girl!"

"Ryan said she did that last night and has been determined to do it again." Shane folded his legs and sat beside the infant, offering her his finger. She wrapped her tiny fist around it and gave him a big, gummy grin. His whole countenance shifted into the most amazingly besotted tenderness. "I don't know much about babies, but I get the impression that this is a big deal."

"It's the first step toward crawling and independent mobility. She's not much past three and a half months old, but she's already working on rolling over. James didn't roll over until he was almost five months old."

He tickled Ashleigh's belly, still gazing at her with that heart-melting affection. "Fascinating critters."

Becky gave a snort of laughter. "Critters? You sound like Aelissm."

With a chuckle, he stretched out on his stomach facing the baby and carefully rolled her back onto her belly. For several minutes, they watched each other, and Becky nearly laughed when Ashleigh tried to replicate the goofy faces Shane made. Slowly, so as not to disturb their game, Becky pushed to her feet with the intention of starting dinner.

"Can I be honest with you?" Shane asked without looking away from Ashleigh.

"Uh, yeah, of course."

"I lied. When Ryan told me she was pregnant, I *was* a little terrified."

"How so?"

"I couldn't imagine being responsible for something so small and helpless or knowing what to do. Now, it seems so foolish to think like that. How many parents truly know what to do? They don't. They just do it."

Becky didn't say anything, sensing that there was more he needed to say. He glanced at her, and for a moment, sadness and regret replaced the amused smile. As he returned his gaze to Ashleigh, his expression softened again, but that adorable delight didn't fully come back.

"When I think about that…. I know I hurt you badly, Becky, but what I did to Ryan was the most heartless and selfish thing I've ever done. She didn't have the choice to just walk away from those fears even if she wanted to. I can pretend all I want that I did it because I didn't want to bind her to a man in love with another woman, but the fact of the matter is that I was a damned coward."

If it scared you so much, why do you have a tattoo on your arm memorializing your lost daughter? She didn't ask because she already knew the answer, and he did as well, but she wanted to hear him say it. "What did you feel when you found out Ryan miscarried? I'm not talking in the weeks and months and years that followed after you'd had time to process it and realize what you lost. How did you feel the moment you found out? Were you relieved because you were off the hook?"

"No," he replied without even the slightest hesitation. "I was devastated. But I spent a lot of time and energy trying to convince everyone—to convince *myself*—that I wasn't."

"And if she hadn't miscarried, would you have let her go on handling everything by herself?"

"I would hope not, but I don't know, Becky. I was so screwed up, and I kept doing things that screwed me up worse. Maybe I was at the point of losing myself completely, and maybe Ryan miscarrying was what jerked me out of it."

No, you'd have come around and done the right thing, given the time to realize you needed to… and wanted *to. That* would *have been what jerked you out of it.*

Becky tilted her head and studied the droop of his

head and the frown that furrowed his brows and said nothing. She only frowned at him until he looked over his shoulder at her again.

"What?"

"I guess it's my turn to wonder if this is real."

"If what is?"

"You baring your soul."

He shrugged. "I made a promise to you to tell you everything. Remember? Keeping things to myself—even to protect you—only ever hurt us both."

"I…." She sucked in a breath and let it out, then sat on the couch with her hands knitted between her knees. "I appreciate it. I feel like I'm getting to know you all over again, and it's comforting. For so long in there, you were so closed up that I didn't know who you were anymore. I also believe what you said on Thanksgiving. You didn't change at all. The Shane I loved was always there, beneath it all. He just got lost."

"That's exactly what Aaron said on Sunday. But I'm finding my way back again."

"Yes, you are. And I'm very… very glad."

"Are you now?"

She slipped off the couch and prowled over to him. "Mmm-hmm."

Grabbing him by the chin, she tipped his head

toward her and kissed him, lightly at first but then with increasing demand as a ravenous desire seized her. For a moment, he kissed her with equal zeal but quickly hit the brakes when she lowered her body to the floor, propping herself up on her elbow.

"Uh, Becky? We have an audience."

"So? I guarantee you she sees her parents do this all the time."

"Yeah, but I think she's getting hungry."

Ashleigh had grabbed his finger and was now trying to pull it to her mouth. When he didn't cooperate, she squealed.

"I guess she is. All right, little girl. We'll get you some dinner."

Shane picked the baby up before Becky could and carried her into the kitchen, bouncing her and distracting her with an assortment of funny sounds and faces while Becky warmed a bottle and rummaged for something quick and easy for her and Shane to eat. There was a package of boneless, skinless chicken breasts in the fridge.

Grilled chicken sandwiches it is.

It wasn't until she took the chicken off the burner that she noticed Shane had stopped making those silly sounds. She glanced over her shoulder. He gazed out at the dark night with Ashleigh fed and asleep in his arms. Craning her neck, she took note of his troubled frown. What thoughts disrupted his enjoyment?

"You all right?" she inquired, joining him at the sink.

At first, he didn't answer, so she followed the direction of his gaze. The pines and firs stood nearly black against a glittering indigo sky but the faint light of the waxing moon tipped their branches with silver. In all the times she'd surveyed the view out this window while she'd stayed here after first moving home, she hadn't ever noticed that the sulfurous mine tailings where she and Luke had found Carol's body were visible through a narrow gap in the trees. In the moonlight, the pale yellow mound glowed faintly.

"I don't know how the hell he did it," Shane said quietly.

"How who did what?"

"Luke. And you, for that matter. I'll never understand how either of you found the courage to face what happened up here." He glanced at her, then back out the window. "I want to understand because I feel like it will always be a wall between us if I don't, but I'm not sure I ever will. I don't know if something like that can be comprehended unless you were there."

"Trust me, Shane, I saw it, and I *still* don't understand it."

"I'm glad you and Luke had each other to lean on."

The comment brought back to mind others he'd made, and Becky began to understand that he was right—she and Luke *had* turned to each other to deal with their grief and shut him out in the process. Maybe he hadn't found Carol tied to the post atop the mine tailings with a bullet hole in her chest and maybe he hadn't been JP's target, but he had lost as much as either of them had. More, she thought bitterly, because his two best friends had turned from him.

I'm sorry, she thought, but she couldn't quite bring herself to say it. "The more I think about it, the more I realize how much you and Carol had in common. Neither of you had many close friends you could turn to and very little family. I guess it's not so surprising she would turn to you. I mean, aside from the fact that you *are* a good friend."

"Does this mean you're going to forgive me for what I did that night? That you believe what I told you about it?"

She nodded. "I am, and I do." Turning her back to the window and the sight of the mine tailings and the memories that haunted them, she slid her hand across Shane's cheek. "As to understanding how we faced it… you don't need to, and I don't want you to because it's bad enough Luke and I had to deal with it."

"But—"

"It won't be a wall between us anymore." She leaned over and touched her lips lightly to his. "The only thing you need to understand—and accept—is that knowing you *want* to understand for my benefit is all I need from you."

He met her gaze and attempted a smile, but it didn't reach his eyes. "It's stupid, I know, but it's instinctive to want to take away your pain—even after I caused you so much—and when I can't, I feel like I'm failing you and failing to fulfill the promise to comfort you."

"I get that, but you aren't failing me at all."

She opened her mouth to say more, then closed it and sighed. She could offer a million words to reassure him, but none of them would convince him because, in a way, he was right. But if so, it was true that she'd failed him by not being more considerate of his needs.

"It's a testament to our bond that we lasted as long as we did. You're right, Shane. We didn't have a chance back then; we were too young to know how to overcome what JP did to us all." Again, she leaned over to kiss him—more deeply this time. When it ended, she touched her forehead to his and murmured, "But we're older and wiser, and time has healed many of those heartbreaks. Now… *now* we have a chance. Because you didn't give up on us."

She lost track of how long they stood like that, but eventually, their emotions settled enough for hunger to distract them. Since Shane had Ashleigh, she finished putting their sandwiches together. It wasn't only a disinclination to disturb the sleeping baby that prevented her from asking Shane to help; it was the look on his face. Ashleigh was therapeutic for him.

With the sandwiches done, she plated them and carried them into the living room. Luke and Ryan wouldn't mind if they ate on the couch, and it would be more comfortable for Shane as it appeared he had no intention of relinquishing the baby even to eat despite the fact that his arm must be getting tired by now.

"This was a great idea for dinner, Becky," he said, picking up his sandwich with one hand.

"It does seem a rather fortuitous decision, doesn't it?"

"And delicious. Thank you."

They briefly debated watching a movie, but decided against it, instead enjoying the quiet. After they finished eating, Becky washed the few dishes she'd used and again joined Shane on the couch. He lifted his free arm in invitation, and she snuggled willingly into his side. They didn't talk much—didn't need to—content to enjoy the simple pleasure of each other's embrace.

A few minutes after eight, the front door opened, and Luke and Ryan stepped inside looking tired but relaxed and happy.

"Isn't *this* a cozy scene?" Luke asked his wife.

"Very cozy."

"You're home early," Shane remarked. "I thought you said you were going to catch a movie. We weren't expecting you until ten or eleven."

"Didn't feel like it," Luke said. "It's been a long school year so far, and home is much more appealing than a crowded movie theater."

"That's all well and good, but you were supposed to take a few hours to enjoy each other," Becky reminded them.

Ryan glanced at her husband with a sly gleam in her eyes. "Don't worry. We did."

"Glad to hear it."

"Hey," Luke said, directing his comment to Shane. "Before I forget, Mom and Dad want you and Austin to join us all for Christmas. You two don't have any plans, do you?"

"Not that I know of," Shane replied. "We usually just have Christmas by ourselves. I'm sure he'd love that. I know I would."

"I hate to interrupt because you seem to be quite enjoying my daughter, Shane, but I need some relief here, and it's getting to be time to feed her again." Ryan gently lifted her daughter from his arms, then blushed. "I'm sorry. That was probably too much information."

"Not at all," Shane assured her.

Ashleigh woke crying, and Ryan took her into her room, nodding for Becky to follow.

"How was she?" Luke's wife asked. "Thank you both again. Luke and I really needed that."

"It was our pleasure. And Ashleigh was great. Shane's had her most of the evening."

Ryan regarded her with a lifted brow. "Really."

"Yep. We had an interesting conversation, too, in which you were brought up." Becky leaned against the dresser while Ryan sat in the rocking chair and nursed her daughter. Maternal curiosity and longing needled her, and she tried with limited success to ignore it.

"Did you know he has a tattoo for Angel?"

"No, I didn't." Ryan's brows rose. "Wow."

"Does that bother you?"

"No. I…." She paused. "I feel somewhat vindicated. And reassured that I was right about him."

"Right how?"

"Right that he's a good man who's just made some stupid, hurtful decisions. It's reassuring because it means he wasn't the poor judgment call I've thought he was. He's showed me a lot in the last couple years, but I'm assuming that to get a tattoo, he's felt this way a lot longer than he let on. He didn't just come to these realizations a couple years ago, did he?"

Becky shook her head. "No. I think he started realizing it even before you miscarried."

She glanced through the door into the living room. Luke and Shane were chatting, and the smiles on their faces drove home yet again how much she had missed the easy friendship that had bound them all those years ago. The soothing warmth of nostalgia entwined with hope saturated her, and for the first time, she began to believe—not just hope—that she could trust Shane completely again. "Do you sincerely believe he's done running?"

"Now more than ever."

"Good. Because I think you're right. And I'm going to do something I thought, not so long ago, I'd never do again."

"And what is that?"

"I'm going to hope that the future with Shane I used to dream about might yet come true."

Twelve

"WHAT DO YOU MEAN you might have to sell the ranch?" Becky asked. Her heart pounded, sending wave upon chilling wave of dread washing through her as she glanced between her parents and the Robinsons. Nothing in any of their faces was reassuring. They were all gathered in the Robinsons' spacious living room the morning after her evening with Shane and Ashleigh, lounging on the couches and recliners and pretending everything was all right.

Beside her, James wasn't faring any better; he worked at the frayed cuffs of his favorite MSU Bobcats sweatshirt, accelerating the shirt's demise. Half a dozen scenarios prowled through her mind, and she shivered, noting how her parents and the Robinsons carried on a silent conversation of frowns and head shakes as if they were debating how to break whatever other terrible news to her and James.

Finally, Jessie spoke up. "We hope it won't come to that, but it's something we have to consider."

"Why?" Becky demanded. Her tone had sharpened, so she drew in a deep breath and let it out. "We've been working on plans to expand, and business has been great. What did the doctor say?"

"This isn't about what the doctor said," Jim replied. "It's about what this has made me—us—admit."

Beneath the familiar grumpiness was something Becky had never before heard from him—a note of resignation.

"Before I ask what *that* means, will someone please tell me what's going on with your health? Because I am worried half to death, and no one's told me anything but *don't worry*."

Again, the older adults glanced between one another, until at last Andy spoke.

"Jim will need open heart surgery—a triple, possibly a quadruple bypass. But the doctor's bigger concern is kidney failure. His kidneys aren't working as well as they should because his high blood pressure is preventing them from getting the blood they need. So, the doctor wants to get that issue under control first. The prognosis is good, though, because Jessie was concerned enough to ask the right questions that uncovered all the issues."

"How long until he'll need the surgery?"

"The doctor thinks we can hold off for a couple months while we get the kidney situation under control," Jessie answered. "The measures we need to take will also help improve his heart health."

"Jim will be okay, right?" James asked.

"I'll be just fine," Jim said. "Except for this damned diet the doc's putting me on. And he says I'm to take it easy until further notice. That might kill me before my heart or my kidneys fail."

"Oh, knock it off," his wife chided. "You big baby."

"You'll do it, though, won't you, Jim," Becky said. "For us if not for yourself."

Jim muttered something about pushy doctors and even pushier wives and kids but promised he'd follow the doctor's orders.

"Glad to hear it," Becky said. She stood and

crossed the room to give him a big, long hug. "Because we love you, you old bear."

"I know you do," he whispered, hugging her tightly in return. "You're a good girl, Becky, and I love you, too. I'm blessed to have you here to browbeat me. You're as close to me as my own granddaughter. You know that, right?"

"I do, but don't you start talking like that. You save those words for a good long time down the road. Okay?"

"Yes, ma'am."

After she returned to her seat, she asked him and Jessie to explain why they might need to sell the ranch. Because they didn't need the money. For one, they had great insurance, and for another, the Royal R had been turning a good profit since they'd turned it into a dude ranch, allowing them to set aside a sizeable nest egg.

"We aren't getting any younger, and we don't know how much longer we'll be able to keep working the ranch," Jessie said. "And our daughter, who would have been happy to take it over from us, has been dead almost fifteen years."

"Yes, but Jess could—"

"Our granddaughter has made it clear that her dreams lie elsewhere," Jim said. "We had a good long talk—several—with her this week. She loves ranch life, but she has ample opportunity to indulge in it on the Lazy H and has no desire to run her own. She wants to be a photographer like Skye, who has already offered to bring her in as a partner in Hammond Photography when she's ready for that kind of responsibility."

"And she's good at it. We only want her to be happy," Jessie added, "so it isn't fair of us to push her into something she doesn't want to do at the expense of what makes her happy."

"She's fifteen," Becky said flatly. As soon as the words left her mouth, she winced at their hypocrisy. At fifteen, she had been certain about Shane… and twelve years later, despite the rocky trail back to each other and the lingering but fast-fading wariness, she still was. Jessie Hammond was a strong young woman with an unusual self-assurance for her age—with her parents, grandparents, and upbringing, how could she not be? She wouldn't change her mind. "Isn't there *some* way? Maybe set her up as the owner and have Mom and Dad take over the rest of the operations. They already do a lot of it, anyhow. And I could take over more duties, and I'm sure Shane would pitch in, too, so they could."

"That's what we're hoping to do," Jessie said

gently.

Again, Becky realized, her voice had risen. She clamped her mouth shut and willed herself to calm down.

"But to make that happen, we have to convince a strong-willed teenager she wants to do it."

Sighing, Becky lifted her hands in a show of peace. "Whatever you need from me, I'll do it. You've both worked so hard for this place that I don't want to see you have to leave it. And I don't want Jessie to lose this incredible inheritance simply because she doesn't understand *what* she's losing, nor do I want some rich out-of-stater to turn it into something unrecognizable from what you've built."

"Believe me, darling, we don't want any of that to happen, either. And we're not giving up yet. We just want you to be aware of the possibility that we might have no other choice."

Becky nodded. "I understand."

"Now," Jim said, "that's all we had to talk about, so you go enjoy your day off. And tell Shane we say hello when you see him."

"I will."

She and Shane hadn't planned to get together until later in the day, and as she trudged through the biting wind and knee-deep snow back to her cabin to stoke the fire, she hoped he was home and up for some company. For the moment, she was holding her own against the implications of this morning's conversation, but she'd lose her grip eventually, and when she did....

Interesting that he's the first person I want to run to right now.

If he wasn't home, she could track down Luke with the assurance that her cousin would understand—after all, he knew how special their hometown was with the same deep-seated belief that nowhere else would ever be home—but he wasn't a ranch kid and he hadn't spent his entire childhood here like she and Shane had.

"Just admit that you want to see Shane," she muttered, climbing the steps of her porch.

She opened the door and stepped inside just as her phone rang. Without thinking to check the caller ID, she grabbed the cordless and answered. "Hello?"

"Hi, Becks. It's been a long time," Justin replied.

Not long enough. Her lip curled into a sneer. "What do you want, Justin? Because I'm pretty sure I told you to stop calling me."

"You did, but it's been weeks. You said you'd

think about my suggestion and call me. Have you even thought about it?"

She swore under her breath. Why hadn't she just told him no the last time he'd called and made it absolutely clear that they were over? Well, she'd better do it now. "I *have* thought about it, yes. And I haven't changed my mind. We're done and over, and I'm moving on. You should, too."

There was a long pause, and in the silence, she heard the familiar chatter of Teton South guests gathered around the massive dining room table in the ranch's main house. She pictured the Royal R's table at the height of the summer tourist season and nearly choked. How much longer would she have that? And why hadn't she appreciated it as much as she should?

"No," was all Justin said.

"No?" She closed her eyes and counted to five. It didn't help, but already facing a far larger tragedy, she vowed to be as diplomatic as she could. "Look, Justin, we had a great time together… at first. But then things—"

"We can have a great time again, Becks."

"No, we can't. It was never going to last because we are too much alike and too different in all the wrong ways."

"Yeah? And how do you know that? You've had two serious relationships, and as I recall the first one didn't work out so well."

"Maybe it didn't end well, but even so, it put our relationship to shame. You want to know why? Because he *listened!*"

"Baby, this is ridiculous. We've been together for six years. How can you just throw that away?"

"We *were* together six years together because I was too indecisive and confused to realize you would never be able to give me what I need. I hate to be such a bitch about this, but you aren't giving me the opportunity to be nice. So let me say it again. I am moving on with someone else. You and I are done. We will never be together again. Please leave me alone now."

"You're moving on with someone else?"

"Yes, I am." She stopped just short of telling him she was moving on with the very same someone who'd broken her heart before. Bringing that up would only give him more ammunition. "Goodbye, Justin."

With a deliberate gentleness, she ended the call and sank into her couch. Not thirty seconds later, her phone rang again. This time, she glanced at the caller ID and, seeing Justin's number, ignored it. Before her answering machine picked up, she bounced off the couch, quickly tossed a couple logs in the woodstove, and zipped out the door with a prayer that Justin would just hang up instead of leaving a message. If he didn't, she promised herself she'd erase it without listening. She had enough else to worry about.

Shane's truck was parked in front of his cabin when she pulled up, and he met her on the deck, which meant he must've either heard her truck or watched her drive up. It didn't matter. He was there, and without a word of greeting or explanation, she threw her arms around his neck and clung to him as if he could keep her world from spinning out of control. It was some time before she became aware of the frigid wind and stinging snowflakes, and immediately, she noticed that he wasn't wearing a coat, only a thin, long-sleeved black T-shirt. He didn't complain, but he was shivering, so she suggested they go inside.

The heat radiating from his woodstove was almost as soothing as his presence, and it was with considerable relief that she sank to the floor in front of the fire with him and let him wrap her in his arms.

"How did the talk with the Robinsons go?"

"Fine, I guess. Jim's not doing so well right now—looking at the possibility of heart *and* kidney failure—but he can avoid it with surgery and by taking better care of himself."

"Well, that's a good thing, right? It could be a worse."

She nodded. It could be a *lot* worse. Terminal cancer had crossed her mind more than once in the last week.

"But you're upset. Why?"

She didn't immediately answer, instead chewing on the inside of her cheek and wondering if it was all real or only the product of her over-stimulated imagination.

"Talk to me, beautiful. What else is troubling you?"

"Jim and Jessie are worried they might have to sell the ranch. And Justin's an asshole."

All the worries—that Jim wouldn't be able to stick to his new diet and routine, that something would go horribly wrong with his surgery, that her family might lose not only their jobs but the only home she and James had ever known, and that Justin just couldn't get it through his head that they were broken up—came spilling out, and Shane listened patiently. Not only listened, she noted, but *heard*. It struck her that, had this happened when she was dating Justin, she wouldn't have opened up to him like this; she would've called

Luke. There was another sharp divergence between her current and former boyfriends—she would have brushed aside whatever words of comfort Justin might have offered, but when Shane promised her everything would be all right and that he'd help her deal with whatever happened, she believed him.

* * *

Shane was more excited about spending Christmas Eve with the Conners, Eppersons, and O'Neils than he'd been about any holiday in years. He always enjoyed the holidays he spent with his father, but the promise of a boisterous, love- and laughter-filled afternoon and evening inspired in him an anticipation and delight that had long been absent from his life. It was that heartwarming stew of emotions that had him out his door and heading to his father's bunkhouse an hour early.

At his knock, Austin called, "C'mon in!"

When Shane stepped inside and closed the door behind him to keep the swirling snow outside, he spotted Jeremiah lounging in his recliner with a book open in his lap.

"Merry Christmas, Jeremiah," Shane said. "You spending it with the Hammonds again?"

"Yep. They're great people."

"I'm sure the feeling is mutual. Or they wouldn't invite you to their family gatherings."

Jeremiah responded, but Shane didn't hear him, distracted when his father mentioned his mother and realizing that Austin was on the phone.

"He's right here, so I'll ask him again." With his hand covering the mouthpiece, Austin turned to Shane. "It's Kelly. She wants to make sure you won't come for dinner tonight."

"Nope. We're going up to the Conners', remember?"

"I know they invited us, but this is important, Shane."

"More important than spending the evening with people who actually love us and care about us? I don't think so."

"Shane...."

"I have nothing to say to her and no desire to spend an evening with her when I could be spending it with our friends."

"All right." Austin sighed. Into the phone, he said, "I'm sorry, Kelly. He's not interested. Yes, I'll tell him, and merry Christmas to you, too. Bye."

Austin hung up the phone and glared at Shane, who responded to his gaze with a nonchalant shrug.

He was in too good a mood to let himself be pushed around, especially where the woman who was-but-wasn't his mother was concerned.

"I've said no every time she's called since she and her husband arrived at that cabin at Georgetown Lake four days ago," he remarked. "Did she think I'd change my mind on the day she wants us to come when we already told June and Ben and Luke and Ryan that we'd spend Christmas Eve with them? Come on, Dad. I know you'd rather enjoy the evening than spend it with your runaway ex-wife."

Austin's glare deepened into a scowl. "I don't appreciate the attitude, but yes, I would rather spend the evening with our friends. However, I think you should sit down with her. If not tonight then sometime while she's in Montana."

"Why? I have no desire to assuage her guilt… or whatever it is that brought her to the decision that she needed to meet me."

He kept his tone even, but beneath the surface, old hurts stirred, awakened by Kelly's insistence.

"I know of *something* she can give you." Sighing, Austin shook his head. "We'll talk about it later. Since you're here so early, I assume you're anxious to head up the mountain."

"You can give me three guesses why," Jeremiah remarked with a wink, "but I need only one."

"When you actually make a move on Heather Brown," Shane retorted good-naturedly, "I'll gladly take the brunt of your smart-ass comments. I'll even smile no matter how thick you lay it on, but until then… shut up."

Jeremiah laughed. "You're on, McGuire."

"Speaking of Becky, you remembered to bring her present, didn't you?" Austin asked

"Of course I did."

"Is it a ring?" Jeremiah asked.

"No. Not yet."

"Why the hell not? You know you want to put one on that finger of hers."

"It's not about what I want. It's about what *she* wants, and I have some work yet to do before I fit that description."

"Excuses, excuses."

"Says the guy who can say barely two words to the girl he wants without turning tail in embarrassment."

"I'm just biding my time."

"Sure you are. And you'll go right on biding it until she's found some other rich doctor or lawyer type. Only this time, she'll marry him. Don't wait, Jeremiah, because waiting doesn't get you anywhere. Trust me on that."

"Says the guy who's got the girl but is waiting until—"

"See you later, Jere," Shane said, chasing his father out the door. "And merry Christmas."

The ranch hand was absolutely right, Shane thought on the drive up to June and Ben's cabin, and the closer he came to seeing Becky again, the further from his mind Kelly slipped. He already knew he was going to ask Becky to marry him; he'd known it as soon as she'd said yes to giving their relationship a second chance, and he'd wanted it much longer. Regardless, he refused to take that giant step until he was certain she trusted him again. Not just enough to tell him about her worries over Jim's health and her family's uncertain fate but enough that she could give her heart back to him and know without a single doubt that he'd hold on to it and cherish it for the rest of his days.

Parking at the Conners' cabin was tight with five extra vehicles in the driveway, but he tucked his truck in beside Becky's. Undoubtedly, she'd decided to drive her own vehicle so she and James didn't have to squeeze into the single cab of her parents' truck, which was parked on the other side of hers. He also recognized Luke's black Dodge parked beside his parents' trucks, and Becky's maternal grandparents' Jeep Cherokee was parked next to that. He didn't see the O'Neils' Suburban, but he figured they'd walked over from their cabin. To his dismay, Ashleigh and Eli Connelly's SUV was there as well, and he pulled his truck in beside it.

"And here I was hoping for a pleasant afternoon," he muttered. "Hopefully Matt isn't with them."

No such luck. As soon as he followed his father into the Conners' cozy, decked-out log cabin, he spotted Ryan's brother sitting on the loveseat holding his niece.

"He promised to be nice," Ryan assured him after she greeted him and Austin.

"And why would he do that?"

"Because I told him to. And because I told him why he should. Yes, Becky and I have been talking about you again, but only good things. I swear."

Despite her words, Shane was shocked when Matt rose awkwardly to his feet and limped over, hesitating only a moment before shaking Shane's hand.

"My sister told me it was time to let the past go," he said. "And she was pretty convincing. I'm not saying we'll ever be friends again, but for my sister's sake,

I *will* let go of my grudge. If she can stand you after what you—"

"Matthew…" Ryan warned. "Shane's made his apologies, and he's making amends. Besides, I am *happy*—ridiculously so—so you have no reason anymore to be mad at him."

"Thank you, Ryan," Shane murmured. "You're an amazing woman. Luke's a lucky man."

"I'm very well aware of it, too," Luke agreed, joining them.

"Do you always have to pop into a conversation like that?" Shane asked with a chuckle and a shake of his head.

"Like what?"

"Right at the perfect moment to impart some pearl of wisdom."

Luke shrugged. "It's a useful party trick."

"Is that Shane?" June called from the kitchen. "Tell him to get his butt over here."

Shane looked for Becky on his way to the kitchen, where June was working on dinner with Aelissm's assistance, but she was nowhere to be found. He stepped into June's open arms, and in that moment as she gripped him tightly, he almost believed that all those years of pain and loneliness he'd spent enshrouded in bitter memories hadn't happened. The whole of Northstar was home, but this right here—his family and friends—was the best of it.

"I'm glad you came, Shane," she whispered. "I thought maybe you'd want to spend Christmas Eve with your mother. Austin told me she invited you some time ago."

"You are more my mother than she ever was, June, and there's no way I'd miss this. Thank you for inviting me. It makes me feel like I'm part of the family again, and I really missed that."

"You were always part of my family, Shane, even after you and Luke parted ways."

He hugged her again. "Not to sound greedy, but when are we opening presents? After dinner?"

"Dinner still has a while to cook yet. I hope you didn't bring anything. You know the rules."

"No presents for anyone but the kids. But I have something for Becky."

"What kind of something?"

"Something special." When her brows lifted, he shook his head and smiled. "No, not a ring. Not yet, anyhow."

"In that case…." June glanced over her shoulder at Aelissm. "Are we done enough in here for now?"

"Yep," Aeli replied. "Hi, Shane. Merry Christmas."

"Merry Christmas to you, too, Aeli."

June called for everyone's attention and told them to find someplace to sit, then popped her head out the back door. Moments later, Becky entered with her brother and her grandparents—James and Eleanor Conner—right behind them. If he had to guess, he'd say she and her brother had been showing off the work young James had been doing to improve his football skills; tucked in the crook of Becky's elbow was a snowy football, and James's pants and coat bore numerous splotches of melting snow. She glanced up and caught Shane staring, and a wide grin brightened her features.

That smile is the most beautiful thing in the world, he thought, still amazed by it after all these weeks of seeing it. He didn't miss the scowls or sneers she'd greeted him with in the past, not even for a second.

She pushed her way through the throng of people gathering around the tall Christmas tree that commanded attention from the front right of the living area and pressed a kiss to his cheek.

Ben announced that it was her brother's and Kyle's turn to hand out gifts this year, so Shane took her hand and pulled her over to the couch. They sat on the floor in front of Luke and Ryan and curled up together with the same intimate comfort as the married couple.

Presents were passed out with the youngsters amassing the largest piles. The only gifts the adults received were from the kids—mostly handmade crafts. While everyone opened their presents, Shane slid the small jewelry box out of his pocket and pressed it into Becky's hand. She regarded him with unveiled surprise, and opened it without looking at it until she'd removed the lid. At first, her only reaction was to press her fingertips to her lips. Then she lifted the delicate sterling silver chain with its phoenix pendant out and stared at it.

"You kept it after I sent it back to you," she whispered.

"I guess I had hope, even back then."

She wrapped her arms around him and held him for a long time. "Thank you. For giving it back to me *and* for holding on to that hope."

"What can I say? I love you."

She tightened her arms for a moment before she leaned back so he could fasten the necklace around her neck, and though he didn't expect her to repeat it, she did.

"I love you, too. Always have. Even when I wanted to hate you."

Suddenly, Shane realized the room had become very quiet. Even the kids had ceased their excited chatter, and when he loosened his hold on Becky enough to glance about the room, he saw that every pair of eyes was trained on them. Heat climbed his neck. Many of those gathered understood the significance of his gift, and those who didn't could guess from the others' reactions.

June was the first to comment. "I do believe the last thing JP broke twelve years ago is on the mend."

Shane searched Becky's exquisite gray eyes for any sign to the contrary. There was only hope and conviction, and at once, he was claimed by a certainty that she was beginning to trust him again. "Yes, it is."

* * *

Becky didn't like the scowl on Shane's face, and she didn't like that she'd seen it more than a few times since Christmas Eve at Uncle Ben and Aunt June's. She fiddled with the phoenix on her necklace, which she hadn't taken off since he'd put it on her, and watched him pace his living room with his cordless phone pressed to his ear. They'd been headed out the door to ring in the New Year with Luke, Ryan, Alex, and Ashleigh when Kelly had called. Again. She'd called four times that Becky knew of since Christmas Eve, but those had all been to Austin. Maybe the woman had gotten tired of Shane brushing her off.

"What do you want from me?" he asked. After a pause, he said, "Yes, I am well aware that you're only going to be in Montana three more days, but don't count on me changing my—"

Another pause, longer this time.

"What's the point? Is this something you need to do to clear your conscience? Fine. Consider it cleared. I don't need any—"

Shane's lip curled at the second interruption. Impulsively, Becky snatched the phone from his hand and punched the call-end button. He stared at her in surprise for a heartbeat, then laughed and kissed her.

"Thank you. I think she planned to keep after me until I gave in just to get rid of her."

"She still wants to sit down with you?"

He nodded. "And the more I think about it and the more insistent she gets, the more certain I am that Luke is dead right. This isn't about making things right with me or helping me. This is about her checking something off her to-do-before-I-die list so she can meet her maker with a clear conscience." Gathering her into his arms, he inhaled and let it out slowly, and she felt some of the tension leave his body. "Damn, that woman is stubborn."

"Maybe you get it from her, then," Becky teased. "Your stubbornness."

"What stubbornness? If I were as stubborn as her *or* my dad, I wouldn't have done any of the stupid shit I have. I would have locked horns with Luke instead of backing down and letting our issues chase me away from you. And if I'd stuck with you, none of the rest of it would've happened."

"Hey," Becky murmured, brushing her fingertips over his cheek. "Let's not think like that tonight, okay? That's all in the past, and everything is how it should be. Or at least getting there. But you know there is *one* way to get Kelly to leave you alone."

"Yeah? What is that?"

"Sit down and talk with her. Just get it over with."

"No."

His defiant tone elicited a shiver of concern from her. Maybe he was sincere in his desire to leave the past with his mother buried, and maybe *that* didn't bother him, but her tenacity was most certainly getting under his skin. Becky bristled. Why couldn't the woman just take no for an answer and leave well enough alone? Shane and Austin had done just fine without her and would keep on doing just fine.

"Not stubborn my ass," she said fondly, hoping to redirect him. "Come on. It's already after five, so let's go."

"How's Jim doing?" Shane asked once they were in the warmth of her truck.

"Good so far. He's staying on track with the new diet, and we've all made adjustments around the ranch so he has no reason to do anything but sit back and relax. It hasn't been easy on him—you know how much he likes to putter around the ranch even when he has a full roster of hands to do all the heavy lifting—but he's cooperating."

"I'm glad to hear it. I'm pretty fond of that old boy, and I know he's family to you."

"He's pretty fond of you, too." She smiled, recalling that Jim had been asking her to say hello to Shane for him on a more frequent basis lately. "I think he's glad we're back together. I, uh, forgot to tell you last week, but I sort of said you might be willing to help out more if that means they won't have to sell the ranch. Sorry if I over-stepped my bounds."

"You haven't. I love that place, and I'd hate to see

it bought up by someone who'd turn it into anything but what it is. With my job, I don't know how much help I can be, but I'll do whatever I can. Have they talked to Jessie about it at all lately?"

Becky shook her head. "For the moment, I think they're taking a wait-and-see approach. But eventually, even if Jim's able to get his blood pressure under control and keep his kidneys out of danger, they'll have to revisit the issue of what will happen to the ranch when they die. Ugh. I don't even like thinking about that."

"I'm sure you don't." Shane let go of the shifter to grip her hand. "But maybe Jessie will come around as she gets older, and they'll be able to work something out with her so she gets the ranch but doesn't get saddled with all the responsibility."

"I hope so."

Wellman Creek Road hadn't been plowed since the last snowstorm had dumped another six inches to what was already on the ground, and Becky fell silent so Shane could concentrate on navigating. The rocks and potholes were completely buried, making the usually bumpy ride into a comfortable one. His truck rolled through the fresh snow with no trouble, and she allowed the rolling motion to distract her. It was a bit like being in a boat, she thought, rocking with the waves.

By the time they arrived at Luke and Ryan's cabin, Luke already had dinner mostly done. Becky greeted Alex and Ryan, who were stacking a few board games on the coffee table, and joined her cousin in the kitchen.

"Crap, Luke," Becky said. "I was going to help with that."

"Not a big deal. But out of curiosity, what took you guys so long?"

"Kelly called. More specifically, she called *him* this time instead of Austin."

Luke lifted a brow. "Determined, isn't she?"

"That's the nice way to put it." Becky grabbed the bowl of grated cheese and sprinkled it over the top of the chicken enchiladas Luke had already settled into the casserole dish. Her eyes briefly sidetracked to Shane, and she was glad to note that the irritation had vanished from his handsome face, if only for a moment. "This is really starting to get to him. I'm worried."

"Perhaps it would be best, in that case, if he just gets it over with."

"That's what I told him, but he shut that idea down fast enough to give me whiplash."

"You think I'd have more luck? Not likely." Luke slid the enchiladas in the oven and leaned against the counter beside the sink to study the man at the center of their conversation. "I don't like that he's closing up. He's come so far, and I'd hate to see Kelly's selfishness take even the tiniest bit of that away from him. I'd say she'll give it up once she heads home, but I doubt it. She has enough money to fly back here with little more than a moment's notice."

"That's what I'm afraid of, too, that she'll keep pushing him until he snaps and does exactly what she taught him to—close up and run to protect himself."

Luke shifted his attention to Becky again. "I thought you said you were beginning to trust him and trust that he won't leave again."

"I am, and I do, but he's closing up about her, and I don't like it. How much longer until he starts closing up in other areas of his life again?" She folded her arms across her chest. "Because you and I both know that he tended to keep things to himself even before JP screwed us all up."

Nodding, Luke hugged her. "Guess it's up to you to make sure that doesn't happen."

"Thanks," she said flatly.

"You can do it. You want to know how I know

you can?"

"How?"

"He loves you."

"But will that be enough?"

"Yep."

"You're usually right, and I hope you are again."

Becky turned around and looked out the window above the sink. With a thick blanket of clouds covering the stars and the waning gibbous moon not yet risen, the forest was pitch black and there was no light to illuminate the mine tailings where JP had murdered Carol. She thought of her conversation with Shane the night they'd babysat Ashleigh.

"I don't think I ever realized until recently just how much what JP did hurt Shane or how much he lost when Mike and Carol died." She slipped her hand around Luke's arm and rested her head on his shoulder. "He didn't just lose them. He lost us, too, and we were pretty much the only friends he had left—the only *good* friends. We had each other, but he had no one because I pushed him away."

Luke shook his head.

"Yes, I did," Becky affirmed. "I resented him for sleeping with Carol and in turn for helping JP hurt you, and even though I loved him, I never forgave him for that, and so I couldn't trust him like I should have. He thinks I chose my friendship with you over him because us finding Carol together gave you some mystical means of helping me through it that he didn't have, but that's not right. Not entirely. We were broken even before we were together."

"I'm sure a lot of that is right, but I didn't exactly help matters."

"None of that was your fault, Luke."

"Maybe it was. I've thought about this a lot since the two of you broke up, and I couldn't admit it then, but I came between you. I didn't mean to, but I did. Shane reminded me of everything that happened, and I couldn't get past that… and I put you in the middle."

The timer beeped, so Luke paused to slide the enchiladas out of the oven. He set them on the stovetop to cool and returned to her side. "We've all come a long way since then, and I firmly believe you'll last this time because everything is how it would have and should have been."

"So, you're saying you're glad he and I are together again?"

"Yep. I thought I made that clear weeks ago." Without giving her a chance to reply, he called, "Grub's up."

Subject closed for discussion, she thought as Shane, Ryan, and Alex ambled into the kitchen to serve themselves. Luke might believe it was his fault she and Shane had broken up, but she would never blame him. In fact, she was done blaming any of them for what happened. Even Shane's mistake with Carol because that was the result of JP's manipulating, too.

They took their dinner into the living room and turned on the TV with the idea of watching each time zone ring in the New Year while they ate and played games until it arrived in Montana. They talked and laughed, and Becky soaked up the familiar camaraderie between her, Luke, and Shane, even with the sense of newness Ryan added to the mix. In fact, she liked it even better than their trio, not only because Luke was happier than she'd ever seen him but because they were evenly balanced now—two couples instead of a triangle that had ensured someone was left out. Alex was an added bonus.

A few minutes before midnight, Luke broke out the poppers and sparkling cider, and they counted down the last seconds of the year together.

"Three… two… one…. Happy New Year!"

Immediately, Becky turned to Shane, struck by an idea. "Luke and I have decided—and I think Ryan will agree—that you need to start this new year off fresh."

"Hey, don't bring us into this," her cousin said, draping himself around his wife like she could shield him from Shane's reaction.

"Too late."

"What do you propose?" Shane inquired.

The carefree, flirtatious smile that graced his features made her hesitate. She didn't want to chase it away, but she had to.

"You need to talk to Kelly, listen to whatever she thinks you need to hear, and be done with it. Had she never showed up here, I think you would've been able to go on with your life like you always have as if she wasn't part of it, but she reminded you that she is, and you need closure, Shane." She wagged a finger at him. "And don't you dare say no to me again. Every time she calls, you tense up. You're closing up on me again, Shane, and I've grown too fond of getting to see the inside of your heart."

He watched her with a defiant gleam in his brown eyes but said nothing.

"You remember what you said to me on Thanksgiving about a clean cut healing better and faster than a scrape made over and over again?"

Grudgingly, he nodded.

"Make the clean cut."

He held out a moment longer, then sighed in resignation. "All right, you win." He took her by the chin and kissed her soundly. "Promise me you'll never back down when you're right."

"That's an easy promise to make," she murmured against his lips. Turning away just long enough to lift her glass of sparkling cider in a toast, she said to everyone present, "Here's to us. May this be our best year yet."

Thirteen

"I DON'T WANT TO KNOW how much this place costs a night to rent," Becky remarked when she climbed out of Shane's truck and took in the so-called "cabin" his mother had rented at Georgetown Lake. The place was monstrous, perched on top of a low, lightly forested hill with a commanding view of the frozen lake and the surrounding mountains. Its sprawling yard sloped right down to the lakeshore and the private dock. She noted two stories from the driveway on the uphill side but figured it had a full daylight basement. Its uniform, milled logs had been stained a pale dove gray, and the trim was white. Not very cabin-like at all in her estimation.

"I don't want to know that, either," Shane said, taking her hand, "but I'm curious to know if it's for show or if she really has that kind of money."

"She really has that kind of money," Austin answered.

"She's even more selfish than I imagined," Becky muttered under her breath.

Shane ignored her comment. "Earned or inherited?"

"Why don't you ask her?"

Austin led the way down the snow-free walk to the front door, and Becky and Shane lagged a few steps behind him. Outwardly, Shane appeared to be composed, but he gripped her hand tightly. She gave it a reassuring squeeze.

They'd left Northstar three hours ago, and even though it was now nine o'clock, the sun had barely risen high enough to clear the wall of mountains. The deep, untouched snow was striped with long, cool blue shadows and bars of gleaming golden light, and where the sun touched, the feathery hoarfrost that coated everything glittered like millions of diamond flakes. Thin wisps of the fog that had fed the frost lingered out over the lake and glowed in the sun's rays, giving the magnificent scene an ethereal air.

"Are you doing all right?" Becky asked Shane, careful to keep her voice too quiet for Austin to hear.

"I'm a little nervous and a little angry, but I'm all right. I'll be glad to get this done and over with so I can get back to my life."

The front door opened before Austin had a chance to knock, and a man of average height, a slender frame, graying medium brown hair, hazel eyes, and a surprisingly welcoming smile invited them inside. Becky glanced over his attire, noting his comfortably worn, light-colored blue jeans and the white polo shirt tucked into them. A simple black belt adorned his waist, and on his feet, he wore only plain white socks.

Clean-cut, Becky surmised, *but relaxed. Not at all the pretentious stiffness I expected.*

He closed the door behind them before introducing himself while his guests removed their boots and coats.

"I'm Glen Hansen, Kelly's husband."

"Austin McGuire," Shane's father said, shaking the man's extended hand. He stepped back and gestured to Shane and Becky. "My son, Shane, and his girlfriend, Rebecca Epperson."

"A charming couple," Glen commented. "I'm delighted to meet you all."

Shane shook Glen's hand, and then Becky did.

"Please tell me, Ms. Epperson, how shall I address you?"

"Becky will be just fine," she replied. "Thank you."

"Come into the living room and make yourselves comfortable. Kelly will be down momentarily."

Despite her predisposition to dislike anything and anyone associated with Shane's mother, Becky immediately liked Glen. His politeness was free of the aloofness she'd experienced with some of the Royal R's more affluent guests, and his smile was quick and open. He led them from the entryway into the cavernous living room. The un-cabin-likeness of the exterior continued in the interior; the logs were stained the same dove gray that barely allowed any of the wood's natural character to show through. The lush carpets were eggshell white, and the L-shaped couch and recliners were a few shades darker than the stain on the logs. Splashes of light and dark purple added a touch of color to the otherwise colorless space. Two-and-a-half-story-high windows dominated the angled south-facing walls, offering a spectacular view of the lake and mountains. The pallid color scheme reflected the light streaming through them, giving the room an airy feel. A horseshoe-shaped loft rimmed the vaulted living room, and from what she could see, Becky guessed there were three, possibly four bedrooms upstairs, two on either side of the space open to below.

"Would you like a tour while you wait for Kelly?" Glen inquired.

"No, thanks," Becky replied. "Will she be long?"

"No."

Becky sat on the couch next to Shane and was nearly engulfed by its deep cushions.

Glen briefly excused himself to fetch coffee and muffins from the kitchen, which sat beyond the neighboring and rather formal dining room in the eastern wing just off the living room, and Becky almost asked him not to bother because there was no way she'd be able to eat or drink in here without worrying she'd make a mess.

Shane stood and walked to the windows with his hands stuffed into his pockets. "It's an amazing view, but I like the one from my front deck much more. I also like that my cozy little cabin doesn't distract from it."

"This place is gorgeous but definitely not our

style," Becky agreed.

He met her gaze over his shoulder. "You know, I like this 'our' and 'we' idea."

"Do you?"

"Yep. And I like that you came with me today. Makes this easier."

"Let's just hope it won't take too long," she mumbled.

Glen returned with a tray of refreshments and set it on the wide glass coffee table, then claimed one of the recliners. Neither Shane nor his father hesitated to take a cup of coffee, so Becky grabbed one for herself and added a splash of hazelnut creamer.

"What is the story behind this place?" she asked.

"I beg your pardon?"

"I've seen this house before, but I didn't know it was a vacation rental," Becky explained.

"It isn't, per se. It's a timeshare, and one of Kelly's colleagues wasn't going to use all of his allotment this winter, so we asked to rent a portion of it." Glen smiled. "I've never been to Montana, so naturally, when Kelly decided she wanted to connect with Shane and we couldn't get reservations a the Ramshorn Hot Springs, I suggested this place rather than trying to hotel it."

"I imagine this is much more comfortable," Austin said. "Just how big is this place?"

"Indeed it *is* more comfortable. Five bedrooms—three upstairs, two downstairs—a den just through those French doors behind me. There's also a game room downstairs. I told Kelly that if this place ever comes up for sale, I'd buy it in a heartbeat. I'd love to retire here."

"I know Kelly is some sort of cancer specialist—I think she said gastro-intestinal—but what do you do, Glen?" Austin asked.

"I'm a school superintendent."

A guy who works with kids married to a woman who hates them, Becky mused. *That must make for interesting conversation at mealtime.* "And you and she have no kids, correct?"

"That is correct." The momentary flash of regret—nothing more than a brief flattening of his lips—indicated a disagreement. "Kelly never changed her mind about not wanting children."

"I'm assuming this was your idea, then," Shane said quietly, staring out the window.

"Yes and no. I suggested it a long time ago," Glen replied, "but we hadn't spoken of it in years until Austin's cancer scare."

"She knew about that?"

"She happened to call the day Jeremiah noticed the spot," Austin answered before Glen could, "and I thought she might be able to tell me if I should be worried enough to go see the doc."

"I think she realized she'd lose any chance to connect with you if something were to happen to Austin."

"She's not wrong about that," Shane said under his breath. "I didn't want to come, but Dad's been bugging me about it… and Becky finally convinced me. If it had been up to me, I wouldn't be here right now. Or ever."

"I'm sorry you feel that way, and I know Kelly has made mistakes, particularly where you and your father are concerned, but—"

Shane held up his hand. "You don't have to explain her mistakes to me. For one thing, they aren't *your* mistakes. For another, I've made enough of my own to understand how they gnaw at you even when you don't regret them."

Becky met Shane's gaze and patted the couch cushion beside her. "Come sit."

He obeyed, and just as she tucked her arms around him, a door opened upstairs. Becky craned her neck to see, and spotted a woman the right age to be

Shane's mother head from the master suite above the kitchen and dining room toward the stairs. She was slender, willowy even, and though she walked with perfect straight-backed posture, the fluid grace of her body kept her from appearing stiff. Her silver-streaked red hair was cut into a stylish bob, and when she reached the living room, Becky saw that it framed a delicate, pixie-like face with possibly the most flawless ivory skin she'd ever seen. *Elegant* was the adjective that popped into her mind when she tried to describe the woman. She certainly did *not* look like she was fifty-two, and her faultless beauty might have been intimidating if Becky didn't know well that that sort of exterior attractiveness often hid a selfish interior, and she thought immediately of Justin.

You promised Austin you would give her the benefit of the doubt.

Upon closer inspection, there was little resemblance between Shane and Kelly. Becky thought he might have inherited her cheeks and the shape of her eyes though not their emerald color as his were the same rich brown as Austin's. In every other way, he was very much Austin's son, and she found that comforting.

"Hello, Kelly," Austin greeted.

"Austin. Thank you for bringing him."

"Becky here had a lot more to do it than I did."

Kelly turned her gaze on Becky and smiled politely. There was nothing overly aloof about her, and in fact, her expression was more inviting than Becky had expected, and yet, she didn't immediately *like* Kelly as she had Glen.

"Becky?" the older woman asked, brows lifted in surprise. "The same he dated in high school?"

"Yes, ma'am," Becky replied.

"I thought that ended… unpleasantly… some time ago."

Becky bristled but bit her tongue just before the words *none of your damned business* popped out of her mouth and reminded herself to play nice. "It did, but it was worth salvaging."

At last turning to her son, she greeted him with a note of something in her voice that sounded to Becky a lot like apprehension. "Hello again, Shane."

"Dr. Brennan," Shane replied.

"Please, call me Kelly. There is no need for formalities."

The woman lowered herself primly into the recliner next to her husband, crossed her legs at the ankles, and folded her hands in her lap. The uncertainty lingered, as if she didn't know where to begin now that she had Shane here. As the silence dragged on while Kelly and Shane eyed each other, Becky's irritation rose.

"You still grow gardenias?" Shane asked at last.

Kelly leaned back in shock. "You remember that?"

"I remember the scent. Dad told me you grew them."

"Yes, I did and do. They remind me of my grandmother, who grew them at her home in the South." She smoothed her expression and affected that polite smile again. "Tell me a little about yourself, Shane."

"It sounds like my father has kept you pretty well informed, so I'm not sure what I can add."

"I'd like to hear it from you, if that's all right."

She doesn't care, Becky thought, noting the forced cheerfulness in Kelly's voice that was contrasted by the way her gaze wandered. Perhaps she was simply uncomfortable with the situation—that was certainly understandable and excusable—but if she were truly interested, wouldn't her attention be focused on Shane? *She's just asking to be polite and make conversation, but look at her. She doesn't want to be doing this any more than we do.*

"If it's all right with *you*," Becky snipped, "I think

we can cut out the pleasantries and get right to the reason why you felt the need to disrupt Shane's life. The faster the better so we can close the door on this and get back to what really matters."

"Who are you to speak to me like that?"

That haughty tone pushed irritation over the edge into anger. Rage boiled in her gut, and she clenched her fists to keep it bottled up. "I'm his girlfriend, and I've watched the thought of having to talk to you and relive your abandonment wear on him for weeks now."

"As I recall, you broke his heart when you betrayed him with his best friend."

"Do *not* go there. You know nothing about why we broke up." Becky knew she should stop right now, but she couldn't. She leaned forward as the accusations exploded out of her. "Do you have any idea of the damage you did to him when you left? I cannot believe anyone could be so selfish."

"You have no idea why I left."

"I don't need to know why. You are his mother, and a mother doesn't abandon her child. She doesn't leave him to grow up believing he wasn't good enough for her... or for anyone else." In her fury, her thoughts threatened to scatter beyond her grasp in a cyclone of allegations, so she paused to inhale as deeply as the adrenaline-fueled quivers of her body allowed. She exhaled slowly, and her heart rate dropped a tiny bit. "For a while in there, I thought he didn't care who he hurt when he walked away because he was just as selfish and because walking away was exactly what you taught him to do. You know, like mother like son. But I look back, and I see how wrong I was. His decisions aren't at all like yours. He hurt us because he didn't think he was good enough for us, that we deserved better, and he couldn't stand in the way of us getting it."

To her credit, Kelly sat through Becky's tirade with an unshakable composure. Becky bit back the rest of what she was compelled to say and waited for the older woman to reply, but that moment of silence stretched into a minute, then two. It dawned on her that she hadn't said anything Kelly hadn't already considered.

"Are you finished?" Shane's mother asked in a calm voice.

Abruptly, Becky jumped to her feet. "I need some air." Turning briefly to Shane and giving his shoulder a squeeze, she whispered, "I'm sorry."

She headed directly to the dining room and out the door onto the broad deck overlooking the lake without bothering to fetch her boots or coat from the entryway. Austin joined her soon after with her boots and jacket and said nothing while she put them on. Standing side by side, they leaned on the railing and stared out over the lake in silence.

"I didn't mean to go off like that," Becky murmured.

"I'm sure you didn't, but you don't need to apologize to anyone for defending Shane. I'm curious, however. Did you mean what you said?"

"Every word."

"Good."

Becky glanced at him. He wasn't looking at the lake anymore, and when she met his gaze, she saw the question as plainly as if he'd spoken it aloud.

Can you trust him again?

"I want to trust him," she admitted. "And I'm starting to. I love him, Austin. I never stopped, and if I had only bothered to look beyond the pain...."

"You have now, so make the best of it." He wrapped an arm around her shoulders and squeezed. "I love Ryan dearly, but she and Shane never had what you and he have. Some people might say teenagers are too young to know what real love is, but you two... you knew."

"I hope you're right."

"No, you don't. You *know* I am."

"What do you think Shane should do about Kelly? And don't say it's not your place to make the decision. I'm not asking you to. I'm only asking for your opinion."

"I honestly don't have one on the matter. He's a grown man, and he knows what he needs better than I do."

"Maybe, but you're still his father, and he'll always value your opinion." Becky sighed. "I think what he needs is closure—to hear why she left so he can see that he's not like her and that he won't keep making the same mistakes."

Austin laughed. "Oh, my girl, you aren't just *starting* to trust him. You *do* trust him."

Becky grinned despite the persisting anger at Kelly because he was right. "Don't go booking the Ramshorn to plan and host our wedding just yet."

"I wouldn't dream of it, my dear."

"Yes, you would. I get the feeling you've been dreaming of it for a very long time."

Austin's only reply was a sly smile.

* * *

"She's quite spirited, that one," Kelly remarked after the door closed behind Austin.

"Spirited, stubborn, honest," Shane agreed, "and fiercely loyal."

"And correct. I was selfish."

Glen rose from his recliner. "I'd best leave you two alone."

Shane watched him disappear into the den before turning back to Kelly. Again, he caught himself studying her, searching her face for any sense of familiarity. Other than a few shared physical traits, there wasn't much beyond recognition from their cursory meeting a month ago. She was otherwise a complete stranger.

This is all so bizarre.

Deciding Becky was right that it was best to get everything out into the open, he asked, "Why did you leave?"

"To properly answer that, I should start with why I got involved with your father in the first place," Kelly replied.

When she didn't immediately begin, he waited a few seconds, then prodded. "All right. Why did you get involved with him?"

"Youthful rebellion."

It wasn't quite the answer he'd expected, and his brows lifted briefly. "You don't strike me as the rebellious type."

"Those years with your father taught me a lot of humility and how to appreciate what my parents did for me instead of resenting the limitations and expectations they placed on me from a very young age."

"What kind of expectations?"

"The usual—good grades, honor roll, so many activities I never had time to breathe or consider what *I* might want to do. By the time I hit high school, I already knew exactly where I would be going to college, what area of medical study I would pursue, and even where I was likely to do my residency because my parents had planned everything down to the letter. I graduated high school with top grades, was the valedictorian, and then off I went to the college they chose to start on the path they'd laid out."

"So what happened?"

"My roommate. She was born and raised in Montana and had a spirit as free as her home, and in listening to her talk about how her parents had let her not only choose her own path but also encouraged her to make mistakes, I hated my life. She had so much energy and so much excitement about becoming a doctor, and all I felt was dread."

The very thought of the constraints her parents had placed on her made Shane's skin crawl, and the first inkling of pity wormed its way into his heart. In that situation, he would have rebelled, too. Thankfully, his father had never required anything but his best effort, leaving the rest up to him to decide.

"What a terrible thing to do to a kid. How could you ever hope to be your own person?" he wondered. "June—she's Becky's aunt—told me about a girl from her high school whose parents did the same thing to her. The girl was anorexic, stressed, and anxious, and one day at school, she had a major breakdown and had to be taken to the hospital in an ambulance."

"I came close to that point a few times, but fortunately, I never reached it." She peered out the windows, and for a few moments, her eyes lingered on Shane's father. "I met Austin the summer I graduated from college with my bachelor's degree. I was to spend three months out here with my roommate and her family before we both headed off to medical school. Her mother was an OB-GYN at the hospital in Devyn back then, but they moved to a bigger city years ago. My roommate and I stayed in her family's guesthouse, and we were allowed to come and go as we pleased. Being freshly legal to drink, we spent quite a bit of time at the bars."

"Dad said that's where he met you. He was in

town with a buddy, and you and he hit it off."

"We did," she said with a fond smile. "The first week I was here—May twenty-first. He was very charming, handsome, and like my roommate, he saw *me* instead of a checklist of goals to meet."

"Sounds like Dad."

"He was exactly the opposite of everything in my life, and I was smitten with the freedom of that. We dated just a couple weeks before I slept with him. We used protection, but we weren't always careful, and only a month into my trip, I realized I was in trouble. I was pregnant. I waited another month until I told my parents. They were naturally furious and demanded I have an abortion."

Shane squirmed a bit in his seat. The direction of the conversation hit a little too close to home but not because his existence had come so close to being terminated. Immediately, Ryan and Angel flashed in his mind, and he flinched. He may have handled the situation terribly, but he couldn't imagine ever being so heartless as to demand she abort their child. That was a choice only she could make, and he'd never for a second thought it would ever enter her mind. "Obviously you didn't go through with it."

"No, and I wish I could say it was some instinctive

maternal love for you that drove me, but it wasn't. It was another means of rebelling against my parents. I knew even at twenty-two that I didn't want children. Ever. It simply isn't in me to be a mother, and the five years I was yours proved it. I was terrible at being a wife and even worse at being a mother. If it weren't for Austin…. He was so great with you and he loved you so much that he more than made up for my shortcomings."

"What did your parents do when you told them you wouldn't have an abortion?"

"They threatened to cut me off if I didn't do it, come home, and continue on toward my career as a physician. The date I was supposed to start school came and went, and they made good on their threat. So I took a job doing some clerical work at the hospital in Devyn."

"I'm a bit surprised they didn't come out here and try to drag you back with them."

"What could they legally do? I was an adult."

"Doesn't mean they couldn't try."

"That is not how they operate. They believed I'd get tired of struggling to make a living and come crawling back. It didn't take long before I wanted to. When December hit and the temperatures plummeted, I began to understand just what life so many miles from real civilization was like. But by then, I had little choice."

Kelly stopped her narrative for a moment and studied him with a quizzical frown.

It was all too clear now that he had in fact buried all the pain and bitterness of her leaving deep inside and that he'd been wrong to think he felt nothing about it anymore. At once, a trickle of anger and panic seeped into him, chilling him at the same time it made him want to hurl his empty coffee cup across the too-pristine living room. *How much more of this do I want to hear? How much more do I* need *to hear?*

Shane rubbed his palms over his knees as a lump formed in his throat, wishing Becky was with him on the couch instead of cooling off outside. Of course, learning that Kelly had wanted to leave even before he was born would have set her off again, so perhaps it was best she wasn't inside to hear it.

Despite his desire to escape, curiosity gnawed at him, and he understood that he wouldn't be able to bury it again until he'd heard it all. And maybe then he wouldn't *have* to lock it away. Maybe, as Becky had said, he'd be able to let it go just like he'd let go of his self-loathing over his mistakes.

"Does this make you uncomfortable?" Kelly asked.

"Very, but the can of worms has popped."

He had a good enough sense of how she'd ended up with his father that he wanted to ask why she'd stayed so long, but he couldn't bring himself to say the words.

"When did you…" he began, but his voice sounded strangled to his ears, so he cleared his throat and tried again. "When did you tell Dad you were pregnant?"

"A couple weeks before I was supposed to go back. Contrary to what I expected, he was ecstatic. Concerned how we would make things work, of course, but happy and determined. I used to think he handled it better than I did because he was wiser, but I've come to understand that's just who he is. Without his support, I likely would have given in to my parents and had the abortion, and while I may have failed you both miserably in the end, I couldn't do that to your father. He loved you so much, even before you were born."

Shane thought back on his childhood, remembering his father's patience when Austin had taught him to rope and ride, his unfailing support when Shane had decided he wanted to play football and his clumsy but determined attempts to help him practice, and even the anger when Shane had wrecked his first truck on a mountain back road. They had struggled financially, and there were times they'd scraped by only because of the generosity of the Robinsons, Hammonds, Strutherses, Carlyles, and other Northstar ranching families, who had found work for Austin—and Shane, when he was old enough—even when they didn't need the help. There was one thing he'd never questioned and had taken for granted too often—his father's love.

Gratitude for everything Austin had done for him in his life overwhelmed him, and Shane pushed to his feet. "Excuse me."

He ducked outside through the door in the dining room and, without a word, wrapped Austin in a crushing hug. When his father hugged him back, he thought they might crack ribs.

"Thank you for my life," he whispered. "Every second of it. I'm sorry I haven't been a better son or done more to repay everything you've done for me."

"But you have, Shane. You've made life worth living. I don't expect you to understand that now, but when you have kids, you will."

It was a long while before they let go of each

other, and immediately, Becky embraced Shane.

"Do you need us to come back in? I promise I'll keep my mouth shut, and if I can't, I'll just come right back out here so I don't interrupt."

"It'd be nice to have you both in there. She's not done yet, but there's really only one thing left that I need to know."

"Why she left?" Austin asked.

"No, I've figured that out. I want to know why she waited so long."

"I wish I could tell you, but I don't know the answer myself."

Becky took Shane's hand in both of hers, and they headed back inside, slipping their untied boots off and shrugging out of their coats before they reached the pale carpet of the living room. This lifestyle—the sacrifice of fun and adventure to keep possessions spotless that his mother seemed to enjoy—did not suit him at all. It made him miss the dirt and mud of the ranches he and his father had worked together, and he wanted to get out of here.

"Sorry about that," he said to Kelly after they returned to their seats on the couch. "If it's all right, I'd like to get through the rest pretty quickly and get out of here so I can process it all."

"Fair enough."

"I think I know why you left… but tell me any-how."

"I saw where my life was heading, and it was noth-ing like what I'd once thought my life would be. I wanted out. It's selfish, yes, but it's the truth. I never expected my rebellious affair would alter my life how it did."

"Then… why didn't you leave right after I was born? Why did you wait five years?"

"Believe it or not, I loved you both. I tried to make it work, I did, but I couldn't do it, and that love became resentment."

"Why did you finally do it?"

"Austin, you never told him?"

"I don't know that I've ever understood exactly what happened," Austin said. "So I figured it best if I didn't tell him because I couldn't explain the whys I knew he would ask."

"He's always tried to speak kindly of you," Shane added. "So what happened?"

"In January, when you were five, you got sick at school, and Austin was out working on the ranch and couldn't be reached to pick you up, so I had to leave work and drive all the way home through a snowstorm to Northstar to get you. On the way, my car broke down, and if it weren't for the kind motorist who stopped to give me a ride, I might have been stranded out there for a lot longer than the hour I was. I finally got to the school to get you, and you were so miserable and bawling…. I snapped. I called my parents and begged them to let me come home, promising them I'd get my life back on the track they'd set for me. They stipulated that I must divorce Austin and give up my parental rights to you, certain I couldn't become a top doctor in my field if I was a wife and mother. And they believed it was possible to strike my *indiscretion* from the annals of my life."

"Yet you married Glen," Shane said. "Don't get me wrong. He seems like a good man, and I like him."

"His parents were good friends with mine," Kelly replied with a placating smile.

"I guess I have another question," he said, realizing there was something more he needed to know. "Then I think we're done."

Kelly waited expectantly.

"Why have you kept in contact with Dad all these years?"

"I thought I could completely sever ties with you, but I couldn't. I never wanted children, but I had a son, and I couldn't just forget that… even if it took me four years to admit it that I felt guilty for abandoning you and that you were better off without me."

Shane agreed with that last part and remembered saying as much to his father once or twice since Austin had first revealed that he and Kelly had talked a few times since she'd left.

"If that's all you want to know," Kelly said, rising, "I'll get up and fix us all something for brunch and leave you three alone to talk."

She fetched her husband from the den, and together, they adjourned to the kitchen, which was sectioned off from the dining room by only a snack bar that jutted out from the southern wall and didn't put much of a barrier between them and Shane, his father, and Becky. Still, the space was large enough that Kelly likely wouldn't be able to hear much of their conversation, especially not with the noise of preparing a meal.

Shane rested his head on the back of the couch and thought through everything she'd told him, comparing it to what he knew. His father hadn't told him much, perhaps unable to comprehend Kelly's situation, and as he pieced together the new information with his memories, Shane realized that his resentment of his mother hadn't come from Austin's explanations.

In fact, as he'd told Kelly, his father had painted her in a rather favorable light. It was the heartache inscribed on Austin's face whenever he had talked about her that had given him the impression that Kelly was selfish. She was, both in her rebellion and in her decision to run home to her parents, but Shane couldn't blame her. Even if he couldn't empathize with the soul-crushing pressure her parents had put on her, the very idea of it was constricting enough that it was easy to imagine how it had eroded her ability to make her own decisions or to embrace independence.

"You're awfully quiet," Becky said. "Are you okay?"

"Yeah. Just processing," he replied. He lifted her hand to his lips and kissed her knuckles. "Thank you for talking me into doing this. You were right."

"Wait. What did you just say? I'm right?"

He leaned in to give her a kiss, and she tried to escape, so he put his arm around her shoulders and pinned her against him, then went after her mouth so quickly she couldn't evade him again. Giggles erupted from her. "Yes, you're right. But don't let it go to your head."

"All right, you two," Austin interrupted. "As happy as it makes me to see you obviously absorbed with each other, we *are* here for a reason and we all have lives to get back to, so let's wrap this up."

Shane lifted a brow and gaped at his father. In the confusion of these revelations, he hadn't considered how seeing his ex-wife might affect his father. Since Austin and Kelly had spoken a few times over the years and had sat down with each other at least once that he knew of—a month ago when she'd stopped in Northstar on her way through to Seattle—he had assumed they'd worked out whatever jitters seeing each other again might have spawned. Apparently not, Shane thought, noting the pallor of his father's face and the strain in his eyes.

"All right," he said, standing. He offered first Becky then Austin a hand up, then started toward the kitchen. His father laid a hand on his shoulder, and he turned to face him.

"Whatever you decide to do, Shane, I support you. But now that you've heard what she has to say and have what you need to make a decision, I'm finished with her. I've kept her informed of your life over the years, and I've done my best to be civil and polite about it for your sake because I figured we might have to sit down like this someday, but it's never been a comfortable thing for me."

Shane only nodded and led his companions into the kitchen. Because Glen and Kelly were busy cooking and because he was still testing his decision in light of the new emotions regarding his mother, he didn't immediately broach the subject of their future. He waited until everyone had their food and was nearly finished eating before he did. With the lack of conversation and downcast gazes, he was glad he hadn't jumped right back in because the awkwardness firmed his resolve.

"So what now?" he asked at last when Glen got up to clear dishes from the snack bar. "Where do we go from here?"

"That's up to you," Kelly replied, "but I don't believe reconnecting is possible because we don't know each other. We'd have to start fresh."

Inexplicably, he laughed. When everyone stared at him, he turned to his father and Becky, "How many times have I said or thought exactly that? Seriously though, do you want to start fresh and get to know me or do you just want to know that I'm all right so you can let go of that guilt?"

"The latter," Kelly admitted. "We have nothing in common, and other than money—which I'm certain you won't take because you are so much your father's son—there isn't anything I can offer you. You don't need me, and you never did."

"I appreciate your honesty, and I believe we are in agreement. I don't need anything from you beyond what you've given me today, which is understanding. I love my life, and I wouldn't trade it for anything in this world."

"Closure," Becky murmured. "That's what you both want from this."

"Yes, closure," Shane said.

Relief washed across Kelly's face, erasing the strain and making her look at least a dozen years younger. Everyone stood at the same time.

"Glen, it was a pleasure meeting you," Shane said, extending his hand to Kelly's husband. "I'm sorry I won't have a chance to get to know you."

"Agreed, but it's best for everyone this way."

Glen stayed in the kitchen to clean up while Kelly walked them to the door, waiting patiently while they donned boots and coats again. At last, it was time to leave, and Shane felt no regret whatsoever. This was right.

"Thank you, Austin, for everything you've done over the years," Kelly said. "Because of you, I am finally able to embrace the decision I made knowing it wasn't just the best for me but the best for all of us."

"I didn't do it for you, Kelly," Austin replied. His tone wasn't dismissive or angry. It was gently matter-of-fact and perhaps a touch weary. "I did it for my son."

"Come on, Dad," Shane said and ushered his father outside. "Let's go home. And why don't we take a good long horseback ride someplace to remind us of how lucky we are?"

"Only if Becky comes with us."

"You bet I will."

Shane turned back to his mother. Again, she was a stranger, someone he only vaguely recognized, and any flicker of a desire to open a line of friendship to her that he might have felt mingled with the pity for her parents' hardheartedness died away. "Goodbye, Kelly," he said with a serene certainty it was the last one they'd ever say or need.

"Goodbye, Shane."

As he pulled the door closed, he exhaled in relief, then hugged his father and Becky at once. "Unless I'm remembering the good times, I don't want to waste any more of my life looking back. From now on, I'll be looking forward."

Fourteen

WHAT A MISERABLE DAY.

Shane stood at the window nearest his woodstove and watched a particularly strong gust bend the pines and rattle the bare branches of the scrub willows and quaking aspen that lined Shale Creek just across the road from his cabin. The wind picked up the powdery snow that had fallen last night and drove it in obscuring plumes across the Northstar Valley. Miserable but harshly beautiful.

"All right," Becky said, joining him. She tucked herself against his side, and without a thought to what he was doing, he draped his arm around her. "The first load is in the washer. How should we spend our time while I wait for it to finish?"

"We could stand here enjoying the cozy warmth of the fire while feeling sorry for your parents and Max and Chris for having to separate cows in this, or…." He swiveled to face her, slid his hands down her hips and behind her thighs, and hoisted her off the ground so quickly that she squealed. "We can do a little laundry of our own. Well, some prewash preparation, anyhow."

"Huh?"

"Don't you remember the old joke about the newlywed couple who were too shy to talk about sex so they called it 'doing the laundry'?"

"I do, but as I recall, the punch line was about how the husband didn't want to disturb his napping bride, so he did a small load by hand."

"I know that's the punch line. But I'm talking about getting the clothes ready to go in the washer, beautiful. I don't think we're ready to actually do the laundry just yet."

Becky giggled, and her gray eyes sparkled in the most enticing way. "What, pray tell, does this prewash you speak of entail?"

Without a word, he carried her to his couch and settled her down, then trailed kisses up her neck and along her jaw to her lips and slid his hand under her pale gray cable-knit sweater, skimming the heel of his hand and then his fingertips over the silken skin of her waist and ribs. He was careful to stay clear of more sensitive areas, not wanting to push her further than she was ready or willing to go, but by the way she responded to his touch, he didn't need to be so cautious. Nevertheless, he took his time and kept his caresses tender and playful, savoring each pounding beat of his heart and each titillated hitch of her breathing.

If the sensations weren't so wonderful, he'd wonder again if he were dreaming, but she was here with him, and the heat and soft curves of her body beneath him reignited the passion she'd kindled the day of her brother's birth. Unlike that day, though, there were no dark memories and no agonizing doubts about their future to diminish the enjoyment of this moment, only a vow to cherish every moment she gave him.

In danger of drowning in sweet oblivion, he nibbled her neck with clownish fervor, and she was soon shrieking with laughter. Pleased with himself, he sat back and grinned as he waited for her to catch her breath.

"That is the most exquisite sound in the world," he murmured. He brushed her hair back from her face and leaned down briefly to press a kiss to her cheek. She beamed up at him. "And the most breathtaking sight. After all these years, you have no idea how beautiful you are, Becky."

"Keep telling me just like that and I might figure it out." With a finger under his chin, she drew him to her for a lingering kiss. "For the record, you don't have a clue how beautiful you are, either."

"Sure I do. If I weren't such a sexy beast, I never would have caught your discerning eye."

She laughed breathlessly. "You only joke about being sexy. You don't actually believe it. But that's all right because it allows your best attribute to shine through."

"And what is my best attribute?"

"Your spirit. You're independent and free, but you're also loyal and kind, and though you're hesitant to give your heart, when you do, you give it all. You see the beauty in even the simplest things and even in the things others think are ugly."

She glanced away when she said that last bit but not before Shane caught the glint of bitterness in her eyes. How did she ever think herself ugly? he wondered, but he knew the answer. As a young girl, she'd been the awkward outcast, the too-tall, too-skinny ranch girl who didn't fit in with what was popular. Even though it had hurt her that her so-called friends hadn't accepted who she was, she'd stayed true to herself, never judging those who judged her. Luke had seen the true beauty in her, and when he'd extended an offer of friendship—genuine, love-her-for-who-she-was, flaws-and-all friendship—Shane had seen it, too, and in that moment, he'd given his heart to her. Too bad it had taken him so long to realize that.

"You know what your best attribute is?"

"No. What?"

"Your heart."

She lifted a brow in skepticism.

"I'm not the kind and loyal one here. You are. I have never met anyone so accepting as you who loves everyone for exactly who they are. Not even June and Luke. And we both know how exceptional they are."

Her doubtful expression softened into a shy smile. "Thank you." She arched up to kiss him again. "No one has ever made me feel as desirable as you do."

"Not even Justin?" he joked.

"Definitely not Justin." Again, she laughed. "Unlike you, he's too obsessed with his own reflection to

all that pressure from her parents and having to be perfect all the damned time…. She acted the only way she knew how by bowing down to her parents. Hooking up with Dad is the only thing she ever did on her own, and I feel sorry for her. Can you imagine being so afraid of disappointing your parents that you couldn't think for yourself? Probably not because your parents loved you and let you be yourself."

"You amaze me, Shane. I'm not sure I could forgive her if I were in your position."

"I doubt that. You've forgiven me, haven't you?"

When she hesitated, his heart tripped. Was he wrong to think that? Then she tilted her head up, and he was rewarded with the most tender smile he'd ever seen.

"Yes, I have."

She pivoted into his lap, straddling his waist, and claimed his mouth with a distracting mixture of adoration and passion. The way she threaded herself around him and pressed her body so firmly against him cleared every thought from his mind but those of how much he loved and wanted her.

His phone rang, and they both growled in annoyance, then laughed. Becky bounced off his lap to fetch the cordless handset from the dining room table, and

Shane let his head fall back against the couch. She handed him the phone, and he poked the button to take the call.

"Hello?"

"Shane, it's Jessie Robinson. Jane told me Becky headed down to your place to do some laundry. Is she there yet?"

Thinking of their laundry joke, Shane nearly laughed, but there was a note of urgency in Jessie's voice that concerned him. "Yeah. Here she is." He handed the phone to Becky. "It's Jessie."

Becky's brows dipped in a frown. "Hi, Jessie. What's going on?" she asked, walking over to the window.

Shane tried not to eavesdrop on her conversation, but his good intentions dissolved when she said, "Oh God, I hope he's all right."

Immediately, he feared something had happened to Jim, but she seemed to be only mildly concerned.

After a few moments, she said, "Yeah, of course. No, I'm sure Shane wouldn't mind. See you in a bit." She ended the call and turned back to him. "We're needed at the ranch. The wind brought a couple big firs down on a section of fence of the north pasture and cows are getting out."

"Who got hurt?"

"Chris. Clipped his leg with the chainsaw—gust of wind caught the branch he was cutting, and that knocked the saw into his thigh just above his knee. Anyhow, Jessie says it isn't too bad, but Belle's taking him to the ER to get it properly cleaned and stitched. The dummy wanted to do it himself, but Dad and Jessie wouldn't let him."

"Smart on their part. All right," Shane said, bouncing to his feet. "I'll get ready while you get your clothes in the dryer, and then we'll get up to the ranch. Your truck or mine? No point in taking both since we're both coming back here after."

"My truck's still warm." She sighed. "I guess we'll have to finish our fun later… and my laundry. I have a lot left to do."

Shane's brows rose at the sudden playful lilt in her voice. "Do you now?"

"Mmm-hmm." She sidled over to him and walked her fingers up his chest. "I like that idea of a little pre-washing… but I think I want to finish the laundry—washing and drying."

"Just so we're clear, you're talking about sex, right?"

"Yes, I am."

Shane clasped her face and kissed her gently. "As much as I want to spend all night making love to you, I'm not sure it's a good idea to take that step yet. We decided to take it slow, remember?"

"I do remember, but I'm sure of this. It wasn't a mistake the first time nine years ago, and it won't be a mistake tonight… or whenever in the near future we get around to it."

"But the first time—"

"Shane, shut up. I want this." She tilted her hips against his body in an inarguable declaration of her intent. "I even came prepared."

Shane swallowed hard and swore. Then he laughed. "What does it say about me that you have not once but twice been the one to buy the condoms?"

"It says you respect me and are so considerate that you let me decide when I'm ready to get physical. And believe me, Shane, I'm ready." This time when she kissed him, she caught his bottom lip between her teeth and tugged. "But that'll have to wait. Go get dressed for the cold."

Shane groaned with pure need but did as he was told, and in ten minutes, they were climbing into her truck, which was semi-warm from her drive over. Fifteen minutes later, Becky pulled up in front of her cabin and dashed in to don her cold-weather gear. Shortly after that, they strode into the main ranch house to check in with Jessie. Becky's brother was in the kitchen helping her prepare lunch for the guests, but other than a quick hello, Jessie didn't give him time to chat before sending him into the pantry for ingredients.

"You seem to end up spending a lot of your days off helping us, Shane," she remarked. "But we sure do appreciate it."

"You won't hear me complain about it," he assured her.

"Give me just a minute and I'll have a couple thermoses of coffee ready for you."

While they waited, he asked how Jim was doing with his diet, thinking of the dread that had coursed through him when he'd thought briefly that something had happened to the rancher.

"He hates it," Becky replied, "and he whines about it incessantly, but he's sticking to it."

"He'd never admit it," Jessie added, "but he's already feeling better, and his kidney function is improving."

"Damn glad to hear that. I hope he keeps it up."

"Limiting his physical activity is a more difficult

for him. Speaking of which, he knows he's only supposed to be supervising the repair of the fence, but he'll want to do more."

"Don't worry, Jessie," Becky assured her. "We won't let him."

"Even if he gets nasty about it—and he will; he's been ornerier than a bear shitting barbed wire when it comes to accepting his limitations—don't let him push you around. If he gets too bad, just send him right on back to the house."

"Yes, ma'am," Shane said. "And thanks for the heads up."

"Here's your coffee. I've already saddled your favorite horses—they're waiting for you in the corral—and Jim and Chris took the tools and supplies out to the break in the fence before Chris cut his leg. I haven't heard anything yet, so I don't know how far Andy, Jane, and Max have gotten, but I imagine they haven't finished rounding up the cows that got out." Jessie hugged them both. "Thank you again."

They wasted no time stowing their thermoses in their saddlebags and mounting and headed out through the gusting wind and swirling snow to the north pasture. As Jessie had guessed, Becky's parents and Max were still chasing cows back into the pasture through the break in the fence. Jim sat on his black gelding just outside to guide the bovines back through. Chris had cut and cleared enough of the fallen trees that repairs could be made as soon as the rest of the cows were back inside. The wind sighed and moaned through the pines and firs and sent branches crashing to the ground, making an already miserable job dangerous as well.

With two extra riders, the task of rounding up the cattle became much easier except that several tried to escape back to the better shelter of the forest beyond the pasture. Shane couldn't blame them—the trees did provide a bit of relief from the cutting gale—but he cursed them regardless.

"Jane, Andy, Max!" Jim called. "Take these to the pasture by the barn. Shane, Becky, and I can get the last couple. Just five-sixteen and six-oh-nine left out there."

"You aren't going to do any damned such thing," Jane barked. "Shane and Becky can handle it. You just keep doing what you are, Jim. Last thing we need right now is you keeling over."

Jim grumbled but retained his post.

"I hate five-sixteen," Becky grumbled. "She's always a pain in the ass. And six-oh-nine isn't much better."

"No, but find the densest patch of trees," Shane replied as they rode back into the woods, "and you know that's where we'll find them. They're smart cows, and they know how to survive."

Sure enough, the two cows were hunkered down in a thick stand of bushy young spruces… and refused to leave. At last, Shane slapped the larger and older of the two—five-sixteen—on the rump with his rope, and she and her companion took off toward the break in the fence. He and Becky managed to get them back into the pasture without any further trouble.

"That was easier than expected," Becky said, eyeing the cows. "What are you two plotting?"

She swung her leg over her horse and secured his reins to a fencepost near the break. Shane followed suit, then trudged through the half-powdery, half-wind-packed snow over to Jim, who was inspecting the damage from his perch on the back of his black gelding. It was a simple post-and-barbed-wire fence, but the trees had taken out two posts. They couldn't dig holes for new ones; the ground was not only snow-covered but frozen solid.

"What do you think, Jim? I don't think stretching barbed wire that far is going to keep these cows in, but we can build a section of jackleg pretty easily. There are plenty of dead lodgepoles right over there, and they're the perfect sizes."

Jim nodded. "I think that's what we'll have to do for now. We can come out here and fix it properly when the weather calms a bit. Make it tall enough to sit right over the old fence."

Shane picked up the chainsaw, which was propped on the trunk of the larger of the fallen trees, and headed out to cut poles. First he cut and notched the thicker logs for the legs, enough for seven pairs— more than enough to cover the break and six feet of the undamaged fence on either side. Becky laid out the pieces while he cut, and Jim kept his eye on the two cows, who paced the fence line like they wanted to get back to their shelter.

"Don't even think about it, ladies," Shane muttered as he cut and hauled the last of the poles in one hand and balanced the chainsaw on his shoulder with his other.

Becky nailed a set of leg logs together in an X like a large sawhorse, then another, and Shane stood the first in its place while she stood the other eight feet away. Together, they lifted one of the thinner poles off the ground and settled its ends into the cradles of the legs. He drove a nail into the pole, securing it to his set of legs, then waited while Becky did the same at her end. He nailed two more notched logs into another X, stood it halfway between the first two sets and secured it to the top pole with a nail. The first section of jackleg was now set, but even with Becky holding it, the wind buffeted it, and it rocked precariously, so he nailed the end of another pole halfway down the leg from the joint on the pasture side and attached it to each of the other two sets of supporting legs. That made it secure enough that Becky could let go and help him hold the opposite end of another rail, which he nailed above the first spaced evenly between it and the joint. They added a third a below it to complete their first section of the jackleg fence. He'd add a diagonal rail to the other side to strengthen the section when they'd finished the rest of their repair. Jim turned his horse around to inspect their handiwork.

"You do good work, kids," he said, rubbing his hand up and down his left arm. "And you're quick."

"Thanks." Shane studied him, noting also the rancher's pinched expression. "You all right?"

"Fine," Jim replied gruffly and immediately dropped his hand. "Let's just get this done so we can get home and get warm."

Shane set the bottom rail against the legs and nailed it in place, then leaned another top rail just over the end of the first and stood another pair of legs in the middle of it like he'd done with the first set. Jim seemed content to watch them work.

Then cow number five-sixteen, noticing their distraction, darted through the remaining gap in the fence at a dead run. Jim let out a wordless bellow and wheeled his horse around to give chase.

"You two get that fence done!" he called back.

"Jim! Let her go! You can't…." Shane let his voice trail off when it became clear the rancher couldn't hear him. Or isn't listening. "Dammit, Jim!"

"We have to go after him," Becky said frantically.

"We have to get enough of this fence done to keep those cows in, or they'll just do it again."

They worked quickly together, but Shane found himself glancing constantly into the woods. The stand where they'd found the two cows wasn't that far away, and it shouldn't take Jim that long to roust five-sixteen out of it again. As the minutes ticked by, dread settled in the pit of his stomach. As soon as they had enough of the fence in place to keep the cows in while they finished the rest, Shane launched into his saddle and pointed to six-oh-nine, who was looking for a way out.

"Keep her in here. I'll find Jim."

Because there were too many tracks in the snow for him to figure out which were Jim's, he headed straight to the stand of spruce. Sure enough, there was five-sixteen, but Jim was nowhere in sight. Dread exploded into terror, and he decided finding the rancher was more important than convincing a stubborn heifer to move. He circled around the area and saw no sign of Jim. He tried calling, but heard nothing in response but the mournful wind. Then he spotted the blurry outline of a black horse with its head down through a curtain of blowing snow.

As he neared the horse, he began to make out a prone figure sprawled in the snow at the gelding's feet.

"Jim!" Shane cried, dragging his buckskin mare to a halt beside them. "Jesus Christ. Jim!"

The rancher's face was beaded with sweat despite the freezing temperatures and was frighteningly pale beneath the windburn. He stared sightlessly skyward, clutching his chest and gasping for breath.

Heart attack.

Shane jumped down from his horse and knelt beside the older man.

"Cows," Jim gasped.

"Forget the goddamned cows. We have to get you

to the house. Can you—"

The agony that flashed across Jim's face cut off Shane's question and answered it. No, he couldn't stand up or walk. Taking Jim's free hand, he pulled the man's arm around his shoulder and lifted him out of the snow. The rancher was lighter than he expected, but maybe that was just the adrenaline pulsing through him. With some maneuvering, he managed to push Jim into his saddle. Since it as clear the man wouldn't be able to ride, either, Shane climbed up behind him. He clucked his tongue to his mare, hoping she'd follow and was relieved when she did—one less thing to worry about. Good horse. The cow can take care of herself for a few hours.

Becky saw them coming long before they reached the fence and raced toward them. "What happened?"

"Get to the house and tell Jessie to call 911. I'm pretty sure he's having a heart attack."

Swearing, Becky leapt into her saddle and took off at a gallop despite the slippery footing. Shane prayed she'd make it to the main house without a mishap. The Royal R had already had too many. When he rode through the break in the fence and onto smoother ground, Shane nudged the gelding into a lope. Jim groaned, and Shane tightened his hold on him.

"Hang in there, Jim."

* * *

Becky gripped Shane's hand as they neared Jim's hospital room. She hadn't heard any substantial news other than he was out of the woods and had no idea how severe a heart attack he'd had or what his prognosis was.

"He'll be fine," Shane assured her, giving her hand a squeeze. "He's too stubborn to let this beat him."

"I know. I just keep seeing…."

The image of Jim pale as the blowing snow with his face contorted by pain and leaning back against Shane, too weak to hold himself upright in the saddle, was branded into her mind's eye, as was the grim tension on Shane's face when he'd told her to hurry to the house ahead of them. And her break-neck race to tell Jessie that her husband of fifty-some years was having a heart attack. It was a miracle they'd made it without going down in the treacherously uneven snow and howling wind, and an even greater one that Jim hadn't died out there in the storm.

He's alive, she reminded herself, choking a little as the what-if questions threatened again. What if Shane and I hadn't been out there? What if Shane hadn't found him so quickly or been able to get him into the saddle? What if…?

"I know, beautiful," Shane whispered as if he'd been listening in on her thoughts.

He didn't need to, though; she'd asked those questions out loud and fretted non-stop since the ambulance had arrived to take Jim into Devyn.

He knocked on the open door to announce their arrival. Peeking her head inside, Becky spied her parents and brother and both Jessie Robinson and her granddaughter Jessie Hammond. All she could see of Jim was his blanket-enshrouded feet, as the rest of him was out of sight behind the wall of the room's bathroom.

"Is that Shane and Becky I hear?" Jim asked.

His voice sounded strong, she thought.

"Yes, sir," Shane replied.

"Well, get in here."

Becky didn't know what to expect to see when she stepped far enough into the room to get her first glimpse of Jim, but him sitting up in bed with a broad grin and healthy color in his face once again was definitely not it. Of everyone gathered, he was easily in the best mood. The others all looked beat—as physically and emotionally drained as she felt.

"I'm thrilled to see you looking so remarkably

hale, Jim," Shane commented.

"I am. All thanks to you and Becky. Doc says it was a fairly minor heart attack and that your quick actions kept the damage to a minimum."

"Glad to hear that." Shane sat in the chair young Jessie vacated and pulled Becky down onto his knee. "Next time we tell you to let us handle something, you'll listen, right? Because we're all so fond of you that we're willing to let you boss us around if it means we get to keep you with us a while longer."

"Speaking of bossing you around, did you get that damned cantankerous cow back in?"

"Yes, sir. She wasn't happy about it, but we got her and the other back with the rest of the herd and moved into the east pasture. We also got the jackleg finished."

"Excellent. If that old cow wasn't such a good mother and such a good leader, I'd have turned her into steaks and burger years ago."

"No, you wouldn't," Becky remarked, "because she's too much like you and you like her."

Jim chuckled. "I guess you're right."

"Did June and Ben make it up to the ranch before you left for town?" Andy asked.

"Yep. They and Max and Mae have everything

under control."

"Very kind of them to hold down the fort," Jessie said. "And of Luke and Ryan to pick up the slack at the Ramshorn so they could."

"It's good to have friends to help in a time of need," Shane murmured.

"Damned right," Jim replied.

Becky looked to the elder Jessie. "So, what happens now?"

"They're going to keep him tonight and maybe tomorrow night for observation to make sure he's stable and that this hasn't further damaged his kidneys. His bypass has been moved up to this Friday, and in the meantime, he's under strict orders to stay in the house and rest."

"What about after the surgery?"

"Much of the same for several weeks. Recovery will be slow, and he'll have to go easy on himself until the doc clears him to ease back into work."

"But he will be able to?"

"Oh, yes. He'll be in better shape after." Jessie gazed pointedly at her husband. "But the diet will continue so he doesn't clog that heart of his up again. Right, Jim?"

He grumbled, but it lacked his usual disdain and

his eyes sparkled. Apparently, he was in too good a mood to complain. "Yes, ma'am."

Relieved, Becky stood to embrace the rancher. "I'm so glad you're okay," she whispered. "You scared the hell out of me."

"Scared the hell out of myself, too, but luckily, I had a couple guardian angels watching over my obstinate ass."

On the verge of breaking down in tears, Becky straightened and swallowed her worry as she returned to her place on Shane's knee, taking his hand and twining her fingers with his. He wrapped her in his free arm and kissed the top of her head.

"We should head home to the ranch to relieve Uncle Ben and Aunt June," she said after a moment, suddenly wanting to escape the blatant reminder of what had happened this afternoon… and what might have happened.

"You'll do no such thing," Jim said. "You have both done enough today. Go home and rest."

"But—"

"We're on our way home," Jane interrupted. "And Chris and Belle left the hospital an hour ago after they stopped in to check on Jim. You probably passed them on the road."

Becky had completely forgotten about Chris's injury and ducked her head guiltily. "How is he?"

"He's fine. He reacted quick enough when the branch knocked the saw that he barely got clipped. The cut isn't deep and needed just eight stitches. He'll heal up in no time and can get back to work in a few days as long as he's careful and goes easy on his leg."

"I have some vacation time saved up," Shane said, "and I'd be happy to lend a hand if you need one."

"Shane, you're not going to waste your vacation time working for us," Jessie said. "You've already done so much for us."

"First of all, I wouldn't be wasting it. I enjoy ranch work. Secondly, if you won't let me do that, I'll stop by in the evenings after work to help. You and Jim and Andy and the rest of the Northstar ranchers did a lot for my dad and me, especially when I was growing up—giving us work even when you didn't need the help and inviting us to family gatherings so we didn't have to spend holidays alone—and I haven't forgotten that. Consider my assistance a small payment toward that debt."

Becky glanced sharply at Shane, stunned by the intensity and sincerity in his voice and expression. She'd never guessed how deeply his gratitude for the people of Northstar ran, and to hear it now amplified her appreciation of him. He was a good man—a better one than he knew.

"You don't owe us anything," Jim said. "You never have, and you sure as hell don't after today. If anything, we owe you."

"You stubborn old bear, just let me do this, all right? You guys do need the help right now, and I'm willing and able to do it."

"Yes, sir, Mr. McGuire," Jim replied with a mock salute. Then he pointed a finger at Shane. "On one condition."

Shane set his jaw and waited.

"You take my sweet Becky girl home tonight and keep her from worrying about me because I know she will, but I'm fine, and she's earned a night of relaxation. So have you. Then, if you want, you can both help Andy and Max separate cows tomorrow."

"You've got a deal."

Becky opened her mouth to object, but he dragged her head down to claim it, no doubt with the intent to silence her. She submitted, too tired to fight it and wanting it too much to ignore it. Jessie Hammond and James let out whistles, and she glared at them the moment Shane relinquished her mouth.

When she met her parents' curious gazes, heat climbed her neck and cheeks. They glanced at each other, and Jane's lips flattened in amused defeat at her husband's smug I told you so grin.

Becky stood to hug everyone in the room. When she arrived last at her mother, Jane laughed.

"Looks like I might have been wrong to think you getting back together with Shane was a bad idea," she murmured. "Go home and let him pamper you. We'll see you tomorrow."

Becky started to turn away but her mother tugged on her hand.

"After lunch," Jane said with a knowing wink.

Blushing again, Becky snatched Shane's hand and dragged him out of the room. Was she really that transparent?

"Don't even think about going back to the ranch!" Jane called. "I'll call my brother and tell him that he and June are to send you packing. I know they'll agree with me."

Becky popped her head back into the room just long enough to stick her tongue out at her mother.

"Love you, babe!" Jane remarked, grinning.

"Guess that's out," Shane said as they walked down the hall.

"Yeah. Dammit."

"You have your laundry to finish, anyhow."

"Yes, I do, and I hope you don't plan on sleeping much tonight."

It was Shane's turn to blush, and she kissed his cheek.

"You really have that much energy left after everything today? Because I sure as hell don't."

"Okay, maybe I'm shooting for the moon, but you're not getting out of it."

"Who says I want to?"

"Glad we're on the same page."

They were halfway down the hall when young Jessie called after them. They stopped and waited for her to catch up.

"Thank you," she said. "For saving my grandpa's life. I know the doctor said it was a minor heart attack, but if he hadn't gotten treatment so soon, the damage could've been a lot worse. And even if the heart attack didn't kill him, if you hadn't found him, he could've frozen to death."

"Jess," Becky said, "please don't thank us. He's family, and you always do whatever you can to keep family safe. Don't you, Shane?"

"Yep."

"Yeah." Jessie smiled with an odd gleam in her hazel eyes—her mother's eyes. Jim's eyes. "I thought you'd say that."

She hugged them both, asked them to drive safely, and headed back to Jim's room. They watched her vanish inside, then turned away.

"What was that all about?" Shane wondered, glancing back over his shoulder.

"No idea."

Becky asked him to drive home. Between her worry over Jim and the hours spent out in the frigid wind, she didn't trust her dwindling energy to hold long enough to get them home safely. She melted into the passenger seat of her truck and shivered. She hadn't yet had a chance to fully warm up.

"A soak in the hot springs sounds lovely," she mumbled, "but I think I'm going to have to settle for curling up in front of the fire with a hot man to warm me up."

"Should I be insulted or complimented?" Shane asked as he pulled out of the hospital parking lot and drove toward the highway.

"Huh?"

"Well, you said you'd have to settle for me, but then you called me hot, which relegates me to the realm of sex objects rather than the category of husband material. Back in the day, I might have been okay with that. Not so much anymore."

She blinked at him, confused. The day's events had turned her brain into a muddled mess, and though his words reached her, their meaning was mostly lost on her. Did he mean he wanted to be husband material? Was he thinking that far ahead? She shook her head, too tired to work through the tangled mess of questions springing up. "I meant I'm going to have to settle for the fire over the hot springs."

"Good because I don't want you to ever just settle for me. Settling means it isn't one-hundred-percent right and that there might be something or someone better for you out there."

"Shane?"

"Hmm?"

"Shuddup."

He glanced at her, and though he chuckled, his eyes were distant.

"I'm not settling for you, Shane, and I never have." She rested her hand on his thigh. "I'm glad you were with me today."

"Me, too." He offered her a tender smile that told her she was cherished and warmed her from the inside.

"Why don't you take a nap on the ride home?"

"Yep."

This wasn't the worst day of her life—the day she and Luke had found Carol Landers's body and the one when JP had nearly killed Luke up at Sawtooth claimed the top two spots on that list—but it came close. With body and mind in agreement that she'd had enough, she tipped her head back against the head rest and let her eyes slide closed. In her last moment of awareness, Shane again took her hand, and that simple connection and the security that came with it eased her into blissful sleep.

Fifteen

FAR TOO SOON, Shane roused her. Unwilling to open her eyes, she muttered, "We can't be home already."

"We can be and we are. Come on inside, and I'll make dinner while you get back to your laundry."

"Dinner?" She opened one eye. Sure enough, they were parked in front of his cabin.

"Yes, dinner. It's six o'clock, and neither of us has eaten anything since breakfast."

It was only six? It felt so much later, and she started to say she wasn't hungry, except that she was famished. "All right. Just lemme peel myself outa this seat."

Before she knew it, Shane was out of the truck and leaning in her open door. With one arm behind her shoulders and the other beneath her knees, he lifted her out of the truck and bumped the door closed with his hip.

"What the—"

"It's cold out, and I didn't feel like waiting."

"How do you have the energy left to carry me?"

"I don't. I'm faking it."

He carried her up the steps to the porch, and she watched his face for any sign of strain but found only the glimmer of a teasing smile. Maybe the exhaustion was making her loopy, but he looked damned sexy in the glow of the porch light with stubble dusting his jaw and his breath coming out in silvery clouds.

Whatever doubts she still had about Shane—if there were any left at all—were tellingly silent. He'd risked his own safety to get Jim to the house, busted ass to repair the fence after, and been by her side through it all to hold her together as fear threatened to overwhelm her. The day's events had stripped away the excuses while the weariness had given her the single-minded focus to dismiss every reason why making love with him tonight might not be such a good idea and left the only thought that mattered at the moment.

I want this. Her lips twitched. "You'd better not fake it later."

"We should probably reschedule, Becky. It's been a hell of a long day, and we're both—"

She cut off his objection with a fierce kiss, curling one arm around his neck with a firm demand to erase any doubt from his mind about what she wanted. When she buried her other hand in his hair and angled her body closer to his, she shifted their balance, and he twisted his body as he stumbled with a captivating agility, and instead of taking a header off the steps, he instead crashed back against the door. The tightening of muscle beneath her ignited a primal instinct, and she tugged on his lip with her teeth, begging him for more. After only a moment of hesitation, he gave in with a passion that left her lightheaded. He set her on her feet, and she rested the length of her body against his, sliding her hands under his coat in search of warmth as he fumbled with the keys and the lock.

The door swung abruptly open, and it was only Shane's quick reaction that kept them from tumbling through it to the floor. He hoisted Becky off the floor again, and she wrapped her legs around his waist, clinging on for the ride as he kicked the door closed.

The cabin was a little chilly because he kept the thermostat on the furnace low, using the woodstove as the primary source of heat. Becky didn't care. She'd be plenty warm soon enough. She dropped her feet to the floor again and unzipped his coat, then peeled it over his shoulders and down his arms. Her coat and their boots followed immediately after, and she grabbed the front of his shirt to drag him to the stairs up to his bedroom in the loft.

"They're in the nightstand drawer," she said, shocked by the sultry huskiness in her voice.

"What?"

"The condoms. I snuck up here this morning and put them in the nightstand drawer."

"Excellent. No wasting time looking for them."

Becky leaned back, surprised. "You're not going to try to talk me out of this?"

"No, I'm not. You've always known what you wanted, and if I'd just trusted that, I might've—"

"Don't say it. Not now. Not tonight." She jerked his layered shirts over his head and tossed them aside, then skimmed her hands over his bare skin and touched her lips to his phoenix tattoo. "Not ever again."

He stripped off her sweater and the tank top under it and let them fall to the floor on top of his. When he kissed the curve of her neck, she shivered. "Never again," he whispered, "because I trust it now."

"Promise me, Shane."

"With every breath and every beat of my heart." He took her face in his hands, caressing her cheek with his thumb, and held her gaze, then kissed her gently. "I promise I will trust you to know what's right for us."

"Good. Because I need to be close to you, and snuggling just isn't going to cut it tonight."

He picked her up again and carried her around the bed to settle her gently down before unbuckling her belt and sliding her jeans and Hot Chillys down her legs and off. The calloused roughness of his hands sent ripples of goose bumps across her skin as he slid them sensually around her calves, up her thighs, and over her hips. He climbed onto the bed and trailed kisses from her navel to the hollow of her throat, and anticipation burned through her.

She wanted to roll him onto his back and run her hands over every inch of bare skin, but at the same time, she needed exactly what he was giving her right now, so she settled for smoothing her hands down his chest and stomach until she reached his belt, turned on by the sinewy planes and angles of his body beneath skin that was contrastingly soft. She squirmed to shove his pants down, and he paused in his caressing to shimmy out of them.

Needing to be pampered, she let him stroke her into relaxation, but eventually, her hunger for more became insatiable. With fevered intent, she dragged her fingertips down Shane's body and back up again before digging them into the meat of his back. Curling up, she bit down on his neck, satisfied when he gasped in surprise.

"I guess this means play time is over," he asked with laughter and desire making his voice hoarse.

"Yes. It is."

Patient, tender caresses became urgent, frenzied as their control slipped and spiraled into oblivion. The rest of their undergarments were discarded, but Shane wasn't done torturing her yet. He cupped her naked breasts in his hands, massaging them and teasing her nipples before flicking his tongue over them. She inhaled sharply. By the time he lowered his hips and pressed his arousal between her legs, she was more than ready. She rocked her hips toward him and a pleading whimper escaped her.

"Not quite yet," he murmured, lowering himself

to nibble from her jaw to her shoulder and back again. He claimed her mouth in a hard, demanding kiss, then sat back on his haunches and opened the drawer of the nightstand.

Becky darted her hand into the drawer before he could, wanting to sheath him herself. As she slid the condom down the length of him, he tipped his head back with his jaw clenched and let out a low-throated groan that fanned her already ravenous desire into aching need.

"Shane," she uttered.

She wanted to tell him she loved him, that she was sorry for every tear they'd cried and every wasted second they could have been together. She wanted to tell him to hurry up already, that no one else had ever made her feel so weak and so powerful at the same time. She wanted to tell him all that and a million other things, but the words were lost in the pounding pulse of carnal physicality.

When he stretched out above her again, the urgency in the hands that raced over her body with irresistible intensity dragged a sharp cry from her. She couldn't remember the last time she'd felt like this—she had never been so physically motivated. Not even their first time together. When she tilted her hips again, it was pure instinct that drove her, a primal need to mate. At last, Shane obeyed, driving deep into her, and she gasped.

"You all right?" he asked.

She could only nod and abandon herself to the smooth, rolling pace he set. She gripped his hips with her thighs and hooked her arms under his with her hands splayed over his shoulder blades, enjoying the movement of flexing muscle as much as the feel of him buried inside her and the incredible sense of connectedness. They raced together toward climax, and she expected him to back off and prolong it, surprised and gratified when he didn't. Their breaths became pants for oxygen mingled with the groans and whimpers of pleasure. The orgasm exploded through her with the force and brilliance of New Years fireworks, trembling through her body long after the peak subsided.

Still joined with her, Shane braced himself on his forearms with his forehead resting on her shoulder as he fought to catch his breath. After a moment, he lifted his head and gazed at her with the most exquisite love shining in his eyes. "You are the most incredible and beautiful woman," he whispered. "I love you."

She traced every treasured feature of his face with her eyes, then laid her hand lightly against his cheek before arching up to kiss him. "I love you, too."

Becky's nose tingled, and she sneezed. It was such an odd thing to happen that she started laughing. And couldn't stop.

Shane regarded her with unveiled amusement. "A little nasal orgasm to finish you off, huh?" With a reverent kiss while she continued to laugh, he pulled away. "I hope you're not coming down with that cold your brother's had."

"I hope not, too."

He started to climb off the bed, but she snagged his hand and jerked him back down beside her.

"Where ya goin', hot stuff?" she asked.

"Thought I might get a fire started since it's a little chilly in here. And I don't know about you, but I'm hungry."

"All that can wait."

"I'm under orders to pamper you."

"And you are."

Because it was in fact a bit cool in the cabin now that the heat of their lovemaking was subsiding and because she wasn't willing to let him go start a fire, she wriggled under the blankets and snuggled up to him with her arm and leg draped over him. He tucked his arms around her and sighed contentedly. With the fervor of passion fading, she took the time to more fully appreciate the lines of his body, most particularly those of his phoenix tattoo.

Letting her fingers dance over the elegant curves and angles of it, she murmured, "Looks like your hope was well placed."

He captured her hand and pressed her fingertips to his lips. "It seems it was."

"I'm glad you held onto it."

"I love you too much to ever let it go."

His stomach growled, and they laughed.

"All right, all right."

The mundaneness of the evening did nothing to lessen that sense of unity that had blossomed at the height of their passion and in fact made her feel even closer to him. She helped him with dinner, he helped her with her laundry, and afterwards, they sat on the couch together, and she watched him sketch a pair of sandhill cranes in the midst of their courtship dance with wings spread and long, graceful necks arched toward each other. His pencil frolicked across the page of the sketchbook, and as the details emerged, she could hear the birds' trumpeted calls.

She edged closer to him, resting her head on her shoulder, and continued to watch him work. He was entirely unbothered by her presence, and once or twice, he paused to give her a kiss or a touch to let her know he wasn't ignoring her. After their tumultuous day, she needed this quiet closeness as much as she had needed the sexual release to clear her head.

"Why sandhills?" she inquired.

"They mate for life."

The way he said it—distracted with his brows knitted in concentration—made her wonder if he'd thought before he'd answered or if the artistic bridge between his subconscious and his voice had allowed the words to bypass his mental filter. What did it mean? Perhaps more importantly, what did she *want* it to mean? She pushed the question away because trying to answer it would only bring a thousand others she had neither the desire nor the energy to work through tonight. Best to just enjoy the moment and accept that whatever would be would be.

The ease with which she was able to do exactly that was an answer in itself.

I want this to be the rest of my life.

* * *

Becky woke to full, bright morning, the soothing sensations stirred by Shane's hand as he idly rubbed her back, and a tingly, smug satisfaction. She was more aware of her body—of her slow, deep heartbeat, of the length of bone and muscle, of every inch of her skin, and of every thrum of sensation—than she had been in years. Her body felt so *alive*. For several minutes, she lay beside him on her belly with her head pillowed on her arms, enjoying his entrancing ministrations and in no hurry to leave the warmth of his bed. Because he seemed distracted, she turned her head toward him thinking he might be sketching again. He wasn't. Instead, he was sitting up, alternating between watching her and looking out the window behind the bed. He smiled when their gazes met.

"Good morning, beautiful."

"G'morning," she replied. "Find me fascinating?"

"Immensely."

"Did you sleep all right?"

"When you *let* me sleep," he teased, "I slept marvelously. How about you?"

"Well enough that I feel a little guilty. After yesterday, I shouldn't be able to."

"After yesterday, I'm surprised you were as energetic as you were last night. I'm also surprised that you're awake already."

Becky buried her face in her pillow to hide her grin and the blush that warmed her face and groaned.

"Sorry," she muttered.

"For what? I'm not complaining. A little shocked is all because we'd agreed to take things slow." He kissed her shoulder and chuckled. "There was nothing slow about last night."

She groaned. "So I've been a bit sexually frustrated… for nine years."

Shane peered at her with brows lifted. "Nine years, huh?"

"Yeah. Let's just say I'd forgotten how good sex can—and should—be. That one night with you was easily the best sex I've ever had, but last night…. Well, last night raised my expectations even higher." She propped herself up on her elbow with her fist against her cheek. "I used to think it was the birth control pills that muted my sex drive when I was with Justin. Now I think it was him."

They lapsed into silence, and Becky appreciated that Shane didn't play the macho card like Justin would have had she paid him that kind of compliment. She didn't like comparing the two men, and she hoped Shane didn't compare himself to her ex. They were so different, and Shane was easily the better match for her. Passively, she thought about the dread of pregnancy that had accompanied her liaisons with Justin even though they were always careful. That dread was conspicuously absent this morning. The difference was the man and how she felt about him. Despite Shane's past history, she was committed to him.

"What would you do if I were to get pregnant?" she asked lightly.

"Start looking for a house to buy or property to build on. I should probably do that anyhow."

"May I ask you something else?"

"Of course."

"After what happened with Ryan and losing Angel, do you still want kids?"

"I might not deserve them, and I have no idea if I'd be a good father or not," he said slowly, "but, yes, I do. More now than before, but with the right woman. With you. I can't imagine anyone else as the mother of my children."

Becky rolled onto her side, facing him, and studied him with narrowed eyes while she let his words sink in. His expression was one of complete vulnerability, and she didn't doubt that he meant every word. That persistent maternal nudge she frequently felt when she spent time with Luke and Ryan's daughter returned a thousand times stronger.

"It doesn't freak you out that I've thought about

it, does it?" he asked when she hadn't said anything after half a minute. "Because as I recall, you've always wanted two kids. Or has life changed your mind?"

"It doesn't freak me out at all." She leaned forward to kiss him, taking her time to enjoy the taste of him and the way he submitted to her with that endearing vulnerability leaving him unsure of himself. Knowing that he'd given her the power to destroy him if she wanted to and trusted her not to was an incredible thing, and it wove another thread into the bond between them, further strengthening it. "It makes me love you more. And no, life hasn't changed my mind. I still want those two kids." Echoing his statement, she added, "Maybe even more now than I wanted them before."

Unlike their frantic couplings last night, this time when they made love, they drew it out, allowing themselves more than an hour to indulge each other in every sensation and emotion that came with. And after, they made breakfast together and lingered over it curled up on the couch while they enjoyed the stunning, clear-skied morning. Finally, around noon, Shane went out to start his truck, and they started getting ready to head to work on the Royal R, taking their time doing that, too.

"My mother *did* tell me not to show up to work until after lunch," Becky mused.

"So she did. I'd ask if you're up for one more round before we head out, but I'm afraid neither of us would be able to stay in our saddles. I don't know about you, but my body is on the verge of resembling Jell-O."

"Oh, yeah." She laughed. "I am so very tempted, but as it is, I'm already going to have a hard enough time not blushing every time I look at you today because I'm sure last night and this morning will be written all over my face for everyone to see."

"You *do* have a wonderfully honest face. I've always loved that about you."

She smiled shyly. "Thanks."

"You ready?"

"As I'll ever be."

After checking to make sure everything in the cabin was turned off, they hauled her laundry out to his truck. The day, though stunningly clear, was bitterly cold. So cold that what little moisture remained from Friday night's snow had frozen, making the very air glitter in the sharp sunlight. Becky figured the temperature was at least fifteen degrees below zero. Normally, she didn't care about working in the brutal cold and enjoyed the razor-edged beauty of it—she had the gear to keep her nice and toasty—but today was a different story, and she was not looking forward to freezing her backside off when she could be snuggled up with Shane in either his cabin or hers.

She was in no hurry to get to the ranch for another reason, and she hesitated to acknowledge it because she didn't want worry to spoil her good mood. It was impossible to ignore it, and as soon as Shane turned onto the ranch road, questions about how Jim was doing and how Jessie was handling everything swamped her. She knew well enough both the agony of a friend's death and the paralyzing terror of nearly losing someone she loved but doubted she could fully comprehend what Jessie must be going through right now. She and Jim had been married over half a century. They were partners and best friends and lovers. They had stood by each other through all the joys and sorrows of life and had survived several heartbreaking miscarriages and the tragic death of their only daughter, Erica. They truly were two halves of one whole.

Unbidden, her gaze sought Shane's familiar and reassuring visage. They'd gotten back together only recently, but it would gut her if anything happened to him.

"I love you," she said, abruptly overcome by the need to make sure he knew it.

"I love you, too." He glanced at her. "What's on your mind? Or do I even need to ask?"

"You don't. I was just thinking about how Jessie's doing with all this."

"I'm sure she's doing the best she can, just like everyone else, and holding on to the positive. She's tough."

"Yes, she is."

"I know it's probably impossible, but try not to worry because worrying doesn't solve anything. It just makes you miserable."

"That's for damned sure."

"Besides, there's nothing more that we can do for Jim other than what we're here to do—make sure the ranch keeps running smoothly so they can both slide right back into their routines when the time comes."

"Right you are, oh wise one."

"I thought Luke was the wise one of our trio—quartet now."

"He is, but you have your moments."

"Why, thank ya, ma'am," he drawled, making a show of tipping his imaginary cowboy hat.

Despite herself, she smiled. "I know I've said it

already, but I missed you all those years we were apart. And with everything going on right now, I'm doubly glad I have you back."

"That makes two of us."

"Technically, it makes four of us because Luke and Ryan both seem to be pretty happy about it, too. Five if you count your dad… six with my brother, seven with my dad, nine with Jim and Jessie, and maybe even ten with my mom. Her comment at the hospital yesterday makes me think she's on board with this, too."

Shane chuckled. "It's nice to know we have so much support."

"Isn't it?"

Without Jessie at the ranch to make lunch for the guests—of which there were eight even this late in January and well into the off season—that duty fell to Jane, and sure enough, when the main house came into view, Becky spotted her mother's truck parked beside the kitchen door. Glancing at her watch, she saw that it wasn't quite as late as she'd thought; they'd arrived right in the middle of lunchtime, which meant everyone else should be at the main house as well.

Shane parked in front of the house. Hand in hand, they walked inside and into the dining area where everyone but Becky's mother—who was in the kitchen—was gathered around the table. As one, the employees of the Royal R Ranch turned toward them, and Becky cursed the blush that stained her face. When Max let out a whistle, she hid her betraying face against Shane's shoulder.

"Look at you two, showing up to the party when the day's half done," Chris teased.

Lifting her head, she grinned sheepishly. "Yep. It's written all over my face."

"Like a naughty teenager."

Shane cleared his throat. "I know the Royal R promises a part-of-the-family experience, but this isn't exactly appropriate mealtime conversation."

"Thank you, Shane," Andy said. Though he was clearly as amused as everyone else about their predicament, he didn't appear to be as amused that Chris and Max had brought it up at the table.

Both cowhands ducked their heads, hiding behind their coffee mugs.

"You two *are* just in time, however," Becky's father continued. "We just finished clearing the rest of those trees before lunch, so we're ready to move cows as soon as we're done eating. The fence repair looks great, by the way."

"Thank you," Shane replied.

"Have a seat and grab some lunch. Jane made extra in case you showed up early."

"I appreciate that, but we had a late breakfast."

Becky thought she heard Chris mutter *I'm sure you did*, so she reached over and smacked the back of his head, defiantly holding his gaze when he glared at her, daring him to retaliate.

"I'll go saddle horses for Becky and me while she gets her laundry put in her cabin," Shane said. He gave her a quick kiss on the cheek and headed back outside.

Their laundry joke popped into her head and her face warmed again, so she retreated to the kitchen where her mother was arranging a selection of cookies on a tray for the guests' dessert.

"Hi, sweetheart," Jane greeted. "Did you have a restful evening with Shane? And did you get your laundry done or do you need to use our machines?"

I will never be able to think of laundry the same way again. She wasn't hungry, but she snagged a cookie. "Yes, I got it done, and yes, I had a very enjoyable evening with Shane."

"Other than looking rather embarrassed…" Jane paused to give her daughter a once-over appraisal. "…you look happy and a lot better than you did when you left the hospital yesterday, so I find myself again admitting that Shane is good for you. No, don't worry. I'm not going to tease you. From what I heard a moment ago, I think you've already been teased enough."

Becky smiled, catching sight of the man in question out the kitchen window. She watched him walk all the way to the corrals before she asked about Jim.

"He's doing very well. They're going to let him come home this afternoon."

"Thank God," Becky breathed. "Anything more about whether or not they're going to have to sell the ranch?"

"No, but little Jessie has been pretty adamant about not wanting it. They were talking about it with her when we left, but that girl's as strong-willed as anyone I know."

"What will we do if they sell?"

Jane shrugged. "Whatever we have to. If it comes down to it, your father's cousin in Wyoming said he'd always have jobs for us."

"You mean the cousin who took Dad in after his parents died and made him feel so unwelcome that he left as soon as he was legally able to do so?"

"That was a long time ago, and maybe they're not exactly in close contact, but they've made amends.

Besides, it won't come to that."

"I hope not because I don't want to leave again now that I'm back home where I belong."

Jane embraced her. "You won't have to. With your animal sciences degree and your AI certification, you could get a job on any ranch you wanted. Plus, Shane has a great job with the Forest Service, and I know he'll do everything he can to make sure you don't have to leave again."

Becky leaned back, eying her mother. "Do you believe he's thinking that far ahead about us?"

"Isn't he?"

Jane's tone was light without a trace of skepticism. She wasn't questioning Shane's intentions but rather her daughter's grasp of them. Becky thought back to his response when she'd asked him what he'd do if they found themselves in the same situation he and Ryan had. *Start looking for a house to buy or property to build on.* Then he'd added that he should do that anyhow.

"I believe he is," she said. "Yes."

"I know I've had my misgivings about him after everything he's done, but your father is right. He's proven his worth beyond doubt in these last few months. More than that, he's in love with you." Jane glanced out the window then back at her daughter. "So you'd better get out there and head off trouble before it starts."

Becky stared blankly at her. "Huh?"

"I'm pretty sure that's Justin's truck I see coming down the road."

"No, it can't…." She stepped up to the sink and peered out the window. At first, she didn't believe her eyes, but as the black truck rolled closer, the silver emblem on the doors became undeniably recognizable as the Teton South Ranch's brand. Justin must've spotted Shane because he detoured to the corrals. "Son of a bitch!"

She raced outside toward the barn and corrals, stumbling once or twice in the choppy snow of the yard in her haste, and somehow made it to Justin's truck just as he stepped out of it.

"What the hell are you doing here?" she demanded.

"Well, hello to you, too, Becks. You know why I'm here."

"No, I really don't. I thought I made myself very clear that I had no intention of getting back together with you."

"You did, but you're making a mistake, and I'm here to prove it."

"The only mistake I made was not leaving sooner. Go home, Justin. You aren't welcome here."

"I believe that's up to Jim and Jessie to decide, and since I'm a paying guest, I—"

"They're at the hospital because Jim had a heart attack yesterday, so my parents are in charge of the ranch for the time being, which means it's up to them who is and who is *not* welcome here, and I guarantee that you fall into the second category."

"Becks, come on."

"No."

Hearing the crunch of snow beneath boots, Becky glanced away. Shane trudged over, standing close beside her but not possessively close—more protective, ready to assist her should she need it. Undoubtedly, he'd heard the anger in her voice even if he hadn't caught the exact gist of the conversation.

"Everything all right over here?" he asked in a surprisingly pleasant voice.

"We're fine. Thanks," Justin replied.

"Doesn't sound like it." Shane leaned back to inspect the design on the truck's door. "You must be Justin."

"Yes, I am. If you wouldn't mind, I'd like to continue my conversation with Becky."

"Actually, I *do* mind, but before this goes any further, you might want to ask who *I* am."

Shane's tone remained admirably level and non-threatening, but his eyes had hardened and he stepped closer to Becky. She wondered what he was playing at inviting Justin to finish the introduction, and she tensed. This couldn't end well. She trusted Shane to keep his head, but she wouldn't put it past Justin to let his arrogance and pride get the best of him and prayed she'd be able to keep a lid on the simmering tension.

Justin glanced over Shane with an unveiled impatience and the thorough perusal of a man sizing up his competition. Standing as they were within a dozen steps of each other gave Becky her first true comparison, and the differences were stark but not physical. Justin was taller by a couple inches, and Shane had a slightly heavier frame, but they otherwise had very similar builds. The difference was in how they carried themselves. While Justin's features and posture spoke of impatience, Shane was the picture of composure. Except his eyes, Becky noted. His usually warm brown eyes were alert and unfriendly.

At last, Justin asked, "All right. Who are you?"

"Shane McGuire."

Becky's heart pounded as she waited for Justin to

put the name to what she'd told him about the man attached to it. At first, he regarded Shane with a questioning frown. Then comprehension widened his eyes, and he jerked his head toward Becky.

"Shane? *That* Shane? The guy you dated in high school who—"

"Yes," Becky interrupted. She waited to the count of five. "And the one I'm dating now."

"You've got to be kidding me!"

"No, I'm not. Get out of here, Justin. Go home to Wyoming." She hooked Shane's finger with hers, and he folded his hand around hers. "There's nothing for you here."

"I cannot believe you're getting back together with the asshole who broke your—"

"She asked you to leave," Shane said quietly.

"What are you going to do if I don't?"

Shane didn't reply.

Justin's brows dipped briefly in confusion and irritation. Then he jumped into his truck. Before he slammed the door, he snapped, "This isn't over, jackass."

He gunned the engine, spraying snow everywhere as he spun away. Becky leaned down to brush several clumps from her legs and stared after him for a while before turning to Shane. She waited for him to mutter something sarcastic like *fantastic* or *wasn't that fun* or comment on her questionable taste in men, but he stood silently as her ex drove away, his gaze trained on the black truck. It wasn't until after Justin disappeared beyond the tree line that he looked back at Becky. His lips twitched into a sad smile.

"Looks like he might have noticed the beauty in you after all."

Sixteen

IT WAS ONLY A QUARTER to five when Shane turned off the highway onto the Northstar Mountains Scenic Byway, but he found himself fending off yawns and fond thoughts of his bed. After four days of ranch work on top of his duties for the Forest Service, he was wiped, and today's dull meetings about the management of upcoming timber sales had tested him. More than once, he'd almost dozed off. He'd decided to take tomorrow off from his regular job and give himself a few hours to recuperate. Besides, Jim's surgery was tomorrow, and he wanted to be available to Becky because she would undoubtedly fret about him.

He didn't mind the work, especially not helping out on the ranch because it meant he got to spend more time with Becky than he usually did during the week, and it wasn't actually the work that was wearing him down. Justin was stubbornly refusing to leave. It wasn't competitiveness that grated on Shane; on the contrary, if Becky decided she'd rather go back to Justin than stay with him, he'd step aside. It was the man's arrogance and the way Justin talked to Becky ground down his patience. He now fully understood what she'd meant when she'd said Justin didn't notice anyone but himself. She may as well have spoken to him in German or Italian or any other language he didn't understand because that's all he heard when she spoke—indecipherable sounds that resembled words but held no meaning for him.

Shane's grip had tightened on the steering wheel, so he flexed his fingers. What was it going to take to get through Justin's thick skull and convince him that his cause was lost? Short of a knock-down-drag-out brawl, he had no idea.

He set the question aside and frowned when he turned onto Elkhorn Road toward his cabin. The lights were on inside. As he drove closer, he spotted Becky's truck parked around to the side, and his frown deepened. The plan was for him to stop at his cabin just long enough to pick up a check for rent and take it to Pat and Aeli before he headed to the ranch to help Andy and Max prepare stalls in the barn in anticipation of the rapidly approaching calving season while Becky and her mother cooked and served dinner and entertained the ranch's seven remaining guests. So what was she doing here?

She greeted him at the door with an enthusiastic kiss that chased away his weariness. He didn't have to ask the question because she answered it before he could.

"I'm hiding from Justin."

"One, why are you hiding from him? And two, how much longer do you think it'll be before he notices that your truck is frequently parked here and starts pounding on my door looking for you?"

"In case you haven't noticed, he's not exactly observant, and in answer to your first question, I'm hiding because he's been up at the ranch half the damned day. Mom sent me down to pick up the mail to give me an escape. And I think she hoped he'd finally get the message that I was ignoring him because I didn't want to talk to him and leave."

Shane bristled at the news. "What was he doing there for half the day? Why didn't someone—anyone—make him leave?"

"We were all too busy."

"I thought today was supposed to be a slow day. That's why I didn't take off work to help."

"It *was* supposed to be a slow day, but we found out this morning that we have a party of twenty-eight coming in on Tuesday and staying through Sunday. It was a madhouse. Mom, Mae, Belle, and I have been running around all day cleaning and stocking the cabins."

"Twenty-eight? Are you kidding?"

"Nope. They're overflow from the Ramshorn—unexpected guests for a wedding they're hosting on Saturday."

"That's a lot of unexpected wedding guests. And this isn't exactly a great time for it."

Becky shrugged. "It's a terrible time for it, but there's nowhere else in Northstar for them to stay and it's good money for the ranch, which means good money for us hands during the slowest part of the year."

"Guess that means I should probably use some more of my vacation time, regardless of what Jessie says about me wasting it working on the ranch. I don't understand why Justin was there half the day. What was he doing all that time?"

"For once, he made himself useful by entertaining the guests with an impromptu competitive roping demonstration. They were impressed by his skill but not so much by his suggestion that they check out the Teton South if they wanted to visit a top-notch guest ranch. The one couple who's stayed here before said they've been to his ranch and prefer the Royal R."

"I'll bet that pissed him off."

"Not as much as me laughing about it." Becky flopped on the couch and sighed. "Why is he so convinced that he'll be able to change my mind? I was with him for six years. He *knows* how stubborn I am once I set my mind on something."

"Yes, you can be stubborn, but you're also too nice to people who don't deserve it." He sat on the couch beside her and caressed her cheek before lightly kissing her lips. "And like I've said before, you're an unforgettable woman."

"You've never said I was unforgettable."

"Maybe not in those words, but haven't I told you how beautiful you are, inside and out?"

"Yes, but that's not the same thing."

"Yes, it is."

"Maybe to you, but not to Justin."

"Why do you think he's here?"

"He's here because he can't stand to watch one of his possessions slip away."

Shane shook his head. "No. If that were the case, he would have let you go because possessions are easily replaced. He may not even realize it, but somewhere in that self-obsessed mind of his, he knows your value and he knows you're irreplaceable."

Her scowl shifted into curiosity. "You're being awfully generous to him."

"Would you prefer I hunt him down right now and kick his ass? That offer's still open."

"No, I don't want you to do that."

"All right, then." Standing again required more effort than usual, but he managed even as he wished they could stay right here and enjoy some quiet time. "I need to take a check to Pat and Aelissm. Shall I meet you at the ranch in twenty-five?"

"Why don't I come with you? Then I'll come home with you after work tonight so we can… release a little tension."

"I can honestly say that I may not have the energy for that tonight."

"Fine. Then I'll just have to stay the night again so we can start tomorrow off on a high note."

He held out his hands and hauled her to her feet. "As you wish, beautiful."

Shane wrote out a check, locked his cabin, and climbed in behind the wheel of his truck while Becky slipped into the passenger seat. When they stepped inside the restaurant of the Bedspread Inn, the place was dead. Only one table by the front windows and two stools at the bar were occupied. As they walked to the back of the restaurant, they found Aelissm chatting with the occupants of the barstools—John Hammond and Old Matt Carlyle in for their traditional Friday after-work beers. She greeted them with an apology to Becky for renting a room to Justin.

"If I'd been here when he came in, I would've told him there weren't any vacancies," she said. "But neither Pat nor I worked that day."

"You wouldn't happen to know how long he's planning to stay, would you?" Shane asked.

"He's reserved the room for eight or nine more days."

"Damn," Becky muttered.

"Anyhow, here's rent. We'll see you later, Aeli."

"Yep. Hey, Shane?"

"Yeah?"

"Try to get some rest soon because you look like crap."

"Thanks, Aeli."

Shane smiled as he and Becky walked away. It was good to have regained Aelissm's respect, and he'd take any teasing she chose to lavish on him because her brand of affection was one more piece of his life he'd lost that had been put back in place, and he'd missed it, too, just as he'd missed all the rest. Becky had said that he was returning to his old self, the one he'd been before Mike's and Carol's murders had sundered their world, and more and more each day, he felt it. That, along with the promise of spending the night with Becky in his arms, boosted his energy levels.

His good mood was short-lived, obliterated when Justin walked through the door into the restaurant.

"Give me a goddamned break," Becky muttered. When her ex approached them, she said, "What now, Justin?"

"I'm just here for dinner, but since you're here, too, will you talk to me now?"

"No. We have to get back to work. And besides, I've already said all I'm going to say... repeatedly. Come on, Shane. Let's get out of here."

As they started to walk away with their hands knitted tightly together, he called after her.

"I can offer you a ranch, Becks. What can *he* offer you?"

Shane cringed as Becky turned back toward Justin. He had to give the guy credit for knowing the most efficient way to poke everyone's buttons.

"He doesn't have to *offer* me anything," she snapped. "I'm perfectly capable of taking care of myself."

"Sure… because I got you the job on my family's ranch, which has opened the door for you." Justin beckoned her, holding out his hand as if he actually expected her to take it. "That job is waiting for you, and so am I. And it sounds like you're going to be needing both before long."

"What are you talking about?"

"I've heard the rumors. The Robinsons are going to sell. With Jim's health and no one to take over the ranch, they'll have to, and when they do, you'll lose your job *and* your home."

"I'm not going to lose anything."

Her voice quivered, and fury lanced through Shane. To this point, she'd been optimistic, but the uncertainty in her voice rang loudly, and if the smug twitch of his lips was any indication, Justin was counting on it. Shane clamped his jaw shut to maintain his silence. What he wanted to say wouldn't do any of them any good.

"Come on, Becks. Think about it," Justin continued. "Jim's going in for risky surgery tomorrow. What if he dies? Jessie won't have any choice but to sell."

Becky let out a small whimper, and Shane's composure snapped. He took a step toward Justin, fighting with everything in him to contain his temper. Right at that moment, he wanted nothing more than to smash that arrogant smirk right off Justin's chiseled face. "Way to be a total dick, Sutherland. She's already worried enough about Jim's surgery, and here you are reminding her of everything that could go wrong tomorrow and after. No wonder she left you."

"I'm just looking out for her. She needs to think about these things and be realistic."

"No, you're not looking out for her. Right now, she needs reassurance and kindness and compassion. Are you giving her that? No, you aren't. You're trying to use her fears to manipulate her into—"

Shane bit off the rest of his accusations and stalked away, aware that he had about two seconds until he did something they'd all regret. He clenched his hands into fists and gritted his teeth to keep the explosive rage contained. *Don't do it. The last thing Becky needs right now is you getting into a damned fistfight with her ex that won't solve anything.*

Becky followed him, curling her hand around his upper arm, and nearly shoved him out the door and across the deck to the steps. The bell on the door jingled again as they descended the stairs.

"You're being foolish, Becks, and the girl I know isn't a fool. He's got your head all screwed up!"

Shane stopped abruptly, prepared to whip around and give Justin what he was begging for, but the pleading pressure of Becky's hand on his arm and quiet voice stopped him.

"Don't, Shane."

It required every shred of his willpower and Becky's soothing presence to get him to his truck, and he didn't dare look up to see where Justin was until his door was closed. When he glanced at the deck of the Bedspread, Becky's ex stood at the top of the stairs glaring at them with his arms folded tightly across his chest. He turned the key in the ignition and backed away from the inn, and he didn't speak until he was out on the main road and heading toward the Royal R.

"I'm sorry. I had to walk away or I was going to

hit him."

"I know." She paused, and when she spoke again, it was with a firmer voice. "Before you beat yourself up for losing your temper, I want you to consider something."

He glanced at her, waiting for her to elaborate.

"You walked away. If the situation were reversed, he wouldn't have."

They sat in silence for a while, and the anger drained out of him, allowing Justin's words, echoing what he'd thought so many times himself, to bob to the surface of his thoughts. Becky was a strong, independent woman, but the need to take care of her was instinctive, and in the low that followed the high of his fury, those thoughts seeped through him like poison.

"I know it's an old fashioned idea that it's my job to take care of you, all the more so because you don't need me to, but the expectation is there… and I want to. *I* need to, but Justin's right. What *do* I have to offer you? What happens if Jim and Jessie end up having to sell the Royal R? I know it's painful to think about, but it's a very real possibility."

Becky gaped at him. "You're not seriously thinking I'd ever go back to him?"

"No. If he were the last man on earth, I wouldn't

want you to go back to him because you deserve so much better than to be talked down to like that or manipulated." He sighed. "I'm just saying that there's probably someone a lot better out there for you than me. Someone who can give you everything you need and want."

"Don't let him get into your head, Shane. And don't withdraw again. You have so much more to offer me or any woman than you know because you have a good heart and because you only want the best for everyone."

"I *do* want what's best for you," he murmured. "And I'm not sure I'm it. I want to be, Becky, more than I've wanted anything, but I don't know that I am."

"What if you *are*?" She leaned across the cab and kissed his cheek. "Last time I checked, I'm pretty sure we agreed that that is for me do to decide, not you."

"Of course it's your decision."

"I'm glad we've re-established that because everything that's happened recently and how you've been here for me when I needed you is pretty solid evidence that you are in fact the best man for me."

As he parked his truck in front of the main house, she leaned over again and kissed him long and hard, leaving little room in his mind for doubt.

"Not only that, you're also the only man I *want*. Always have been. So please don't leave me again."

"I'm not going anywhere."

* * *

Despite the occasional bellows of the heifer preparing to calve, the quiet of the barn was a refreshing respite after a week of avoiding Justin and three days of the chaos that was the Royal R's second-largest guest count ever. Becky perched on top the four-foot-high front wall of the birthing stall with her back resting against the corner pole. Shane was similarly seated on the adjoining wall. If for no other reason than the peacefulness, Becky was glad she'd volunteered them for calving duty when they'd found the cow—the notorious five-sixteen—well into labor early this morning. She'd made the offer with the hope that, when Justin arrived, they'd be able to use it as an excuse to ignore him, but until this moment, she hadn't realized how much she needed even this watchful break.

Becky was heartily sick of Justin despite the fact that she had seen very little of him. Over the weekend, she and Shane had found ways to avoid him, and since the wedding party had arrived, she'd been too busy with guests to give him any attention, but he'd found excuses to hang around, all under the guise of "helping." It was pathetic, really, that the son and heir of a multi-million dollar ranching empire would be wasting his time on the considerably smaller Royal R Ranch… and without pay.

Speaking of the prick, I wonder when he'll show up. She didn't doubt that he would. He was leaving for home tomorrow, but it wasn't in him to give up until he'd made every possible attempt. Some might think it was a sign of his devotion to her, but she knew better. That wasn't Justin's modus operandi—it was Shane's.

Becky's lips twitched. If there was one benefit to having her ex in Northstar, it was the foil he provided; he made her appreciate Shane so much more than she already did. He was so wonderfully different from Justin in every way, and Becky was glad she'd listened to her heart and given him this second chance.

The man-sized door to the right of the big live-stock door at the front of the barn opened, and her father and Max, who'd been out checking the rest of the herd for any other cows in labor, stepped inside.

"Please don't tell me Justin's back again," Becky said when they reached the stall.

"Not yet. When's he supposed to head back to Wyoming?"

"Tomorrow morning."

"Let's hope he doesn't come back. Ever."

"Amen to that," Shane muttered.

"What's the matter, McGuire? Don't like the ex trying to muscle in on your territory?" Max quipped.

"Has nothing to do with territory. He's a self-centered asshole who doesn't know how to take no for an answer, and he has no respect for Becky's wishes whatsoever."

"Never has, as I recall."

Becky rolled her eyes at them. "I'm right here, you know."

Hearing several vehicles, they all walked to the barn door and stepped outside to watch the procession as their guests headed down to the Ramshorn for the wedding rehearsal and the rehearsal dinner.

Max sighed happily. "Ah. A few hours of peace and quiet."

"Perfect timing, too," Andy added. "Last thing Jim needs right now is that much excitement. He and Jessie just got home, by the way, which is why we're here."

Becky wanted to cheer, but she contained her excitement. Barely. "How's he look?"

"Good. Tired, but that's to be expected. I'll keep an eye on this girl for you so you two can go see them, but before I let you go, how's she doing?" Andy asked, returning to the stall and leaning over the door to look over the heifer.

"She's struggling a bit, but she's not far enough yet to tell if we're going to have to assist," Shane replied. "Becky's pretty sure she's having twins again— her third set in four pregnancies, I understand. And Becky says she's never rejected a twin?"

"Nope. She's never had a problem delivering, either, so hopefully she won't this time. Still, I think it was wise to bring her in. If nothing else, you two have a warmish place to wait and watch."

"Any more heifers getting ready to calve?"

"Not yet."

"I don't know that I'm ready for calving to begin just yet," Max said. "Seems like it's coming fast this year."

"We've been busy and shorthanded, so time's flying." Andy lifted his gaze from the cow to Shane. "I hate to ask, but with Jim out of commission for most if not all of calving, we could really use your help."

"You don't have to ask, Andy. I'll be available for weekend and evening shifts."

"Are you sure?"

"Positive. It's the slow time of the year for us

forestry techs, and if I need to use a couple more vacation days, it'll be pretty easy to schedule them."

"It won't piss off your bosses?" Max inquired.

"They all grew up on ranches. They get it."

"We appreciate it, Shane," Andy said, clapping him on the shoulder. "All right, you two. Get on over to the house."

They jogged across the yard to the main house, but as they neared, Becky slowed to a walk as nervousness settled over her. She didn't understand it. Jim's surgery had gone perfectly according to routine, and his recovery was right on schedule. That was something to celebrate, and she *was* relieved to have one less worry. But the issue of the ranch and her family's tenuous situation remained unresolved.

"Everything will work out," Shane murmured, giving her hand a squeeze.

Just like when he told her how beautiful or strong or smart she was, she believed him. She exhaled and smiled, glad to have him here to help her through whatever came.

Jessie and Jane were just getting Jim installed in his favorite recliner when Becky and Shane stepped inside, and the rancher appeared to be both enjoying the fussing of his wife and Becky's mother and exasperated by it. Other than looking a tad pale and tired, as her father had noted, and a bit winded from his walk from the truck into the house, he was in good spirits. When he spotted Becky and Shane, he grinned broadly and waved them closer.

"Just who I wanted to see," he said with a surprising exuberance. Maybe he wasn't as winded as she thought.

"It's good to have you back," Shane greeted, shaking the rancher's extended hand.

"Believe me, I'm ready to be here. I was going stir crazy sitting in that hospital."

"I'll bet."

"Becky, come here, girl, and give me a hug."

She leaned down and embraced him carefully, mindful that he was barely healed enough to be sent home, a fact proven by the lack of strength in his arms. "Welcome home," she murmured. "We've really missed you and Jessie around here."

"I hear you've all managed just fine without us, however. Do we really have twenty-eight guests here right now? A third of the way through February?"

"Thirty-five if you count the seven that *aren't* part of the wedding party. You should've seen this place last night at dinner. It was packed."

"Considering that our capacity is forty plus the help, I imagine it was. If business keeps going like it has been, we may need to expand operations a bit more than we've already talked about. When you have a few minutes to spare, I'd love to sit down with you and see what you can come up with."

"No business talk, Jim," Jessie scolded.

"Can't I at least thank Shane for stepping in?"

"That's fine, but stay away from topics that'll get you all worked up."

"Yes, ma'am. Would you mind getting these two kids some lunch since it sounds like they may not be able to join the rest of us?"

With a nod, Jessie and Jane disappeared into the kitchen.

"We are grateful for all the help you've been, Shane," Jim said. Pausing barely half a second, he queried, "So, you think you'll stay with the Forest Service until retirement?"

Becky stared at the rancher with narrowed eyes. What an odd question to ask.

"That's the plan. There's only one job that'd make me leave it," Shane answered. "And since I'm not likely to be able to buy my own ranch without winning the lottery, which I hear you have to play to win, I'd say the chances of that other job opening up are pretty much non-existent. Besides, the Forest Service job pays well, comes with great benefits, and I do enjoy it."

"Not as much as this, though," Jim prodded.

"No, not as much as this."

"What are you up to, Jim?" Becky inquired.

He regarded her with such uncontrived nonchalance that she wondered if she'd imagined the probing tone in his voice.

"I'm carrying on a conversation. Why? Do I sound like I'm up to something?"

"I guess not." She caught the faintest twinkle of mischief in his eyes and thought, *Ah-ha! You* are *up to something. But what?*

Jessie returned with sandwiches for Becky and Shane and scowled at her husband. "Jim Robinson, what did I tell *just* you? No business talk for at least a couple days. You'll have more than enough excitement to set your recovery back days with all the guests running around without adding the stress of business to your plate."

"I was just asking Shane about his job with the Forest Service."

"Sure you were."

"I was. Wasn't I, Shane?"

"He was, Jessie, but we'll get out of your hair. We need to get out to the barn, anyhow," Shane said. "Five-sixteen's in labor. Becky thinks she'll have twins."

"No surprise there, but why's she in the barn? She's never had a problem delivering before."

"Jim," Jessie warned.

"We'll let you rest," Becky said, taking Shane's free hand.

They vacated the living room, taking their plates out to the barn to eat their lunch. Nothing had happened in their absence, and Andy and Max left to tend to other duties.

Once they were alone, Shane asked, "Feel better now?"

"Much. I didn't expect him to look so good so soon. It's a major relief." She took a bite of her sandwich and chewed it thoughtfully, then swallowed. "I feel like everything will be all right and go back to the way it's always been… and stay that way for at least a few more years, maybe even until Mom and Dad are ready to retire and James is out of the house and it won't matter so much if Jim and Jessie have to sell."

"I'm glad to hear you sounding so positive about it."

She shrugged. "Like everyone keeps telling me, there's nothing I can do about it so there's no point fretting."

With a bellow, the heifer regained her feet, and Becky observed her for a moment. She saw the cow's sides heave with an obvious push.

"It's go time," she told Shane.

They scarfed the rest of their lunches and set their plates on a nearby stool, then returned to their perches atop the stall rails to keep vigil. Given five-sixteen's half-wild disposition, they wouldn't venture into the stall until they had to. She was distracted enough to tolerate them being as close as they were, but that was no guarantee she'd allow them closer.

For a while, they talked quietly about the task at hand, but when a pair of the calf's hooves appeared, they fell silent, mindful of the clock as the minutes ticked by with no sign of the calf moving farther into the world. After close to three-quarters of an hour passed with no more progress, Becky climbed cautiously into the stall, watching the heifer for signs of irritation while she inspected the calf more closely. The cow craned her head around and let out a distressed call but didn't otherwise take issue with Becky's presence. She was too exhausted already to care.

"Crap. We're gonna have to pull."

"Think we can do it without the jack?" Shane asked, joining her.

"Guess we'll find out," she replied. "But would you grab it just in case?"

She stripped down to her black tank top, hung her coat and sweater over the wall where she'd sat, and scrubbed her arms and hands down in the wash bucket Shane brought over and hung on the hook on the corner pole. First, she checked the position of the calf, sliding her hands along its exposed legs until she felt its nose. It was in the right position and on the small side, so the veteran heifer shouldn't be having trouble… unless Becky was right and they were dealing with twins. If so, it was possible they were wedged in.

Gripping the calf's slimy legs, she waited for a contraction and pulled. A tiny bit more of the calf emerged. She heard the barn door open but didn't look to see who entered, too focused on her chore to care. Shane joined her in the stall, set the calf jack out of the way but close enough for easy access, and glanced toward the arrival as he washed up. He positioned himself beside her, and she let go of one of the calf's legs so he could take it.

"You are a master of shitty timing, Sutherland,"

he remarked.

Of course it's Justin. Who else? Becky glanced over her shoulder at the person now standing at the stall gate for confirmation.

"At least I'm a master," her ex retorted.

"If you're just here to exchange juvenile insults, go the hell away," she snapped. "We're busy."

If he said anything in reply, she didn't catch it because the cow's bellow drowned out everything else. With her push, Becky and Shane pulled. At first, the calf didn't budge, but then something gave, and out came its head. With the next contraction, they were able to free its shoulders, and with one more push from the heifer, they dragged the calf free. They lowered it to the straw, and Shane immediately set about clearing its nostrils and mouth so it could breathe, then carried the little bull around to his mother's head so she could clean him.

When Shane came back, Becky slapped his lifted hand in a high-five. "We make a good team."

"Don't we?" he agreed.

Five-sixteen gave another push and another bellow, and another pair of hooves appeared, confirming Becky's suspicion of twins. As she had with the first calf, she checked the position of the second. Again, it was turned right. The calves must have been wedged, she decided, though not too badly or it would have required a lot more effort than it had to pull the first.

"Ready for number two?" she asked.

"Yep."

"Pity about the twins," Justin mused. "Wonder which one she'll reject."

She'd almost forgotten he was there. "This is her third set of twins, and she hasn't rejected a calf yet."

With the first calf out of the way, five-sixteen should be able to push this one out herself, but she was worn out, so Becky and Shane each took one of the calf's legs. In between contractions, Becky monitored the position of the calf's head, which seemed determined to angle up, and twice she had to push the nose down against the legs.

"You know you wouldn't have to shove your hands inside a cow on my ranch," Justin said as if the idea disgusted him—not the general idea of doing it but of Becky doing it.

Of any woman doing it, she thought with a scowl. "I'm AI certified, Justin, and I've done this most of my life. Do you really think I have an issue with, as you put it, shoving my hands inside a cow?"

Conversation ebbed again as she and Shane

worked and the calf at last began progressing forward with relative ease.

"I can't believe you want this," Justin muttered. "You're covered in crap."

"What about Becky has ever given you the impression that she's opposed to getting her hands dirty?" Shane asked.

Becky answered before Justin could. "It's difficult for him to understand why I love this because he and his family believe a woman can't do this kind of work or shouldn't want to even if she could."

"Seems a little contradictory to me—" Shane grunted when Becky's hands slipped, leaving him with the brunt of the pulling. "—since it's women who give birth."

Before Becky could grab hold of the calf again, the rest of it slipped out of the birth canal with one last determined push and bellow from the heifer. Shane settled the calf on the straw-covered floor, and Becky squatted to clear its nostrils.

"Baby number two alive, breathing, and looking perfectly healthy," she said, flicking the gooey afterbirth from her fingers. The mother shifted and craned her head to nose the second calf, a little heifer. She eyed Becky with something that looked distinctly like relief and gratitude, and in that moment, Becky sensed the inklings of a bond between them. "You're welcome, Mama. Congrats. Try to remember this the next time you want to give us a hard time, all right?"

"Do *not* insult my family," Justin snarled as if the arrival of the second calf hadn't interrupted.

She rolled her eyes. "I'm not. I was illustrating the insurmountable differences between us in the hopes that you'll figure out what I've been telling you for months. Because the broken-record routine was old weeks ago. Now it's just sad."

Justin scoffed. "You think Shane is any better?"

"He's right here in the stall with me, isn't he? Covered in the same *crap* I am." Becky rose to her feet. "I *know* he's better because he hears me and loves me for exactly who I am—with all my flaws, which he doesn't seem to think I have—rather than who he wants me to be."

Because the heifer was still cleaning the first calf, Becky climbed out of the stall to fetch a towel to dry the second with.

"You don't know what you're losing, Becks."

"I'm not losing anything. I have everything I want and need right here in Northstar, on the Royal R, and with Shane."

"And what happens when you lose it all? You're going to come crawling back to me, begging my parents for your old job, and begging me to take you back."

"That's quite a fanciful dream, Justin."

She walked past him back to the stall, but he grabbed her arm and jerked her toward him. She whirled on him, and when her fist connected with his jaw, he drew his back in reaction. Shane hurdled the stall gate, landing between them and barely lifting his arm in time to deflect the blow, and decked Justin hard enough to send him staggering back several steps.

"Put your hand on her again, and I will knock you the fuck out."

Becky shivered with the chilling promise in Shane's low, deadly tone.

Justin ran his tongue over his busted lip and spit blood onto the barn floor. "You want her? Fine. You can have the bitch."

Shane shook his head and smirked. He didn't immediately respond, probably talking himself out of retaliating for the insult. When he spoke, his voice was admirably level, almost pitying. "That's what you don't get. It's not about what you want or what I want. It's about what *she* wants. Maybe, if you were capable of comprehending that, she wouldn't have left you."

"And you think you're what she wants?"

"I hope I am. Guess I'd better find out so we can settle this ridiculous argument." Turning to Becky, he took her hands in his, and she was too distracted by how his eyes softened to notice how slimy they both were. "I'm really sorry, beautiful, because this isn't how I wanted to do this."

Her heart—pounding from the exertion of delivering the calves and the tussle with Justin—beat faster. When he kissed her, it raced, knocking so hard against her ribs she thought the world would be able to hear it.

"Marry me, Becky," he murmured for her ears only.

"There was a time I thought I'd never hear you ask that," she breathed. Somewhere in the back of her mind, she wondered if this was just a ploy to get Justin to leave once and for all, but her heart knew it was real, and a whirlwind of relief and joy and gratification and a million other happy emotions filled her. How long had she been waiting to hear those words? Years—a decade. Loud enough to make sure Justin heard, she said, "Yes, Shane. Yes, I'll marry you."

Shane lifted her up, hugging her tightly, and she

dipped her head to kiss him. When he set her down, she slipped her hand around his arm and turned to Justin.

"There was nothing here for you before, but now there *really* isn't," she said as kindly as she could manage. "Go home to your beautiful ranch and your loving family… and leave me to mine."

"This is how it ends, then? You're going to throw away six years?"

I'm not the one who threw it away, she wanted to say but decided against it. "This is how it ends."

Justin glanced between them, then pinched his eyes closed. The muscle in his jaw worked, and when he opened his eyes again, Becky winced at the pain in them. Understanding had finally broken over him, and while she was glad her time with him was done, she *had* devoted a large chunk of her life to him, and sorrow wormed its way into her heart. She never wanted to hurt anyone. Not even him.

"I'll leave you alone to say whatever else you need to say to him," Shane murmured. He touched his lips to her cheek and slipped back into the stall to check on the calves and the heifer.

"I'm sorry, Justin. This isn't how I wanted to end things with you, but I tried to be polite, and you refused to listen… just like you always do."

He only nodded and turned away without another word. After almost two weeks of interminable attempts to sabotage her relationship with Shane, she was shocked that he'd just… walk away.

"At last," she sighed. She leaned over the gate of the stall and grinned at Shane. "That *was* a real proposal, wasn't it?"

"One-hundred-percent genuine. I love you, Becky, and I knew long before we got back together that I wanted to spend the rest of my life with you. Why do you think it's been so easy to wait for you to figure out that I'm never leaving you again?"

"There you go again, surprising me."

"You don't believe me."

"I said yes, didn't I?"

"Not about that. You still don't believe how beautiful you are or why I'd know without a doubt that you're the woman for me."

She joined him in the stall and hooked her arms around his neck with a wide smile. "I'm beginning to figure it out."

"I may not be able to give you a ranch, and I don't know what will happen in the coming years with the Royal R, but I promise to love you and support you in whatever way you need me to for the rest of our lives."

"That's all I need." She grinned. "James is going to be beside himself when he finds out."

"Him and Dad both. We'll have to break it to them gently so they don't keel over on us." He touched his forehead to hers and tucked his arms around her waist. "I'd hoped for a better proposal, maybe a quiet dinner with roses and candlelight, not covered in afterbirth in a barn before I've even bought the ring."

Becky laughed. "Actually… for us, it's perfect. Even the most romantic proposal you could put together wouldn't suit us half as well. And the only ring I want is the one you give me at our wedding." She kissed him again. "Can't wait to see the design you come up with."

Epilogue

OF ALL THE PHOTOGRAPHS Skye Hammond had taken of their wedding, Shane figured it would be a tie for his favorite between his and Becky's first kiss as husband and wife and one of the shots of them standing in the open main door of the barn where he'd proposed nearly a year and a half ago. The memory of them covered in goo and happier about it than any two people had a right to be made him smile. She was right about it suiting them perfectly. Their wedding, which the Ramshorn had of course planned and organized, did, too. They had been married in the vibrantly green pasture behind the main ranch house with the craggy northern Northstar Mountains as a backdrop. They and their small wedding party—just Luke and Ryan as their best man and maid of honor—had been on horseback, as had the pastor, while the guests had sat on straw bales.

The reception was currently under way in the center field of the ranch compound, and wedding guests meandered amongst the picnic tables the Conners, O'Neils, and Hammond clan had brought in. Everything, down to the Mason jar candle centerpieces and mouthwatering barbecue, embodied the Western theme. Though he'd seen the Conners in action on several occasions now, he was every bit as amazed at their talent as he'd been at Chloe and Ryder's Meadow Lake wedding.

Shane stood with Luke near the wedding party's table, sipping a glass of iced tea. He glanced around the large gathering, not quite believing his eyes. He'd never imagined so many people would come to his wedding, but nearly the entire population of Northstar had turned out along with a few others, including Becky's old friends, Jenny and Andrea, who had been shockingly pleasant, gracious, and genuinely congratulatory despite their disbelief that she was the first of them to get married.

Jake Sterling approached and clapped him on the shoulder. "Looks like you've made your amends."

"It certainly seems that way," Shane replied. "You heading out?"

"I'm afraid so. Wish I could stay for the rest of the festivities, but work calls. Congratulations, Shane. I'm sure this feels like it's been a long time coming."

"It does, and I'm relieved today is here at last."

"Pass my love on to your lovely bride, will you?"

"Of course I will."

After Jake left, Shane's gaze found its way back to his bride for the ten-thousandth time today. At the moment, she was talking with Ryan a few tables away with Ashleigh perched on her hip. He supposed he looked handsome enough in his tux and crisp black cowboy hat, but Becky was purely breathtaking in her lacy, layered ivory gown with her long, dark hair pinned back in a simple, elegant French twist and a lace veil cascading down her back from a diamond-studded comb. The halter-style neckline with its flirty V revealing a hint of cleavage called attention to her proud, graceful shoulders and neck, and the asymmetrical hem, which was higher in the front than at the back, showed off her beautiful, hand-tooled cowboy boots, but the most exquisite part of the dress was how classically Becky it was. It embodied the very essence of everything he loved about her.

"If anyone still doubts that you two will make it," Luke remarked, "the look on your face right now will cure them of that delusion."

"Guess that means I'm grinning like a fool."

"In the best way."

"Luke?"

"Yeah?"

"Pinch me, would you? Because there's no way all this is real. Am I really married to the woman who's haunted my thoughts and dreams from the moment I was stupid enough to break her heart? And have we all put that god-awful summer and all its consequences behind us, conclusively?"

"Yes, you are, and yes, we have."

"I guess that means we won."

"Won what?"

"JP's game. He divided us for a while, but in the end, we've won."

Luke frowned thoughtfully, then smiled. "Damned right we have."

"Shall we go track down our wives and get the rest of the formalities out of the way so we can get to the fun part of the evening?"

"Are you referring to dancing … or your wedding night?"

"While I'm quite looking forward to tonight, I'm actually referring to dancing. I'm in no hurry, and I fully plan to enjoy every moment between now and then."

When they reached their wives, Shane leaned in to kiss Ryan's cheek. "I don't think I've said it yet, but happy third anniversary to both of you."

"You said it this morning," Ryan said. "At least four times. But thank you again."

"Really? Four times?"

"Well, your mind was elsewhere and rightly so. Next year, we'll have to do something special for our double anniversary."

"Absolutely."

"I love that idea," Becky replied. Immediately, she turned impatiently to Luke. "Did you tell him yet?"

He glanced from his cousin to his wife. "No, I haven't because I thought we were waiting until tomorrow because today is their day."

"I'm sorry," Ryan said. Her broad grin contradicted her words. "But we got to talking kids… and it sort of popped out."

"Tell me what?" Shane inquired with a brow arched, pretty sure he knew what their news was.

"It looks like Luke won't be the only one of us to have an almost-birthday baby."

"You're pregnant? Congratulations!" Shane hugged her. "How far along and when are you due?"

"Ten weeks and mid January. Not quite as close to my birthday as Ashleigh is to his, but close enough. We really didn't mean to break the news today because, like Luke said, today is your day, but we had our first appointment yesterday and got to hear the heartbeat."

"Don't apologize, Ryan. I can't speak for Becky, but that news is a pretty amazing wedding gift."

"You say that now," Becky remarked playfully, "but you might change your mind later tonight."

"Oh?"

Suddenly, her expression turned shy and her cheeks reddened as if she'd realized what she was thinking might not be the most appropriate topic with a couple hundred people nearby who might overhear. He didn't think he'd ever seen her look quite so adorable.

"Well, since we had such a long engagement...."

He waited for her to finish her thought, but she only chewed on her lip.

"You want to start working on the first of those two kids you've always wanted and sooner rather than later," he guessed, keeping his voice quiet so they wouldn't be overheard. Luke and Ryan undoubtedly caught what he'd said, but they were polite enough to turn away for a moment, and Ashleigh was too young to understand or repeat it.

Becky nodded. "I want to try for a honeymoon baby." The playful spark returned to her gaze, and the grin that curved her lips was pure mischief. "Does that freak you out?"

The comment brought back the conversation they'd had the morning after Jim's heart attack, and he found himself grinning, too. When Ashleigh reached for him, he took her lifting the toddler over his head to her delighted squeal before setting her on his hip. He couldn't believe how much she'd grown despite watching the changes as they happened, nor could he believe she'd be two years old in just a few months. Shaking his head, he turned his attention back to Becky. "Why on earth would it freak me out? Whatever you want, I want."

"All right, newlyweds," Luke interrupted, holding his hands out to take his daughter. "There's a lot more excitement yet to come, so let's get the toasts out of the way, shall we?"

"Wait," Ryan said. "I haven't heard yet why Becky's ring is a square knot instead of a phoenix, which seems to be your thing as a couple. She said I had to ask you, Shane."

He lifted Becky's left hand and brushed his thumb over the result of his design. A single diamond sat in the center of two slender threads of white gold shaped into a square knot. "We've already risen from the ashes, so I wanted something more representative of us moving forward together. A square knot is surprisingly strong for how simple it is. Just like us."

"That is a powerful sentiment, Shane." Ryan nudged Becky. "What'd we do to deserve these two thoughtful men?"

"I have no idea, but I'm pretty sure they'd say they're the lucky ones."

"We are," Shane and Luke said at once.

They returned to the head table, and Becky and Shane took their seats while Luke and Ryan remained standing. With his wife's arm around his waist, Luke tapped his glass of sparkling cider with a fork. A hush fell over the crowd, and people quickly returned to their tables in anticipation of the toasts.

"I'm going to keep this fairly short and sweet

because what I need to say won't take many words, and the bride and groom are anxious to get the dancing started. So here goes." Luke shifted toward his newly married friends. "Shortly before you got back together, I asked you to make a promise to yourselves to let go of the traumas we've faced and to stop letting them prevent you from enjoying the blessings in life. That we are all here today is proof that you've done that, and I could not be happier for you both. I've waited for this day for a long time, but at last, I have both of my best friends back and back together… for the rest of our lives. Congratulations to you both, and may this be the beginning of the happiest chapters of your lives."

Ryan, rather than making her own toast, simply raised her glass and added, "To the couples who were meant to be together."

Shane dipped his head in a nod to acknowledge her sentiment that they hadn't survived not only because she and Luke were meant to be together but that Shane and Becky were meant to be as well.

Austin stood and lifted his glass. His toast was simple, but it took him a few tries to get started as he choked back tears. "To Becky, my lovely daughter-in-law, thank you for helping my son find his way back.

And to Shane, you have been the light of my life, and now that light shines twice as bright. I am so proud of you, and I love you, and I am glad you've at last found everything you were looking for."

Becky's parents said much the same, adding that they were honored to welcome Shane to their family.

James's toast was the quickest of the families'. All he said was, "I finally get to call you my brother! Oh, and thanks for making my sister so happy."

June and Ben, Pat and Aelissm, Becky's Conner grandparents, all the Hammond and Carlyle families, and many others added their congratulations and well wishes, leaving the Robinsons to make their toast last. Jim and Jessie waved their granddaughter and Becky's family over to them.

Jim was misty-eyed, Shane noted. "We congratulate you both, but we don't have a toast so much as an announcement that we've been waiting some time to make."

"About the fate of the Royal R Ranch," his wife clarified. "We've made a decision."

"We aren't going to sell. Ever."

Relief radiated from Becky, and Shane wrapped an arm around her shoulders and squeezed.

"You convinced Jess to keep it," she said with

relief saturating her voice.

"No," the girl said, "they haven't. I won't inherit the ranch."

Matching frowns of confusion spread across every face around them, and total silence descended.

Becky stared at them, dumbfounded. "What?"

Shane noticed the smiles on the faces of her parents. This announcement was no surprise to either of them, and in fact, it appeared that they were in on it.

"Jess suggested we will the ranch to Jane and Andy," Jessie said, "but when we brought it up to them, they had a different idea because they apparently want to retire someday, too. Which left us with just one choice of who will inherit our ranch… and we can't think of anyone better because she loves it as much as we do, and we know she—and her new husband—will continue to build and protect it."

"The Royal R will go to Rebecca Epperson, now Rebecca McGuire," Jim announced, "whom we have long been blessed to consider our honorary grand-daughter."

If Shane weren't already sitting, he would've collapsed into his chair. Becky dug her fingers into his arm, leaning awkwardly over the table as if she couldn't hold herself upright.

"No, I can't..." she whispered.

"Yes, you can. At any rate, it's a done deal," Jim said. "You've earned it, girl. Without you and Shane, I might not be here right now, and as I said, we know the Royal R will be safe in your hands when we're gone."

Shane and Becky sat paralyzed by shock as the Robinsons sat down.

Beside them, Luke cleared his throat. "I believe that's it for the toasts, which means it's time to get the dancing started."

Some of the fog of disbelief lifted enough for Shane to rise to his feet and help his wife to hers. When she told him to wait a moment, he frowned, watching in surprise as she reached under one of the layers of her gown's skirt and, with Ryan's assistance, peeled the lower skirt off, converting her gown into a sexy, more practical dress for dancing.

"Put your eyes back in your head, Shane," Luke said under his breath. "You'll have plenty of time for *that* later."

Shane took Becky's hand and led her to the dance floor. Guests gathered around, but he didn't pay them much attention, too consumed by the glitter of happiness and excitement in Becky's eyes... her gorgeous, honest silver eyes. He held his arms out, and she stepped into them.

"Justin's argument was moot," she said, threading her arms around his neck, "because it looks like *I'll* be giving *you* a ranch."

Shane tipped his head back and laughed. He settled his hands into position, and as the band began to play, he led Becky in their first dance as husband and wife with all the confidence and poise their lessons with John and Tracie Hammond over the last year had given him.

"So, Mrs. McGuire, there's one question I never got to ask you."

"And what is that?"

"Have I proven beyond a doubt that you can trust me again?"

"You absolutely have." She took his face in her hands and kissed him long and deeply to the cheering of their family and friends. "Everything that was broken is healed, and everything that was wrong is right again now. And we have the rest of our lives to enjoy it… together."

* * * * *

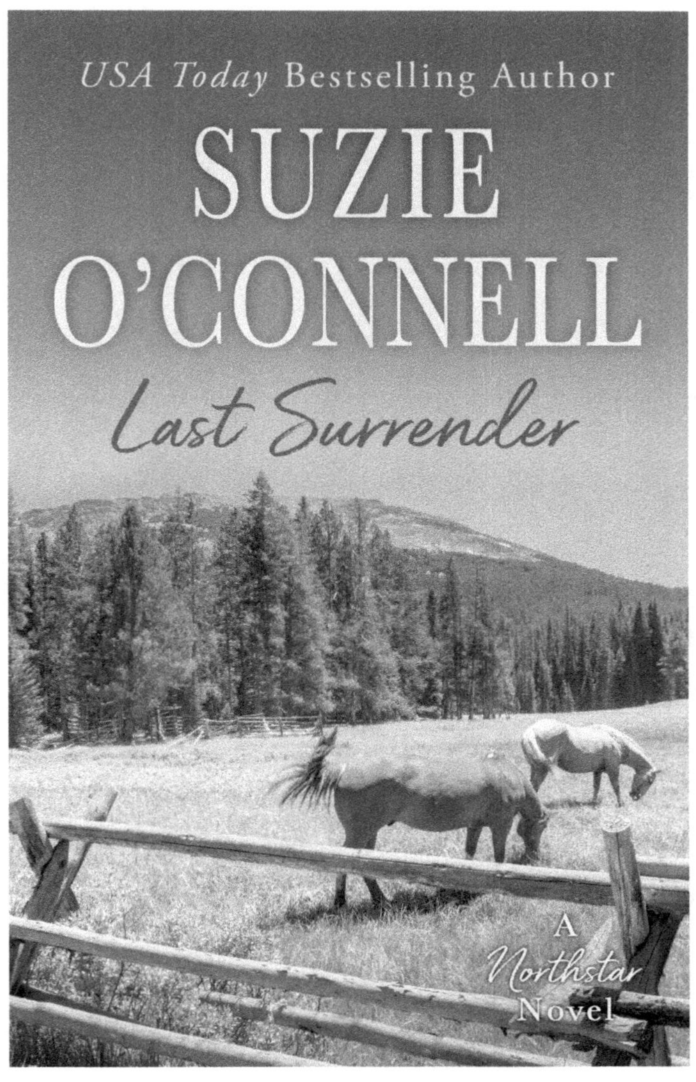

USA Today Bestselling Author
SUZIE O'CONNELL
Last Surrender
A Northstar Novel

Last Surrender

Horse trainer Heather Brown is strong, confident, and successful, and as far as ranch hand Jeremiah Mackey is concerned, she has it all. So why does she keep walking away from good men?

It's Heather's thirtieth birthday, and she's newly single. Again. With a talent for finding Mr. Right-for-Everyone-Else, it's time to try something—or someone—new. Jeremiah certainly fits the bill. He's different than any man she's dated, but with her family openly hostile to him, how can it last?

Jeremiah has made a lot of mistakes in his life, and he's spent time behind bars because of them. But eleven years ago, he was given a chance to turn his life around, and he took it without looking back. With Heather by his side, his future is looking brighter than ever… until someone from his past starts playing deadly games.

AVAILABLE NOW

Visit www.suzieoconnell.com for more information.

About the Author

Suzie O'Connell is the *USA Today* bestselling author of the Northstar romances. The series is the product of a love affair with Southwestern Montana that began with a two-week adventure at her stepsister's rustic cabin in her teens. That love affair shows no sign of abating.

She has been writing stories for as long as she can remember, and her love of writing and of Montana pushed her to earn a Bachelor of Arts in Literature and Writing from the University of Montana-Western. What else would you expect from a self-professed mountain-loving nerd?

When she isn't writing, you'll probably find Suzie in the mountains with a camera in hand and enjoying the beauty of Montana with her husband Mark, their daughter Maddie, and their golden retrievers Reilly and Angus.

Find Suzie online at www.suzieoconnell.com